HELLBEAST

THE ARC CHRONICLES BOOK 3

MATTHEW W. HARRILL

Copyright (C) 2015 Matthew W. Harrill

Layout design and Copyright (C) 2021 by Next Chapter

Published 2021 by Terminal Velocity – A Next Chapter Imprint

Cover art by Yocla Designs

This book is a work of fiction. Names, characters, places, and incidents are the product of the author's imagination or are used fictitiously. Any resemblance to actual events, locales, or persons, living or dead, is purely coincidental.

All rights reserved. No part of this book may be reproduced or transmitted in any form or by any means, electronic or mechanical, including photocopying, recording, or by any information storage and retrieval system, without the author's permission.

First Printing & Edition, 2015

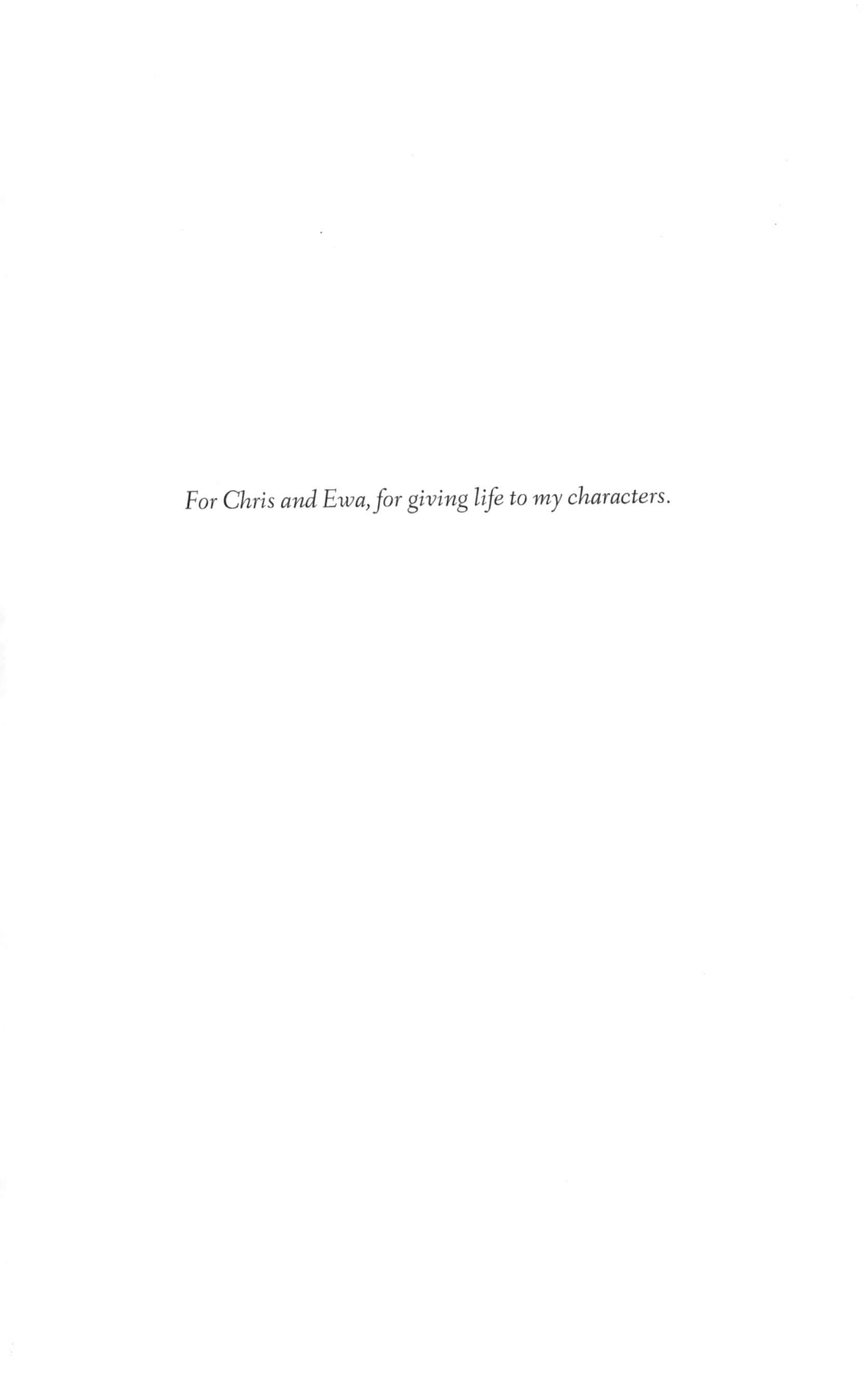

For Chris and Ewa, for giving life to my characters.

THE ARC CHRONICLES

Hellbounce, Book 1
Hellborne, Book 2
Hellbeast, Book 3

PROLOGUE

"Ellis, come away from there! You know it's dangerous. Anything dangerous..."

"...could hurt Jess," the eleven-year-old Ellis finished the sentence, watching his younger sister as she crept toward the remains of what used to be a house.

All bushy-blond hair and fearless bravado, Ellis put on a face of mock-concern until he was sure his mother believed him and turned back around to watch her programs. She wasn't really interested in his safety or Jessica's, his nine-year-old sister. She wanted the neighbors to think she was. His mother was all about image.

The door clicked shut, and after counting to thirty, Ellis winked at Jess. The two of them resumed their exploration of the ruined structure. It was a sunny afternoon in June, and the birds chirped in the trees. It was perfect for exploration.

Ellis had watched, with his sister, transfixed by the scene only a week or so before, when the house, for no apparent reason, had collapsed in on itself. A group of people had been outside; cops had shown up and then left as if nothing was wrong. The house was ruined, but it had become a magnet for every daredevil kid from the nearby high school, all of them wanting to discover the treasure hidden beneath the mound of rubble. Ellis had waited, biding his time, as those bigger kids burrowed through what remained. There were tunnels under the wood and 'the haunted house' quickly became a local Worcester legend.

His Mom had told them expressly to stay back and then turned away, muttering something about poltergeists. They had gotten closer and closer every day, until they found the hidden den under the wood.

With one last glance for his mother, Ellis pulled a flashlight from under his shirt and beckoned for his sister. Jess needed no further invitation and skipped with good-natured innocence alongside him.

Shifting some of the ruined wood to one side, Ellis wormed his way down a tunnel in the rubble, being careful not to touch the precariously wedged supports. Jess followed him down, and soon enough, they were sitting on the cozy, if somewhat putrid, couch discovered in what must have been a basement before the collapse.

Ellis turned the flashlight on, Ellis shining it around. Jess following his every move with the excited devotion of a younger sibling. Dust trickled down from above, and he held his breath as part of the building settled. It was all right; their tunnel was still there.

"Where's the light coming from?" Jess asked, pointing to their left.

Ellis followed her arm. A glowing red mist had begun to float across the floor, like lava in one of those volcano movies. Silent, creeping. Ellis watched in mute fascination as the red glow oozed toward them, spreading up the sides of their den.

"Ellis," said Jess, uncertainty in her voice. "I don't like this. I want to go home."

The red began to glow white in the center. Sparks began to fly out, what looked like lightning, touching the wood and setting it alight. There was a stink of rotten eggs, and Ellis covered his mouth. A growl from behind the light made the walls of the den shake. Suddenly, this adventure was no longer fun.

"Ellis," Jess whined, pulling at his hand.

"Yes. Let's get out of here, Sis."

Letting his now-terrified sister crawl ahead of him, Ellis pointed the flashlight forward, up the tunnel leading to distant daylight, keeping equal watch on their escape route and the growing glow behind them, now white and hot. More noises followed up the tunnel, and Ellis urged his sister on.

When he climbed out into daylight, Ellis made sure to replace the wood as best he could and then set to brushing the dust off his jeans and his sister's red and white striped dress.

"Come on; let's go. Maybe Mom won't know where we were."

Jess led him by the hand. They had only taken a few steps when there was an almighty crash behind them, followed by a blast of heat. The stink of rotten eggs was overpowering. The birdsong ceased and flocks of the small creatures took flight at the sound.

Ellis stopped walking and turned. The entire house had disappeared, leaving a red crater where the doctor and the sportsman had lived. The middle glowed white... something was moving down there. Jess stood mute beside him, right on the edge of the crater where the light was an angry red. A roar of recognition and movement toward them was enough for Ellis.

"Run!"

Across the yard they hurtled, round their mother's brown Ford and into the safety of their own house. Inside, Ellis ran past his mother, who was engrossed in her favorite game show, bounding up on the couch and spreading the green and pink flower-patterned curtains wide. Jess joined him, her slight hand quivering on his arm.

In the distance, figures had begun to stumble out of the crater. Huge and distorted with engorged heads, glowing eyes, and elongated arms, they began to fall into ranks.

Jess twitched the curtain and one of the creatures caught sight, pointing, and roaring. Jess screamed.

"What is it?" their mother called from the other couch, feigning interest.

"It's the monsters," Jess said in a timid voice.

Ellis couldn't move. The giant was looking straight at him.

"There's no such thing as monsters," their mother said, finally clambering up. She wandered across the living room, peering over their shoulders.

Ellis finally broke eye contact with the advancing creature to watch his mother. Her mouth hung open, and her face was as pale as a ghost. The growing pack of monsters outside had begun to advance on their house.

"Kids, I want you to get down in the basement," she said, her voice as quiet as his sister's voice had been. "Now. Run!"

Agent Marcus White, the pride of Anges de la Résurrection des Chevaliers, or ARC, prowled the tunnels of the facility known to the operatives as 'Tartarus'. The base beneath Mount Gehenna, the scene of the demon horde's last major attempted incursion just over nine months ago, was as secure as any facility on the planet. Only a skeleton crew remained; a mere hundred or so of the legion of whom had once fought and died for Eva Scott, or Eva Ross depending on who one listened to. Marcus did a lot of listening to himself; there was usually nobody else on patrol with him for obvious reasons. Marcus knew as well as anybody of his affliction. He had embraced it. Despite his excellent record as a soldier, Marcus was quite crazy.

"My name is Legion, for I am many," he uttered the words for the thousandth time, shouldering his Tavor TAR-21 bullpup rifle. Not standard issue. A gift from an Israeli friend, it was a weapon he would not be parted with.

Marcus glowered out of the cave entrance to the mountain's exterior, the scene of the grisly battle with the Behemoth.

"Come out to the coast, we'll get together, have a few laughs," he said, quoting one of his favorite movies. Marcus adjusted his parka against the wind blowing through the entrance and settled onto a grey metal bench bolted to the cavern floor.

"Well yes, you would say that," he replied to voices in his head, voices telling him he was a babysitter, nothing more. "This might look like a bum deal to you, but it is a great honor, a privilege even, to guard this entrance. Important things happened here. Earth nearly became Hell. We drove them back. We stopped it. Yes, you might say we did nothing of note, but you weren't the ones out there fighting, none of you. I elected to stay here. I was chosen to protect this facility."

The voices laughed at this proclamation of self-importance. He wished he could send them away, but he was lucky to hear himself think. Only when Marcus dreamed did the silence truly descend upon him.

"You can say what you want; I'm alert and ready. If they try it again, you can bet they won't get through us."

Marcus closed his eyes, attempting to force out all the faces looking at him. Before long, they disappeared, along with any sense of the passing time.

With the denial of sight, he imagined flickers of light and shuffling feet approaching from his right. Opening his eyes, Marcus examined his watch. Twenty minutes had passed. The wind had died down and the crisp breeze mingled with the fresh tang of the ice inside the entrance. Invigorated, Marcus stood and stretched.

"Babysitter," he guffawed to the voices. "I babysit you more than this place. It wouldn't exist but for me. I... shut up! Quiet!"

For once, the voices died down. In the distance, back down the tunnel where ice and natural rock formations were replaced by concrete, there was a flickering of red, a pulsing glimmer. Marcus picked up his rifle, checking it was loaded and ready. He crept back down the tunnel to find the source of the glow.

Resisting the urge to call ahead, Marcus edged along the concrete corridor, leaning out ever so slightly into the junction from where the radiance came. It was a white corridor, square in construction and only recently hollowed out. The lights ended midway down. The far end of the hallway was in complete darkness. Except for the red glow beneath one door. There were strange bumps and growls coming from inside the room.

"Time for us to be heroes once again," he muttered under his breath. The voices remained strangely quiet.

"My chance for glory," Marcus continued, trying to fill himself with courage. Edging into the darkness, he refused the use of his night-scope, relying instead on the sullen glow.

As Marcus reached the door, the light winked out.

"Hey, hey you!" he called, tapping the door with the butt of his rifle. "What are you doing in there? Open up!"

The noises ceased, and the door was pulled slightly ajar.

Taking this as an invitation to enter, Marcus pushed the door wider and moved forward. He could see nothing. Instinct told him there were forms in front of him, maybe two or three.

"What are you... hey!"

Quick as lightning, hands belonging to someone much, much stronger grabbed him.

"Help!" Marcus screamed. The voices just laughed at him. He grabbed the door frame with one hand, trying to kick out at his shadowed nemesis. With his free hand, he reached around and pressed the emergency button, setting off the base alarm.

Emergency lights glowed red, the bulbs cycling round in their plastic casing. Marcus screamed at what he saw.

The door slammed shut and the ARC soldier's screams were abruptly cut off, the noise of sinew and cartilage crunching and pulling apart the only remaining sounds.

Ten minutes later, a squad of three ARC operatives entered the corridor clad in black, each wielding a standard-issue M16. Flicking the lights on, the leader observed the scene with disinterest.

"Who was up here?"

"White. He was serving extended guard duty for his assault on the Afghan locals outside the main entrance. This was the safest, most isolated place we could find."

The leader nodded. "Makes sense. What have we here?"

A red trail led off down the corridor into the warren of hallways honeycombing Gehenna beneath the mountains' surface. The leader pushed the door open with his rifle, shining a torch into the room.

The stink of offal and the heavy iron tang of blood assaulted him. Any lesser man would have puked, but the leader had seen worse in his time in Special Forces. "At least he's out of his misery. Get the rest of the squad up here and secure all entrances."

The leader pulled a sat-phone out of his pocket and hit a button. A pre-dialed series of numbers flashed up on the screen.

"Get me Director Guyomard."

Two camels sat side-by-side, evidently content to wait for their owner to invite them to stand. One chewed feed, its jaw moving laterally. The animals did not need feeding but the treat helped cement the bond. Their owner had been with them for a while. He knew their temperament.

It was the middle of the afternoon; the temperature approached forty-five degrees Celsius. The sun blazed in the cerulean desert sky, roasting the crusted hardpan. There was little, if any, moisture in the Gobi Desert. Camels were the only creatures able cross the great expanses and not perish. They were also much more anonymous than off-roaders.

He had been crisscrossing the desert for six months now, seeking any sign of clues relating to a Holy City in the sky. The Convocation of the Sacred Fire had been convinced of the city's existence long before its media debut only weeks ago. His job was to find the answers.

Now, an unprecedented event overshadowed his urgent mission. In mid-air, maybe three or four hundred feet above ground level, perhaps two miles in the distance, a cloud had formed, moisture spinning from nowhere to coalesce directly above the waves of heat radiating from the ground.

The cloud, which should have been forced up by the thermals, remained stationary, ever growing, black and threatening. Sparks of lightning began to appear around the outer rim of the cloud, dancing about its surface. Then something the watcher had never witnessed began to occur. Bolts of lightning launched up from the ground, touching the base of the cloud and working their way up until a continual chain of lightning fed the center. The bright white core of the cloud began to expand; the noise generated by so much concentrated heat from the combustion was almost too much for him.

And then, as quickly as the pyrotechnics had started, the show stopped. The lightning winked out and the cloud was finally forced into the sky. The only indication it was ever there was the tangy stink of concentrated ozone.

The observer reached under his robes, bringing out a sat-phone. He pressed one button, a prepared number.

"This is Baxter," he said in a posh English accent. "Sir, it has begun."

CHAPTER ONE

IMAGES FLASHED BY AS EVA STARED INTO THE DISTANCE, watching everything, seeing nothing. The sun blazed over Lake Geneva, the calm waters reflecting the sunshine back as if seeing it once was not enough for mere mortals. Majestic mountains grew out of the top of the treeline, some still dusted with snow despite the season. Boats bobbed carefree on the surface of the lake. Eva wished she could appreciate the stunning beauty of the Swiss backdrop, but she was empty; she had lost everything. Nina was gone.

Again, Eva replayed the events in her mind and came to the same conclusion.

"There was nothing I could do. It was executed without fault: Rick's death, Elaine's escape. They had it planned to perfection."

Gila Ciranoush, all dark-haired Egyptian gorgeousness and Eva's closest friend, ceased the conversation she had been having by phone. "They did and we have to find out how."

"We know how," she argued.

"Yes, we do. However, we are in a sorry state. We have to take stock of what we have and where we go from here. Precipitous action now could have the direst consequences."

"But they have Nina. They have my daughter."

Gila reached across and placed a sympathetic hand on her arm. "Yes, they do. They have your daughter, but we all know they are not going to harm her. If they had just intended blood and sacrifice, Elaine would not have been cradling her so. They want more. They want you."

"Then why are we sitting here in a car driving as fast as we can away from the scene?"

"Because the most obvious answer is not necessarily the correct one. They want us to go. We will find a way, but we will go there on our terms, not theirs."

Eva turned away, watching the ambulance in front of their car. Inside, Madden and Swanson were both unconscious following the events at the Orpheus portal. The hidden sensor at CERN had been presumed a failed project, but—to their detriment—was really a portal to Hell.

"At least we got Asmodeus," Eva said with slight satisfaction, referring to the demon Lord who had perished in the collapsing portal, the energy slicing him in half. "You are right. Perhaps we do need to rest, but I can't. Nina is only days old. I barely had time enough to get to know her."

"Yet she knew you and from what you explained, knew you well. Eva, your daughter is courageous, small as she may be. She knows you will never abandon her."

"It feels like I have."

Gila's phone sounded, and Eva turned to contemplate the scenery as her friend attempted to do the job of reassembling the ARC council and whoever else would listen. Whoever was left. A sign flashed past. 'Évian-les-Bains'; they were halfway around Lake Geneva, heading Eva knew not where.

"Oh, that is bad news indeed," Gila said to her mystery caller. "Have you contacted headquarters? No? Well, protocol may still be in place. Swanson is out of action for the foreseeable future, and if you can't get hold of the Council then I guess it falls to me. I will do what I can. See to it the facility is secure."

Not looking up from the phone, Gila dialed another number. "This is Director Ciranoush. Tartarus has been breached. Assemble Legion reserves."

The title caused Eva to turn from her contemplation of the endless expanse of water. "Director?"

Gila smiled. "They accepted it. Nothing else matters. Sometimes people just need someone to tell them to do what they had already decided. The base below the portal has been compromised. Demons made an incursion and slaughtered some of the forces stationed there. You understand the consequences of their actions, yes?"

Eva nodded, wishing there were some way this could be otherwise. "The Well of Souls is being used to open portals to Earth. So soon?"

"It sounded like the knife was all they needed to complete whatever ritual they intended to undertake. No longer are hellbounces the only way back from Hell. Still, it could have been worse. No trace of the demons was found. But one hallway in the mountain was encrusted in ice."

Memories came flooding back to Eva, countless apparitions of ice-white portals with tentacles, dark and slimy, writhing and probing. "The others are hunting the demons."

"Just as they hunt us. It seems our planet is safe for nobody. We are in a mess, Eva. If we stand any chance of doing what we need to do, we need to know we have a solid foundation at our backs. Somebody has to take charge. If we lose the keystone, the bridge will collapse."

Gila made a lot of sense. Given only a year before she had been a researcher, a custodian of Coptic history in Cairo, she had come far.

Eva's training in psychotherapy left her always analyzing, always seeking the reasons behind why people were the way they were. Gila had always had the confidence to back her decisions. Unconsciously, Gila was asking Eva to have confidence in her. Desperation, and perhaps a touch of guilt, was forcing her to take the necessary steps. Gila was, after all, the one responsible for destroying the Orpheus portal. She was ultimately responsible for stranding Nina in a place only the dead were meant to be.

Eva closed her eyes, reaching out to her daughter for the first time since CERN. The psychic connection had existed since conception, before there was anything Eva could call a child growing within her. It had saved them both on several occasions, but now there was nothing. There was less than nothing. There was an absence, and it left Eva numb.

She opened her eyes, and the guilt lay heavy on Gila's face. "It was not your fault, Gila." The words were nigh on impossible to speak, but they had to be said. There could not be this wall between them.

"I had no choice," she responded, unshed tears brimming in her eyes.

"I know. It can't get any worse for me at the moment." Eva paused and then laughed, the sound cynical. "Of course, it can always get worse. Nina's last words to me were 'Find me'. That is all I have of her inside. It is the only force driving me. What you did rid the world of a dreadful curse. Asmodeus was a parasite, sucking the human race dry for his own needs, his own pleasures. Giving all God's creatures more time to prepare might make the difference. It certainly saved Madden and Swanson. While there's life, there is hope."

The words made Eva feel better, if only for a moment or two. She glanced out the window again to see a small lake ferry racing them for a moment, smoke billowing from its black-tipped red stack. The Swiss flag fluttered in the breeze and passengers waved with enthusiasm. Eva forced a smile, only the corners of her mouth tipping up and then they were past. The boat chugged on in the distance, the moment gone. If only they knew.

"It just makes me wonder. If I had never thought to question; if I had accepted my place with Brian, given him no cause for jealousy, worked at the hospital, could all this have been avoided?"

"From what we have seen, you have had your path arranged far earlier than you could possibly have imagined. Asmodeus played this game long before you were born."

"You think I would have met Madden anyway? The demons would have had us sleep together and end up on Mount Gehenna? The cult? Bodom? CERN?"

"I think the route may have been a little different but yes. The alternative is you would have ended up on a slab in Iuvart's office, which doesn't bear thinking about."

The phone rang once more. Gila's face paled, and she answered it without speaking.

"I understand," she said in due course and put the phone down. "We have to stop. I need to speak to Swanson." Gila leaned forward, tapping on the glass dividing them from the driver.

"Oui, Director?" The French chauffeur inquired without turning.

"Please signal the ambulance to pull over."

The driver pulled their car out half a lane and Eva saw the reflection of headlights on the back of the ambulance. Hazard lights flashed in response. At the next available break in the road, the two vehicles pulled over, traversing the oncoming traffic to pull to a halt in a dust-filled layby thirty feet from the waters' edge.

Climbing out of vehicles with ease served as another reminder. To Eva there was one very important thing missing. For so long she had been on the move with Nina inside her. Eva focused on the ambulance. The very same vehicle had taken her to hospital. The paramedic, Nina, was seeing to her husband and Swanson Guyomard, member of the ruling council of Anges de la Résurrection des Chevaliers, known simply as ARC. The rest of the staff that had taken them to the hospital had disappeared and were presumed subordinates of either the demons Asmodeus and Belphegor, or of Benedict Garias, the ARC director whose guilt had been proven, but the extent of his responsibility in the recent events had yet to be determined. Either way, they had vanished; Eva presumed by design.

She scuffed at the rough chunks of limestone gravel and watched eddies of the white dust cloud in the onshore breeze. While still a lake, Geneva was enormous and had size enough to cause waves tugged along by the wind to lap against the shore. The daytime heat was mollified somewhat. Part of Eva wished she could dive into the water, maybe to sink into oblivion where she could find her baby daughter.

The edge of depression, Eva knew it well. She had seen it in many patients over the years. Consciously trying to avoid such thoughts, Eva looked about. Near the road was a sign proclaiming the land border between Switzerland and France. Eva laughed.

"What is it?" Gila asked, turning from the ambulance.

"It just dawned on me; I'm perpetually confused as to which country I'm in."

Gila glanced at the road sign. "Yes, I can see how you could get a bit lost. But the people on one side of the sign are no different to those on the other, much how it is with any land boundary. In fact, if you track the language variations across Europe, you can see how everything changes from one side to the other. Some say if one listens carefully enough, dialect changes from street to street in some cities."

"I thought you just studied ancient languages and texts?"

"I do, but while mankind has evolved, the tricks of language remain much the same. Even in ancient history, the dialects changed from town to town. Some hypothesize the aberrations are what gave rise to the variations in ancient religious practices."

"Different dialect gives rise to different interpretation," Eva concluded.

"Exactly! We will make an ancient historian of you yet."

The ambulance door opened from the inside, swinging on silent hinges, and Eva's heart jumped. She missed Madden whenever she was apart from him; he was the rock she depended upon.

Inside the pristine white of the ambulance was a space crammed with two beds. Into each was secured a body with blankets and strapping. Swanson Guyomard, descendant of the ARC founder, Jerome, was a man who once had looked so smug, so carefree. In the year Eva had known him, his hair had thinned, and his face had become worn. Worry lines had developed as they jumped from drama to crisis.

Next to him was her husband. Eva leaned in; Madden was out cold, sedated. It had taken far more than the normal dosage to keep him under because of his unique nature. Madden was a Hellbounce, a man who had died and gone to hell and returned in his human form, one harboring a deadly peril. Inside him a demon lay dormant, just waiting for him to lose control enough to let it erupt from within, ultimately destroying all vestiges of the man remaining.

His long brown hair was loose about his shoulders; Eva's fingers itched to arrange it. Whatever he was, whatever he had been or might become, he was her husband, the father of their abducted daughter, and she loved him.

Both men had been incapacitated in the collapse of the Orpheus portal at CERN, home of the particle accelerator known as the Large Hadron Collider. They were on their way to the ARC retreat to heal and recuperate. Nina, the blonde paramedic who had been so steadfast during Eva's labor and for whom Eva had named her own daughter, checked his vitals.

"Give him a few minutes to come round," Nina advised Gila.

Eva waited, watching her husband sleep. In the end, she stepped away from the door.

"He should have healed," she wondered aloud.

"Like the bullet wound?"

"Exactly. He has the demon inside of him again."

"Maybe it was more. The cold touch he received from Belphegor? Who knows what happened to him when he received the touch of Asmodeus."

Eva felt real worry for him. It was a feeling she had not experienced in a long while; she was not used to Madden looking vulnerable. More than his frailty was the constant worry he would be a target for the denizens of the netherworld lying beyond Hell. Whenever a hellbounce had been injured, portals had sprung into life. Tentacles straight out of nightmare had reached through, pulling the injured demon into their domain. Somebody beyond the limits of imagination and reality had a game plan and a reason for hunting demons.

"Swanson? Can you hear me?" Gila's searching voice came from within the ambulance and Eva peered back inside.

Gila leaned over Swanson, whose unfocussed eyes were open. His eyes twitched, trying to peer at the light outside.

"Swanson, we need to talk. This is an emergency."

Swanson turned his head, mumbling a few words in Gila's direction and closed his eyes once more.

The frown on Gila's face betrayed her frustration. Instead of pressing the injured man for comment, she climbed out of the ambulance.

"It was worth trying. Nina, let us get to the retreat with as much haste as we can manage. The sooner they are settled, the sooner they will mend."

The paramedic climbed back into the ambulance to secure the passengers and Gila led Eva back to the armored Mercedes.

"Anything I can help with?" Eva enquired.

"Not unless you know a way to permanently seal Hell away from earth." Gila shook her head at some inner turmoil. "If they had only concentrated on the greater good rather than becoming the politicians ARC was never supposed to have. Maybe we would have some direction."

"The Council?"

"Yes. They are hidden away, not speaking to anybody. We have reports around the globe of lightning in clear skies. Pressure building where there is no reason and the ground giving way and pits full of fire opening up. The other side has always been ready for this, and we don't have long to react. The longer we leave it, the more like Hell earth becomes.

. . .

In quick order, they were back on the road and into France. The road took them away from Lake Geneva for a while, passing Bouveret, Rennaz, and Villeneuve.

Eva wanted to continue talking, but there was nothing for her to say. The men in her life were both strapped to a bed, and until they recovered, her daughter was alone with a psycho of a wet nurse. *'If you can hear me, Nina, I will come for you,'* Eva thought.

As they passed through an industrial estate, the lake came back into view on Eva's left. Dense forest crowded the flanks of the mountains to their right. Through it, the highway cut like an arrow.

Ahead, appearing to emerge from the water on a shallow base of rock, was a castle with red-tiled towers atop pale yellow walls.

Gila breathed a sigh of relief. "At last."

"Our destination is the castle?"

"It is indeed. If ever we needed a place to feel safe, a castle on a lake is it. The ARC Council refers to the building as the refuge. To the public it is 'Château de Chillon'. I only have one name for it though: Fort Guyomard."

CHAPTER TWO

A WEEK PASSED, DURING WHICH EVA GREW INCREASINGLY BORED and frustrated at the lack of anything resembling information pertaining to either her husband or Swanson. Gila had remained at her side for a couple of days and together they had explored the ancient castle, sometimes joining the frequent tourist parties filling the stunning structure with life.

The castle itself appeared to Eva to be divided into three sections: the area the public saw, the private ARC residences, and an area she could not gain access to despite her most thorough efforts. Thus, when Gila was called off on council business and Eva was left completely to her own devices, she attempted to find a way into the hidden section of the castle by any means possible.

By the fifth day, Eva had determined there had to be access via the roof. Currently, she was leaning out from under a narrow overhang buttressed with aged wood reeking of decay. Having no other recourse, Eva checked the courtyard below and seeing nobody about, hooked one leg over the guardrail.

"It would be unwise to take such a drastic course of action, young miss," said an elderly yet still strong voice, rich with culture and accented just the way Eva imagined a stereotypical English aristocrat would sound.

Eva's heart missed a beat. "Steadman," she admonished the elderly gentleman who was officially curator for the castle. Eva believed, as with everything else inside the fortress, he too had hidden facets.

Eva pulled herself back onto the walkway. "How long have you been watching me?"

Steadman gave her a look seeming to say 'I can see right to the heart of your schemes'. He wore morning dress of a dark jacket with tails, black and grey pinstripe trousers, and matching grey waistcoat and pocketed handkerchief on his left breast. With neatly trimmed if thinning hair and his perceptive gaze, he was a man in complete control of his domain.

"Long enough, young miss, that I can see what it is you are attempting to accomplish. Yet, not too long I could not prevent you from your foolhardy undertaking. Come now."

Steadman held out his right hand, signifying Eva should walk ahead of him down the slender pathway.

"You know why I was doing it?"

"I do. And such a course of action would be considered folly; this castle is over a thousand years old. There are a hundred different buildings merged together. Trust me when I say there is no way into the restricted rooms across the roof. ARC is not a brotherhood of cat burglars after all."

"I just want Madden back."

"You will have to trust and be patient, young miss."

"Why? What's the problem?"

Steadman gave her a knowing smile. "I did not say there was a problem. As to the reason for your separation, I couldn't possibly comment."

. . .

Steadman left her at the bottom of the stairs, specifying with a pointed finger that she should return to her rooms. Eva had been given quarters in a cottage lining the inside of the courtyard. She shared half of it with the public; the building was one of those on the tour. She was the only person with access to her private rooms.

Collapsing in a yellow-cushioned chair, Eva watched the dust settle about her, the motes catching the rays of sunlight as they shone through the grilled window panels. The room was full of the scent of burning coal, as the fires were kept burning all year round to ward off the chill of so much rock. Eva's attention focused on the specks of soot glowing in the back of the fireplace, sending little radiant lines of 'soldiers' up the surface. She imagined the armies of Hell, impatient, eager for the chance to advance in much the same way, while she sat here doing nothing.

"I haven't lost my daughter for this," she said aloud to no one. "Demons, a year of living dangerously, my own blood spilled on several occasions, and all I have to show for it is a fancy prison cell in this damned castle in the middle of nowhere."

Eva continued to stare into the flames. Images came to her, short-lived, appearing in her mind as impressions. In the flames, somewhere on the other side, there was a woman carrying a baby. Her baby. The child screamed and the bearer paid it no mind, her only purpose to nourish it long enough to bring about the end. There were others with them, grossly distorted figures in robes. This was a procession. Next to the woman, a large silhouette crouched, and Eva felt the hunger, the wanton and unabashed gluttony of the creature as it watched over the woman and her prize. The woman turned her head, looking straight through the flames at her and smiled. It was a reflection of her face! The eyes were red, glowing like coals; the smile was full of wickedness. This procession led to an altar, crusted black with ancient blood rites. The other Eva lay the baby down on the altar and pulled out a knife with a glassy blade. Sweeping her arm up in a grand gesture, she plunged the knife down.

Eva screamed, looking around the room. The fire had died somewhat, the coals now not much more than embers, glowing with sullen obstinacy.

Had the fire hypnotized her? Had the vision been accurate? Eva focused on herself, seeking inward. Whatever had happened, she came to only one conclusion: if she had to wait any more, her daughter would be gone forever. The thought lay heavy on her mind and on her heart. As much as she knew the loss, coupled with so much dormancy, was leading her down a spiraling path on the way to depression, she began to hatch a new plan.

Checking she was alone, Eva peered out of her cottage. There was nobody in the forecourt; it was pitch black but for the occasional spotlight focused on the walls, lighting the castle for those who passed in the night along the highway nearby.

Slipping into one of the great halls used for banquets when not open to the tourists, Eva looked about. The leftovers of one such event still remained; messy tables, no doubt left for the morning staff, were covered in an abundance of cutlery. Amidst this was exactly the tool Eva desired: a carving knife. About a foot long, this had obviously been used for something bloody judging by the stains. Eva ran her finger along the blade, leaving a narrow line of red where the skin separated. It would suffice.

Stalking out of the hall, Eva went in search of the next part of her plan. In truth, she had no idea what she was doing, but Nina's cry filled her mind. This overrode anything resembling sanity.

"Madame, may I help you?" A French accented voice asked from an open doorway Eva had just passed.

Eva stopped, turning on the spot, and appraised the blonde girl in the grey dress and pinafore, standard uniform for the castle staff, as she stepped forward.

"I think you can," she answered, a numbness overcoming her better judgment. "I need to find a place. You are going to help me get there. You see: I lost my daughter."

"Oh no, how dreadful. How did this happen?" The concern on

the young woman's face was absolutely sincere; despite this, Eva began to stalk her.

"She was taken from me, only days after she was born. She is an innocent, *the* innocent. Thrust into a world she can't possibly know or understand. Sin took her there and only sin can save her."

"Oh no, Madame. There is no way sin can offset sin."

Eva shook her head. "No, you are wrong. Sin is not just an act of wrongdoing. Sin is a gateway. Sin is a portal to another place. Sin is a means to an end."

Pulling the knife from behind her back, Eva continued hunting the girl, who began retreating into the room. She ignored the girl's gasp of fear. The subsequent screams for help just washed over her, convincing her she was doing the right thing.

"You will help me find her," Eva droned, grabbing a fistful of blonde hair and raising the knife, preparing to plunge it down exactly the way the dark version of her had done in the dream.

The maid screamed; her eyes focused on the blade.

Eva saw her own reflection in the polished metal of the knife and hesitated. This mask of rage was not her. This was not who she had spent all her life striving to become. She was a doctor. She preserved life, in her own way.

Releasing the hair of the maid, Eva just stood there, numb, watching herself in the blade, so close to committing the worst of sins. Her breath came in ragged gasps, and she doubled over, vomiting on the floor. The pain filled her middle now, radiating out anguish and loss. She began to sob, hoarse noises never seeming to contain enough air. Her vision faded. Her face in the knife was the last thing Eva saw before she blacked out. Eyes glowing red, teeth filed to points, grinning in satisfaction.

Eva stirred. She was comfortable and felt a lot better. Moving her pinkie against her ring finger and finding no ring there, Eva realized she had returned to the harshness of reality. Without opening her eyes, she concluded she was back in her quarters, her wedding band missing, lost in the collapsed cave housing the Orpheus sensor. But she was not alone. There was breathing in the room and a scent so familiar it made her feel whole.

"Hey you," said Madden's deep voice from across the room. Eva's eyes sprang open.

"Madden!"

He smiled at her, all warmth and confidence, the feeling suffusing her with joy but never quite undoing the knot of pain at her core. Madden rose gingerly from his seat and came to sit on the edge of the bed beside her.

Eva grabbed his head, clutching him to her as she planted a kiss on his warm lips. Madden reciprocated but then groaned as she attempted to pull him closer.

"What is it?"

"Careful," he said, wincing. "They only let me up this morning."

"Why? What happened? Where have you been?"

"They have had me shielded. I was very badly injured at Orpheus. Worse than you knew. That blow from Asmodeus crushed everything in me. I was in pieces. As I understand it, I was safeguarded from those beyond by the residual energy from the collapsing portal. Once we were away, they used the same technology Ivor Sarch had been developing to keep a portal open, except they reversed it and used it to keep them shut. They did it in the ambulance, but more so here. Eva, the other side can't know about this castle. The technology is in its infancy. Powerful, but it is not strong enough to stop the inevitable. Portals will open, and I need to be healed."

"But you are hellbounce. You can heal quickly."

Madden held up his hand. The cold had spread crystalline veins up his arm to the elbow. "Not as quickly as I once could. They only let me out this morning. They had you sedated after your little stunt. Now, you are going to have to do some answering of your own."

On the tail of his words, Gila, Swanson, and Steadman entered the room, along with a couple of the castle staff, a man and a woman. Mercifully, Eva suspected for sake of both their wits, the poor girl who Eva had assaulted was not among them.

"While you were recovering," began Steadman, "Doctor Scott attempted several times without success to breach the restricted area. She became quite adept at eluding me." With this comment, the elderly curator arched an eyebrow at her.

"At least we know the defenses are secure," Swanson commented, receiving a glare from the unnamed pair across the room.

"The charge leveled is very straightforward," Steadman continued. "Eva Scott assaulted a member of the castle staff with the intention of grievous bodily harm."

The couple glaring at Swanson now settled their gaze on her. There was undisguised hostility there. Eva suspected had she been alone with them, more than hostile looks would have been traded. Thank God for Madden.

There was no point being coy here. "It wasn't bodily harm. I intended murder. For a moment, I was going to kill her. I would have killed anybody crossing my path."

The woman gasped and the man took a step forward.

"You would have killed my Shelly?" His accent betrayed his English roots. His face was beetroot with indignation at this disclosure.

"May you go straight to Hell for even considering such an act," his French companion, a short woman of middling years spat.

Swanson nodded in the background, understanding on his face.

"Are you her parents?" Eva asked.

"We are," replied the Englishman, tall and rangy, with short grey hair. "What you did was unforgiveable. What you could have done was worse. If you had a daughter, could you imagine what life would be like if you lost her?"

The comment hit Eva like a well-aimed punch to the stomach. "I... I... I'm so sorry. I wasn't myself. I would never..."

Shelly's mother began to retort but Swanson stepped in. "Look. There was no harm done beyond a bit of a scare. This was all clearly a misunderstanding. You and your daughter have served well in the castle. I understand if you feel you need to press charges; it's your right and you are entitled to move forward, but for now, we need some time with Doctor Scott alone."

The tone in Swanson's voice when he said 'alone' brooked no argument and with one final glower from Shelly's mother, the couple left.

"The depression. Is it bad?" Swanson asked after Steadman had locked the door.

"It is my fault," the ageing curator said, his voice heavy with sympathy. "I should have seen the signs. I thought her desperation to reach you was borne out of loneliness."

"No, Steadman, my actions were my own," Eva said, smoothing out the sheets of her bed. "I miss my daughter. She has been gone a week, and I yearn for her more than ever. She is in great peril. I saw an image in the fire. A vision. A dream. I could not tell. Nina and Elaine were there, as well as great shadowy monsters, contorted and evil. They all wanted to consume Nina, but something worse prevented them. I knew I had to get there by any means necessary. The quickest way to Hell was murder, then suicide."

"I guessed as much when I heard what was happening." Madden took her hand. "I do a lot of hand holding it seems. You are a nightmare."

"I wish I could make it up to the family. The poor girl must have gone through hell. What will happen now?"

Swanson looked over at Gila, who nodded back.

"They are castle staff, not ARC," Gila said. "They will be offered compensation. If they choose to pursue the matter, well, let's just say the case will never reach the authorities. We do not have carte blanche to do as we will in this world, but these are exceptional circumstances. You and your daughter are far too crucial to get caught up in so trivial a matter."

"Attempted murder is not trivial," Eva argued, amazing herself with the words coming out of her mouth, even though she was the culprit.

"Yet we will take these steps for you. It may be what you saw was, in fact, your daughter reaching out to you. It is acknowledged you have a preternatural link. We have seen evidence of this far too many times to deny it."

"Also," added Swanson, "the boundaries are thinning. As Hell and Earth come closer, it may be Nina can reach you. The enemy has a plan, and the time has come for you to see the final part of the castle. Eva, if you feel up to it, we have something to show you."

CHAPTER THREE

Eva stepped with care over a pile of bricks as the five of them made their way through the crypt underneath the castle. High brick-vaulted arches rose above them, festooned with thick black electricity cables that fed the lighting this far underground. Dampness permeated the air and left a musty taste clinging to the back of Eva's throat.

"We always end up in cellars or crypts, it seems," she observed, placing her hand on the wall only for the stone beneath to crumble. It was clear why there was wreckage everywhere. These foundations were not solid.

"We deal in death," Swanson said from in front of her, tripping as he turned to look back. "ARC might not be on the surface an organization of such limited vision, but look at our ultimate objective. Demons are the reason Jerome Guyomard founded this organization. We plan against the day we have to fight creatures most people don't believe in. Those who do believe in them fear them. We guard across the globe against the threat of incursions from a place that should not exist. Our singular goal, as things stand, is to rescue a newborn from the very place we never want to see on our doorstep."

"ARC: We will keep the demon from your door," Madden quoted in the sort of voiceover one heard in commercials. "Catchy, no?"

"I'll alert the media wing of the organization," Swanson answered wryly. "You can be the poster boy when demons start invading."

"It doesn't seem very stable down here," Eva announced, wiping dust-covered hands on her jeans. She started to tie her hair back, and then thought better of it.

"Looks can be deceiving, young miss," Steadman said as he hopped over the rubble she had just passed.

Eva grinned at the old man. "Yes, so it would seem. You are very light on your feet all of a sudden."

"Steadman was a procurer of antiquities in his younger days," Gila interjected. "It is a skill set that one cannot easily put aside."

"Rick was much the same," Eva said in somber tones, remembering the great brute of a man who had remained at their side and protected the two of them after Elaine revealed her true nature. "He paid the ultimate price despite those skills."

"He did," Swanson agreed, "and we shall miss him. He was one hell of a man, Eva. But don't get too down about it. Rick Larrion understood the risks and, despite his quiet demeanor, he was vociferous in retaining his place with you. He almost came to blows with other agents to assist in his capacity. On the front line, there was no better man to serve. Honor his memory by never forgetting the man."

"Amen," Madden said; the irony of his demonic half not lost on anybody.

Gila turned a corner in the crypt, where the end of the brickwork met a roughly chiselled rock face. Winking at Eva, she pushed an inconspicuous section of the stone, watching it slide back into place. There was a heavy 'clunk' from behind the rock, and the section dropped back, sliding out of sight.

The gap revealed a metal frame on which the stone face had pivoted. Beyond, the walls were dark, the stone of the underworks covered with what appeared to be carbon panelling.

"It's not sanctified, is it?" Madden asked.

"Not at the moment," answered Gila. "If demons find their way into this area of the castle, they would never get this far. Trust me, when I say the defenses have been disabled for you, and you do not want to ever see them in action."

Madden looked about them, his face tentative.

"Ladies and gentlemen," Steadman announced, "if you would be so kind as to proceed in, I will seal the entrance behind you."

"One way in, one way out," Swanson said to Eva with a wink.

Eva led the way, tugging on Madden's arm to encourage him along. The black hallway had the distinct ARC reek of sterile cleanliness, with the promise of something ancient at the end.

The rock slid into place behind them and from this side, Eva could see the complexity of the mechanism holding it in place.

"That must weigh…"

"Upwards of twenty-five tonnes," Swanson provided. "Welcome to the ARC retreat, where the secrets with secrets of their own are kept secure."

The hallway opened out into a room about thirty feet square, with several smaller rooms accessed through archways. Judging by its shape, the ceiling was evidently buttressed in the same fashion as the rest of the crypt but more of the dusky material hid any brickwork. Lighting came from many small bulbs hanging on nearly invisible wires about two feet from the ceiling.

"This is hidden?" Eva looked about the room. Servers and computers crowded one side. The rest of the retreat was dedicated to shelves of documentation.

"Hidden, bombproof, infra-red proof," said a familiar voice. Jeanette Gibson, member of the Council and head of ARC's media wing entered the room. "Satellites can see nothing but the castle. If nuclear war erupted, we would be protected from both radiation and the electromagnetic spike. There is one way in and one way out; we could control most of the world's media from this one room. If the castle crumbled, this would remain the only standing structure within the walls."

Eva crossed the room and clasped her blonde-haired ally in a brief hug. "It's good to see you, Jeanette."

The woman Eva had once only believed to be the ABC World News anchor held her at arms' length, examining her with a look of approval. "You have done well. You have come such a long way in such a short time. You're definitely not the innocent I met in Alabama. I'm so incredibly sorry about your daughter."

"She's not lost yet," Madden protested.

"Indeed, Madden Scott. It seems you are proof anything is possible. Human, demon, human, demon. Hellbounce doesn't apply to you."

Madden laughed. "When you put it in such a way, it's more like 'Hell-yo-yo'. The beast within is always ready to explode. I have more control this time."

"It's for the best," Jeanette concurred, "for control is needed now more than ever. With events transpiring as they have at CERN, it has begun; as much is clear to anybody able to interpret the signs."

Eva glanced at Gila, who nodded.

"Eva was party to the information as I received it."

"What neither of you know is the extent of how personal this has become."

There was an edge to Jeanette's comment, and it hooked Eva. "What exactly do you mean? What's happened?"

Jeanette opened a black leather folder on the table nearby, placing several photographs where Eva could see them.

"Look familiar?"

The images awoke several latent memories in Eva's mind. "The mountain... my street... Swanson... your house in Sweden... I don't recognize this last one. But they all look damaged."

"It has begun in earnest: the demon attack on Earth. The very event we were charged to guard against."

Eva turned to Gila. "This is what they were telling you? No wonder you didn't want to pass the information on."

"Some of it," Gila admitted. "I did not know all of the locations and the extent of the damage until now."

Eva studied the photographs again. "A fiery pit where my house used to stand. It's a fitting end for a truly despicable hellhole."

"Unfortunately, the demons that emerged from the portal did a lot of damage before they were stopped. Two children and their mother were killed in a nearby house."

Eva put her hand to her mouth. "What were their names?" she asked, afraid for the answer she knew was coming.

Jeanette flicked through the dispatches. "Ellis and Jessica. Their mother was..."

"Roxanna," Eva finished. "They lived next door. Oh, dear God, we have to do something about this."

"All in good time. In Sweden, Eyvind and Rikke Moeltje perished when the house collapsed. On Gehenna, a number of ARC operatives were killed."

"And this last photo? It looks deserted."

"You couldn't be more right. That's the Gobi Desert, in Mongolia. A lightning storm of immense proportions erupted in a clear sky and disappeared just as quickly."

"The Gobi Desert," Madden pondered. "The same place where the Convocation of the Sacred Fire intended to send you to protect Nina."

"Indeed," Jeanette said in agreement. "All incursions were ended after a brief interval. Portals from this frozen dimension opened and the demons were taken. They are being picked off before they can do too much damage. In this, the enemy of our enemy..."

"Is a worse enemy," Eva finished. "They are taking demons for the exact same reason Hell's minions are coming here. They're strengthening their forces. The stronger they become, the easier it is to cross. Asmodeus said as much."

"Undeniably. These places all have one thing in common. You two."

"You think they are tracking us?" Madden spun to Eva. "Could such a feat even be possible? Did Asmodeus have that kind of power?"

"I don't think it was necessarily him."

"What do you mean?" Swanson asked.

"Ivor Sarch. He is a demon."

"Impossible," Swanson declared. From the tone of his voice, it sounded as though Swanson wasn't certain.

"There was writing on the wall in the sepulchre Iuvart safeguarded. You were there. It read Rosier and Garias. Iuvart was clearly a different entity entirely. Who else was closer to Benedict Garias than Ivor Sarch?"

"We have safeguards," said Jeanette.

"Designed by whom?"

"The technology wing of ARC."

Eva threw up her hands in exasperation. They could not see it or were still bound by some kind of influence.

"And who runs the department and what are their key interests?"

"Benedict Garias. He is at fault, but he would never willingly become a traitor to humanity. They research demon science, armor and weapons, emergence tracking… and energy… Oh dear God, what have we let ourselves become?"

To Eva, it was as if a bubble of steadily building pressure had popped and everybody could see with clarity for the first time.

"Gila, you read a quote about Rosier when we found the name. Do you remember?"

Gila looked baffled. "No, I'm sorry I have no recollection."

"Open up one of these computers and search on the name."

Gila flicked on a nearby monitor and sat down at the desk. A few taps on the keyboard and she started to read aloud.

"Rosier is listed as second in the order of Dominions, and with his sweet and honeyed words, he tempts mortal man. He is considered the patron demon of tainted love..." Gila looked up at them from the desk, "... and seduction."

"You were hoodwinked. All of you. When we stood in the Council chamber, Ivor Sarch said barely a word. He didn't need to. The vote had already been decided because demonic influence was enough for him to sway the people he needed to convince to vote him onto the Council. It may be Nina was protecting me from the influence, just as she has done on so many other occasions. I was as susceptible as any before I was pregnant." Eva looked pointedly at Madden, who had the grace clear his throat in embarrassment.

"Yes... um... we were definitely caught under the spell for a while. As fun as the night was, we had no idea other than in Moynagh's for a brief moment we were being played."

"I could see it in the chamber and none of the rest of you were aware. I went into labor at precisely the wrong moment. He has been playing ARC for fools the entire time. Ask yourself this: his shielding technology— could it also have been used for tracking?"

Swanson slammed his hand down on the table in frustration. "Of course. It must be the reason they wanted the amniotic fluid they collected from outside the ambulance. They weren't just using it to open a portal. They have some way of finding you from Hell. Something tells me it's not all fire and brimstone down there, you know. Look at these photos. Every picture is a place we have been. Is this targeted guessing or practice?"

"We need to know more about what they were doing. Will Benedict Garias still be at ARC Headquarters?"

Jeanette referred to her tablet computer. "There is no record of any arrival or departure after I left which was before the lockdown; whatever else is wrong with the organization, they take threats like this very seriously. The last we heard was he had disappeared with Sarch. I have no more news yet."

"We need to get there then," Eva decided.

"There's more to it than just prying information from Garias though, Eva," Swanson countered. "What do we do with any information we get? Yes, we know your theory is very sound about Rosier, but he is gone. Zoe Larter, despite her unsavory affiliations, is dead. Killed by the very creature she served, willingly or otherwise. I must say I have mixed feelings about her involvement. It disturbs me somewhat that I do not regret what happened as much as I should."

Madden reached out and took her hand. "She had her eyes on your prize, for one reason or another."

"True, but if there is one thing we have been taught by this, it is that all life is precious. Benedict may be our only hope of understanding this situation of course, but..."

"But he is only a means to an end. You know what I want, Swanson. If they are finding a way through to us, then I want to find a way through to them. There has to be another way to make a portal."

Swanson considered this for a moment. "We have always found there is a certain residual energy reading when gateways have been open. The longer they remain open, the stronger the signature. It might help us detect a more likely location to benefit us. Orpheus was open for a while and it was a portal of massive power. If we can get down there, maybe we can get the readings we need to calculate accurate locations. We could turn their technology against them."

"Good. I don't want to waste any more time. I suspect there isn't anything positive we can learn from here. Ancient documents put us on the path, but technology is going to open the door. I have a ticket for a one-way express train to Hell. My daughter is there waiting. One other thing." Eva held up her left hand and wiggled her fingers. "I gave you my wedding band when I thought I was going after Nina. I would like it back, if there is any way we can find it."

"There was a lot of wreckage down there," Gila said. "We left quite a mess."

Jeanette smiled. "Oh, you would be quite surprised how much rubble angry scientists and their friends can move when they realize their precious science project has been heartlessly misused. Plus, it was in part ARC funded. We want to get to the bottom of this as much as those working there. I'm sure there is a way down, so let's..."

The end of Jeanette's sentence was drowned by the wail of a siren. A repeated 'whoop' of a noise threatened to deafen Eva, and yellow warning lights blinked on as the main power in the room was extinguished.

Eva looked at Madden in confusion as a loud rumble from somewhere nearby made the walls shake, sending clouds of dust from atop ancient manuscripts into the air.

"What is it?" Madden shouted at Swanson, his voice just audible above the noise.

Swanson shook his head and tried to flick on another of the screens. Nothing happened. Another shudder shook the room and then the rock door opened.

Steadman stumbled in; his forehead marred by a huge gash with blood pouring down. He waved at them, urging them to come to him.

Eva didn't need any further invitation. Madden grabbed her hand and the two of them dodged around falling shelves, heading for the door.

"What is it?" Eva heard Swanson yell from behind them.

"Lightning!" shouted the elderly curator. "Lightning from a clear sky. It's right above us!"

"Oh crap," Eva heard Madden say as they passed through the doorway. "They've found us. They know we're here."

CHAPTER FOUR

THE SALVO OF EXPLOSIONS CONTINUED AS EVA AND HER companions made their way back through the crypt, clinging for dear life to the warmth of Madden's good hand. With every blast, fragments of the ceiling jolted loose, shards of rock from the roof plummeting down, threatening to blind her. Dust was everywhere, the scent mingled with heavy ozone. Eva felt her hair begin to rise with the build-up of static electricity. One peek revealed the same thing was happening to everybody around her. Had they not been fleeing for their lives, it would have been time to stop and laugh.

"Go to Hell, get an afro." Madden said exactly what she was thinking. "So much for the protection."

Eva smiled. The last things to fail him would be his humor and sense of camaraderie. By the appearance of it, Madden's comments worked. Despite the imminent carnage, Gila, Jeanette, and Swanson all had grins on their faces. Eva began to laugh. In her black business suit, Jeanette, especially, looked ridiculous with her blonde shoulder-length hair standing on end.

Madden pulled his phone out to get a picture.

"Don't," warned Swanson. "You can see what's happening. If you turn your phone on, with this much electricity in the air, you will probably electrocute yourself and attract a bolt of lightning down on us to boot."

Madden paused in the act of switching his phone on. Instead, he pocketed the device.

Another series of blasts hit the castle above. A crack appeared along the ceiling, a deep rupture appearing with the groaning cracks of breaking rock.

"Young miss," said Steadman. "It is time to move with haste. The next room is safer."

Eva needed no more urging, and hastened under the brick-buttressed arch. Taking a deep breath, she willed the rest of them through in silence, afraid any noise she made might bring the roof down. One by one, her companions appeared from the dust-filled cavern. Eva touched them all on the arm to reassure herself they were all right. Steadman, Gila, Jeanette, Swanson.

"Madden?" She called. "Where's Madden?"

Through the arch, there was a colossal crash as the roof gave way, tonnes of rubble pouring down from above. Dust blew through, blinding everyone.

"Madden!" Eva shrieked.

"Here," he replied from within the arch.

Eva grabbed him, kissing him hard. "What were you doing?"

"I'm dead. Better those with a real claim to life went first."

"You are not," she contradicted him.

"Kids, how about we argue the semantics of what it means to be alive when we don't have a severe chance of all ending up dead?" Jeanette spoke with the authority of someone who expected to be listened to. "Steadman, where now?"

"Cars are useless," the old man called back. "We have a boat tied up at the dock. We ought to be able to reach it from here if the outer walls are still standing. It should get you to Geneva."

"Great, nothing quite like a nice paddle in the face of Hell," Madden bellowed above the thunderclaps.

Swanson grabbed Madden's shoulder. "If it's the boat I expect it to be, no fear there!"

"Through the next section, up the stairs, across, and down. The boat is tied up at the mooring. Go!" Steadman pointed in the direction they needed to take. Another barrage of lightning shattered the structure above and there was a cacophony of noise as bricks hit the water nearby.

"Where are you going?" Eva called to the old man.

"Someone has to secure the retreat. The entire history of ARC is there, young miss. Good luck." Steadman pointed once more and started toward the collapsing crypt.

"Wait! That's suicide!" Eva moved after the old man and found herself held immobile by her husband.

"Eva! Remember the real goal. We have to find Nina. We have to rescue our daughter! He knows what he's doing. Let him go."

Eva allowed Madden to turn her and lead the way out of the castle. The last Eva saw of Steadman, he was disappearing into the ruined crypt, one hand holding a cloth over his mouth against the dust.

They followed the trail through the remainder of the crypt. The lightning flashes became much more palpable, virtually non-stop in their frequency.

"Keep your eyes lowered when we get out," Swanson advised. "Your natural inclination will be to look up, and this close you will go blind. Also, stay below the height of the walls. You are less likely to attract the lightning. Go! Go!"

Eva scurried out of the crypt, up the stairs, and out onto the walkway leading to the moorings. Keeping her eyes fixed on the flagstone pathway, she acknowledged Swanson was right; it was very difficult not to look upward. The air stank of weird scents. The ozone was mixed with sulfur and phosphorous; it felt as if the very air was ready to open up a furnace.

At the end of the walkway, Eva turned right, hugging the wall as she descended the stairs.

"Hurry," Swanson called. "This isn't a good place to be. Metal railings are everywhere."

Eva noticed, beginning to panic. She stumbled on one step and only Madden's quick hands caught her. She gave his hand a quick squeeze, not turning her head.

At the bottom of the steps, they were partially shielded from the electric assault by the walkway above.

Madden looked about them. "This is it?"

There were two dinghies with small outboard engines tied up under the stone supports for the pathway. Eva's heart sank. "We don't stand a chance."

"Not here," Swanson called from the back of the group. "Keep going?"

More lightning. Fragments of sulfur began to filter down through the air, settling on Eva's head.

Shielding her eyes from above, Eva peered ahead. "The path ends in Lake Geneva, Swanson."

"Keep going. Around the corner."

There was nothing obvious in front of Eva, just water between her and the tree-lined shore a few miles in the distance. She leaned out to find the stone blocks of the path had crumbled into the water. More importantly, another boat was moored. Black sides, low at the stern with cream leather seating. It would have been beautiful but for the apocalypse happening around them.

Eva grabbed the wall and jumped across the gap to the remaining stone dock. The wall was high enough they were totally shielded from the bombardment if they ducked, so she dropped to a crouch.

Madden followed her an instant later, pausing in admiration when he saw the boat.

"Nice. Sunseeker Portofino. That should get us there quickly enough," Madden approved. He jumped aboard and was in the pilot's seat in seconds.

Eva followed him onto the boat, standing close as he fired up the engine, feeling the unfamiliar rocking as their transport reacted to the overhead pyrotechnics. "Is there anything you don't know?"

Madden laughed, waving Swanson, Jeanette, and Gila aboard. "Love, I lived in Jamaica. Plenty of boats about and abundant work for a mad driver like me. Everybody sit down. Swanson, cast off."

Once the boat was free, Madden gunned the throttle; the luxury boat surged forward onto Lake Geneva. In the distance, the sun reflected off the surface of the lake, turning the pristine blue water a beautiful silver. Scarcely a cloud dotted the sky; vapor trails from a plane's exhaust the only markings.

"How far to Geneva?" Eva requested of Swanson, the noise of the engine significantly less than the thunderclaps, yet still loud enough she had to shout.

"Maybe forty miles. Don't worry; this little beauty should get us there quickly enough. She handles thirty-odd knots, so I reckon forty miles should take us about an hour."

Madden opened the throttle and the boat leapt ahead. "Something tells me an hour is not going to be fast enough."

There was another series of booms and Eva could not resist. Turning back to the castle, she beheld for the first time, the enormity of what was happening.

"Lightning strikes from a clear sky," she said aloud, causing everyone but Madden to follow her gaze back to the castle.

"Chillon won't stand for much longer," Swanson said.

The castle, though it still stood, was black and charred from the continual lightning assault. In many places, the building was on fire and several of the rooftops had collapsed from view. Above the walls, bolts of purple-tinged lightning shot down from an amoeboid tear in the sky. Other lightning, more yellow in color, shot up from the castle.

"The light in the center is growing," Gila observed.

"It grows with each strike," Swanson agreed. "We're seeing a portal initiated from their side entirely. This is how they are doing it. Madden, hold to the left of the lake. Not too close to the shore. We want to get on dry land as soon as we can, but we don't want to run aground."

"Why? Surely this is faster? It's definitely a damned-sight more luxurious."

"I have a faster way," Swanson said and pulled out his phone. "This is Director Guyomard. There is an incursion event in progress at Chateau de Chillon, Lake Geneva. I need full air support for extraction. Use this signal to triangulate."

"Nice," Madden called as he kept his eyes forward. "Remind me to keep you around all of the time."

Eva had not taken her eyes from the castle and the image was affecting her sight. It was compulsive viewing though.

"The portal is growing in size. It's enormous."

"This is no Hellbounce for sure," Gila observed, her hand tightening on Eva's arm. "Look!"

The lightning took on a curve as the light at the center of the tear in reality began to spin clockwise. Even from this distance, Eva could see the electrical discharge struggling to keep up. The portal rotated until it was horizontal. All remaining was an elliptical light directly above the castle. It was surrounded by a whipping vortex and a stygian show of power. Despite all she had seen in the past year, nothing had prepared Eva for what was to come.

The portal expanded and a creature from nightmares emerged, landing directly on top of the ruined castle, sending bricks from the walls flying outward hundreds of meters at the impact. It was massively muscled, with black skin looking more like the shell of a lobster. Its shoulders and legs were wrapped in sinew and the enormous paws with which it braced its landing must have been the size of a double-decker bus. Worst of all, was its ungodly face. Set lower than its shoulders, almost mid chest, two bright yellow eyes hungered above a circular mouth, with teeth pointing in all directions. Eva had seen the Behemoth. This thing looked worse.

"Madden, can this boat go any faster?" Eva asked as she watched the monster find its feet.

"Why, what is... oh no." Madden had turned to see what had fallen through the portal, only the occasional spark remaining.

The monster rose to its full height, at least twenty-five meters high, leaned back and roared.

Eva put her hands over her ears and screamed. If the lightning caused a noise, this creature threatened to shatter windows for twenty miles.

"We aren't going to last very long if they know where we are and they keep dropping those on us," Madden said, unbalancing them as he turned the boat hard to port, embracing the coast as much as he was able.

"Let's hope they don't," Jeanette said.

The demon had begun to dismantle the castle, roaring with a hunger as if it were missing something.

"It's like a cat unable to catch its mouse," Gila observed. "But it's going to tear apart the castle looking for you. Maybe it is the portal technology finding you and not the demons."

"Let's hope so, or we are all dead."

"More portals!" Eva shouted and pointed. Just as soon as the tear in reality had closed, the smaller ice portals had begun to open, tentacles attempting to seize the obsidian giant.

The demon roared in pain every time one of the tentacles touched it, but swatted around with those colossal fists, destroying anything coming after it.

"It's like a spider trying to trap an elephant," Madden said. "Those tentacles aren't going to do any more than irritate it."

Madden was correct. Within few moments, all the portals had winked out.

"It appears they want to hunt the demon. Imagine the boon they will suffer if they succeed in turning it."

"Quite frankly," Swanson said, glaring at the ruin of Castle Chillon, "I'm in a mood to help them. My family has been heavily connected with Lake Geneva and Chillon especially, for generations."

The demon, now the ice tentacles had retreated, began to dismantle the castle in earnest, crushing the ancient brickwork as it sought its prey. It roared in frustration as it stamped down on one section of the castle, the roars becoming pain as something too small to see fought back.

"It's Steadman," Swanson crowed. "He's still alive and has activated the defenses."

"What defenses?" Eva asked, squinting as she tried to see what Swanson saw.

"The retreat is self-sustaining," Jeanette provided. "It has power for months. Swanson decided it would be a good idea if one could reverse the polarity and output the power as a massive electrical shock. All in one go. You just witnessed it."

"But surely if Steadman is alive and has unleashed that, there is nothing left. He is defenseless." Eva grabbed Madden by the shoulder. "Cut the power."

"What?"

"Do it. Steadman helped us. He got us out. I'll be damned if I can't at least do something to pay him back. Does this vessel have distress flares?"

"Should have," Swanson answered. "Standard for any ocean-going vehicle."

He knelt and retrieved a solid-looking metal case from under Madden's feet. Opening it up, Swanson revealed a flare gun and ammunition.

"I suppose you want me to fire these at it?"

"No, fire them up in the air. Madden does this boat have a horn?"

Madden nodded, not saying anything, still regarding her in disbelief.

"Do it. Both of you."

As instructed, Swanson began firing flares into the air, while Madden let off blast after shattering blast of the horn.

It took maybe ten seconds, but the demon ceased stomping the ARC base out of existence and turned toward them.

"Keep it up, but let's go!" Eva ordered.

Even from this distance, she felt the demon's eyes narrow on her. The roar turned from violence to one of hunger. The hunter had found its quarry.

With one enormous leap, the demon left the castle and entered Lake Geneva, submerging in moments and causing a wave. From the cacophony of noise before, the relative silence was unnerving, the boat's engine and little else. The demon was under the water, seeking them from beneath.

CHAPTER FIVE

"Okay, you got its attention, love," Madden said. "I hope to God you have more to this plan."

"Sorry, nothing comes to mind."

Madden slammed his hand down hard on the steering wheel, causing the boat to veer and Eva to lurch to her left. "Dammit Eva, what were you thinking?"

Eva glared at her husband. "I was thinking better us than them. If this demon is after me, or you, then it's going to get us, come what may. Why should innocents die because of a blood feud? Why, after he saved us, should we do any less for Steadman when he is clearly doing his job to its utmost?"

"A blood feud? Is that what you think this is?"

"Why not? They are using the very essence of what makes us 'us', the very fluid that supported and nourished our child in the womb, to locate us. Iuvart repeatedly referred to me as a 'Child of David'. Why me? What was so special about me? Why is my blood and Nina's so crucial to their endeavors?"

"The Scroll of Judgment. They thought only you could open it," Gila contemplated.

"Exactly. What if we are the last surviving Scions of David? What if the introduction of demonic essence was enough to reverse the Scrolls intended purpose?"

"You mean like your blood corrupted the Well of Souls?"

"I like to think of it as 'enhanced' it, but yes. If opening the scroll fully opens the portal between realms and the bloodline is tweaked by demonic essence…"

"The portal isn't going to just open Hell to earth. It could be used to open anywhere. Here, this ice realm… heaven…"

Eva nodded at Gila. "God would look damned strange with horns and a forked tail."

"So that begs the question: Why would they send a creature of such massive size after you? And why now? There is something here not making sense."

"Maybe the enemy decided they don't need me alive to make use of my body."

"Or it's pure coincidence," Madden countered. "They are trying to fill the earth with their own kind; it could just be you are a good point of reference to send something likely to cause a lot of damage. The longer it's here, the more the balance tips in their favor. We need to find a way to send the demon back."

Eva peered at the boat's wake, studying the indigo depths of the lake for any sign of movement.

"How deep is Lake Geneva?"

"A few hundred meters at its deepest, but it varies," Swanson said. "What are you thinking?"

"The demon was a good twenty-five meters tall. Just gauging how long it might take to catch up. Your helicopter, will it be armed?"

"Probably. It will be Swiss military. As a country, the Swiss are well defended. The majority of those undertaking national service keep their weapons with at least a nominal amount of armament. The same can be said of their air force. They consider their navy without equal."

This brought a guffaw from Madden. "Only the inhabitants of a landlocked country would say such. Eva, what's your plan?"

"Is there a way to get us off the boat while it's still moving?"

Swanson considered this for a moment. "They could probably winch us up if it were called for."

"Call it in. Here's what we are going to do. Let us assume this demon has the mentality of a cat after a mouse. It appears huge, but not too bright. Let's be honest, a little light and sound show was enough to draw it into the lake. Like the Behemoth, it is designed to be a battering ram and hold ground while the balance sways.

"So let's leave the mouse where it is, on the lake. They might have been targeting us, but the demon is presumably left to its own devices once it's been cut off from home. Fix the boat so it's headed in one direction and then get us off. Launch some kind of weapon to disable the demon and hope we have a bit of help."

"Help?" Madden asked, turning in his seat.

"The enemy of my enemy is my friend. At least until the point it becomes my enemy. The demon is swimming in the water. Water freezes."

Madden broke out into a smile. "Good plan." He pulled Eva toward him and kissed her. "How long do you think we will have to wait?"

Not really wanting to let go, Eva revolved to look out onto the lake. "Not very long." She pointed. "The demon is following us in the water."

Gila grabbed a pair of binoculars and looked in the direction of the castle. Saying nothing, she watched and then passed the binoculars over to Swanson.

"Dear God," he breathed. "That thing's enormous. It has to be moving as fast as we are, if not faster. Good eyes, Eva."

"We're gonna need a bigger boat," Madden quipped, the movie reference bringing a smile to Eva's face.

Eva took the binoculars and watched for herself. There was a bulge in the water, nothing more than a couple of the demon's shoulder ridges cut the water like sharks' fins. "It's moving fast but still a couple of miles off. We need to cut this fine. Where's your helicopter?"

"There," Swanson pointed at a black speck in the sky above the left shore of the lake. "We need to get past the headland before we take any action. If you want to trap this entity, I suggest doing so where it is going to be able to put its feet down."

"We're gonna have to be right at the entrance to the city," Jeanette warned.

"Right. I'll get on with warning people."

The ARC directors became a flurry of activity, while Madden kept his eyes on the lake. Eva watched their pursuer building a head of water as it chased them.

The hunt was agonizing. Fighting against an element Eva presumed the demon had never before encountered, it nevertheless gained on them with creeping regularity.

Eva divided her attention between the demon and the helicopter, the tiny object gaining form and definition as it neared.

"Where are we?" Madden shouted above the noise of the engine, maxed out as fast as it could go, but still not fast enough; the demon was under a mile away now, the bulge in the water rising higher than the boat as the fiend gained momentum. The water was cresting, the now-elongated head of the demon visible under the surface, its bright yellow eyes staring straight at her. Even through the binoculars, she could feel the hunger, the urgency driving this monster onward.

"Thonon-les-Bains is over there on the left. We need to get past Yvoire on the next headland to stand a chance of your plan working. The water gets shallow as it approaches the city."

"Still another ten miles," Madden said and proceeded to curse.

"At the rate it's gaining on us, we won't get much farther, Gila concurred with a desperate glance astern.

"Distract it," Eva suggested.

"With what?" Madden replied. "Harsh language?"

Eva considered the boat and its contents. There were fluorescent lifejackets and rings stowed in one compartment. She took these and threw them into the lake. "Counter measures. Got any more flares? Set them off."

Swanson did as bidden, aiming for the floating refuse and firing the remaining three flares at the surface. In the meantime, the chopping of helicopter blades increased in volume; their rescue was overhead.

"Time to go," Swanson decided as a tethered rescue jacket was lowered to the boat. "Madden. Use this rope to tie the wheel in place."

Madden took the looped rope, regarding it with doubt. Behind, the demon loomed in the water. "No. Not yet. We need to keep on going as long as possible. You get the ladies out of here, and then we tie it off."

"You're first," Swanson said to Eva, approaching her with the rescue jacket.

"No, I'm waiting here with Madden."

"No, you aren't," Madden shouted back. "Swanson, get her out of here. Knock her out if you must. One of us needs to be alive to rescue our daughter!"

Eva couldn't argue with him. The reminder of a greater goal here subdued her, and in no time at all, Eva allowed herself to be strapped in.

"Yvoire," Madden called and pointed. "Hang in there, gorgeous; it won't be long."

Swanson jerked the tether to indicate readiness. Eva found herself swaying through the air, the downward gust propelling her hair all over the place.

The sense of urgency lessened between vehicles, even with the helicopter only a few meters above them. Behind, Eva watched the titanic demon as it reached the jettisoned items. As she had hoped, it slowed; massive fists reached for the rescue gear. Lifting them aloft, it crushed the remains in one huge paw, shoulders and head appearing above the water. It screamed in rage. The boat's horn blasted in defiant response and the chase was once again on; the demon moved faster than before, making up the lost ground. Water rose ahead of it, eight, ten metres high, the top of the wave cresting white. It was a sight rarely before been seen on Lake Geneva: a tidal wave.

Eva found herself pulled in by two somber-faced men in blue uniforms and ear protectors. One unclipped the harness while the other lowered a second to the boat. In quick order, Eva was ushered to a seat on the far side of the helicopter where hand signals indicated she had to strap herself in, which she duly did.

From her vantage point, she could see the wave but not the boat, as the shoreline hurtled by beneath them. They had passed the land jutting out into the lake and were now above the strait leading into Geneva. The city was visible up ahead, the populace unaware for the most part, of what was causing the evacuation.

A head popped into view from below, the dark hair of Gila flapping in the wind. Clutching her belongings, Gila took the seat next to Eva, smiling at her in encouragement. Eva tried to say something back but the noise of the rotor blades was so loud; any verbal communication was lost. She settled for a thumbs-up.

Below, the demon-borne wave had closed to within a half a mile of the boat. The momentum of the water caused the wave to grow. It must have been a quarter of the way across the lake. Boats anchored at moorings were thrown landward by the sudden rise in water. Houses were devastated in the wake of the flooding.

Another head, the blonde locks of Jeanette Gibson, who allowed herself to be unclipped with a minimum of fuss. They were far down the strait now, the land encroaching on both sides and the wave growing higher. This wasn't just the momentum of a huge body under the water; other forces were at work.

Jeanette took a seat opposite and, after a moment of searching, passed headphones to them both.

Eva placed them over her head. Instantly, the noise of the helicopter disappeared.

"Your husband is either the bravest man I have ever known, or a complete damned fool!" Jeanette shouted through the microphone on her headset.

"Why?"

"He wants to pilot the boat all the way to Bellevue."

"Where?"

"Up ahead where the coast narrows on both sides. You have Bellevue on our right and Collonge-Bellerive on the left. The lake is shallower there and the shore closer. It's a bottleneck. He wants to lead the demon up against the shore."

"He's insane. What good will we get from giving the demon the ability to stand?"

"We have a little something planned for the creature. This isn't an assault vehicle, nor is it the only bird in the sky."

Swanson appeared on the end of the tether as the winch ceased movement. He sat next to Jeanette and grabbed another set of headphones. The demon was only a hundred meters behind, the wave gaining on the boat and Madden now, threatening to lift and tip them.

"Are we set?" Swanson asked.

"All ready," Gila replied. "How about downstairs?"

"Your lunatic husband has this idea he can swing away at the last minute. He has the boat set in the right direction and I swear he's staring the demon down as it closes in."

"Get the winch down," Eva screamed. "Get him out of there."

Her stomach clenched in knots as the wave came closer and closer to the boat, rising as the lake shoaled to the point the wave was only just below them. In the midst, the demon hungered, moving with more purpose now its target was within reach.

They crossed an invisible barrier and Swanson waved a command to the airmen, who began to winch once more. Eva waited for signs of her husband, but the tether sprang up and the helicopter lurched.

"He fell off!" Swanson said, peering out of the open side of the helicopter. "He's all right. Trying again."

The wave, right behind them now, crested as the demon fought through the water, finding its feet on the floor of the lake. It roared, a noise threatening to deafen Eva despite the headgear and the helicopter. The wave continued, tipping the boat as it was overtaken. Eva saw no sign of Madden.

"Where is he?"

"Got him!" Swanson called. "Sortons d'ici! Volez à Genthod!"

The helicopter swung away, gaining height and speed as the blades churned the air. Underneath, the demon plunged on the helpless boat but another noise intruded. Eva watched as two missiles launched from afar streaked across the surface of the lake, slamming into the demon's chest and exploding.

The damage wasn't mortal, but the demon threw its head back and roared as black ichor erupted from its chest. As it did, portals erupted all about the demon, the air chilling in an instant. Some portals opened beneath the water; the water froze around the legs of the demon. From the vantage point of the retreating helicopter, Eva watched in mute horror as tentacle after tentacle whipped out of the icy apertures to snare the giant demon. The monster screamed in pain and rage as it became caught in this web of icy death, and the screams turned into panic. Then from above, much as the portal had opened horizontally to allow the demon to earth, an enormous aperture formed, the air beneath freezing the surface of the lake. The demon struggled as one enormous tentacle uncoiled and lazily wrapped itself about the waist of its victim. It tightened and lurched, the demon screaming. The tentacle pulled the demon from the lake, snapping its legs where they were trapped in the frozen water, hauling it, dripping black blood, into the portal.

As before, once the prey was captured, all portals winked out, leaving a lake frozen for a mile in every direction.

Unable to contain her patience any longer, Eva unstrapped herself from the seat, leaning out of the helicopter's open door.

The black strap used to winch them up hung loose, flapping in the breeze, the harness on the end devoid of human life. Madden was nowhere to be seen.

CHAPTER SIX

"Madden? Madden!" Eva turned back to her companions. "He's not there."

"He was just there," Swanson said, by all accounts as confused as she was. He called on the pilot to circle around.

The helicopter banked. Eva was thankful she had hold of the inside of the helicopter as for a moment she was face-down above Lake Geneva, air the only buffer between her and the lakes' frozen surface. Below them, the lake was solid around the feet of the demon, black blood running over the ice, repelled as if it were oil. Of the boat, only a smashed hull poked through.

"What if he's in there?" Eva quelled her panic with deep breaths.

"He's not," Swanson answered, "and he's not on the ice, so he can't be down there; the ice stretches too far. He would have been a mess had he hit the surface. It's like falling on concrete from this height. There has to be another answer. Let's get on the ground where we can think."

Eva wanted to argue, but with the rush of wind on her face and the overpowering 'thud' of the helicopters blades, she had to concede he was right and took her seat once more.

. . .

It was only a few minutes later the helicopter settled on a neatly manicured lawn next to a beautiful mansion in what she presumed was Genthod; the journey felt like months to Eva.

Already a couple of local men had emerged from nearby houses, rifles in hand.

"Tense situation," Jeanette observed and hopped out before anybody could stop her. She approached the men; her hands held up in a gesture of pacification and began speaking.

Before long, the men turned away and Jeanette returned to the helicopter. She had noticed something by the evident look of amusement on her face and leaned in.

"You had better get out here."

Fearing the worst, but confused by Jeanette's reaction, Eva threw her headset down on the seat and jumped down to the springy turf below. She turned and put her hand over her mouth in a moment of hilarity; Madden was tangled in a web of netting attached to the belly of the helicopter.

"Do you mind if someone lets me out," he said, his voice reeking of embarrassment. "This really isn't dignified."

Relief swept over Eva. Caught up in the moment, Madden looked ridiculous. She began to laugh.

Swanson and Gila came to see what the fuss was and in short order, the mirth at Madden's expense was overwhelming.

At length, he said, "If you really don't mind, I'd love to get my feet on the ground."

Swanson nodded and the airmen, grinning themselves now, untangled Madden from the netting.

Eva helped him up, squeezing him tight.

He squeezed her back. "There's nothing like a thrill-ride for the constitution."

"How did you get there?" Gila asked.

"The harness wasn't on properly as you saw. I hung on for dear life and the harness started swinging. There wasn't a lot of length on it and I saw the netting. I figured my best chance was to hook myself under the helicopter. Unfortunately, I was a bit stuck. You lot didn't notice; I presume because your attention was held by something bigger."

"You must have had quite a view," Jeanette's voice was full of admiration at his feet.

"You could say so. Believe me; you don't want to be the nearest animated object to an insane giant demon jumping out of a lake if you can help it. The demon knew I was there. I really don't think being attacked bothered it. It was more irritated to be losing its prey."

"You're safe. I don't care about anything else." In an arched tone, Eva added, "One of these days you and I are going to have a serious talk about your apparent lack of self-preservation."

Once more together, the passengers climbed back aboard the helicopter, Swanson ordering the pilot to fly above Geneva rather than go straight to CERN.

"Did the ice stop much of the wave?" Jeanette asked, looking at Madden.

"No, it had passed when the demon took out the boat. I can imagine it might have dissipated somewhat without the driving force behind it, but there was a lot of water on the move."

"And the lake only got shallower," Swanson added. "Oh dear God, look."

"Oh no," Eva said aloud, surveying the carnage in front of them.

Geneva was under water, the streets flooded and cars piled up against buildings where the tsunami had hit them unprepared. Parks were underwater, the trees flattened by the power of the wave. The city was a mess.

"Looks like it spread a good mile on either side of the main point of impact," Swanson observed. "Most of the water is standing. It looks from here as though it went a couple of miles right through the center of the city. "

"The World Meteorological Center wasn't spared," Eva pointed out.

"I've got to get down there," Jeanette decided. "You can land me on the roof. I don't care what Johan Klaas thinks he is doing by adhering to protocol. This city needs help and ARC has to be responsible for it."

In quick order, the helicopter touched down on the roof of the ARC headquarters, the elliptical glass construction having sustained damage to the first four stories judging from what Eva saw of the missing glass.

"The wave must have been thirty feet high here," she said, terrified at the mere prospect of witnessing a wall of water so high bearing down on her.

"This wasn't even in the main path," Swanson replied.

"Don't you worry about this mess," Jeanette said in a tone signifying she would suffer no argument. "I'm on it. We did what we could with the time and resources we had. With any luck, most of the city was evacuated. The Swiss are tremendously resourceful when the right buttons are pushed. You go get these readings. If you plan on going ahead with this insane scheme of yours, or if we can get earlier warnings about portals, maybe we can mount a stronger defense."

"Good luck," Swanson shouted as Jeanette removed her headgear.

"Get back here as soon as you can," Jeanette shouted back. "It might take more than your uncle and I to sway this."

With a squeeze of Eva's hand as she passed, Jeanette stepped down from the helicopter and waved as it lifted off.

The land stretched out beneath them as the helicopter resumed its brief journey from the center of ruined Geneva to the Orpheus site. The stink of diesel fumes had begun to take its toll on Eva, threatening to turn her stomach. She considered it funny the turbulence during the flight and the rocking of the boat had not affected her at all.

Eva took great comfort in the shared feeling of inclusiveness with her husband and their friends. Given her experiences with Gideon, who had turned out to be the demon Iuvart and Elaine, her daughter's abductor, these moments were rare. Gila was her closest acquaintance and the former Curator of the Coptic museum in Cairo smiled in understanding. Swanson, a man torn between politics and doing the honest, right thing, was as steadfast as they came. His explanations might be somewhat inconclusive, but in his own way, he always had her back and would support her. Even in hare-brained schemes like this.

They followed the road leading right to CERN, the very same road they had chased Elaine down only a week or so before. Eva tried to map out the particle accelerators beneath the ground, but from this height, there was no discernible disruption in the surface along the French-Swiss border.

The helicopter descended as the lush green woodland surrounding the entrance came into view. With the explosion and consequent subsidence, the towering electric pylons once dominating the skyline had collapsed into a depression presumably above the Orpheus cave. They were able to land in a clearing right outside the concrete tunnel.

"What's the status?" Swanson asked when an engineer in a blue boiler suit approached.

"The power drain has been isolated and sealed off. The sensor or whatever you think is down there has no life."

"Turn it back on."

"What?" The engineer pulled off his yellow hard hat and scratched at a receding hairline. "We've spent the last week moving heaven and earth to power the sensor down, and now you want it back on?"

"Look, when we return, you can turn it off again, right? We need to study what's left of the sensor and to get any answers we need it to function, at least nominally."

Eva interrupted Swanson's belligerent demand. "The people that caused this kidnapped my daughter. She's only a week old. If we get down there and analyze the sensor, we might be able to find a clue as to where they have taken her."

Evidently on the verge of a retort in Swanson's direction, the engineer paused, mouth open. "I will make sure it's powered, but as you say, nominally. It's very hazardous down there, and I wouldn't remain below ground any longer than necessary. Don't linger. The roof is still unstable, and any vibration could set off further collapse so you will have to walk."

Eva laid a hand on the man's arm. "Thank you so much. We won't be long."

Dragging Swanson away before he could say another word, Eva entered the Orpheus tunnel for the second time in a week.

"You really need to work on your tone," Gila muttered as the four of them walked down the concrete tunnel, cracks in the ceiling making it all the more precarious.

"He is a bit out of touch with the common man, isn't he?" Madden added. "Ah, what it must be to be a Guyomard, to enjoy such a life of luxury."

The gentle mocking hid none of Madden's fear of this place. Their recent visit had ended very badly for all of them.

"He's right though," Swanson said. "We don't want to be down here one moment longer than necessary. Let's be quick about it."

The tunnel appeared shorter than before; Eva surmised the last time she had been here, every step had felt like a mile in the fruitless chase for Nina.

Nina. She wished the portal had enough power to grant her but a moment's contact, just to let her know her mother was coming.

"You don't have to do this, you know," Madden said.

"Am I so obvious?"

"Yes," Swanson agreed.

Eva looked at Gila who nodded. "It is written all over your face, Eva."

"I'm fine. Wild horses couldn't drag me away. It might actually do some good to see this place in the cold light of... well, without demons everywhere."

"Just one," Madden took her hand.

Eva looked into his deep brown eyes. "If only they were all like you."

"If they were like me, imagine the human race walking on eggshells all day long, afraid of their neighbour threatening to lose dominance over the beast inside, if, indeed, that person was a hellbounce. My demon, whatever it is, must be very minor. I don't feel much threat to my control."

The first door hung wide open, the portal entrance beyond, no trace of the macabre scene greeting them from the last time they were here.

"The team would have been buried with honors, returned to their loved ones if they had any."

Swanson was looking at her; he knew exactly what she was thinking, but it was not hard to guess. Orpheus had nearly claimed them all and left them profoundly changed.

"It was all so senseless, but then Brian was never really one for thinking straight, even when he was alive."

"I don't feel I should really defend the creature, but I suspect Asmodeus and Belphegor did a good job of pushing him just a little bit further over the edge."

Eva's ex-husband had been the first of a new generation of hellbounce, demons randomly spawned back on earth in the host body of their mortal selves. The dagger used to kill the demon Iuvart, the very same blade used to cut Eva open on the mountain in Afghanistan, had properties allowing the wielder to reincarnate anybody they wished. Brian had been brought back to torment Eva and ultimately drive her to this exact place. He had succumbed to the one weakness a hellbounce really had: once they lost their shell of humanity, the demon alone could not survive.

Inside the first room, where they had once imagined the Orpheus portal to be located, they were met with absolute carnage. The walkway once created to provide access to the portal before had fallen from the wall and lay in pieces at the base of the second door. A ramp had been constructed to replace it.

"You two dragged us out through all this?" Madden said in awe. Both men had a look of bewilderment on their faces.

"We didn't really consider the logistics of it at the time," Gila admitted. "It was escape or die, and we were not going to let you perish."

"The sooner we get out of here the better," Eva said. "There are simply too many bad memories.

Eva climbed the ramp to the portal room, fearing what was to come. The doorway, fully open now, was half-filled with rubble. Stepping onto the loose pile of rock, Eva paused as she beheld the devastation inside.

"Jesus," Madden said from behind her as he looked over her shoulder. "How are you supposed to find anything in this?"

"All the action happened at the other end of the room," Gila replied. "Moving closer should make it more specific. Grab hold of the rail and follow it down. We have work to do, and time is running out."

Eva did as bidden and held on tight as she descended the hastily constructed stairs into the Orpheus cave. The treads ended abruptly; the rock and broken slabs of concrete from the ceiling large enough for the workmen to have traversed the cavern without further need for stability.

She watched the roof of the cavern with some trepidation. "These lumps of rock are bigger than I am," she observed, thankful they had made it out of the cavern before the ceiling had collapsed.

"Where did the pool come from?" Madden asked, pointing.

Down to their right, near where Gila had fired at the portal, the entire floor was under perhaps six feet of water, the temporary lighting turning the water a distinct turquoise color.

Eva saw the source. "Down the wall to the right, behind the gantry. It's leaking in."

"Water would compromise whatever integrity is left in the structure of this chamber," Swanson said, his voice now concerned. "I suggest we take the measurements and get out before we become permanent residents."

Up ahead, the Orpheus portal dominated the end of the room. As promised by the engineer above, the machinery whined with power. To Eva's dismay, there was not even a glimmer of light where the gateway to Hell had been.

"Sorry," Madden said, settling his good arm around her shoulders.

Eva turned to see genuine sympathy in her husband's eyes.

"We all had our reasons for returning, none of them the same. The portal was never going to work a second time. It was too damaged."

Madden was right. Where the superstructure had once fed in power from the CERN network, one of the relays now spat sparks, the end glowing red.

"But if we could fix it..."

"We would pass into Hell at a place of their choosing. If beneath is where it deposits us." Swanson was at a terminal, transmitting information to a small tablet computer.

"And what's the portal telling you?" Eva pointed to the screen.

"I can see there is a way to read the signals, both before and after. Eva, we have no idea what's the other side of this threshold; it was never going to be our way in. We have to be cleverer than them. They won't be there— Elaine won't be holding Nina to hand back to you, meek and with apology. They have plans of their own. We won't win this game by plodding on their pre-prepared path."

"As much as they desperately seem to want us to," added Gila. "Can someone help me shift this rubble? I have found Asmodeus."

CHAPTER SEVEN

Eva waited, gnawing the nail off her left index finger as Swanson and Madden heaved at a lump of concrete rubble. What was underneath suddenly made it all so much more real.

Tipping the concrete to one side, Madden let it fall away with the hollow clank of a very heavy piece of man-made construction material. Dust billowed out, disturbed by the movement, as the rubble settled.

Both men leaned in, blocking the view. Eva heard rather than saw Swanson gag. It struck Eva as curious how Madden was unaffected.

"What is it?"

"Looks like dried demon blood, judging from what we have seen before."

The previous incident came to mind, a creature of nightmares chasing them through tunnels from Westlabs, meeting its end at the unlikely hands of a Massachusetts detective, Mike Caruso.

Eva shouldered her way between the two of them. Acrid fumes threatened to overwhelm her, the stench somewhere between blood and sulfuric acid. Holes were burned in the rock floor beneath, disappearing even beyond the limit of her flashlight.

"Asmodeus was sliced clean in half by the portal's collapse; where is he?"

"Maybe his remains caused those holes," Gila observed.

"Or there could be another explanation," Madden offered. "Look under there."

Madden shined his flashlight to an adjacent section of rubble, where a small nook had been revealed. "There's something in there."

"Pull it out," Eva instructed. "It's okay," she said to the others, "I have a feeling he will be fine."

Seemingly emboldened by Eva's confidence, Madden reached in and tugged hard. The object slid out, scraping on the floor as Madden hauled it into the open.

"What the hell?"

Eva shone her light on the object. The light reflected off metal. A large spike thrust up from curved plate, evidence of smaller barbs having been snapped off. The section must have been two feet across; had the demon really been so large? She thought back to the last time they had been here.

"Here's what's left of his armor. One of the shoulder spikes looks damaged."

"He was chopped in half," Madden replied. "I would say he was pretty thoroughly damaged"

"There's more," Gila said.

Eva peered round the shoulder spike. A knife was embedded to the hilt in the metal. Pinioned to the armor by the knife was a crumpled note. She reached over and jerked the blade, wiggling it with the teeth-jarring noise of metal catching on metal. The knife, when it came free was eight inches in length, the blade razor-sharp obsidian, the hilt comprised of heavy bone.

"Nice," Madden admired.

"I don't think so. This was intentional. It's a message as much as the note, more so, perhaps. It's a reminder of what we have lost, what is going to happen."

Eva unfolded the note. Inside was her wedding band. She dropped it into her left hand and placed it on her wedding finger.

"No coincidence," she said to Madden and examined the note. Written in a fine, spidery script, unhurried and stylish, this had been prepared a long time ago. She read it aloud:

"Eva Ross,

You will know by now there is no way to avoid the destiny lying in wait for you. I have the Well of Souls, the Scroll of Judgment, and more importantly, your daughter.

Now you have ended my master, I have the ultimate honor of wielding the blade destined to end the world as you know it. Your daughter will die unless you take her place. I will bend her backward over the altar in the deepest pit of Hell and cut her throat, savoring the gush of blood as her life fades from her eyes. When I ascend to primacy, believe me you will wonder what potency is as far as lust is concerned. Your one night stand in the hotel will feel like a casual fling compared to what I unleash on your domain if you do not comply.

I offer you a trade: Your life for hers. I will grant you this opportunity to join me. Your blood and your blood only can reopen the portal. After, it will collapse, useless. If anybody else tries to come with you, the portal will collapse. You have fourteen days to decide. Wait any longer, I will gut your child and take pleasure in doing so. She will live if you comply, in a world remade by me, in my image. If she dies, your fate will be far worse.

I leave it to you to make the decision.

Rosier."

Eva folded the paper, placing it with care in the inside pocket of the brown suede jacket she wore.

"Well, those words make the decision for me. Fire up the portal. I need to go."

"You do not," Madden countered, his voice angry.

"What choice do I have? They are going to kill Nina."

"There is always a choice," Gila said. "There is more to this than the contents of this letter. 'Ascend to primacy' he says. He's speaking of politics."

"In Hell?"

"Why not? We honestly know nothing about what's going on there. To humanity, it's a place of fire and brimstone, full of mindless demon masses preying on each other and swarming about the place. We know differently. Hellbounces: Neither entirely demon nor human. Satan: Destroyed or at the very least deposed. Ivor Sarch, Rosier, whatever you want to call him, hardly seems upset by the destruction of his master. There are ambitions at play here we know nothing about. Fourteen days? How do you measure days in a realm without a sun?"

"I agree," Swanson added. "It sounds like they want you under their control, playing their game. We have another way."

"But Nina..."

"... Is a pawn in this game. She is your weakness, but I have a firm belief they will not harm her. They are too anxious to get you to Hell. Asmodeus was desperate for it. These ice beings are focusing on you. You have something they want."

Eva looked at the ruined aperture. "If I use my blood to open the portal, will you get better readings?"

"We have what we need, but it can't hurt. No talk of going through," Swanson counseled.

"There has to be a better way," said Madden.

Eva approached the machinery responsible for regulating the power to the portal. As she did so, the entire structure hummed to life and a screen popped out of the computer terminal, glowing a steady blue. Words appeared on the screen:

"Place hand here," she read aloud and proceeded to place her hand on a horizontal section of glass adjacent to the screen.

The screen changed to read 'Verified', and a robotic arm with a needle on the end whirred into life, rotating into position directly above her hand.

To Eva's left, the portal began to glow as power fed once more into the structure. So far, nobody had moved a muscle to stop her. It was all so close.

"Hang on," Madden warned. "The note said this was only going to happen with your blood. You haven't given any yet. There is something off about all this."

The robot arm buzzed as it lowered to just above her hand. Eva watched with interest, her only thoughts of Nina. The needle plunged down and as it did so, Gila grabbed Eva by her free arm, pulling her off her feet.

The needle plunged into the glass screen, shattering it. A sucking noise could be heard from the mechanism. Shortly after another arm appeared, the end containing an empty vial. This was passed into the mouth of the portal where it disappeared. The portal winked out, not a trace of energy left in the entire structure.

"They wanted your blood," Gila said as she helped Eva to her feet. "They never wanted you. This was a trap intended to bypass the need to get you to Hell. Once you cross over, Rosier, or whoever is behind him, wins."

"But now they have Nina."

"Correct, the game is unchanged. They will want you more than ever and will be aggressive in their hunt for you. Remember. Hell is under attack, too, and now they don't have an easy way out."

"We need help," Swanson decided. "It's time to go back to ARC. We have done all we can do here."

Eva turned to leave, trying as best she could to hide the devastation she felt at being denied a chance to find her daughter right then. Light flashed behind her. She turned to see small sparks of electricity dancing over the portal.

"They know we are here," Madden said. "The portal is activated. They're coming straight for us."

"Time to run," Eva decided.

. . .

Their escape from the tunnel was far less memorable than before, mainly because Madden and Swanson were conscious. As she exited the two rooms, Eva watched the same team of engineers who had been waiting above lock the door behind them and weld it shut.

"Nothing's getting through now," Madden said. Still, he appeared to hurry, the sweat on his brow evidence of his stress.

Don't lose control, Eva silently prayed. He was probably right; the way the ice portals opened up on any true blood demon meant they were doomed in such a small space. If it was another of those giants, it still couldn't pass through the restricted doorway.

Up ahead, the helicopter was waiting for them, rotors whirling. As soon as they were aboard, it took off, not even giving them time to sit down.

"What now?" Eva asked when she finally found her seat.

"Now we take over the council by one means or another, and take your dream vacation down under, so to speak. We have some friends who would literally die to come along." Swanson was deadly serious, no trace of mockery or sarcasm in his voice.

"The Shikari?" Gila asked, one eyebrow raised.

"Indeed," Swanson looked out of the window. "All this is for naught if we aren't prepared."

"You think the council will authorize their use?"

"I think the council will have no choice. They are our best hope."

"Who are the Shikari?" Eva asked.

Swanson smiled, his face a mystery. "I wouldn't want to ruin it for you. Words don't do them justice."

The journey back to the ARC Headquarters was a solemn one. The full extent of the demon-bred tsunami was now clear. The wave had washed through the center of the city and out into the suburbs beyond. Houses and treetops poked above a stagnating lake of muddy brown. Even from the air, Eva imagined she could smell the stench of sewage washed to the surface. Emergency services were everywhere, evacuating by boat and helicopter those who had not managed to heed the call to escape the wave.

"Structurally, it looks intact," Swanson observed. "It could be worse."

"But at what cost to people's lives? To their livelihoods?" Eva responded. "The intrinsic value can never be replaced."

"The same could be said all over the world," was his solemn reply. "Those tsunamis in the Pacific, not so long ago? People cope. With help, people rebuild, finding new memories. Humanity finds a way to move on; it's what makes us such hardy creatures. The key now is to make sure we continue as a species."

Swanson was right. For all of his faults, the arguments, and the secrets he kept, Swanson Guyomard only had the bigger picture in mind, leaving the details to others. Eva considered this as the Meteorological Center came into view; he was complicated, but he was probably the biggest humanitarian of them all.

The helicopter touched down and in quick order, Eva was ushered down stairs from the rooftop. The floor below housed what appeared to be the buildings' air-conditioning machinery, which whined as it strained to maintain the atmosphere. The air was markedly warm, full of vile chemical scents as the building struggled to assert itself. Jeanette Gibson was waiting for them at the bottom of the stairs.

"Good timing," she said, falling into step alongside Swanson. "What did you find?"

"Tricks by our enemy but nothing precipitous."

Jeanette looked to Gila for elaboration.

"Ivor Sarch rigged the Orpheus portal to take a blood sample from Eva and deliver it to whatever is on the other side."

"The portal is still active? I thought you took it down."

"So did we," Gila responded. "It looked pretty destroyed when I unloaded a clip of bullets at it and caused it to slice Asmodeus in two.

Appearances can be deceiving. It may be portals to Hell never truly close."

"If the portals remain permanently open, then Asmodeus was meant to die. Do you think his death was planned?"

Eva smiled. Jeanette was as good at reading people as anybody in her own profession. "I think that's what they are trying to imply. It looks like Ivor Sarch or Rosier as you really should call him, planned this all along. We thought Asmodeus was the power behind everything happening between Sweden and CERN, yet he was as much a dupe as anybody. There is a level of politics at play here; the subtlety and magnitude of which we have never seen. This could have been aeons in the creation."

Eva unfolded the note and handed it to Jeanette, who scanned it, her mouth shaping some of the words as she did so.

"I can already guess what you want to do, Swanson. It will take a few days to gather them, if you have a place in mind."

"We need to use the readings taken from the portal to calculate likely incursion locations."

Jeanette looked at Swanson, her face blank.

"What Robbie the robot is trying to say," Madden elaborated, "is we need to find the correct gateway to Hell."

"And then what?"

"And then we go find it, try to slip in unnoticed, find our daughter, and get out of there."

"You want to go yourselves? Very brave of you to volunteer."

"It's Nina," Eva said, her heart beating fast at the mere prospect of a rejected proposal. "I can find her."

Jeanette pressed a button to call an elevator, probably the same one they had entered from below the last time they were here. The doors slid open and the group entered.

"Jeanette, what is it?" Swanson asked. "I've known you for too long for you to hide it. You aren't the only one in this group capable of reading people, far from it."

"You might have to delay your trip just a little bit, Swanson."

"Why?"

Jeanette crossed her arms, leaning back against the side of the elevator, the stress she had been hiding cracking her normally stoic façade. "The ARC Council is in disarray. Johan Klaas is dead."

CHAPTER EIGHT

The elevator doors opened on a very somber ARC office, the reception area empty. To Eva, the room felt cold, as if the air conditioning had been turned to maximum and left on. There was absolute silence and they crept out with caution, as if to make a noise was to disrespect the passing of the Council's leader.

"Where is he?" Swanson asked at length. "Medical?"

"In storage. Since lockdown, none of them has left the building. They might be a contrary and awkward lot, but they respond well to protocol. It was a fight to even gain entrance."

"And Benedict?"

Jeanette smiled, a thin-lipped grim expression. "There we have good news. He showed up not long ago. Security found him out of another part of the building and delivered him here. He's in his own personal lockdown in one of the interview rooms."

"I'd like to have words with him," Madden snarled.

"Give it time." Swanson's face was a barely-concealed mask of fury. "Where are the rest?"

"In the council chamber. They are a very morose lot. All except your uncle. We know he was no fan of Johan Klaas, and I doubt he could even take the end of the world seriously. Be warned though, I suspect Margaret Anderson is plotting her way to the Chair again. The way the rest are reacting to Johan's death, they might even vote her in."

"Not this time." Swanson's face had steeled from angry to resolute.

Jeanette paled. "You wouldn't?"

"Remember why ARC exists and what we stand both for and against. I would indeed." Saying no more, Swanson squared his shoulders and marched to the doors of the council chamber.

"What?" Madden asked. He looked at Gila. "Did I miss something?"

Gila blushed, saying nothing and followed Swanson into the council chambers.

"He feels aggrieved at their treatment of Ms. Ciranoush," Jeanette said, approval all over her face. "Come on in, you two. You won't want to miss this."

Inside the boardroom, only six of the twelve council seats were occupied. The Canadian, Margaret Anderson, had taken the head chair, Petra van Veld, the Dutch treasurer and Sejal Khwaja, the Pakistani who feared Gila would supplant him on either side. A few seats apart, Jose Barroso Partada, the Brazilian head of Grail, the artifact research branch of ARC sat with Gaspard Antroobus, the head of Documents and Antiquities from Belgium. Eva smiled at the pair; they had voted for Gila at the recent failed election.

On his own, Swanson's uncle, Daniel Guyomard lounged with obvious indolence, one arm over the back of his chair as he watched them enter. "About time. Margaret here was about to explain to the rest of us why she should resume her former post. She said something about declaring you renegade and striking you from the council. Right, dear?"

The elderly Canadian woman, without doubt still a force despite her age, flushed in anger at Daniel's description, her tightly bound white hair hiding none of the blood rush to her face. "How dare you breach protocol, especially in this desperate time?"

"How dare I? Because screw you, that's how I dare. Look at you, gathering your cronies about you like a gaggle of old women. Taking the chair under the assumption it was your right. You gave up the right years ago to your boyfriend."

"Get out," Anderson hissed. "All of you get out! You, Swanson, are hereby struck from the Council under clause fifteen of the charter stating..."

"Yes, we all know what it states," Daniel interrupted her, "but you aren't going to be able to enact the clause."

"You have to be the head of the Council to implement an executive order without unanimous backing of the Council, Margaret," Swanson added. "I don't see unanimous backing. Johan dead. Larter dead. Benedict Garias a traitor. Ivor Sarch a demon."

"Ivor is not a demon," Sejal Khawaja spat.

"Could you tell his writing if you saw it?" Eva asked.

This caught Khawaja off guard. "Well, yes. He signed the charter."

"Finally, a word of truth from one of you, Lord be praised!" Daniel raised his arms in a mock-evangelical manner and rose from his seat. Crossing the room, he unlocked a heavy cabinet, removing a document from beneath thick glass. He returned to the table, placing the document before Margaret Anderson.

"There is his signature," Daniel provided, pointing at a handwritten entry low on the document.

"What has his handwriting to do with anything?" asked Petra van Veld.

"We found this letter addressed to me in the Orpheus chamber, only an hour or so ago," Eva unfolded the letter and placed it next to the charter. "Please take a look at Sarch's signature and the note. You will find the script to be a match."

Anderson glared at both, evidently trying to find fault.

"There is some similarity," Sejal Khawaja conceded before she had a chance to comment.

"What has this to do with the Council?"

"Gila," Swanson invited, holding his hand out, palm up in an invitation for her to speak.

Gila flicked her tablet on and began to read:

"Rosier is listed as second in the order of Dominions and by his sweet and honeyed words, he tempts mortal man. He is considered the patron demon of tainted love..." Gila looked up at them as she had in the castle, "... and seduction."

"You voted a demon onto the ARC Council," Daniel accused. "You were misled. Benedict Garias was misled, far earlier than you, I might add. Ivor Sarch was responsible for the portal technology and the shielding now guarding this very building, was he not? Who was his sponsor? The very same man who was misled from the start. The very same man who sat at this table and now sits not fifty feet from here in an interview room."

Swanson nodded at Daniel. "You people have to understand the threat we have always feared, the very peril looming over the earth since before the days of my forefather, is now ready to act."

"This is all stuff and nonsense," Anderson declared. "It is media speculation, probably all generated by her." Anderson pointed at Jeanette. "There are no portals out there. No threat is apparent."

Swanson turned to Jeanette. "See? Blind fools resorting to petty squabbles. They maintain an utter inability to listen to reason. I did not come by this decision lightly."

He turned back to the table and indicated the chairs with his right hand. "Eva, Gila, if you would please take your seats at the table."

"You do not have the authority..."

Swanson silenced Margaret Anderson with a stare. "Ladies, if you would."

Eva took the seat to Daniel's right, straight opposite Margaret Anderson, who looked very uncertain. Gila sat to her right, next to

Gaspard Antroobus, who positively glowed with anticipation. Jeanette took the seat to Daniel's left while Swanson remained standing.

"I invoke clause three of the charter of the Council of Anges de la Résurrection des Chevaliers: In time of imminent demonic threat, a member of the family Guyomard may assume the role of Council Chair, independent of the vote of the Council."

"You've always craved power. The Council will not stand for this," Anderson shot back without hesitation. "The Council is..."

"Fragmented, incapable of acting as a unified body under either Johan Klaas while he was still alive. Still incapable under yourself now and in the future. But under my uncle Daniel Guyomard they will act."

This caught everyone by surprise. Eva looked around the table, gasps sounding, dumbfounded faces showing on nearly everybody, not the least of which was Daniel himself.

"Swanson, I... The honor is too much."

"You won't make this stick," Anderson said, her voice quiet and calculating.

"I beg to differ. First, this is the charter we all signed, and if you do not abide by its tenets, you are out. Second, whatever advantage you think you may hold, consider this." Swanson held up his hand and the room filled with ARC special ops garbed in black, machine-guns held at the ready. Each wore a badge on their uniform, a stylized logo of a Roman soldier, a legionnaire. These were all members of 'Legion', the army once responsible for defending Eva on the mountaintop in Afghanistan. Several looked her way and nodded in recognition, though she knew not who they were in armor. "There is a reason Guyomards have always headed the wings of Security and Global Response, Defense and Tactics. In case they were needed."

"This is a coup, pure and simple," Anderson accused him.

"No, Margaret," Daniel said. "This is salvation." He rose from his own seat and approached her around the table. "If you would be so kind? The chair is no longer yours to occupy."

Anderson rose, her face angry with impotent rage. She glared at Eva. "I hope you are happy."

"I will only be happy when I have my daughter in my arms. If you had bothered to look outside these walls, you would know she was kidnapped. If you had read the note, you would know where we go next. You are most welcome to come."

"None of what you say is real," Anderson's denouncement was as ridiculous to Eva as it was stubbornly illogical.

"I wish you were right; I really do wish you were. I just hope you don't live to see us fail, or you might face worse than the demon guilty of destroying Chillon and ruining most of Geneva. Margaret, I feel for you. What were you ever doing here? Go and hide. Deep, in whatever crevice you can find. If we don't succeed, there will be no place they can't find you."

Anderson huffed at this and stormed from the room.

"Escort her from the premises," Swanson said to one of the commandoes, "See her safe."

He turned to the table. "Anybody else?"

After a moment, Petra van Veld stood, gathering her documents and refusing to look anybody else in the eye. With dignity, she was escorted from the room.

"I will remain," Sejal Khawaja decided aloud. "We all were duped by Ivor Sarch and there are more than worthy people to fill the gaps here. You. Madden Scott. Why do you not sit?"

"With respect, Councilor, you have already had one demon at this table, so I must decline the kind offer."

Khawaja glanced at Swanson.

"It's true. The demon returned with the opening of the portal."

"You can't keep a good hellbounce down," Madden grinned.

Daniel took the proffered chair at the head of the table, squirming. "This is uncomfortable. I'm having a couch installed. Swanson, for God's sake, sit down now. You're far too excitable; you always were. Do you have the readings you need?"

Swanson took his seat. "First things first. I nominate Dr Eva Scott and Dr Gila Ciranoush for seats on the ARC Council, non-sitting."

Daniel grinned. "Non-sitting, eh? Meaning you don't want them tied to Geneva because you have places to go?"

Swanson inclined his head. "Correct."

Already the atmosphere under the new Chair of ARC was more relaxed. Eva knew this would gird them in the dark times to come.

"Do we have any objections?" Daniel asked, looking around the table. "No? So let it be written. We have the charter before us. Ladies, if you would be so kind?"

Gila took a pen proffered by Gaspard Antroobus and duly scribbled a signature on the ancient document, passing both to Eva.

She studied the document for a few moments. Names she knew down near the bottom of the charter stuck out at her, Swanson, Jeanette, even Johan Klaas in a time when he was less obstructive. Further up the names were fading but the first name on the list was still strong: Jerome Guyomard.

Daniel leaned forward. "Yes, it's a piece of history you are penning your name on today. It is as important as the Declaration of Independence, the Dead Sea Scrolls, or the Magna Carta. Yet unlike those, people will probably never know the people who moved behind the scenes to keep their lives normal. They will never see this, whether we prevail or not."

"I'm honored," Eva admitted, "but I'm not signing this until our marriage is ratified."

A small smile crept across Daniel Guyomard's face. "I thought as much, so I arranged to have this made for you. Sejal, if you will?"

Sejal Khawaja rose from his seat, crossed the room to the same heavy cabinet the charter had come from, and removed a document about a foot wide, edged in gilt. He carried the document to her and unrolled it. "Mr. Scott, if you please, you will need to sign this as well."

"Sign it?"

"This is your marriage certificate."

Madden looked over the document, absent-mindedly letting his cold hand rest on Eva's shoulder. The touch was like ice but she endured it, preferring any touch to none.

"Looks more like the Scroll of Judgment," he said, referring to the document he had carried in agony from Egypt to Afghanistan. "Who are all these signatures from?"

"The leaders of just about every major religion in the world. Popes, Buddhists, Muslim Clerics, the Dalai Lama. If there's a name missing from my list, it's not worth knowing about, but it's safe to say your marriage is about the most ratified in history. We have a lot to thank you for, the most important of which has not yet happened."

"Opposition vote, eh?" Eva said to him.

The Pakistani laughed, a deep, rich sound. "You have a lot to learn about council politics, Dr Scott."

"Thank you. This means a lot." Her wishes fulfilled, Eva signed her name on the charter.

Daniel Guyomard cleared his throat, bringing the meeting back to order. "We have several key posts to fill. I would appreciate any suggestions you might have regarding who fills them."

"Let them wait," Eva suggested. "This is happening now. You need to act now. If we survive the end of the world, choose then."

"Eva makes a very good point, Uncle," Swanson concurred. "We need to co-ordinate efforts around the globe to repel the demons. Your department will work in sync with my own. ARC will need a leader when we are finished, but for now it needs a global response."

"We already have our hands full with various government and agency responses to the Nibiru threat," Jeanette counseled. "We need to lock them down. They are losing faith."

"May I suggest the truth at this stage?" Madden looked deadly serious. "These incidents are no longer isolated. People are not stupid."

"Do you realize what a profound change in their understanding will make in the life of humanity? Providing actual proof of Hell's existence? Religion is a delicate issue."

"Talk it over with your contacts," Daniel decided. "See what they think the best approach is and go with it. At this stage, with the media coverage of The Convocation and the Gehenna footage, it's really just affirmation of what they suspect. Swanson, what else do you need?"

Swanson turned to Eva. "Fancy examining a patient? It's essential to know if there's anything we are missing."

CHAPTER NINE

Eva followed Swanson down the stairs into a part of ARC she had never seen before.

"It's not just the one level with the council chambers," Swanson provided. "We could survive here for months on end, as we could in the underbelly of the castle."

"As long as a fifty-tonne demon doesn't drop out of the sky and land on the building," Eva quipped.

"True. The core of this building is of a similar material to the retreat, perfected more as this was custom-built for us. We have light from the rooftop redirected through the core of the building right to the base level. The World Meteorological Organization staff sees the light too but only through mirrors. They have no idea what's actually here. We have a bunker below ground level. When they say lockdown on this building, they mean it."

"You might need it soon."

"Perhaps. That depends on you. The council position you deserve, Eva. Nobody has been through as much as you have. Despite this, you are willing to take on more. You embody the values we seek to promote. Utter selflessness. There are not enough of you about."

"Swanson, I only do what I can to survive, to find my daughter, and see her safe. Any parent who truly cared would do the same."

"And your actions only make you a better person. You have had the pleasure of meeting Benedict Garias. You know how a man like him could never be considered virtuous, selfless. He is a dangerous opponent."

Eva stopped, causing Swanson to turn and face her. "I have dealt with dangerous opponents before. Just look up the records of the inmates... *hellbounces* I have interviewed in Worcester. Are you saying you don't want me in there?"

Swanson watched her for a moment, his face betraying nothing. "I'm saying I don't want you in there to begin with. Let him take out his frustrations on me. You can do plenty from outside the room. Just observe him. You should get a pretty good idea of the man."

They turned a corner and approached a series of muffled rooms. Swanson called them 'interview' rooms, but Eva understood they were plainly interrogation cells. Swanson opened the door to one, and rather than just a plain cell, Eva saw it led to a muffled corridor, one door going into the cell, another to an observation room.

"He can't see or hear us?"

Swanson smiled, a twinkle in his eye. "They have been piping in white noise ever since he was brought here. Have a look."

Eva ignored the window to the cell and walked through into the observation room. Through the window, a frail old man sat staring into nothingness. Wisps of hair hung from his head, as if he had thrown a fit of rage and not composed himself. His hands were cuffed to the table in front of him, the chain looping round a metal bar, and keeping him secure. His jaw was clenched in discomfort.

"What's wrong with him?" Eva asked taking a seat in the confined darkness of the warm room.

Swanson flicked a switch on a panel in front of them. A hissing filled the room, making Eva cringe. "White noise, static. It gets to you after a while. He's been on edge for days."

"But what you're doing is torture."

Without another word, Swanson left the room, closing the door, and leaving Eva in the silence of the soundproofed room. In a moment, he appeared at the door of the interview room, his face an emotionless mask. He entered, sitting opposite the old man. Without making eye contact, Swanson shuffled through a sheaf of notes, giving the interviewee plenty of opportunity to become even more wound-up.

Eva flicked the switch enabling sound; there was silence in the room except for the sibilant rasp as Garias breathed.

"You must love this," croaked the old man, his voice left ruined by throat cancer and no doubt additionally injured by whatever release of rage he had recently experienced. "Power, the Council in the palm of your hand. The ability and backing to do anything."

Swanson kept his eyes on his notes. "You've been proven guilty of treachery. You have misused the funds of governments around the world, and in league with the minions of Hell itself, sought to bring mankind to its knees. The list of those calling for your head would go from this room to the council chamber. Where is Rosier?"

"I have no idea who you are talking about," Garias spat.

Swanson slapped the file of notes shut, and without looking at Garias, stood up, and started to leave the room.

"Wait? Where are you going?" There was a genuine tinge of panic in the old man's timeworn voice.

Swanson glared at him. "You're wasting my time." Giving Garias no time to respond, he exited the room, slamming the door shut to the sound of the old man's strident howls. The white noise resumed, but Garias was unable to put both hands over his ears at the same time because of the cuffs.

Swanson opened the door to the observation room after a moment.

"Thoughts?" He asked as he came in, looking at Garias through the window.

"His surprise at seeing you was genuine. He tried to hide it well. Benedict is all about the control and the power. He couldn't help but attempt to rib you regarding the council. He's shrewd and manipulative; he knows exactly what your presence here means, but he is fixating on you. He doesn't consider your uncle a threat."

"Your reputation is well merited," Swanson approved, his voice remaining neutral. "Anything else?"

"I think the noise is getting to him."

"You don't approve? Would you consider the well-being of a traitor over the future of the human race?"

"I would consider the well-being of any human. The Geneva Convention was created for a reason."

"It was created so ARC could operate outside its boundaries. It was accepted by the global powers that there needed to be an organization outside of these rules with the ability to act swiftly if necessary. What will be eating Benedict up in there is the fact he knows this; he is a direct descendent of one of those who drew the charter up in the nineteenth century. You don't like this, Eva? I have had to deal with many unconscionable tasks during my career. I don't like this any more than you, but it could be the fastest way to your daughter."

Eva was about to let fly with a retort but an image of Nina forestalled her. It always came down to her daughter. "Go on then."

Swanson considered her, his face once again a mask. He nodded and rose, leaving the observation room once more.

Discomforted, Eva felt beleaguered now by the observation room. It was cloying and warm. The air was full of the sweat of conflict.

Back in the interview room, the white noise silenced and Swanson entered, resuming exactly the same habits, reading the notes, not looking at Garias.

"Where is Rosier?" He asked after finally looking up and acknowledging his subject. "I've a finely-tuned crapometer telling me your previous statement was false and you know exactly where he is. I have graffiti on a wall in Worcester, Massachusetts in a cell where Gideon Homes, a known associate of yours kept people slaves for decades. Decades! I have the video and computer evidence taken from the secret Westlabs laboratory with which you are known to have been a close associate. I have funding taken from ARC, the records which have now been brought to light. I have you behind it all. Lives are at stake, the very lives we swore when we joined the Council of Anges de la Résurrection des Chevaliers we would protect. It is all at stake because of the choices you have made. Now tell me where he is!"

"Or what?" Garias responded after a moment. "You will torture me? Do you think my frail body can withstand the assault? You think sleep deprivation or dosing me with sodium thiopental, or more of this white noise will make me any more susceptible to your questions? Do you want to water-board me? You know nothing and you have nothing to offer me."

Swanson glanced at the window from where Eva watched. "I can offer you information. I can tell you where Rosier is."

"Then you don't need me."

Swanson ignored the comment and continued. "Rosier has already returned to Hell. The Orpheus portal, the instrument by which you hoped to follow him, was not destroyed as presumed. It was disabled. Once the commotion died down, Rosier reactivated the portal and left us a little love letter."

Swanson removed a copy of the letter from his notes and passed it over so Garias could read it.

Eva watched, enthralled, as a myriad of emotions passed across the face of the old man. Disbelief was followed quickly by anger and then sullen acceptance. Betrayal, rage. Both were written all over his face as clear as if it had been carved into the flesh of his forehead.

"He said he would take me with him. I would be granted eternal life. He told me Hell was a place of an eternal instant where one exists forever. There is no aging. No death."

"You believed him. Why?"

"I am an old man, boy. A sick old man. I have suffered and still do. I have months left to live. Six at the most. The cancer eating me alive is only held at bay by the fact I give it nothing to feed on."

"You were a dupe, Benedict. Giving you hope was the easiest thing for Rosier to do. You have caused too much harm to too many for you to walk away from this. The best thing you can do is help us. Soon enough, the whole world will know what they face, if they do not already. Everything you think you have accomplished will only serve the purpose of those coming to colonize our planet. Your actions have already cost Zoe Larter her life. Would you cost humanity its future when you stand to gain nothing?"

The light appeared to go out of Garias' eyes as he came to the realization he had been beaten. He worried the edge of the letter from Rosier.

"Asmodeus wasn't meant to kill Zoe, only make it look like he had. He was always out of control. If there was one element of all this I would show contrition for, it is her death. Zoe knew what she was getting herself into. Her eyes were fully open to the potential gain and the risks we were taking. This..." Garias waved the letter about as much as his chains would allow. "This was irrelevant, none of our concern. We were already damned."

"You can't possibly accept your fate with any... oh." Swanson snorted a laugh. "Rosier."

This confused Garias. "What about him?"

"How much did you know?"

"He is a demon. Similar or lesser rank to Iuvart."

Eva shuddered at the memories of Gideon Homes, her mentor in her previous life at Worcester State. Had she not witnessed the subtle changes in his character, she would have been enslaved. Given what she knew now about her bloodline, the line of David, Eva suspected she would have been bred like a captive animal. Gideon had turned out to be the demon Iuvart, watching, brooding over centuries until the right person came along to open the Scroll of Judgment.

"The only detail written about Rosier is that he has the ability to influence men's minds," Swanson said. "Much like he did when the Council vote came about.

"The vote was honest," Garias hissed.

Swanson shook his head. Eva understood what was going on. This man was so far under the influence; they might never discover the whole truth. "If Rosier's influence was the case, then it's a good thing my uncle has replaced Johan Klaas as head of ARC."

This caught Garias off guard. "He wasn't expecting to hear of Daniel," Eva chuckled.

"What..." Garias fumbled for words.

"See, that's your problem, Benedict. You are so blinded by power and your search for supremacy you automatically assume everyone is like you. Could you ever see there were bigger issues at hand than a place at the table?"

"I know exactly what the issue is. Rosier seeks supremacy. You didn't need to show me the letter for me to realise his goals. There are politics at play on a level in Hell making the jockeying for position here look like the scurrying of ants in comparison. Someone down there made a mistake and they are paying for it. The ice coming through is destroying them wholesale. It seems one of their number was crucial in keeping the ice at bay and they were removed from service. They are seeking a way out, a place to stage before they fight back. Earth is their chosen ground, get used to it. As for me, better to be the right hand of the devil than a slave in ice."

Swanson glanced in her direction, the shake of his head almost imperceptible. "Thank you, Benedict. You haven't brought ARC down just yet. I understand our demise was your main goal, wasn't it? Bringing us down? Eradicating the one stumbling block from their path to conquest?"

"You won't win," the beaten man taunted. "You can't. What is humanity against the forces of Hell? Nothing. When Crustallos breaks free of his prison, you will all know suffering."

Garias turned away, evidently prepared to offer no more. Realizing this, Swanson gathered his notes and left the room. Mercifully for both Eva and the former director, the white noise did not resume.

"Did you get any more?" Swanson asked upon re-entering the observation room.

Eva watched Garias, still staring into empty space. "The portal was shut intentionally. Asmodeus was never going to make it back to Hell. If his death was inevitable, then Gila's assault on the portal was inconsequential; the portal caused the cave-in, not her. He believes his version of the truth. Rosier engineered the portal. He probably engineered its closure."

Swanson peered thoughtfully at the window. "What's Crustallos?"

"It must be something to do with the ice. Perhaps it's the creature reaching through the portals and taking the demons?"

"He said 'When Crustallos breaks free of his prison'. Not if, when. Like it's already a done deal. Why would demonkind attempt to flee to earth if the battle is already there..."

"...unless the battle is already lost," Eva finished the sentence. Then a fact dawned on her causing her to stagger back and sit down.

"What's wrong?"

Eva looked Swanson in the eye. "Asmodeus was never in charge. The whole Nibiru masquerade. It was to keep him occupied. Rosier is in Hell with Nina and Belphegor. She was freezing to the touch. There was something changing her. Belphegor betrayed Asmodeus, promising Rosier his place at her side; I would swear it. They took Nina, knowing I would go after her. Swanson, they intend to use us to *open* the breach between Hell and what is beyond. The battle is already lost because all the pieces are now in position."

"So if we don't go there..."

"They invade earth and we lose. If we do go there, they use us to release the boundaries and we lose. Either way, I am not leaving Nina to her own fate. We are going."

Swanson opened the door. "We have planning to do."

CHAPTER TEN

Eva followed Swanson back to the Council chamber, neither of them saying a word. The air smelled stale to Eva; there was no way out of the situation she now found herself in. There never really had been. Her daughter was in a place only the sinners were supposed to go when they died.

There was commotion up ahead as they entered the foyer. The Council chamber stood empty, seats abandoned in chaos. The noise came from a room on the far side. Swanson began to hurry and Eva kept pace with him, her legs aching at the strain of doing so. Eva's grumbling stomach reminded her she had not eaten and she grabbed a pastry from a nearby trolley. The smell of vanilla was cloying and the fat from the pastry made her hand slick but she persisted with nibbling on it.

"What's the fuss?" Swanson called out as they entered the room.

"Incursions, lad," Daniel said from a group on the far side of the room. The group consisted of Swanson's uncle, Sejal Khawaja, the Brazilian Jose Partada and the Belgian Gaspard Antroobus; Jeanette Gibson sat with Gila and Madden alongside some technicians who were busy monitoring calls and cycling through screen after screen of absolute carnage.

"Where?" Swanson asked.

"From what we can see, director, just about everywhere." The speaker was one of the technicians, a woman with dark hair tied back and a recognizable demeanor. The voice was very familiar, reminding Eva of an old ally— often missed, never forgotten.

Eva crept round to the side of the technician, studying her face. Warmth blossomed in Eva's middle as she beheld the face of someone she hadn't seen since Cairo, a year or so ago.

"Tilly? Tilly Cark?"

"Pardon me, it's Tilly Benson now, Councilor," she corrected, her eyes still on the bank of screens in front. I..." Tilly turned in her seat. "Eva?"

"You can't pry her away from these screens, I swear," Madden observed, causing Tilly to look around her colleagues to the other end of the desk.

"Madden?"

"Sharp as a tack, this one," Madden said, smiling.

"Of course, you know each other," Swanson added. "I forget we didn't just pick you up in Cairo. Eva, Madden, Tilly works for me in Frontline Threat Response. Quite the observer. A brilliant analytical mind once we wiped all of those insane patrol-cop rules out of her head."

"And you didn't know we were here? Despite everything?"

"I knew about Afghanistan, but they keep us fairly isolated."

"You know what I said about people you can trust," Eva said to Swanson. She turned to the rest of the Council. "This young lady saved Madden and me, helping us escape the horror of Sloss Furnaces where Iuvart first attempted to resurrect a ghost as a targeted hellbounce. You could do with ten more like her."

"What the hell's going on there?" Madden cried out, calling their attention back to the screens in front of them as he pointed.

Professional to the core, Tilly forgot who she was talking to and resumed her job. "You're watching Chattanooga, just below Lookout Mountain in Tennessee. The incursion happened ten minutes ago."

On the screen, cameras evidently on helicopters filmed an unfolding scene of utter devastation. Eva watched, feeling completely helpless as an army ploughed its way through woodland and housing, leaving it flattened.

"Oh no, there's one, no two of those demons that chased us in the lake."

Eva pointed to the middle of the screen. The enormous monsters were evident, armored, and heavily muscled, pummeling buildings and trees alike.

"You escaped a creature so big?" Bartada said in awe. "I'm impressed."

Around the giants, many smaller creatures swarmed, chasing after anything moving. Occasionally, there were flashes of white.

"The flashes are what we were looking for," Swanson confirmed. "As they hunt us and try to tip the balance, the ice hunts them."

The flashes of white became more concentrated and the smaller demons began to scatter. Their numbers gradually decreased.

"It looks like they are doing to the demons exactly what the demons are doing to us," Tilly advised. "They are shifting the balance, preying on weak and confused demons."

"How do you know?" Eva asked.

"Because the scene on the screen is what we are seeing everywhere. These portals are opening up, depositing large numbers of demons on earth for no reason other than containment. This balance will only be tipped when enough demons, and more importantly, their giant warriors and captains, are on this planet. These armies are largely confused, moving in no logical direction, with no specific target. The only pattern I can determine from my experience is one of following your previous path."

"Or the movement of my daughter while I was pregnant. If only we knew what they were using to track the path. Maybe we could find Nina the same way."

On the screen, the numbers had thinned and one of the large demons was stuck in a parking lot, a red sedan crushed in one of its paws, swinging its arms about as portals erupted around it. Tentacles snared it like prey caught in a jellyfish as more and more portals opened up.

"This is generally how it happens," Tilly informed the assembled notables. "The larger the demon, the more force needed to subdue it and the more portals are opened up to attack."

"They are learning," Madden perceived. "Whoever is doing this is not stupid."

"Crustallos," Eva recalled the name.

Madden looked at her, a question on his lips.

"It's what Benedict Garias called it. The entity behind all this is apparently called Crustallos and is locked outside of Hell. Crustallos is trying to break through. It wants back in to this reality. We have no idea when it was here before. Demonkind are hoping to use me or Nina to prevent Crustallos succeeding."

"Or they are hoping to bring it through," contradicted Swanson. "We aren't quite sure yet, but it looks like the main play is being made by the demon Belphegor."

Madden looked down at his arm. Eva could see a crystalline tinge to the skin, the lights causing it to glitter. "She who was freezing cold."

"Right. It looks like you are going the same way. How fast is the ice creeping up your arm?"

Madden moved his arm about, wiggling the fingers. "Not fast, but it is farther up than I would like. Belphegor looked terrible before the portal."

"We need to get this ended one way or another," Swanson decided. "What else do we know about these demon incursions?"

Eva looked at the screen where the second of the large demons was being pulled against its will into the netherworld. In moments, it was gone, leaving only a trail of devastation mixed with immense ice-covered patches of land.

"We know they are lasting longer, in proportion with the greater numbers they are sending through each time." Tilly replied. "Each army is led by one or two larger demons, attempting to deflect the focus from the smaller demons. Here we have Peshawar," Tilly flicked the screen to show a mob of skull-wearing creatures led by a brute wielding an enormous cudgel. "Here we have the town of Sawhaj." The screen showed close ups of what appeared to Eva to be an army of zombies, wielding blades and ancient shields. Behind them, the town was ablaze, the flames reaching over ten metres into the sky, pierced by the ice portals, which seemed much less effective in the dense heat. "There are many different types of demon. It appears they have different armies."

"The balance tips," Madden muttered.

"Indeed. It's taking longer for the ice to subdue them, but so far we have not committed any forces to the incursions."

"Why waste our own when someone is doing the business for us?"

"I think there's more to it," said Eva. "We have a plan, a mad plan, for those not in the know. We are going after Nina. I intend to rescue my daughter."

This caused all of the Councilmembers who had not been privy to the recent conversations to stand up and stare. A group of worried faces greeted her.

"Are you crazy?" Daniel Guyomard burst out. "We are here trying to prevent earth becoming Hell and you want to go there?"

"At least he didn't say he won't allow it," Swanson mumbled from behind her.

"I damned well shouldn't, but something tells me I'm only being included at the end of this conversation. That's why you want me heading ARC? So, you can go there?"

"Actually, it hasn't been decided who is going yet," Eva offered, "only Madden and I need to go. They are going to kill Nina because they want me there."

"A noble sentiment," Gaspard Antroobus observed, his Belgian accent only slight. "What do you hope to accomplish by going there? If you rescue your daughter, then what?"

"I haven't thought so far ahead," Eva admitted, not being able to see beyond Nina. "They have taken the one thing I love above almost everything in my life, and I'll not give up until I have made every effort." Eva took Madden's hand as she said this. "Do you have a family? Would you not give everything for them?"

Antroobus nodded. "I do, and I understand. I would give anything to help my children, grown though they are, should they need me."

"You won't be alone, either," Madden said. "I'll be by your side, remember"

"I know. Is that really wise?" Eva asked.

"To Hell with if it's wise or not. I'm halfway to Hell already. I might as well go see what I missed by only spending an instant there."

"I'll be going, too," Gila decided, holding her hand up as Eva started to object. "You are going to object no matter who volunteers. You are my closest friend and I feel responsible for you. I have knowledge which will help on this journey. With Swanson needed here to counter the threat, I am also the only member of this council with the real chance of making it there and back again."

Madden chuckled. "She's right. Some of you are a little long in the tooth."

"Jeanette, they are going to need you to keep a lid on what's happening, or if the truth gets out, keep everybody abreast of the situation." Eva looked round the room and Tilly shot up.

"I'll go."

"No, not this time you won't," Eva countered. "You are married now."

"So are you," came the obdurate response.

"True, but my husband is coming with me. I have the feeling we are going to need a small party."

"But one with the means to get the job done," Swanson said. "With the approval of the Council, I recommend we send the

Shikari; Hell is their ultimate challenge. Nothing even comes close. They are far more useful as a covert team than they are as frontline troops. There is only one way to get behind enemy lines in this battle. There is only one way we can end this. Stop whatever arcane ceremony demonkind intends to conjure up. Hit them hard and fast with the best we have. They might not come back from this challenge, but they will relish it nonetheless." There were no objections.

"Done," Daniel decided. "Is there anything else you require, Eva? You have pretty much any resource on earth at your disposal."

"Yes. I would like to see my parents. I would like to take Madden to meet them before we go. If we are to die in this attempt, I would like Mom and Dad to have at least met my husband once, even if they never see us again. Can you organize a plane to Iowa?"

Daniel looked at Swanson, who nodded in affirmation. "It will take a few days to gather the right team anyway; they are all over the world and sometimes a little difficult to find. Plus, it makes no difference at this juncture. You've earned it at the very least. I'd say you have two to three days' grace. We need to find a point of entry at any rate, which reminds me."

Swanson passed the tablet he had used in Orpheus to Tilly. "Wire this in. It has portal readings taken from CERN. It should help us predict likely locations for infiltration."

Tilly did as bidden and in a very short time, the screens of demon armies were replaced by an image of the earth in three dimensions, rotating with red dots in a suite of familiar places.

"America, Egypt, the Middle East. North Europe. Wait, what are these other markings?" Eva pointed at faint yellow dots on the map.

"Zoom in," Swanson instructed Tilly. "These are probably locations based on readings taken from Orpheus, as well as other known portal locations. There's a distinct spike in various spectra when a portal occurs. This was confirmed by readings taken by Ivor Sarch himself at Nag Hammadi."

"So these are potential portals?" Eva asked, staring at the enormous amount of yellow appearing on the globe as the data uploaded. "What if all of these were to open at once?"

"Then demons would flood onto the earth and the balance would be tipped in an instant. Let us pray we don't reach that point. Tilly, narrow it down a bit. We want lower level readings, not all of them. Any place the team is going to enter Hell, we want to be large enough to pass through but small enough they might escape notice. Our enemy isn't worried about subterfuge; they are anything but subtle."

Eva smiled at the irony of Swanson's statement. The moves and countermoves leading to this situation had covered thousands of years on earth.

"Still thousands," Tilly observed.

"Can you narrow the search? Try cross referencing the readings with places of death. Known hauntings."

Madden put his good arm around Eva. "Good thinking. All the places where this has been the worst for us were places of death. We need a location in theory already close to Hell, where the boundary might already be thin."

"Much better," Swanson said as the number of yellow dots diminished. "Okay, what do we have? Birmingham? No, Sloss is a mess. Geneva?"

"Very close, but still underwater and they know we are here," Madden objected. "How about Qina?"

"Too dangerous and it was where the knife was found. It will be swarming with demons. They flock to the residual energy. There." Swanson touched the image, and the map zoomed in on the north coast of an island. "Where's are we looking?"

"Montego Bay, Jamaica."

"What's there?"

Tilly punched the keys in front of her, bringing up the image of a very grand white house in Colonial style, surrounded by foliage.

Eva glanced at Madden; his face had gone pale. "What?" She asked.

"The building is Rose Hall, near where I once lived. It contains the tomb of Annie Palmer, the white witch."

"Small, concealed, underground," Swanson approved. "Perfect. Eva, you have whatever you need to go find your parents. I'll make sure you have protection and all manner of transport. We will see you in Montego Bay in three days."

Swanson lifted a phone from its cradle on the bank of controls. "This is Director Guyomard. No, the other one. The location is set. Freeport, Jamaica. Three days. Summon the Shikari."

CHAPTER ELEVEN

THE GOLDEN CORNFIELDS OF CENTRAL IOWA FILLED EVA'S vision ahead of them. "I feel numb."

"I don't doubt it," Madden said from behind the wheel of the black ARC security vehicle they had been given. No plates, no logo, though Eva swore it was just a souped-up Chrysler Grand Voyager, with two anonymous ARC operatives. Both wore identical suits, had comparable hairstyles, the same rectangular cut-from-granite jaws. Eva suspected if she did something erroneous, one might pull out a long silver memory-wiping device. She decided to call them Ron and Ron since they were so similar.

"Some flight," she said, more out of the need to break the silence than to start any real discussion.

"Mmhmm. If you say so, love."

Eva punched Madden's shoulder, his grip on the wheel not remotely altering; he was getting stronger.

"What? I was tired. It doesn't mean I miss Nina any less just because I was tired. We will all be tired before this ends."

Eva turned to the two agents behind them. "And you two. Ron

and Ron. What's your story? Do I need protection from my mother all of a sudden?"

"We are on war preparations, ma'am," Ron on the left replied, his lips barely moving.

"All ARC Directors must be accompanied by at least one security aide," Ron on the right added. "Our approach is considered non-invasive, unless you have need of us. Just continue as you normally would, ma'am. We will watch over you."

"Just continue as I normally would," Eva echoed. "Yeah right." She turned and looked out the window, watching Sioux Gateway airport disappearing behind them. Their plane waited for them in an ARC hangar, on perpetual stand by for their flight to Jamaica.

"What's on your mind, love?"

Eva sighed. "What isn't? In a few days, we go to a place that should not exist, to find our daughter. Meanwhile, the denizens of said reality are doing their level best to invade earth. It's all a bit twisted. And I'm going to my parent's house to speak with them for the first time in years." She watched the cornfields passing by. The countless squares of yellow bordered the interstate and bisected areas of urban growth, sometimes as far as the horizon.

The scenery had changed in the time she had been gone. Eva hoped this was as far as the change went. So peaceful, so ordinary. So blissfully unaware of what was imminent. If the people here were as they once were, they probably ignored the media coverage, or dismissed it as 'too far from home to worry about'.

They passed quickly through an area Eva knew as Donner Park, and as they approached the banks of the Missouri, Madden took them right on to route twenty, heading east. They passed through the suburb of Morningside and Eva could still remember the house of her early childhood, a place of security, of refuge. Was this why she really had to come here? One more moment of safety before it all ended forever?

In only moments, Memorial Park Cemetery loomed on their

right, stately and serene. Those who lay here she hoped were full of goodness; she certainly didn't want to see them again.

"Off here, past the cemetery then take a left," Eva instructed her husband.

It was all coming back to her: the fenced-off fir trees to the left of the road, the pylons and electrical cables overhead, even the way the cracks in the road had been sealed over with asphalt, making it look like crazy paving. It was all so normal, so quiet.

The entrance to the cemetery appeared on their right, the low white wall bearing the words 'Memorial Park' in black, the Stars and Stripes hanging limp in the utter lack of wind.

"May it always remain this peaceful," Eva said aloud as they passed. "Turn just up here."

At a sign called 'Heritage Place', Madden took a left. "How far along?"

"The seventh house. Everybody always had a lot of space out here. Not exactly urban."

Madden continued down the shallow gradient, slowing the car as they passed a succession of enormous houses. "I can see," he said as they passed a grand house, mostly white with brickwork facia. "It looks like everybody out here made it big."

"There was some success with industry," Eva conceded.

"I'm surprised you wanted to leave."

"It took a lot of effort to get to this. The neighborhood was run-down when I left here. I never wanted to leave. They had to drag me kicking and screaming, telling me it was for the best. It took me most of my childhood years to realize they were right. My parents were always right. I resented them for their choices. I hope Nina never resents us for ours."

Madden reached out and took her hand. "Never. Let's get this done, spend a day or so with your folks, and then we are on it. Here we are. Is this it?"

Behind a succession of massive White Ash trees, two small post boxes, one bright white and the other midnight-black, poked out at the side of the road. They hadn't changed in years.

"Yes, yes. This is it. Pull in."

Madden pulled the car off the road, parking it in front of the left door of the colossal double garage. He peered up at the house, letting out a low whistle of appreciation.

"This isn't how it used to be. The hill slopes off down behind, so dad always had plans to rebuild and extend. I guess he did." Eva opened the door and stepped out. "It's all so familiar. The lawn is the same. The low red wall where I used to sit. The maple." Eva crossed the drive, running her hands down the grey bark. "I remember you. Not as smooth as once you were, old man."

"Want to see if anybody is in?"

Eva's heart skipped as she considered seeing her mother for the first time in years. Their contact had been irregular, only a couple of calls a year and even more rare correspondence. "I'm not sure how they will receive us. It's been a long time and they didn't approve of Brian."

Madden smirked. "Did anyone? After all, you did say your parents were always right. Sounds like they have good instincts."

"It took me a long time to comprehend their intentions. It's funny, the worse a mistake I make, the longer it takes to realize."

Madden joined her under the maple, leaning down and kissing her soundly. "Lucky you stopped with the mistakes. Come on."

With his good hand, Madden tugged at her, paying special care to avoid the chilling touch of the other. Eva followed, nervous, her breath coming in shallow gasps. She frowned. "Oh hell, it's only my parents." Yet when they got to the door, still she hesitated before knocking.

Nothing. Eva stood there motionless, straining to hear the sound of footsteps inside; her mother had always been fond of woodwork and the floors had been no exception. Eva had loved to slide along the polished wooden floors. It was her earliest memory.

"Well, what do we do now?" Madden asked, unimpressed. "We came all this way for an empty house."

"Patience, love. We wait. They won't be far, not at their age. I can show you round the outside, at any rate. It's worth the look. Come."

Eva was the one taking the hand this time, pulling her husband around the side of the house, after she had ordered the Rons to sit and stay, most emphatically and several times.

Out of range of the affluent sophistication of the street-front, there was a dramatic change in scenery. Around the back of the house, the ground dropped away but Eva remembered no more as she led her husband through the gardens.

"I don't recognize this place," she said, feeling a little misplaced. Lush green lawns were swallowed up by dense foliage filling the rise beyond.

"Looks a nice little forest," Madden approved.

The collection of trees was alien to her, juvenile ash mixed with dark Fraser fir made for an odd contrast of light and dark, not unlike the mailboxes. She struggled to find something to ground herself. "The lake is still there. Looks like Dad built up his favorite trees amongst those already here. I don't remember all this, Madden."

She turned to indicate a full-blown two-story mansion emerging behind them from the steep incline. "The house was certainly smaller but it looks like it was torn down entirely and rebuilt. Dad always wanted his family and grandkids under one roof. It was the appreciation of Native American society that gave Dad a lot of his ideas. He had great respect for their ideals."

"So you aren't descended from the Sioux?"

Eva smiled. "Might have been easier if we were. I always thought of Maygan as an unusual name but never gave it any thought I might be Jewish."

"Well, I wouldn't say quite so much. Descended from the line, certainly. This is new side to you love. You've never spoken about your parents before."

Eva sat on the edge of the lake, her legs crossed. Leaning forward, she trailed her right hand through the crisp water, the cold a refreshing contrast to the heat of midsummer. Her dad had done a great job here.

"I guess I haven't had cause to before now. My dad's name is Bud, my mom Jaime-Lee. Dad was a supervisor at a local manufacturing plant. With all of this, he was presumably very successful. You would like him. No pretence. Very straightforward. He saw the beauty in everything."

Madden began to roll his shirtsleeves up. The way he unconsciously folded the cotton, the gradual revealing of well-muscled forearms, left Eva with an inner-warmth fighting the outside heat for control of her feelings. She too shed outer garments in the heat, leaving her sweater in a heap in the shade. She lay down, resting her head on his thighs as he stretched out.

It was hard to forget they were so close to a realm of nightmare. Her daughter was very much in the forefront of her mind. Eva felt guilty for feeling contentment in any form, yet she felt herself surrendering to Madden, whether he noticed it or not.

She stretched with a languid grace, offering up temptation to her husband, who brushed a stray lock of hair from her face.

"Do you think Bud would see the beauty in what I have become?"

"I think so. My father holds true to many Native American beliefs, including, if I recall, accepting the spirit of the individual never dies. What are you if not proof the life force resides elsewhere, to be summoned back? Death is supposed to be a journey to another world. It does make me wonder. Amongst all the chaos, is this not lost spirits simply trying to find their way home?"

"Did they look like lost spirits when you beheld the army of Leviathan on Mount Gehenna?" Madden asked. "Those ice monsters, this." Madden held out his freezing arm, glittering as the sunshine sparkled off the crystalline frosting on the surface. "Are these spirits, trying to find their way in the dark? No, love. This is a far more sinister undertaking. I have no doubts most find their way to their 'happy hunting ground' but I am certainly not one of them and it is not time for Nina to meet her fate. Not for a long time.

"I get it. You are at peace here. I can't afford the luxury, as lovely as you look. I would like nothing more than to take advantage of you here and now, lose myself in your embrace, enjoy what comfort we have left to offer each other. But this arm is a constant reminder. It is a disease, and no one here has a cure. I think the only answer lies in the one place we would never go given a logical choice."

Eva realized Madden was right. This was not the time or the place as much as she wished it was. "Nina would love it here," she said in an attempt to diffuse the situation.

"And she will. She has a lot of childhood to spend here. With us." Madden turned to look uphill. "What's up in the trees?"

Eva smiled. "Dad's burial mound. It was one of his first projects. He spent all his free time up there. The fir trees have always been here. The others he planted to keep the grove private. I'd love to show you inside, but Dad always said we only go in there at twilight out of respect for the shades of the ancestors."

"Sounds more like Japanese tradition. Does your family have a natami?"

Eva recognized the term for a traditional family stone. Each family had their own, placed in a grove in the garden. It was the family's most sacred object. "I don't believe so. Mind you, I was young at the time. You are right though. Many traditions from both cultures share a common theme."

"Let us hope they come together in time for the next threat," Madden said in a low voice. "Or there won't be any of us left."

From the other side of the house there came the sound of an engine as a vehicle pulled up. Shortly after, a door slammed and they could hear raised voices.

"They're back!" Eva exclaimed, excited and nervous all at the same time. Jumping to her feet, she brushed herself down, ridding her clothes of grass and fallen leaves. She appraised Madden's state of dress when he had done the same. "You'll do, let's go."

Eva took Madden's hand and led him through the garden, permitting him to help her up the steep slope. As they passed the house, the words became clear.

"You know what? I don't care what agency you are from, whether you will tell me or not. You will move your goddamned monstrosity from my driveway or I'm calling the cops."

"I'm afraid we can't, ma'am," said one of the Rons. "We are under orders."

"The hell you are. Under orders from whom?"

"From me." Eva stepped out, Madden in tow, and her mother gasped. Recognition. The brown bag she carried dropped to the ground, groceries spilling on the driveway.

"Eva..."

"Hi Mom." Eva stepped forward into a fierce embrace.

"Oh, you have no idea what it means to see you safe."

"I'm fine. Where's Dad?"

Her mother stepped back, eyes brimming. "Honey, I'm so sorry. I had no way to contact you. The brute you called a husband of yours was nothing but hostile when I called."

"I don't understand."

"Eva, your father is dead."

CHAPTER TWELVE

Eva stared out the window at the back of the house without seeing. The view of the garden was different from this angle; the woodlands did not dwarf the lawn, rather a delicate progression from house to the burial mound sitting above and behind the lake, surrounded by firs. The burial mound in which her father now rested.

"Nobody escapes death," she murmured.

The landscape was green and lush, in stark contrast to her mood, the late afternoon sunlight diffused by a haze of moisture formed as the day went on. The theme continued through the house; everything was pale panelled oak: the floor, the walls, even the buttressed roof. Where possible, natural wood had been used, trunks split to form the stairs, branches woven with nest-like care to form handrails. It was like living in a treehouse.

"Here, drink this," her mother said, offering a steaming cup of tea.

Eva took the mug, earthenware brown, painted with tribal markings and sealed with varnish to make it glow in the sunlight. The tea smelled delicious, delicate flowers and zesty aromas.

"Thanks."

"I'm sure you have a lot of questions."

Eva regarded her mother with clear eyes for the first time since she had entered the house. Jaime-Lee Maygan had aged a great deal since they had last been together. As tall as Eva, her hair was completely white. In her early sixties, she still had a youthful complexion, although careworn lines now filled the corners of her eyes.

"I'm sure you do too, Mom. When did it happen?"

A shadow passed over Jaime-Lee's face. "I'll never forget it. We were watching the morning news on television with a mug of coffee, as we had done countless times over the years. There was a flicker and the cult came on the screen, declaring you their messiah, saying you had a child destined to save us all. Your father lurched up, his face pale as winter fog. He took a step forward and dropped to the floor, right over there." Jaime pointed to a spot where Madden was standing, near a white sofa and a deep pile of brown corduroy cushions.

Madden started at being pointed at and stepped out of their line of sight.

"Just there," Jaime continued. "He was probably gone before he hit the floor. You know his heart was never so good, sweetie. Seeing you in peril was too much for him. It's not your fault, of course. It didn't look like you had much of a choice. The pain is still there. It will always be, but I live on. He left me very comfortable. Your father was always one heck of a provider. I will miss him always but you are here now and I can revisit memories of him any time I like. Now. Tell me what is happening. Who are those men outside? Where's this baby? Who is this?"

Eva couldn't help but smile. "Mom, this is Madden Scott, my husband." Eva sauntered over, taking Madden by his bad arm before he had a chance to say anything.

Jaime-Lee gasped. Madden offered his hand before the news had a chance to settle in. "A pleasure, Mrs. Maygan."

"When? How? And Brian?"

"Brian was killed, Mom. He lost his mind. The last time I saw him alive, he was climbing the wing of a plane as it was taking off in Birmingham, Alabama. That was shortly before a missile hit it. There wasn't much left after that the plane exploded."

"Good," Jaime replied, with more than a small amount of satisfaction. "He was always a bad choice for you. And you, Madden. Are you any different?"

Madden smiled, as disarming as he could be. "Mrs Maygan, it's safe to say I would go to Hell and back for your daughter. She means everything to me. She is my world."

"Good. I would settle for nothing less after the thug she married before."

Madden's eyes twinkled as he grinned in silence at Eva.

"So these men? I would like an explanation as to why two Feds were trying to bar me entrance to my own house."

"My fault," Eva admitted. "Occupational hazard. They come with the job. You see, I no longer work in Worcester. I was recently... elected to the Board of Directors for a... Swiss firm. They are my security. I told them wait while I showed Madden the gardens."

Jaime-Lee's eyes widened at this revelation. "They don't sound Swiss."

"It's a multi-national," Madden provided. "Offices all over the place."

"I see. Do you work for this mighty corporation as well? What are they called?"

"Archcorp. No I don't. You could say I freelance for them on a consultancy basis."

Jaime turned back to Eva. "Why don't you tell me what's really going on? I have no doubt there is an element of truth to what you are telling me, but don't take me for a fool. You are skirting around the issue."

Eva took a deep breath, shrugging at Madden. "You're right. When all is said and done, what we have told you is true. Now, no word of this is a lie. Our daughter Nina has been kidnapped. I wanted to come and see you; we are hunting those who took her, but we believe they have taken her to... a very dangerous place. We are tracking her there, but it's new to all of us and there are a great deal of risks. We might not make it back. I just... I just wanted to see you and Dad, to let you know I was finally happy."

"You seem remarkably calm for one who has lost her child," Jaime alleged.

"Mom, what choice do I have?" Eva balled a fist and placed it next to her heart. "It hurts here. I'm in knots when I think about Nina. I would kill to get her back. I'm not the child you left in Worcester all those years ago. I'm much stronger now. Your unorthodox methods gave me steel making me strong. I have to have strength. For Nina, for my baby. She was stolen from me, not a week old."

"Where do they have her?"

"It's one of those militant armies you hear about," Madden supplied, saving Eva having to twist the truth any more. "They are linked to the company in certain ways but are holding Nina for ransom. This is one ransom we don't intend to pay." There was a sincere expression on his face, as if Madden had accepted his fate. Eva felt the same way. If they couldn't rescue Nina, life would not be worth living anyway. It was do or die.

"How long are you staying?" Jaime-Lee asked.

"I wouldn't mind staying the night, if possible. It would be nice to at least try and relax."

"Of course, dear. There's plenty of space in the house. You know your father's plans. Unrealizable now. You might want to ask those two man-mountains to come in for some food. I don't think they will have a good time of it stuck outside the front door all night when their charge is inside. And you will want to see *him* as well. He would have liked to know you would stop by. You know I dragged him up there myself. Bud always wanted to die with those he loved surrounding him and be buried by his family."

"It's the way the natives would have done," Eva agreed, finding enormous respect for her mother's strength, not only physical but also the strength of character to be able to deal with it alone.

"He left something up there for you as well. He said you would recognize it when you saw it."

"Where?"

"In the barrow. There are all sorts of strange curios in there. Take the flashlight. You will need it."

Eva scrutinized the sun, just a couple of fingers above the horizon now, where distant parts of Iowa met Nebraska, the golden ball surrounded by the red stain it left in the sky. "It's close enough. This would be as good a time as any to go and say goodbye."

Eva left her husband and mother to sort out the logistics of housing the two guards and walked back out into the garden, the greens deeper, and the shadows longer as the lush vegetation faded to black. The air was still very warm; the tang of freshly mown grass blew in on the gentle breeze caught in Eva's throat.

She swung the flashlight by the thick nylon strap she clasped as she crossed the lawns, bypassing the beautiful lake to the left, and following the path through the trees. In spite of the size of a copse this small, this manufactured, the densely packed fir stilled the breeze. There was no birdsong, no sunlight, just a dim twilight, artificially created by her fathers' labor. On the flank of the hill, it felt as if she were deep in the woods.

The burial mound stood in front of her, the dark green grass unkempt. Eva marveled at the size. The mound was a good twelve feet in height, and twice as wide. While there was a gravel path around the circumference, it was only a yard or so in width. Fir trees interspersed with smaller ash rose up around her. Eva realized for the first time she was in a shallow bowl, a natural depression on the side of the hill.

Eva followed the path around the mound, the structure perfectly symmetrical. When she reached the far side of the glade entrance, a cut appeared in the side of the mound, ending at a doorway, sealed by a heavy oak door. Eva ran the flashlight's beam over the surface of the door. The wood was finished rough, knots sticking out toward her and catching in the torchlight. The handle was brass and looked recently used, judging by the grimy fingerprints. Eva eased the handle down.

Inside, Eva had expected to find a crudely designed mud arrangement, since burial mounds were not traditionally hollow structures. What met her eyes was far more complicated. The floor dropped down from the entrance and was paved with enormous flagstones. The walls were a similar type of stone, dark and cloudy, while a web of steel supported the domed roof. It looked like the design of the retreat in the Chateau de Chillon. The room should have reeked of mold and decay. Instead, it smelled clean and well kept.

At the rear of the room, a casket had been placed atop several columns of the flagstones, keeping it off the damp floor. Once again, Eva commended her mother's strength, marveling at the feat.

She approached the casket, trailing her fingers with respect over the simple carved inscription: 'Bud Maygan. Father. Husband.' A lock of hair and a ring, her mother's wedding ring, had been placed midway down the casket, and a knife had been left on the floor. Eva picked the knife up and holding a lock of hair in the same hand as the flashlight, proceeded to saw with the knife until it had come free. Placing the lock of her own hair next to her mothers, she then placed the flashlight on the casket and reached to unclasp the necklace she had recovered from Brian's house.

"You gave me this, Dad. It was the only thing I kept hidden from Brian, the only thing I ever really cared for. It belongs with you."

Eva placed the necklace on the casket, resting her hand across the wood. "I'm sorry I wasn't there for you, Dad. I'm sorry you had to see me the way you did. I've had no choice in any of this. I miss you." She held back the tears, but the regret left her somber.

Shining the flashlight around the crypt revealed nothing. The walls were clean, the floor clear. Of course, it was never easy. "All sorts of peculiar objects?" Eva said aloud to the empty room. Moving past the coffin, Eva used the flashlight to follow the contours of the room. She stopped.

The air began to grow cold and there was less light coming in from the doorway. Eva shone the light at the entrance for a moment. A reflection to the right caught her eye, a perfectly symmetrical five-pointed star. She crossed the room to examine it. The star wasn't five-pointed. It was a Star of David, one of the points missing as if erased.

"Just like the mark on my shoulder..." Eva pondered aloud and ran her hand over the star. The stone was smooth and cold to the touch but the star itself was less so. No, Eva corrected her assessment. Not the star, the place where the missing point should be. On impulse, Eva pressed the stone and the area below the star clicked. Off to her right, back near the casket, a stone popped out from the wall.

"Clever," she said, walking back to the misplaced stone. It swung on hidden hinges, leaving an opening behind. She reached in, her arm all the way to her shoulder inside before she found anything. Her fingers brushed the tip of an object made of plastic, smooth and cold in the low temperature of the crypt. Gaining purchase between thumb and forefinger, Eva tugged. Whatever it was came free with little resistance, causing her to step back to regain her balance.

Eva shined the light on her prize. An envelope was sealed inside cling film. It was an envelope with her name on it, written in her father's hand. Setting the flashlight down, she ripped at the edge of the wrap, very curious and suddenly desperate to get at the letter. The plastic came free and she let it go, forgotten in an instant. With reverence, she pried the envelope open, and with the flashlight in hand, she made herself comfortable in the chill of the evening as she began to read aloud.

"Eva. My darling daughter. If you are reading this, it is testament to the fact I never had the opportunity to speak to you in person. This is my only chance. My last chance. I will be at peace, finally.

I must say first how truly sorry I am that I had neither the courage nor the will to oppose them. They have known my entire life who I was, as I suspect you will now know who you are and where your family comes from. I have four points of the Star. That is all I need to explain the meaning. They have waited for us, for millennia it seems. They manipulated me into letting you go, placing you in the clutches of one of their own. They encouraged me at first with money. I am not a strong man, nor a wise man, and I accepted it. Only once you were gone did they tell me directly you were theirs. I wanted so much to be there for you, but those raising you would not allow it. They were not blood kin. They had one job only: to raise you to adulthood and see you had a child of your own..."

Eva sat stunned by what she was reading. "A child of my own," she said to the surrounding gloom. "But Madden wasn't influenced." She began to read again.

"The child would be the key to their goals is my guess. Eva, if you ever have offspring, guard them with your life. They want the world. The whole world and everything in it. If they take your child, for God's sake get it back. Do what I could not. If you are reading this, I am so sorry I was not there for you. I have a greater sorrow. Because of my sins, I might end up back here among you. I know their plans. This barrow is the only place I am safe. They will have had a hand in my death. They are everywhere. Keep the child safe if you have one. It would be better for all concerned if you didn't.

Your father."

"You bastard," Eva whispered to the casket, shell shocked, furious. She screwed the letter up and threw it at her fathers' remains. Then, on second thought, she retrieved the letter, folded it, and pocketed it. Madden would want to know. Eva picked up the knife. The hilt was chilled and there was frost on the blade. The temperature had dropped to the point the hairs on her arm stood up; in her study of the letter and consequent rage, she had not noticed. The air smelled crisp, the tang of ozone strong. The flagstones were slick under her feet. Shining the flashlight around the crypt, she noticed mist pouring down the steps. The darkness was artificial. Something was out there.

Wielding the knife in her left hand, Eva ascended the stairs, exiting the burial mound. There was nothing in front of her but more vapor, so Eva stepped out into the ring of trees.

Fog was everywhere, so dense the trees only feet away were barely visible. An icy breeze on her neck caused Eva to turn, starring right into the faces of two ice demons. Leaning down from above, not six inches from her face, teeth bared, skin white, eyes rolled back in their heads, hands twitching with mindless want, they reached for her.

CHAPTER THIRTEEN

The sky beyond had darkened, and with the strange fog about her, looked an odd shade of green. The two demons, hellbounces who had been captured, faces stretched midway between humanity and monstrosity, gibbered in silence, mouths twitching. They couldn't see her. They were otherwise inanimate. Eva froze, afraid her movement would attract notice.

What they were doing on the burial mound she could not fathom, yet it was clear they had tracked her again. The demons turned, exploring the surface of the mound, and Eva saw the tentacles. At first, it was a wriggling under the skin of the neck of the demon to her left, the end of the tentacle writhing wormlike, a buried parasite. Then she saw the thicker end of the tentacle protruding from the back of each demon.

She had never been this close to them. These tentacles were different. All along the length of the appendage, mouths gaped and snapped shut, gnawing at nothing by reflex. Miniature tongues stuck out and withdrew from each of the hundreds of openings, perhaps tasting the air.

The demons had moved maybe three or four paces away from her when Eva saw the portals they had come from. Up near the top of the mound, an eddy in the fog revealed the source of the eerie light. Three portals, one large with two on either side allowed the tentacles through. The smaller portals were only a few feet across; the central portal was seven or eight feet, its center a putrid darkness of green and brown markings.

Eva took a small step back, intending to flee. As soon as she moved, the darkness in the central portal shifted down. Eva realized it was not caused by an absence of light, but rather something huge blocking it. She flicked the flashlight up at the largest aperture. Something green, scaly, and impossibly enormous moved on the other side in silence. Faster and faster, it moved, the green surface becoming a blur as it descended. There was a color change— from dark green to icy white.

Eva knew she was watching a creature of gargantuan size as it moved. Slowing, it became clear the curved white surface was the edge of a tooth, one at least twenty or thirty feet in length. A fetid stink blasted through as the entity breathed, threatening to knock her off her feet. Eva clamped her mouth shut; it was like ammonia, mixed with the iron stink of carrion. In a moment of profound clarity, Eva realized the creature had been devouring hellbounces. She had endured the stench of their destruction as time after time, when hellbounces had attacked they had been defeated. The portals opened and the tentacles had dragged the creatures into another realm. Not to boost numbers. It wasn't seeking to dominate but to feed. Hell was its hunting ground as well as its prison.

The movement slowed, the green scales returning but more delicate this time, and far more defined with swirls and geometrical patterns. In a hideous, inhuman way, it was beautiful, capturing her attention. Even greater was Eva's shock when they disappeared and an eye, perhaps half as big as the portal beheld her, appeared. Finally, Eva stood face to face with the being which had ultimately been behind all the anguish, all the pain she had suffered.

The eye regarded her, unblinking, the pupil contracting as it focused in on her from within whatever dimension it resided. There was no sound. On the fog-shrouded hill, there was no need. The malevolence Eva felt under the gaze of this gargantuan monster was overwhelming. That such creatures existed should have reduced her to a blithering idiot, her mind reduced to the insanity of one single recurring thought: the eye had been watching her across space, across time. There was hatred, pure and simple. Hatred for her. Hatred for all it could not yet touch. Hatred for the creatures dangling off of its appendages.

For a moment, there was a connection. This was her nemesis and Eva hated it right back.

"I must be crazy," she muttered and took a step toward the eye.

The puppet demons twitched, turning at the command from their master toward her. The eye moved back away from the portal, momentarily startled, and then crowded back toward the aperture, the eye straining to breach the portal if at all possible. There was a definite hunger. It wanted to make contact with her. She still had the knife in her hand.

"No, there is always something bigger, something scarier," Eva said to the eye of this creature, this demon god. "But never forget the little man or woman."

Holding the knife by the blade, Eva flicked it with all of her strength at the portal. The knife spun end over end, passing into the portal and sinking into the creature's eye with a squelch. Eva watched in fascination as the creature failed to comprehend that a being so tiny could wield such a sting and then its eye collapsed, black ichor gushing out of the wound.

The creature screamed in pain, a noise of such immense power it knocked her to the ground. The eye moved out of view, replaced by rushing skin and the creature screamed again, a noise of pain mixed with rage. Enormous teeth gnawed at the portal, unable to gain any purchase.

The demons were whipped back into their respective portals and the tentacles were withdrawn. Eva stepped back from the burial mound, hurrying around the path. The screaming alternated with a guttural rumbling causing the ground to shake beneath her feet. The portal began to widen. Two enormous finger-like appendages poked through, reaching for her, green and slimy, like tentacles with claws. Eva ran for the grove's exit and one of the fingers slammed down in front of her, the claw piercing the earth.

The fog began to swirl as a breeze formed. The air around her was sucked into the portal. The fingers moved in opposite directions around the grove, seeking the source of the monsters' pain. There was a desperation as they pierced the ground again and again. The mound collapsed as they ripped the roof asunder, searching the crypt beneath. The wind increased.

Above Eva, the cloud began to swirl as air spun into the portal. There was another scream of pain and Eva jumped a hole left in the ground several feet deep as the fingers withdrew into the air. The portal was closing and the knuckles of this massive monstrosity were caught in the gateway, which had now begun to contract. There were more screams of pain as the energy forming the aperture squeezed shut. The wind increased, twisting, enveloping the hillside as it gained strength.

Eva didn't look back as she ran down the hill and into the gardens. At some point Madden appeared, grabbing her by the arm and pulling her closer.

"It's dark," she shouted above the rage of the trapped creature.

"No, it's not," he yelled back. "I don't know what you did, but something's pissed!"

Eva turned to see beams of white light shooting in random directions from what must have been the portal. Wherever light struck a solid surface, ice instantly formed. For the most part, the beams shot into the sky. The howling wind reached gale force as the still-open portal sucked the very atmosphere from around them. Eva began to lose her breath. Then, with one final squeal of pain— a noise that shattered the windows of her mother's house, sending shards of glass in every direction— the portal imploded.

The energy caused the cloud to keep spinning, and where the cloud touched the earth, the swirling vortex ripped the hillside asunder.

"Keep going!" Madden yelled. "Twister!" He forced her ahead of him with strength more demon than man, and they reached the house through a door in the basement, dodging glass as they did so.

Slamming it shut, Madden barricaded the fortunately small window frame as best he could with unused planks of wood presumably from construction but the act proved unnecessary.

"Move," Eva ordered him.

Confused, Madden did as bidden.

Eva cleared the wood and looked out of the hole in the door. The tornado had crossed the hill and had followed the path of least resistance toward the golf course. "We're safe," she decided.

"What the hell did you do up there?" Madden asked, aghast and evidently nonplussed she had put herself in harm's way.

"We had a visitor. A large, cold visitor. I encouraged it to leave. We have to find my mother."

"It..." Madden said in her wake, but Eva was already running up the split-log stairs into the main house.

Jaime-Lee was sitting ashen-faced on a wooden bench just behind what had once been windows, staring after the retreating tornado. One of the Rons was with her, a crude bandage tied around his arm. The tornado was now a thin white funnel a mile or more away. She turned when Eva barged into the room, her face a bloody mosaic of lacerations. Fortunately, none of them appeared deep. Eva crunched glass underfoot as she crossed the room.

"Eva, thank God. Were you near that the twister?"

"Did you know this?" Eva demanded as she thrust the letter from Bud at her. She would never refer to him as her father again. There was no excuse for what the man had put her through.

Jaime-Lee read the letter, her face going pale at the onset of shock. At length, she let it fall from her hand, tears in her eyes. "Eva... I..."

"Did you know this?" Eva repeated, trying her best to hold on to her temper.

"No. No, I had no idea. Not in the way it is written here," her mother replied. "Bud always said it was a family tradition to send the Maygan children away to grow and to learn. Who was I to go against him?"

"You were his wife! You were my god-dammed mother! You don't just let your children go, Mom."

"Eva it was a different time, a different generation. I don't even know what half of this means. He was bribed? Blackmailed?"

Eva saw her mother meant every word. This was her father alone. She pulled the neck of her blouse down, exposing the five-pointed mark to her mother. "Yes. Because of this. Because somebody of pure evil believed I was an instrument for their salvation from what caused the mess outside. Bud did you an enormous favor leaving you ignorant. It's a set-up, Mom. Bud was a coward with no strength to oppose those stronger than he was. I got this..." Eva pulled up sleeve of her blouse, exposing the crude scar Iuvart had carved into her arm only months before. "Because Bud was a coward. Our daughter, Nina, currently resides in Hell because he was a coward."

"Hell?" Jaime-Lee looked extremely confused. "There is no such pl..."

"Oh yes, there is. I was on the mountaintop, staring quite literally into the abyss, where endless legions of Hell's army waited to cross over. It was my daughter the cult was after. She was taken despite everything we did to protect her. I watched somebody I had trusted with my safety stand beyond the threshold in Hell taunting me with my own little girl.

"They are coming, driven here by the desperate need to escape the being hunting them. You can't be blind to what's happening. It was here, in your garden, watching me. The invasion is now and the only way we can stop it is to go to a place that doesn't exist, can't exist. Yet we have irrefutable evidence it, in fact, exists beyond everyone's comprehension."

"It's everywhere," Madden agreed.

"See? I'm not mad, Mom. Even Madden..."

"No, Eva. You don't understand. It's everywhere," Madden pointed out of the glassless window and Eva followed his hand.

In both directions, a series of lightning storms lit up the dark sky, concentrated close to the ground.

"Portals," Eva breathed.

"What does this mean?" Her mother asked, bewildered. "Eva?"

"The invasion. This means it is time to go. If we don't stop it, and the number of demonkind outweighs the number of mankind, they will be able to survive here and the earth becomes an unholy Eden. Ron," Eva looked at the hulking ARC agent.

"Josh, Director Scott. My name is Josh."

"Josh, as a member of the ARC Council, I know you have to accompany me. But I want you remain here. Look out for my mother. If this thing goes south, another agent won't make a difference where we are going. We have to get to the plane and Jamaica. The other agent will suffice."

"A difference? To what?" Her mother was clearly still confused.

Eva reached carefully around her, squeezing her with care. "I love you, Mom. If we make it out of this alive, I swear I'll explain it all to you. Until then, listen to Josh."

Eva turned away while she still had the strength to do so. Madden fell into step beside her, saying nothing until Eva closed the front door of the house behind her.

"So you saw the real enemy, huh?"

"It was terrible beyond description, menacing and wicked. It hungers."

"And what did you do to kick all this off?"

Eva grinned. "I stabbed it in the eye."

Madden laughed aloud, a noise as defiant a statement as Eva's own rash act. "There's my girl."

CHAPTER FOURTEEN

The journey back to the airport was fraught with hazards. Terrified by the unearthly attack, the residents of Sioux City hurtled along the roads paying no attention to those around them. Crashes were frequent and several times, they had to switch sides to avoid flaming pile-ups.

Eva sat in the back of the ARC vehicle with Madden while the remaining Ron threw the car along the highway at ridiculous speeds. All around them, sometimes as close as the road itself, but mostly in the distance, portals began to open. Their arrival was heralded by lightning storms so incredibly intense the night was as bright as day. The eerie lightshow and the staccato bursts of lightning put the landscape into bizarre perspective, reflecting the whole world through a negative lens. The noise continued to sound, so much so Eva cradled her head in her arms in an attempt to block out the barrage of exploding air.

Yet they made it, without any actual sign of demons passing from their portals. The engines were already whining, indicating the plane was ready for take-off.

"Get on board Director, Mr. Scott," *Ron* shouted above the noise of the plane. "I'll join you after I secure the vehicle."

"To Hell with the car," Eva shouted, "get on here."

Ron had other ideas and continued with his task. "Get on!"

Eva did as bidden, Madden following her up the steps.

"Director Scott," the snowy-haired pilot greeted her. "If you and your husband will make yourself comfortable, we should be in Jamaica in around four hours."

Eva turned to the doorway. "Why hasn't he come back? The hangar is right near here."

The hangar in which the ARC agent had taken the vehicle exploded outward as a ball of electricity burst into view, flames erupting all over the building. Eva could feel the heat as the flames consumed the structure.

"A portal! Let's get out of here!" Eva turned to the pilot. "*He* isn't coming back, not in this lifetime. Go!"

"You heard the lady," the pilot shouted into the cockpit at his co-pilot. "Take off. I'll seal the door. Director, if you please?" The aviator waved her back.

Eva strapped herself into the nearest available seat, watching from the window as the lightning grew in intensity. The plane began to turn, aligning itself with the runway and the lightning coalesced into a ring of power, the boundary of a portal.

The plane gained momentum and the pilot swung the door shut, locking it and returning to the cockpit without a word.

"Oh no," Madden said. Eva stared out of the window, craning her neck to try for a better view. An army of dark shapes poured out of the ruined warehouse, chasing the plane with inhuman speed and incredible as it was, gaining on them even as they moved faster.

Then an intense white glow and the second wave of portals opened, tentacles from within snatching at the demons as the gargantuan monster beyond sought to feed. Eva saw no more of the struggle on the ground. The plane tipped back as they took off.

Circling about gave Eva the opportunity to witness the chaos beneath. The airport in flames, lightning still licked everything as more portals threatened to open from both Hell and as the nightmares poured through, the place beyond.

"It's not helping us," Madden observed. "It just has more attractive prey at this time."

Eva just stared.

Four hours passed, with Eva watching the same scene repeating below in each new location. Even from their great height, the bursts of lightning were bright, illuminating the cities on the ground. It was much more concentrated around urban areas, the enemy having planned well. Eva hoped the ice demons were equally as successful. Cities came and went. Birmingham, Orlando, all were alight as they passed overhead. There was only respite when they flew over the Gulf of Mexico, leaving the land behind.

"Never thought the darkness was quite so serene," Madden observed from the seat behind.

"This is about the limit of it, sir," said the pilot from the open cockpit. "From the reports, it is mostly concentrated on the mainland."

"Mostly," Eva repeated.

"In all honesty, we haven't had any word from our destination, Director. We are about to begin our descent, so if I could ask you to ensure you are secured for the sake of precaution please."

The plane bucked as they hit turbulence, causing Eva's stomach to jump. She clasped the safety belt on immediately.

So close, Nina, she thought, hoping in the midst of all this insanity, her little girl would get the message. *Hold on kiddo, I'm coming.*

"There's your answer," Madden declared as he looked out the window. In front of them, Jamaica was alight, lightning bursts making the island glow like a beacon in the night as they flew over Cuba directly toward the West Indian paradise.

"Are you going to be able to land?" Eva shouted ahead.

"No choice, Director. We have our orders from Director Guyomard. We have to get you on the ground at Sangster International even if we have to crash the plane. What you are about is more important than any of us."

Eva swallowed hard. "This could be rough. Madden, come round here and sit by me. The window view is fine even if you have to look. If we are going to die horribly in a plane crash, let's at least do it together."

Madden was round in an instant. "Seen one portal lighting storm, I guess you have seen them all." He buckled himself in and held her hand. He wasn't hot, nor was his pulse racing like hers. He was completely at ease. Strange

"Are you okay?" Eva asked, looking into his dark eyes, trying to understand the mysteries hidden within.

"I feel... different. Since the demon returned, it's not the same. Like how I am not anonymous anymore? People used to overlook me but now... it's like I am powerless against everyone."

Eva opened her mouth to reply, but the pilot shouted out, "Portal! Hang on!"

The plane rolled to the right as a ball of lightning erupted in the sky in front of them. The island was now visible, lightning enhancing the normal lighting of a densely populated area. The pre-portal lightshow passed without harm under the wing as the pilot righted the plane.

"Lucky this isn't a 747," Madden said. "They would never have made it.

The plane was coming in from the West and the island stretched out to the left. The pilot was correct; there was not as much activity here in terms of portals but there were still some, dotted about in the night sky.

"Was this me?" Eva's rhetorical question echoed around the cabin.

"Maybe, but this isn't the same as the ice portals," Madden pointed out. "These require power and time. They are almost mechanical in nature. The ice... they are organic. I think this was planned. Perhaps something is going on we are not aware of. Maybe we get into Hell and find it already frozen."

"No...No, I can't think that way." Eva squeezed Madden's hand, the knot in her stomach growing ever tighter. "We have to believe Nina can be freed. Otherwise, what is the point of this? We would already be doomed."

Eva felt the leaden clunk of machinery as the landing gear deployed beneath them. In the near distance, the lights of the runway grew awfully close. It was hard for her to take her eyes away from the window.

Madden made the decision for her, sliding the covering of the window shut. "Don't watch it, love. You will only get more agitated. We get there, or we don't."

"We get there," Eva confirmed, her voice adamant. She closed her eyes, leaning over so her head rested on his shoulder.

The thunderclaps were loud now, the superheated air crackling all around them, drowning out the sound of the engines. The plane dropped without warning as they dodged another portal and then the shudder of the tires hitting the runway announced they had made it onto land.

"Jamaica," Eva breathed with a sigh of relief.

"Not yet!" The pilot barked and threw the engines into reverse to slow them down. "Portal right! We can't stop! Gonna hit!"

There was an enormous wrenching of metal as the wing passed through a portal on the right side of the plane. The lightning was right alongside them for an instant and dazzled Eva as instinct drew her gaze across to an open shutter. A moment later, the plane began to shudder even harder as the wing disintegrated, a flaming mess of a stump left where there had been an engine and a wing only moments before.

"I've lost control! Gonna try and park it. Director, brace yourself."

Eva threw her head down between her thighs, her arms covering her neck. It was a painful position, and Madden covered her with his arms. Eva felt reassured, protected. Even like this, she could feel the plane veering left, still at full speed with the one remaining engine trying to slow them down. There was a terrific series of bumps as the plane left the runway, slewing over the softer turf nearby.

"Enough of this crap," Eva yelled, sitting up and uncovering the window. "If I'm gonna meet my end, it's not with my head between my legs!"

Lights underneath indicated they had made it across the open ground onto another runway. The plane was decelerating but the engine was not very effective and losing power. Above them, clouds boiled, lightning shattering the sky as it danced around its focus. They passed other planes parked alongside the runway as the out-of-control jet headed straight for the enormous glass windows of the nearest terminal. There was a squealing of brakes and a massive shaking as the pilot, in a last-ditch attempt to slow the plane, applied manual braking. The wheels gave way and the plane staggered forward off the landing gear, skidding along the asphalt on its metal belly. Free of restriction, the plane continued to turn so the eventual direction of their skid was sideways.

"Hold on!" Came the final yell from the cockpit as the plane hit the terminal side on. There was a rending of metal, glass smashing everywhere, and the lights in the cabin went out. Eva felt herself thrown from one side of her seat to the other, where Madden stopped her from moving any farther, his strength incredible yet tender.

For a moment, there was blackness. Eva breathed a sigh of relief. The sound of glass falling from the terminal's window frames provided a tinkling counterpoint to the cataclysmic thunder.

"Eva? Madden?" A familiar voice called.

"Swanson!" Madden roared back. "In here." He struggled to open the cabin door, but despite even his strength, the latch would not budge.

"Get out the front. It's the only way. Hurry. This plane is about to blow!"

Eva unbuckled herself, and with the light of emergency lights and flashlights, entered what was left of the cockpit. Mercifully, for her own sanity, there was little left of it and no sign of the pilots. "They perished getting us here. Nobody could have survived. Madden, how many more are going to have to die to end this?"

"If we don't hurry, a whole horde more, including us."

Madden pointed the way. Eva clambered down what remained of the terminal's enormous metal facia. Swanson waited with a team of ARC security, the Jamaicans hanging back. Already fire engines had arrived and were drenching fire-retardant foam all over the incinerated wing.

Once they had made the ground, Swanson grabbed them in a rare show of emotion and, with an arm around both, led them away from the damage.

"Damned pleased to see you. Hope the excursion was worth it."

Madden gave Eva a frown seeming to say *not here* and she kept silent. They headed down a passage away from the plane. There was an excellent view of the runway and Eva stopped when she noticed lights moving.

"Why is a plane out there? Can't they see what is going on?"

Swanson peered in the direction she was watching, and his eyes went wide. "Dear God, those imbeciles." He pulled out a two-way radio. "Tower, this is ARC. Who sanctioned that plane to leave?"

"No-one," came back a crisp answer in well-spoken but Jamaican-accented English. "They won't answer."

"They are dead," Swanson said. "They can't hope to take off."

"What are we looking at? A Cessna?"

"Looks like a twelve-seater from here," Swanson answered. "Good eyes, Eva. I just hope it's one pilot only."

The Cessna had finished its taxi and proceeded to accelerate for take-off without pause. All around the airport lightning crackled.

"No! For God's sake, no!" Swanson punched the wall as a portal began to coalesce right on the runway. Being small, the plane had already reached take-off speed and was in the process of lifting its nose when it plunged into the rim of the gateway, exploding in an enormous fireball as it lost control and flipped onto the runway. In the stark white light of the embryonic portal, the flames looked pale and sickening. The ruined plane lay burning, only the tail perceptible.

"Idiots," Swanson growled.

"There's more," said Madden. "This one's not going anywhere. Look at the flames."

Eva watched as the flames began to reach toward the portal, which expanded rapidly, circular and red, its luminous glow combining with the flames to create an ugly red tear in reality. The light steadied, the red glow clearing, and even from several hundred yards, Eva could clearly see structures reaching up from the ground of whatever lay behind the portal.

"Get the portal shut!" Swanson ordered into his radio. "Eva, Madden. We should get you out of here. It's not safe. We have transport standing by."

"No, Eva said. I'm not going anywhere."

"What? You will..."

Eva turned to her husband with unshed tears in her eyes. "Madden, I can feel her. I can *hear* her."

Madden turned away from the window. Behind him in the distance, a squadron of cars raced to intercept the monstrous beings attempting to hold ground in front of the portal, spraying everything within reach with a viscous fluid of deepest red. Behind them, more warped creatures swarmed from the portal; the runway was rapidly becoming a battlefield. Another plane attempted to land, the demons spraying their fluid underneath. The belly of the passenger jet melted away, the plane crashing midway down the runway, bouncing into the air with the force of the impact and coming back down with an explosion that fractured the wall in front of Eva.

A bestial shriek followed and the ice portals sprang into life. This time however, Hell's army fought back. It was no longer one-sided. The carrion waft combined with the crisp scent of the icy domain, rolling like a wall of fog over the airport where fire met ice. The stench turned Eva's stomach but she ignored it, lost in the linking, trying to understand what it was her daughter was telling her.

The warmth, the connection, faded as the ice spread, frosting the area around the initial portal. Eva strained to feel for her daughter. She shook her head.

"Nothing. She was close. I think she was lonely but safe enough. I felt something from her I never have before. She is at odds with somebody or something."

"Elaine?"

Eva watched the carnage unfold in the distance. With the opening of the portal, the rest of the lightning had ceased. "I don't know, but she's still alive. I don't want to know anything more if I can't get to her. Maybe they are inviting us to try. Swanson, can we go?"

The ARC Director exhaled a groan of relief. "I thought you would never ask. We have a facility about half hour away downtown where you can rest up. It may be the last chance any of us get for some peace."

CHAPTER FIFTEEN

Eight hours later, after a somewhat restful sleep, Eva found herself behind a window stained with muck, viewing with childlike fascination cargo ships loading and unloading their goods. Eva found she could only stand the sight of rectangular boxes shifted from ship to lorry for so long. Freeport was not the impression of Jamaica she had expected to get. A stuffy and already-hot apartment in the corner of a warehouse just reminded her of their reason for being there.

"Not all coconut rum and steel bands, is it?" Madden said from the bed they had shared the night before, not quite a double but with space enough for a close couple.

"We aren't here for the tourism," she replied. "Doesn't mean I'm not interested though."

Madden threw back the bed sheets, dragging on a rumpled grey t-shirt as he rose, his dishevelled brown hair loose about his neck. He gathered her in his arms, Eva enjoying his warmth despite the growing heat.

"Let's get ready and sorted then we'll find Swanson. I doubt they have left us alone without any of the ARC goons for protection. Let's see if I can't show you at least some of my former home while it's still here."

Having lost all her clothing on the ruined plane, Eva made do with what had been left for her. So, once she had cleaned up she found herself in military fatigues, black cargo pants too large until bound with a black belt, tough-but-comfortable black combat boots, and a snug-fitting and somewhat revealing tank top in army green. She wore her hair loose in an attempt to cover as much of her neck as possible.

Feeling very self-conscious, Eva opened the door separating the apartment from the rest of the warehouse. The area inside was vast, probably the size of a football field. Off to the right stood a collection of machinery and several military vehicles, but otherwise the warehouse was empty. Madden sat with Swanson and the remaining *Ron*. All stood as she joined them, Madden's eyes nearly bursting out of his head as he saw how she was clothed.

"Nice," was all he said as he kissed her and offered her a seat at a breakfast-laden table.

Eva was starving; she helped herself to a plate heavy with eggs and bacon. *Let them watch*, she thought.

"So what are the plans?" Eva asked after she had taken a mouthful of delicious, greasy food, swilling it down with coffee tasting rich and smooth, a definite bonus. "Where is the cavalry?"

"Around, most likely," was Swanson's ambiguous answer. "They are an elusive bunch, very independent as individuals. Once their leader, the Mir-Shikar arrives, they will appear. I suspect there may have been some delays due to the incursion last night. Do you realize those lightning storms tracked you right across America? Like an arrow. Gila is off trying to make sense of it."

"Where?" Eva asked, hoping for a bit of female company; despite Madden being her world, Eva sometimes craved the familiarity of sisterhood.

"Where she is necessary, Eva. Trust me when I say the less you know, the less perilous you are to us all."

"Me?"

"Yes, I'm afraid so. Geneva, Iowa, now here. They want you. They want you with a desperation defying logic. Last night was all about the contact with your daughter. They don't want you to lose focus. They want you under their dominion, on their terms."

"As it is," Madden continued, "the Director here was just explaining how the lightning last night has probably depleted them for now. Incursions are happening all over the world and hellbounces are springing up everywhere. The world is beginning to realize they are not alone, but they aren't quite prepared to accept the idea of where the threat is coming from. People are frightened."

Swanson turned his laptop around so Eva could see the screen. A map of the world was dotted red.

"Those are portals?" She asked.

"No, those are riots. Soon, Hell won't have to come and conquer. Demonkind will have its victory handed to it on a silver platter, garnished with sinners of every description. It seems it's deceptively calm hereabouts. I was just telling your husband you have the day to yourself. Go have some fun. It might be the last chance you get. Take your pick of the cars. Just nothing military."

As soon as Swanson said this, Eva dropped her cutlery with a clatter on the table, even though she was reaching to take another bite. "Let's go. I feel a sudden need for freedom."

She rose from the table, hauling Madden along with her. He was dressed in similar attire but couldn't wipe the grin off his face as she marched with purpose toward the distant fleet of cars.

"You should wear those clothes more often," he said.

Eva glanced back to find him admiring her rear. "Maybe I should," she purred, her voice inviting. "You don't look so bad yourself. When did you start working out?"

Madden looked himself over. His shoulders and chest were more defined, his arms now bulging with muscle. "I don't know, love. Since the demon half of me returned, I have felt altered in so many ways. Maybe this is just a side effect."

Eva grinned. "It works for me."

They stopped in front of the cars, a myriad of different shapes and designs.

"Oh, *very* nice," Madden said, admiring a dark-grey Ford Mustang convertible. "Hop in."

Eva opened the door, which seemed to weigh a ton on its own and settled into the furry soft black leather of the muscle car. Madden climbed in the other side and started the engine, the snarl as the pistons fired echoing around the empty warehouse.

"Bet you've driven loads of these," Eva shouted above the roar as they pulled out onto a road flamboyantly signed Coconut Way.

"Never have, never had the occasion."

"What about the racing?"

Madden beamed, evidently pleased she had remembered. "Nobody went for muscle. They love Japanese round here. Skylines, modified Supras. Even the German cars would be better. This has nothing on a good R-eight. But it looks great and it's perfect for showing your wife around at leisure."

Eva grinned back, squinting in the sun. Seeing her distress, Madden popped the catch on the glove compartment, releasing it. Upon opening, it revealed two pairs of aviator sunglasses.

"How convenient," Eva observed.

"Just knew," Madden said. "Had a feeling."

Eva took the larger pair for herself despite them appearing massively oversized. Feeling playful, she passed the smaller set to Madden. It was peculiar but this amused him even more. He put the glasses on and they still made him look great.

Eva leaned back, reveling in the freedom and the fresh air.

"So where to?" Madden asked, keeping his eyes on the road.

"Anywhere?"

"Anywhere."

"I want you to take me on the bank run. I want to see the route you took, the beginning of the journey to... you."

Madden pulled the Mustang to the side of the road, drawing admiring glances and several comments by a gang of children dressed in shorts and t-shirts in various hues of red and green. Eva paid them no mind apart from one child who stared wide-eyed at Madden for a moment and then bolted down a nearby alleyway. The haunted look in Madden's eyes was enough to tell her perhaps she had asked one thing too much of him.

"You never really wanted to come back here, did you?"

He looked forward, avoiding her eyes. "I wanted to show you the sights. Maybe not this sight. If you had died and come back, would you really want to retrace those steps? Would you not spend the entire time regretting your actions and trying to work out how you could have done it all differently?"

Eva placed her hand atop his on the steering wheel. His hand was trembling, slick with a sweat she was sure did not come from the heat. "We don't have to..."

"Yes. Yes we do. It's time I stopped running from my ghosts. If nothing else, I can face up to this for you. I owe you so much."

Madden pulled the Mustang back out into the traffic, blending in with a surprising number of other high-profile cars. At one set of traffic lights, a neon-yellow sports car pulled up alongside them.

"Yo, Kwenga! You back an' racin' man?" Called the owner, a Jamaican with dreadlocks bundled behind his head and sunglasses with bright red frames.

"Kwenga?" Eva asked.

"It means someone with style," Madden said and leaned over to his left to answer the man.

He looked the car from end to end. "In your antique racing car? You're living large on past victories, friend. You race me, you will lose."

The owner of the other car looked furious. "I run da road. Eleven, tomorrow night."

The lights changed and the owner of the yellow car tore off, wheels squealing, leaving tire marks along the road. Madden laughed in reply, waving at the car as it surged through traffic.

"What was he saying?"

Madden grinned. "He liked the car and wants to race me tomorrow night. He didn't like being told I didn't think he was a serious threat."

Eva found she was impressed with the ease Madden had acted. This was definitely his home. "Are you going to meet him?"

Madden shrugged. "The way I see it, either we are in a warehouse full of the deadliest armed force on the planet, or we are somewhere our friend is only going to catch up with us when he dies. Let the little man think about the street race. We have bigger concerns. Here we are. This is where it all started."

Madden stopped the car outside of a bank, the S stylized with an icon representing the world in the middle, all red on a white background.

"The Bank of Nova Scotia," Eva read aloud. "Strange place for a Canadian bank to be."

"It happens. Turell Banks and his gang had been racing me. They were looking for drivers and I was the best. Back then, I had no boundaries; this was all just a bit of fun. Until it went wrong. Turell hadn't gambled on the security inside the bank actually fighting back and alerting the police. Before I knew it, they came running out empty-handed and jumped into the car. They just wanted to flee. It was better to hide, to lay false trails, and the entire time I was driving I had this argument with them."

"Them?"

Madden moved off, turning right onto St. James Street, Corner Street and Orange Street in quick succession. Eva breathed in the aromas of the various miniscule restaurants all over Montego Bay, the aromatic scents of pimento and cinnamon wafting over her in complete synchronicity with the vibrancy of the painted buildings and the colorful clothes of the locals.

"Turell had a brother, Joseph, and their associate Delon. None of them was capable of acting rationally in a desperate situation, which is why I beat them in street races. It made them panic and panicking was exactly what they were doing."

Madden turned right into Love Lane and continued at a sedate pace past large, ornate housing. This merged with another road, with houses harking back to what Eva presumed was colonial times were interspersed with large glades of tropical woodland and enormous mahogany trees. Ferns surrounded the long, straight trunks, and occasionally she would see bananas or other fruit hanging from smaller foliage.

"This is Upper King Street. It's where the final run began." Madden's voice was somber. "I turned in here." Madden pulled to the right, down a tight lane, driving to the end and switching off the engine. An enormous white house loomed over them, making Eva feel tiny by comparison. In the shade of the trees, it felt cool, though Eva admitted cool was a relative term in the Jamaican heat.

Madden closed his eyes. "I'm right, you're wrong. Get used to it."

"Excuse me?" Eva asked, confused.

"It's what I said to the gang. I told them hiding was the best course of action. The cops drove by without even noticing us. It gave us a chance, although it didn't last."

"Why not?"

Madden reversed the Mustang with care out onto Upper King Street, so they faced downhill. "Bank robbery in the middle of the day. There were cops all over the place in seconds. We were lucky to get this far. Before you ask, I couldn't refuse the job. Turell Banks had a reputation, especially with anyone who didn't tow his particular line. Unfortunately, he didn't have as much sense as he did viciousness."

Madden drove them back down into the town center, a look of sincere regret on his face. Eva felt for him. It must have been like the last walk to an execution, although in his case, death had already happened. The Mustang moved at a sensible speed, mindful of people jumping into the road.

At length, they emerged onto a road bordering the water, in the sunshine a deep sapphire blue. Eva gasped at the sight.

"Gorgeous, isn't it? I always loved this view. Welcome to Gloucester Avenue, the 'hip strip'."

"Why's it named so?"

"Clubs, shops, restaurants. It's where those with money hang out. Those beaches you see were built just for them."

Eva looked past Madden to see three beaches protected from the ocean by enormous sea walls.

"I'd love to spend some time there," she said in a dreamy voice.

"I never had much time for them. I was usually driving past them too fast to see anything but a blur. By this point we had the cops tailing us; one of the gang had already been shot and pretty much killed instantly, though I never found out if he had actually died."

The traffic was steady in the late morning, so they had no chance to repeat the car chase, a fact for which Eva had profound thanks. Madden was right about the shops. The walkways outside the shops were bursting with people of all ages, kids everywhere.

"Why so many children?"

"I'll wager they are playing at the Margaritaville. It's up ahead." The road began to bend to the right, away from the sea, and then just as quickly, it turned back. The breeze coming in off the water blew her hair out behind her, cooling her head.

When Eva turned to her husband, the blood had drained from his face. "What is it?"

"There was a roadblock up ahead, past the Coral Cliff Hotel. I knew about it because the road was closed, under repair. Still, Turell insisted I drive up here. The cops were waiting. One took out one of my front tires and the car lost traction."

A building came into view, pale green walls with orange decorations, a plain brown roof and the Jamaican flag streaming with pride on a pole in the breeze. There was a procession of children going to and from the place; there was a great orange waterslide descending from the top floor directly into the sea.

"The Margaritaville?"

"The very same," Madden confirmed. Pulling the car to the side of the road, he got out and walked over to the low sea wall, standing statue-still, beholding a scene in the ocean only he could perceive.

Eva joined him. Boats bobbed in the perfect water in front of them, children splashed around in a protected area by the restaurant to the right. They were all oblivious to the peril was so close to overwhelming humanity.

"The car hit this wall, flipped, and landed on a boat several feet out in the sea. However, I have no memory of the entire episode. All of a sudden, I was swimming. When I climbed out, the cops didn't even notice me. I was changed. Eva, you wanted to see where it all happened. Here. It was here the man who was Madden Scott perished. It was here I was reborn a demon.

CHAPTER SIXTEEN

Eva grabbed Madden, turning him toward her. He was semi-responsive, his arms heavy at his sides. "Do you regret your actions?"

"Not a day goes by I don't."

"Maybe your feelings are why you're different. Because you do regret the actions leading you here."

Madden looked into her eyes, his gaze troubled. Eva imagined she could see right into his soul, laid bare for her judgment, all his deeds and misdeeds on trial.

"I love you," she said, her voice thick with emotion.

This did the trick, snapping him out of his morose state. His smile was full of remorse. He touched her face with his good hand, cured of the scarring the Scroll of Judgment had caused. "I love you, too. I'm sorry. Sometimes, I am reminded of what I am and it gets the better of me. Here, more than anywhere else. Since we still have this day to ourselves, how about we go get a drink?"

Saying nothing more, Eva led her husband into the garish surroundings of the Margaritaville restaurant and bar.

. . .

Inside the restaurant, the decor was no less bright and enthusiastic than outside. Eva had no idea where to look next. Pillars bound with rope gave the interior the feel of a pirate ship. Off to one side of the room, the head of an enormous blue shark emerged from one wall, the fish grinning back at Eva with oversized plastic teeth. Several counters selling food and tobacco were set back in various enclosures, Jamaican women of varying shape behind each. A few people sat enjoying each other's company, oblivious of those around them. Reggae music blared in tin-like tones through ancient speakers near the ceiling. Outside, the sound of countless people splashing in the water filled the lulls in music.

"Happy place," Eva observed, trying to be as understated as possible.

Madden grinned at the comment; he had worked out her humor long ago. "It was one of my favorite places... before."

"Mad One!" squealed a rotund Jamaican lady with a wealth of blue-black hair and an ill-matched bright yellow dress as she came through what passed for serving doors but would have looked more at place in a wild-west saloon.

Setting down two enormous bowls of food, she came bustling toward them at a frenetic pace. Then the woman stopped and stared at him.

"Madden Scott, look at you, man. When you get so buff?"

Madden winked at Eva and flexed his good arm. Eva was impressed with just how much muscle knotted in his bicep.

"I was always buff, little sister. You just didn't notice."

The woman leaped forward, grabbing him round the neck. Madden was careful to keep the cold arm well out of the way.

"Vinette, this is Eva," Madden introduced when the Jamaican finally let go.

Vinette proceeded to look her over. "Yo' wife, Madden? So happy."

Madden looked about the room. "Vinette, we need to talk. Private."

Vinette's face became serious. "One minute." She returned to the double doors, letting loose with a set of Jamaican colloquialisms so fierce and rapid Eva couldn't make out a single word.

Whatever she said, it clearly did the trick. Vinette grabbed the food she had been carrying and indicated they should follow her. Setting her load down, Eva's mouth began to water when she saw the most enormous bowl of nachos, loaded high with salsa and sour cream. The other bowl was terracotta and contained a pint of guacamole, flecks of chili glistening red amidst the pulped avocado. A young woman followed them over and set down three bottles of Red Stripe beer. Eva just stared.

"Dig in, you scrawny ting," Vinette encouraged her. "It's no gonna eat itself." The strong Jamaican accent was still there but the language was easier to understand. Eva did as bidden, choosing a nacho soaked in salsa and sour cream, digging up the guacamole for good measure. The combination of the cool cream and the spices on her tongue was almost too much to bear. Eva moaned in appreciation.

Vinette laughed. "Man, I like her."

Madden swigged his beer. "How are things?"

"Ah you, know. We live. You scare me half to death, walkin' in like so. You know they think you dead?"

Madden glanced toward her and Eva gave him a warning look. This was neither the place nor the topic for this discussion.

"Let's just say my recent demise is a truth I would like to maintain."

"With the hell and powder house you cause by showing up here? People love you. An' there's the problem. You show up here, kids want to make a buck tellin' those as shouldn't be told."

"Who?"

Vinette leaned forward. "Turell Banks, thas who."

"Aren't they in jail?" Eva asked around another mouthful of nachos. "I watched the article on the news last year where they were all arrested at the scene of the crash, right outside here."

"Yeah, dat's right. Babylon had them locked away. But they dark souls now. All three of them. They got the devil in them. There's more, too. Them never find your lover here, Mister 'Big man ting' but them never find anybody in the car."

"Nobody was in it?" Madden asked. "The police were on it in moments. Camera crews were everywhere."

"No, man. Cameras filmed Turell and his crew being dragged out of the water the day of the crash." Vinette leaned forward. "Da car was three month later. Them planted it back in the water, the same wreck. Them want it to look like it all happen on the same day, but there were some as saw the truth. Turell and Delon fell out of thin air into the water. Joseph did the same onto a car down the strip. It was staged."

"Where he was shot and killed?" Madden questioned aloud. "Yeah, I can see it definitely works."

"How what work, man? You crazy?"

"Level with me, Vinette," Madden said raising his hands in a gesture of placation. "Where are they now?"

The Jamaican woman looked worried, genuinely fearful as she looked about the room. "Them break out of jail and take up in them house in Mount Salem. Babylon try several times to take them out, but each time the devil come callin' and Babylon end up ripped to shreds, in a pile. People be afraid to even enter the street."

"Madden, we need to do something about this," Eva decided.

"No."

"But we can. We have the ability, the backup. We can..."

"No. Eva." His face was angry, determined, leaving Eva feeling at odds.

"They are hellbounce. They are stronger than I am, and there are three of them. They took out the cops and any help we can be would jeopardize everything we came here to accomplish."

"But the Shikari..."

"We don't even know who they are or where they are. What we do know is Turell's gang are still in their hideout, and I know where it is."

"What madness?" Vinette whispered. "Hellbounce? What you say? You can't go again' them. There's sometin' wrong with them. They unholy. You see the news on the television. Sometin' bad is comin'. The end. Rastas say Hell is already here. Them say stay away from Mount Salem. People are scared, man. There be tales of noises, late in the darkness. Tings movin', strange shapes, deformed, large, and shamblin'. Nobody goes there. 'Tis a place of fear, some say the Devil himself live there."

Madden rolled back the sleeve of his bad arm, exposing the glittering skin. "They are closer than you think. I got the devil in me, too."

Vinette recoiled in shock. "What you say, man?"

A hand clamped over Eva's mouth, pulling her back. Another hand shoved a blade against her throat. "Him the devil," said a man's deep voice, sounding to Eva like evil incarnate. "Him comin' with us or the lady gets herself cut."

Another Jamaican, swarthy and well-muscled, appeared beside Madden, wearing a green sleeveless shirt and a black baseball cap on backward. What caught Eva's attention was the fact his eyes were wide with madness and his skin rippled as a nonhuman form moved beneath. Eva had seen this before. The man was a hellbounce, and he was having trouble containing the demon. They were this close to their goal and it felt like they might as well have been back in Geneva.

Eva glared at Madden, nodding encouragement as much as she could. Fight back, she willed him. Freeze them.

"What you say, breh?" the green-shirt opposite her asked. "Turell want to see you, man. Him really want to talk to you again."

"Delon, if you harm her..."

"You what?" sneered the man holding her. "You kill us? Man, we already dead. We demon. We stronger!"

As if to demonstrate their resolve, the man next to Madden pulled out a gun, a shiny silver pistol and fired off a shot. Fluid splashed her face, warm and sticky. A thump indicated Vinette had collapsed to the table. Eva feared the worst. She tried to move her head to see and the arm clamped tighter.

"You comin'? Or we do your woman, too. Naah mean?"

Madden clamped his jaw. Eva saw signs. Her husband was, through conscious choice, preparing to do the one thing he could not return from. He couldn't!

Eva made a noise from behind the meaty hand holding her mouth clamped shut. Madden looked at her. In return, Eva glared at him with such fury he recoiled. Closing his eyes and taking a deep breath, Madden nodded. "You leave my woman here, I come, all right?"

"Iree," the man called Delon agreed.

"Put this on," Green-shirt ordered, dropping a burlap sack on the table.

"Joseph, I know where you live. I lived there, too."

This caused a moment of confusion for the emerald-shirted Joseph; it was clear neither of these was the brains of the outfit.

"Up," Joseph ordered Madden, who complied.

"What about her?" he asked. "You said she would be left alone."

"Oh, she will, man," said Delon, who released some of the pressure on her face. A split second later, something hard hit the top of her head, and Eva remembered no more.

Eva's head throbbed. Without moving, she could feel the distinct pain blossoming after being knocked out. She refused to move until she could assess the situation better. A hard surface under her face. The table. A nauseating sweet stench. The tang of iron mixed with spices. Vinette, Madden's friend.

Eva opened her eyes; daylight piercing the windows indicated it was still the middle of the day. She sat up and her head swam.

"Bad idea," she groaned, reaching up to assess the damage. Blood caked her hair, matting it to her neck, but it was not hers. Nothing more than a lump decorated her own head. Eva attempted to focus on the table. There was no point checking the body for signs of life; the back of Vinette's head lay open, the exit wound terrible.

Eva stumbled to the bar, wrapped ice in a bar towel and pressed it to the back of her head. The pain was agonizing but as she held herself steady, her eyesight improved. Madden's abductors had been thorough. The other patrons of the restaurant were gone. The remaining staff lay on the floor, executed the same way as Vinette. The only noise now came from the machinery, the pump sending water down the slide outside. The reggae music provided a sinister counterpoint to the brutal scene. The kids were all gone, no doubt frightened by the gunfire. Bob Marley would not have been *Jammin* to this.

Eva stumbled outside, the strength of the overhead sun making her eyes throb. She tried to hold the ice towel above her head. The shade helped a bit.

"Hello?" she called. There was nobody about. Not a car in sight on the road. In the strong sunlight, Eva squinted, trying to make sense of it all. She grabbed a large floppy green hat from a stand nearby, pulled it down on her head, and shielded her eyes.

"Great," Eva said aloud to the gulls peeking down at her from atop the roof. "Mount Salem it is then."

Crossing the road on wobbly legs, Eva took her time finding the Mustang. When she finally approached the place they had parked, she groaned.

"Typical, of course they would take the car. Why wouldn't they, Madden? It's a goldmine!"

Unperturbed, Eva decided to walk across the parking lot toward an alleyway on the other side. Passing through a gateway made from barbed wire, Eva found herself keeping to the shadows between warehouses to keep the sun off. The clothing Swanson had provided didn't protect her very well from the sun. Letting what remained of the ice drop down her top in liquid form, Eva wrapped the slightly frigid towel around her neck. It gave some respite, the moisture drawing the heat from her body and the thumping in her head easing somewhat.

As a cloud blocked the sunshine, the echo of her combat boots on the worn and broken asphalt was loud but steadily grew quieter.

"Strange," Eva said aloud, feeling the temperature drop more than one simple cloud should have been able to accomplish, and then she stopped.

CHAPTER SEVENTEEN

Eva did not have to turn around to feel the malevolence directed at her from the other side of the portal.

"What do you want now?" she demanded, not caring if she was facing her final doom or not. Her head hurt too much.

The air around her began to turn frigid. The cloud she had presumed was high up in the sky continued to billow out around her, reaching the tops of the warehouses but evidently not much higher. The portal blinked into existence, a ruined eye attempting to watch her. The creature drew back, what must have been a great distance, for her to behold its full shape. There were three eyes down one side of its face, one in the middle black, ruined and missing. Its mouth was stuck off to the right, resembling a flatfish. Two multi-jointed arms on each side of the body flexed and fingers grabbed at air without conscious direction. A snakelike lower half writhed around itself. From just below the mouth emerged tentacles of varying lengths.

The creature was more horrific than something from nightmares. Its very shape threatened to rip away her sanity. There was rugged breathing emanating from the dreadful vision, guttural and deep. It made Eva tremble as her body tensed in order to combat the vibrations.

Worse was to come for Eva when clear as a bell tolls, a baby cried. Eva knew by instinct; it was the cry of her own child, and she stepped toward the portal without thinking.

Join us, said a voice, directly into her head. The being pulsated on the other side of the portal as she listened. She stopped.

"I don't know what you are," Eva said, her voice resolute, "but siding with you is the last thing I will do."

Join us. We have your progeny. Step through. Join us... The abomination flexed its arms, fingers extending toward her from the infinity beyond the portal. The tentacles writhed about its mouth, the two remaining good eyes studied her, probing and curious. Again, the cry of a baby sounded, scared, lonely.

Eva's heart wrenched at the sound. "You are full of deceit," she taunted. "You have nothing to offer me. You follow me around from your cage, hoping for a chance of escape. Do you really understand anything beyond your hunger? Where are your pet demons this time?"

The creature beyond the portal opened its maw in a silent roar of rage, surging toward her. When it slammed against the aperture, Eva stepped back, buffeted by the wind. Off-balance, she turned. A blue van had parked at the end of the alleyway behind her. The same two men who had assaulted her and taken Madden were standing beside open doors, machine guns in hand. Eva was trapped.

A repeated pounding caused Eva to look back toward the aperture. The abhorrent entity thrashed in desperate fury against the portal, impotent in its enormity. It pulled back, jamming one enormous tentacle into the space between realms. The mouths, fanged and gnashing on pure reflex, gnawed at the edges of the portal. The monster screamed in pain as it touched the edges, pure power crisping it black.

"Down!" ordered one of the men.

Eva dropped to the asphalt as both men opened fire on the portal, automatic weapons spraying twin streams of bullets at the creature beyond. The end of the tentacle erupted, spraying black ichor everywhere. Wherever the liquid touched, it melted the surface. Eva scrambled out of the way, staying low as she could to elude bullets and dark acid.

The portal, with a loss of stability, had already begun to close around the shredded end of the tentacle, cutting through it like cheese-wire. The flesh-plug in the aperture blocked any more sound; the mouths all now screaming in silent agony.

Eva continued to crawl toward the questionable safety of her would-be rescuers, who could be seen laughing as they continued emptying clip after clip of bullets. The portal winked out, frost turning to water droplets in the heat of the day. Eva put her hands over her ears as the pair continued to torment the lifeless tip of the tentacle on the asphalt.

The gunfire stopped, the smell of cordite strong in the air, mixing with the stench of acid melting the surface of the alleyway. Eva took short, panting breaths to stop her lungs burning.

A shadow loomed over her. Eva squinted, trying to see what blocked the light.

"You," said the green-shirted man from the restaurant. "Him want you both. Get in de car."

Having been bundled into the back of the decrepit blue van, Eva did her best to remain unobtrusive. The sound of gunfire and the poor woman dying beside her would likely haunt her for many years, Hell or no Hell. She sat on a leather seat made hot in the sunshine, the material cracked with age and sharp under her legs. There was no belt, so she gripped the sides of the seat as she tried to hang on. These two were interested neither in the comfort of their passenger, nor the well-being of those in the cars around them. When somebody had the courage a beep their horn and attempted to remonstrate, green-shirt just pointed a gun at them; it was usually enough.

There was no hint of a working ventilation system in the van, the insides a grey metallic color. This was functional far more than practical. Her abductors drove with the windows raised aside from the occasional invective-filled altercations. The winding down of windows for the enjoyment of cursing did nothing for her comfort. Eva looked through the grime-covered windows at the streets outside. At first, she recognized them. The hip strip was obvious.

When they started up a back-alley which quickly opened onto a different road altogether, Eva lost her bearings.

The green-shirted Joseph began to chuckle, a deep rumble of a noise full of malevolence.

"You got no chance to escape, lady. Turell he bait up yo man for the Massa demon. He a bait up you, too."

Eva cursed in silence, regretting the impulse leading her out here.

Entering a different community, cars were crowded, unused, and rammed up against each other on the sides of the road. Many were shells, completely burned out. People gathered in groups along the sides of the road, looks of fear on their faces. This only gave her abductors more amusement. Boxes, ripped out seats and other rubbish littered the place. Eva closed her eyes as they just ploughed through the detritus, each impact jarring her spine on the uncomfortable seat.

In the distance, a tall building, possibly a hospital, rose out of the woodland. Eva made a mental note of this. And then something unexpected. A church. Pristine and untouched, high glass windows stood in defiance of the ugliness all around. A group of people stood outside, cowering against its walls.

Maybe they are... Eva thought, remembering the conversation they had been having about Madden's old crew.

"Them no innocent," Delon growled to her. "You no innocent either. Massa demon, him come take you home."

They turned the van up Frances Isabella Road, bearing to the right until there was no more road to follow. This was at least clear of debris; the chaos and mess out of sight by all accounts intended to slow and dissuade those tempted to come in here.

Several guards stood outside the house, swarthy and well-muscled, each bearing a machine gun.

"We run road," Delon said to her. "We run Salem."

Delon climbed out of the front seat and opened the side door of the van, waving her out with his gun.

The house into which he led her was a riot of color and architecture. Blues, reds, yellows, blacks. Every panel of wood was adjacent to a different color, every post of the stair rails painted different from its neighbor. The rooms were also on random levels added at different times. It was on a hill and reminded Eva of what her parent's house might look like if it had been built in Hell.

Delon poked her with the muzzle of his gun and Eva stumbled forward, climbing the stairs under the leering scrutiny of the guards. Wide grins met her at every turn, each one returned with a flat gaze of contempt.

Inside the house was more of the same. Stone met wood met cloth-dangling doorways.

A small portable stereo blasted out reggae at a volume almost loud enough to to blow the speakers. Near this sat Madden, bound to a chair with a cloth tied around his eyes.

Eva started to say something but Delon slammed the butt of his rifle between her shoulders, forcing her onto her knees.

"What?" yelled Madden above the noise of the music.

In response, Delon pushed Madden's face to an uncomfortable angle with the muzzle. "Go on, man, say it two time."

Madden clenched his teeth but remained silent. Evidently, this was not the first time they had had this discussion.

Shoved by rough hands into the chair next to Madden, Eva remained silent, staring at Delon. He tied her hands with strips of rag cut from a garment judging by their tie-dyed staining and then stepped back, admiring his work. "You goin' nowhere." He patted the gun. "I'm watchin' you."

After this strange tirade, Delon turned the radio off, presumably so he could hear if they said anything or tried to move, and with one final glare, left the room. Eva sighed and counted to thirty in her head. The door slam came after only a few seconds, the inevitable creaking of badly nailed floorboards ten seconds later. Madden had been right. They weren't the sharpest tools in the box.

Madden sat completely still, as if trying to gauge the nature of his fellow captive. He appeared fine but then they hadn't been apart long. He began to grin and spoke in a low voice.

"You pissed him off big time, pal. Don't you know captives are supposed to avoid eye contact? This lot are like a bunch of silverback gorillas. Stare at them and they charge you."

"A wise man once told me Turell's gang weren't blessed with an ounce of sense between them. I had no idea what he was saying."

"Eva," Madden gasped in relief, appearing to relax. "How?"

"They came back for me. Evidently, orders were both of us. As it turns out, I was actually glad to see them. I had another visit."

"The ice?"

"I awoke alone, your poor friend Vinette dead next to me, the restaurant full of the slaughtered. I had a bit of a headache. Vinette said Mount Salem, so I set off after you. How long do you think they have had you here?"

"When Delon and Joe finished tying me here, Turell came in and they had a massive argument. It seems whoever is pulling the strings wanted both of us. They set off only a few minutes later, so perhaps an hour? There's more. They referred to you as the ice witch. They did so with fear in their voices."

Eva's chest constricted at the name given to her. "I think it's been tracking me. The... whatever it was beyond the portal, it spoke to me, trying to entice me with Nina's cries to cross the threshold. It went mad when those two showed up, grabbing for them and getting stuck in the portal. There's currently a huge lump of monster flesh decorating an alleyway down near the shore."

"I know why it reacted the way it did, the way the ice has reacted when one of my kind is near. Eva, they are hellbounce. All of them, I can sense it. Once again, they are drawn to me. The trouble is I don't think they have the faintest clue what they are; they just have an overwhelming sense of invincibility."

There was a clamor from outside. Yelling mixed with the breaking of fences.

"Turell's here," said Madden. "If he was violent with a volatile temper when he was alive, he's only gotten worse with rebirth. We need to get out of here if we stand a chance of finding Nina."

"I can see," Eva whispered. "They tied me, but didn't bind my eyes."

"Is there anything to hand?"

"No. This room is empty except for us."

Madden ground his teeth in palpable frustration.

An idea came to Eva. "You aren't going to like this, but I have a plan. There are woods out behind the house. If we can get out there we can escape and hide, but you are going to have to lose control just a little bit."

"Are you crazy?" Madden panicked.

"It's the only way. We are tied up and at their mercy. If you can make your wrists stretch, just a little, then you can loosen the bindings and untie me. You are going to have to do it consciously this time. Just think about Nina. This gang of yours is keeping us from rescuing her."

Eva waited while Madden wrestled with the decision. The conflict on his blindfolded face was understandable, the frown barely concealed by the material around his eyes. He began to take deep, steady breaths. At his wrists, an alien form swirled beneath his skin, seeking the bindings and stretching his wrists, enlarging them. Sweat glistened on his brow, his mouth became a snarl and his arms began to shake with the tension of the conflict within. Then Madden flexed his shoulders and the bindings ripped clear of the seat.

Standing, he took several deep breaths as he calmed his heart rate and tamed the inner demon. "Don't ever ask me to lose control in such a way again," he said as he pulled the blindfold from his face. He rubbed his wrists, which were now their normal size, and bent down to untie Eva.

She gasped when she saw his face and he moved back.

"What is it?"

"Your eyes, they have gone red. The irises are yellow."

"Strange, I feel fine."

They had no more time for conversation, as the commotion outside moved closer to the door Eva had come through.

Eva moved slowly back, toward the window she intended to use. Something sharp touched her back and she turned. A Jamaican stood there, his face a mask of fury, eyes bordering on the insane.

"You goin' no place, woman," he said in a strong accent. "Sit. Back. Down." He raised the hunting knife toward her throat.

"Turell, no." Madden said, pleading. "Don't do this."

Behind them, the door burst open, Delon smashing through the timbers and leaving the door hanging as he was thrown through the entrance. Behind him, outside, stood the biggest man Eva had ever seen. Bald-headed, wearing sunglasses, and sporting a massive beard, he had tattoos all the way down his arms and legs. With a t-shirt bearing the words *Dimmu Borgir*, black shorts and enormous hiking boots, he looked like a bigger nightmare than the pump-action shotgun he was carrying.

The stranger grinned at Delon and entered the house, not paying attention to anybody else. "This is what it feels like to be prey," he said in a deep rumbling voice and reversed his gun, smacking Delon in the head hard enough to draw blood. "Demons don't go to Hell twice. It's a one-time deal."

An instant later, the room began to chill as Delon crashed to the floor, his head wounded. The ice-beast would find her again. Eva was the first to come to her senses, turning and punching Turell between the legs as hard as she could. Still watching his underling lying prone, he crumpled.

"Quick!" Eva urged Madden. "Now!"

They scrambled over the windowsill, dropping about six feet to the rubbish-strewn back yard, running as fast as they could for the safety of the trees beyond.

Eva glanced back, spotting Turell and Joseph escaping the same way. The stranger stood at the window, staring in silence as the room froze behind him and the place beyond hell claimed another victim.

CHAPTER EIGHTEEN

Madden pulled Eva beyond the cover of the treeline. "Come on. He's bad news, whoever he is, but the Banks brothers are after us in their own back yard! We have to keep moving, or you are dead and I'm deader."

"Where do we go?" Eva sought an escape in the trees, scared to let go of Madden's hand lest she lose him. They had only gone twenty yards or so. Already the imposing foliage leaned in above, piling additional pressure into the atmosphere.

"It doesn't matter where, as long as we keep moving. They can sense me, remember? Our only hope is to injure them. Your friends will be along to finish them off. Today the enemy of our enemy is our friend."

Eva stopped, infuriated by the reference. "What do you mean, my friends? I didn't ask for this. I just want Nina back."

"Sorry, poor choice of words," Madden apologized, contrite. "Look out!"

Eva twisted to see Joseph clambering over a rotten mahogany log. His mouth fixed in a triumphant grin, he crouched atop the log to spring at her. Madden picked up a moss-covered rock and threw it with such force it knocked Joseph back several yards, leaving him sprawled on the ground behind. The air instantly began to cool.

"Faster," Madden hissed, and they ran off to the left, avoiding the trail.

Running slowed in moments to a walk thanks to the tangled greenery. Pushing aside foliage, Eva elbowed and shouldered her way through the dense woodland. Plants grew thick at every height, ferns and bamboo crowding in at ground level, while above the larger trees fought for supremacy. The smell reminded Eva of the reptile house at a zoo she had once visited, the conditions forced and alien. Branches and vines dragged across her, leaving smears of dirt, moss, and who knew what else on her skin. Strangely enough, Eva appreciated the extra camouflage. She was pallid at the best of times.

Madden fared no better, the pace slowing as he led her through a copse so dense it took both of them to push through gnarled old vines, overgrown with new, younger shoots.

"It's like nobody has been through here in years," Eva observed, brushing an enormous swallowtail butterfly, black with yellow markings and as big as her hand, from his shoulder. Above, the sweet piping call of a strange green bird with long black tail feathers seemed to indicate they were safe.

"Of course they haven't," Madden whispered in reply. "Just look at this place. These woods got crowded in behind developments as they built the estates. There's just nowhere for them to build in here."

"How far do you think it is to the hospital grounds?"

Madden lifted a branch up so Eva could pass him by, letting it back down with care to camouflage their path once she had done so. "Not too far as the crow flies. Maybe half a kilometer the way we are going."

"Great. Half a kilometer of tangled roots. Glad I left my hair down now."

"We could escape onto the streets nearby any time you want, love. The problem then is we lose any advantage we have by staying ahead here. Line of sight would be immediate. Turell would be on us in an instant, faster than us in a car."

"But he knows where you are anyway."

Madden stopped, perching on a log after brushing aside a small green lizard with red frills raised in indignant fury at being displaced. Looking back for a moment, he frowned, and continued ahead.

"He knows pretty much where I am. It's more of a vague directional sense than pinpoint accuracy. Just like it always was when we were on the run from Iuvart."

The mention of her former friend and guide always sent a chill down Eva's spine. It really brought home just why they were doing this. Nina. Their daughter was at the end of the jungle, at the end of every path she chose to tread.

"Where is he now?"

Madden closed his eyes, seeming to listen to the forest. After a moment, he raised his arm, pointing directly back up the path they had been following. "He's coming. I can't say how fast, but it doesn't seem he is in the immediate vicinity."

"I punched him hard enough."

Madden grinned. "I don't doubt it, Eva. But hellbounces can heal at quite a pace. I think he's trying to sneak up on us. As crazy as he is, I would have thought he would just charge through the foliage until he found us."

"Unless he's under orders from another. They *were* told they had to take us both."

"You think a scenario like Brian?"

Eva shuddered, causing her hand to slip on moist rocks, dislodging them from the slope they followed. Her feet slipped out from under her with the force of the fall, dislodging yet more rocks, sending them down to the valley floor and resulting in birds flying squawking in every direction. Brian Ross was a worse prospect than Iuvart for Eva. The persistent hounding, the knowledge he had been out there the whole time she was crossing Europe for ARC. Had it not been for Nina's fortitude, Eva was sure she would have lost the baby.

"Maybe," she answered when she found her footing again.

"Typical. You find the only place in the forest where a rockslide can happen. I wouldn't worry about Turell. I can handle him when the time comes. The other guy, the one with the beard. I was just glad to get away from him."

Madden held out his hand. Eva took it and holding tight, dropped down to a lower part of the valley floor, where larger tree trunks dominated and the sun shone through. For a moment, Eva was glad to feel the warmth on her face. Madden jumped down after her and then held his hand up.

Eva strained to listen. "There's nothing."

"Exactly."

"But the rocks..."

"No, it's more profound, as if the very woods are afraid. The silence is more widespread than just here. Get back into the shade."

Madden pulled Eva behind him underneath an enormous ebony tree, the trunk wrapped with an interconnected network of vines, fitting it securely like a second skin. He watched the valley behind them. Soon it became clear as to why the woodland remained silent.

Turell Banks emerged into the light of the glade, a huge machete in one hand. He swiped it about him, dismembering smaller plants as if they had offended him somehow.

"Come out, man. I know you in there. You and you little lady frien'. Come out, or maybe I come in dere and show her what a real man be like, eh? Maybe I show her anyway."

Madden made to engage him and Eva grabbed his arm. "Don't," she whispered. "He's trying to goad you. It's only words, Madden. Just words."

Madden pulled free of her grasp. "No. This ends now."

"But he's stronger than you."

"We don't know if he is for sure. Eva, wait here. If this goes bad, follow the valley to the left. Keep going left. In time, you will find something resembling civilization. Get to Swanson."

Madden kissed her with a passion totally at odds with the situation, as if they had all the time in the world. "I love you, wife."

Before Eva could respond in kind, he darted off to the right, disappearing into the trees. A moment later, he appeared from a different part of the woodland, entering the glade with fists balled.

Turell started to say something but never got the chance. Madden rushed him with inhuman speed, spearing him with a tackle before he had a chance to even lift the machete.

Eva watched in awe as Madden grappled with Turell before the Jamaican flipped him over, leaving him prone on the forest floor. Madden flailed with his legs, but Turell had him across the shoulders, knees immobilizing Madden on the ground. She was right. Turell had a stronger demon element than Madden and it showed. The strength, the ferocity. The pain showing in Turell's face as he began to dominate the struggle. Raising the machete, rusty with dried blood, Turell grinned with savage satisfaction before bringing the huge blade around in an arc. Eva was helpless in the trees. Tensing herself for the blow leaving her a widow for the second time, Eva closed her eyes.

The blow never came. More sounds of struggling led Eva to open her eyes, fearing the scene. Madden had grabbed Turell's right arm at the wrist and was bit by bit bending it backward.

"This is what it feels like to lose control," he said, his face slick with sweat. He twisted the wrist and there was a sharp crack. Turell screamed in pain, the machete falling from his hand to lie flat on the forest floor.

Throwing Turell off, Madden rose to his feet. "And this is what it's like to feel what awaits you when you go where you belong." Madden grabbed Turell about the throat with his crystalline arm.

Turell gasped, putting his hands to his throat. "Mad One, what you done, man?" He staggered back, bumping into a tree trunk, and leaning against it, numb.

"I've marked you, Turell. You should never have come back. Demons only go to Hell once." Madden bent down to retrieve the machete. Turning the blade, he considered it for a second, before throwing it with a nonchalant underarm cast. The blade flew straight as an arrow, pinning Turell through the middle to the tree behind.

Turell screamed in pain and Madden jogged toward Eva, escaping the inevitable.

"Madden, look out!" Eva screamed.

Turell pushed himself off the tree, the blade still embedded in the trunk. Pulling himself down the blade, he began to expand, his face stretching and his shoulders bulking. His eyes went black, filming over completely. Teeth grew as the jaw cracked wider to accommodate them. His legs lengthened, forcing the body up, and causing the machete made gash to slash as the blade tore his body open.

Mist began to form on the floor of the glade, underneath Turell's feet. The Turell demon continued to swell, the size of it ripping clothes apart. Fingers became talons, hair fell out as the skull elongated. The demon bellowed a challenge to Madden, who stepped out of the glade, stopping by Eva. He was panting heavily; the fight had surely taken more out of him than he would care to admit.

She put her arm around his waist, the attempt to hold him up felt like she was fighting to balance a marble column. "Since when did you become so heavy?"

"I don't feel any different. Must be all the muscle I've gained. Look."

Madden pointed back to the impaled demon, now totally transformed. Eva felt no fear. The floor of the glade and the tree trunks around Turell were now frozen, the portal opening beneath him, but it was not the gateway beyond to which Madden referred. The demon was freezing from the throat out, where Madden had grabbed at Turell in his human form. Leathery skin was becoming brittle and cracking, oozing black ichor down its chest and to the forest floor where it hissed on the frozen ground. The demon began to comprehend this, the revelation of its true self now complete. It panicked, bellows of rage changing to screams of desperation.

The portal formed and four tentacles whipped out, grabbing the demon by each limb, but then one touched the black blood, and all four moved to absorb it. Only once they were done did they resume their work, wrapping around thickly muscled arms and legs, ripping Turell asunder and withdrawing the pieces into the realm beyond the portal. One last tentacle emerged, pointing its tip in the direction they were standing. They could clearly hear a baby's cry before it too withdrew.

"Never heard it cry before," Madden observed and then looked his bad arm, the skin glittering almost up to the shoulder. "What am I becoming?"

"Whatever it is, hold it off until we have Nina back. I don't think we want you revealing your true self before then."

Madden looked into her eyes and she could see he was beginning to change there, too. Just a couple of crystalline flecks in his iris but they were clear for anyone to see. "If it comes to it. End me before anything bad happens. I don't want to lose you and Nina to this. Promise me. Promise me you won't leave it too late. I don't want to be whatever Belphegor became, and I might end up being changed against my will."

Eva clutched her husband to her, holding him close, burrowing into the good side of his chest. "I love you, Madden. I promise if it comes to it, I will carry out your wishes."

"Let the others know, too. I won't put them in danger."

"You can tell them yourself. Can we get out of these woods now?"

Madden looked past her into the glade. "They are gone. We are safe."

Eva followed Madden in silence for the rest of the trail through the dense woodland. By the time the trees began to thin, they were thoroughly covered in moss stains, their skin a mixture of greens and browns. It maintained the illusion Madden's arm was still normal.

Madden paused when they reached open ground, turning back and staring for a while. He leaned close to her, his mouth right beside her ear.

"What is it?" Eva asked.

"We aren't alone. There's another back there. It's been trailing us. It knows we are aware."

"A demon?"

"A hellbounce. Eva, run. You see those buildings in the distance? Get to the hospital. I'll be right behind you. Now, run!"

Eva ran with all the strength she could muster. Hearing Madden close behind gave her confidence. The shattering roar from the edge of the trees did not. Eva tried to get a look at what was chasing them.

"Don't!" Madden shouted. "Keep running!"

Obeying, Eva looked forward. The main hospital building was to her left, concrete-grey and ten stories high. She ran toward a series of run-down buildings. In the distance, there was a thumping sound of footfalls as something big and heavy pursued them. Eva reached the first building and ran around it. Madden followed on her heels, but whatever it was following had closed the distance.

The demon shattered the corrugated steel walls of the ancient hospital outbuilding and barreled right through. Rearing onto hind legs, the demon stretched out blood-red arms and roared, black eyes narrowing as it identified its quarry.

"Down!" yelled a female voice.

Eva turned back, spotting a woman with long brown hair in a red top and jeans sporting a sniper rifle. She dropped beside Madden to the ground without a moment's pause.

The woman fired off a single shot, hitting the demon in the face. An instant later, its head exploded, the body crumpling to the open ground of the deserted hospital hinterland.

"Bishop!" yelled a deep voice, somewhat familiar to Eva.

"Coming," called the woman, clearly Bishop. "You two. Up. Come with me."

Bishop waved the rifle in their direction, and unwilling to risk a bullet herself, Eva hurried forward.

Rounding the corner of another building, Eva stopped dead in her tracks. Madden bumped into her back. "What the...? Oh crap."

The enormous man from Turell's house turned to regard them, the shotgun still in his hands.

CHAPTER NINETEEN

Eva stood mute, stunned by the sudden turn of events. They had escaped the forest just to be captured?

"Is this it?" The giant looked Madden over. "Him? A demon?" He pulled his shades off, revealing he had eyes not unlike a demon himself; they were red around the edges.

"You will find I can be full of surprises," Madden snarled. Under the skin of the hand Eva held, she could feel the demon begin to stir. He was at breaking point.

"If he's the demon, you're Director Scott," the giant assumed. "Funny, I was expecting someone less... commando."

His two companions chuckled at this. Bishop began scrutinizing a black gadget held by the other man.

"Scope, any other readings?" The giant stood at ease, his shotgun loose in one hand. Eva had no doubt he could wield it in an instant.

"Negative, sir," said the third member of this unusual trio, a thin man with glasses and a scraggly beard, wearing a red t-shirt bearing a picture of a mountain above the words 'Crook County, Wyoming'. "Between our hit and the one perishing in the house, only one of the trio is unaccounted for."

All three turned to Eva, suspicious and unwilling to trust Madden to answer.

"My husband fought and killed the last, Turell Banks, just moments ago in the forest."

This had some small measure of success, the trio all appeared impressed to some degree.

"I froze its throat and skewered it with a machete. The ice portal did the rest."

"Who are you and what are your intentions with us?" Eva demanded.

"Director Scott, we are the Shikari. The scrawny drink of water over there is Scope, our sniper. This hellion is Rachelle Bishop. My name is John Wolverton."

"Just three of you?" Madden seemed somewhat crestfallen.

"Enough to rescue your ass, demon," Bishop bit back. "The Mir-Shikar could end you all one handed." She indicated Wolverton, who did nothing to contradict her. It appeared humility was not in their nature.

Eva felt the hostility, or was it barely-suppressed violence? All three were on the edge. What had they gotten themselves in to?

"Load up, kids," Wolverton ordered. "Let's get back to civilization before we have any more revelations or these two decide to go on another hike in the forest."

Scope disappeared into one of the outbuildings. A second later, Eva jumped as a ferocious growl tore the silence apart. A Hummer, painted matte black, knocked the doors aside, crawling to a stop beside them.

Bishop opened the rear door and nodded to Madden. "After you."

Eva sat between her husband and their rescuer or potential executioner— she hadn't decided which yet. Wolverton sat up front with Scope, the sniper driving. Eva studied Wolverton as he stared out the window. There was so much reeking of alpha-male about the man, yet he did not seem to need to impose himself on others. He also had the look of a man who didn't need to engage in needless banter. Eva turned to Bishop.

"Why 'Shikari'? I don't know the origin of the word."

"It comes from the Indian subcontinent, from back during the origin of Anges de la Résurrection des Chevaliers," said Scope. "Those with power and influence maintained squadrons of big game hunters, also known as shikari. They were famed for their advanced training and expert use of local knowledge and weaponry. Basically, if you wanted a hunt to be a success, you used the shikari. Jerome Guyomard was such a person."

"And we have always had them?"

"Yes ma'am. The Shikari are the elite squad of, shall we say, problem solvers in the organization. Anywhere an issue requires intelligent, forceful resolution, you will likely find one or more of us."

"How many are there?"

"Enough," Bishop continued. "There are always enough. You, it seems, warrant the single largest gathering of the tribe in decades."

"A tribe? How do you see yourselves as a tribe?"

Bishop leaned in toward her. "You have a problem with our self-perception?"

"No," Eva shot back. "I was promised the best and it seems I have it. I want to know I have every chance of finding my daughter."

Bishop's stern demeanor fractured into a slow grin and Wolverton chuckled in the front seat of the Hummer. "I told you she has balls, Rachelle."

"Do demons scare you, Director?" Bishop studied her, as if this question was key.

"No. After what I have seen, the only thought scaring me is of not seeing my daughter again."

"Good. You will need to steel yourself with positivity where we are going. I knew Elaine, you know?"

The admission caught Eva by surprise. "How?"

"Legion. I was in your army under Gehenna. Elaine was in my squad. She desperately wanted to be Shikari, but chose to aid you. We all know why she chose her particular path now."

"She has my daughter."

"Not for long," Bishop promised.

The remainder of the return journey to Freeport was silent. Eva chose to enjoy the time with her husband, sitting close to him while doing her best to avoid the crystal-enclosed arm. To his credit, Madden kept it away from her.

When they pulled in to the warehouse, a radical change had occurred. Whereas before the structure was nearly empty save for a few vehicles and empty crates, now it buzzed with activity. All windows blacked out, the main space had become a hangar for two helicopters, banks of missiles sticking out to either side. Several black-armored vehicles were lined up along the bottom of the steps leading up to their apartment. In between, tables had been set up containing just about every type of weapon imaginable. In places, plated armor, the likes of which Eva had not imagined possible, hung from frames.

"What is all this," Eva wondered aloud.

"These, Director, are all the toys," Wolverton informed her. "The full resource of Global Response at our disposal. Whatever you need. It's candyland. Let me show you around your team."

Wolverton led Eva to a nearby table, where a young-looking man had an assault rifle in pieces, assembling it with his eyes closed.

"Most impressive," she said when he had finished in what seemed a mere matter of seconds.

The young man stared at her without emotion for a few seconds before turning to Wolverton.

"This her?"

"Director, this is my son, Luke. It's his first mission with the tribe."

"You realize this could well be your last," warned Eva.

Luke smiled. "I'm a peaceful loving creature, Director."

"With a penchant for firing assault weaponry with unequalled accuracy," Wolverton boomed, causing several of the as-yet unnamed group to look up from their tasks with grins on their faces.

"Oh I don't know, boss," said a short, slightly built man with closely-shaven white hair and matching beard. "I've come close a time or two. Matt Tanzer, Director Scott. Munitions. You need something blown apart, I'm your man."

Eva nodded a greeting and looked past him at an enormous pile of c-4 explosives. "Are we safe? What if it goes off?"

"Then we stare it in the face and make sure everybody knows we aren't afraid," said an enormous black man from across the warehouse. This raised whoops and hollers from the rest of the team. He crossed the distance between them in several giant strides. "J.D. Shelton, lady. Hand-to-hand if we need it. Aikido, shito-ryu, Tae-Kwon-Do among other things. The J stands for Jawara. It means peace-keeper in Sanskrit."

Wolverton extended an arm and the two gripped each other's forearms, warrior style. "Glad you could make it, brother."

"You think I would miss this? The other side? I'm going there anyway. Might as well get a head start."

"If you get stuck in a tight spot, make sure you have this one at your back," Wolverton recommended to her. "Now, next we have Kris Elliot. Mercenary recruit with training in South Africa. He fought for several companies before we found him."

"The rest weren't extreme enough for me," said the small, bald man with a grin. His accent was unmistakably South-African and the expression on his face utterly psychotic.

"Scope and Bishop you already know, and this is Jenn Day."

A short, blonde woman with a pretty face and blue eyes smiled in greeting, putting down a long dagger she had been sharpening. "Pleasure to meet you," she said, extending her hand.

Eva took it. There was steel in her grip. "Fighter?"

"Medic, though all here have rudimentary knowledge. Still, detailed knowledge of anatomy makes one a more efficient killer."

"Over there we have Wolfgang Stufflebeam and Forrest Everret Kyle, ordnance and heavy weapons. If you can carry a tenth of what they lug around, I'll be impressed."

"Nice," Madden admired. Neither man was big, yet both packed mini-guns and RPGs.

"It's amazing what the human body is capable of doing, given the right incentives," said a woman as she looked up from some complex and unidentifiable electrical equipment. She rose from the desk and extended her hand. She had white hair but a very youthful face around green eyes.

"Ellen Covlioni, Director. I transferred in from Media on the recommendation of Director Gibson. I've been on mission near your hometown until they pulled me here. If there is a way to communicate back to earth from down there, I will make it happen. I'm the lifeline for Emdy here."

A slight man with black hair and dark skin raised his arm. "I am recording the journey and interpreting what we see in terms of a biblical sense."

"Are you Indian?" Madden asked.

Emdy's answering smile was shy which was odd for Eva to see in such robust company. "Bangladeshi."

"This is a journey for posterity as much as it is a rescue mission," said a familiar voice.

Eva turned to find Gila, decked out in one of the figure-hugging black combat suits hanging around the warehouse. She hugged her friend close. "I've missed you."

Gila held her at arms' length. "It's only been a couple of days, yet look at all the trouble you've gotten into. You should try on your armor. It takes some getting used to."

"It appears very revealing," Eva admitted, dubious about wearing it. "What have you got on underneath?"

"Not a hell of a lot."

Without looking, Eva reached out and pushed Madden's mouth closed.

"Looking good, Director Ciranoush," approved Wolverton.

"Feeling good, Director Wolverton," Gila replied.

"Director? I think I have a lot to learn still."

Both looked at her. "I have the ARC title of Director but am outside of the system."

"Sometimes even we need clandestine operations," said Swanson as he walked toward them across the warehouse, his eyes widening as he beheld Gila in her new gear.

"There is one more member of my team," Wolverton said, bringing the focus back to the people around them. "Our point man. Porter Rockwell."

Wolverton indicated off to their left. Following his hand, Eva saw a tent set up, a man inside, cross-legged and meditating. He had grey hair past his shoulders and an equally long beard, fading from grey to white. He did not acknowledge them.

"Ah, he's not playing today. Well, he's named for his ancestor, Orrin Porter Rockwell, a gunfighter. Some say he was an assassin for Joseph Smith."

"The founder of the Mormon Church?" Madden asked.

"Does it surprise you?" Rockwell said in a cold voice without opening his eyes. "Many here belong to the same church. Some of the most violent gun masters in the Wild West were Mormon."

"I just guess I never expected Mormons to be mixed up in this."

"It's our earth, too. We will defend it with hostility."

"So there you have it," Wolverton concluded. "The Shikari. To a person they are rock-hard, intelligent, resourceful, adaptable, and unafraid to die. Any given mission may be their last, and they embrace their fate."

"So you are the best of the best?" Madden asked.

"Ha! The best of the best need not apply. The Shikari are far beyond your normal military. If you wanted someone to go to Hell, you would choose the best of the best. If you want someone who can take you to Hell and back, you choose us."

"I suggest you go try on your own combat suits," encouraged Gila. "The amount of gadgetry and sophisticated weapons they expect you to carry is no small amount. I took the liberty of having them placed in your room."

Eva looked down at herself, covered in sweat and muck. "Do I have time for a shower?"

"You have as much time as Hell allows," Swanson answered. "We move at the next sign of an incursion."

Eva observed her figure in the full-length mirror. It amounted to a cat suit, felt paper-thin, but was impossible to tear. It was also warm but breathable, the sleeves ending in gloves gripping anything she touched like glue. Black as night, it hugged her figure, leaving her belly flat and her breasts snugly accentuated. She turned to admire her rear.

"I should wear one of these all the time," she said to herself.

"You're telling me," Madden answered from the doorway to the bathroom she had already used, only his head peering round. "Hubba hubba." Madden wiggled one eyebrow and made some growling noises.

"Come on then. I've shown you mine. What are you packing?"

More self-conscious than she had ever before seen him, Madden stepped into their room and quite literally took Eva's breath away. The combat suit did the same thing to Madden it had done to her but in a masculine way, emphasizing the muscles on his chest, his thighs, the bulging contours of his arms and broad shoulders.

"Right back at you, handsome," Eva complimented her husband.

She crossed the room to admire him up close. From there it only looked better. For a suit doing a great deal to homogenize gender in certain areas, it accentuated so much more.

Eva ran her hands over his chest, feeling the blood start to pump inside her in a way she had not felt since the lake by her home. Madden reciprocated. Normally the gentleman, he picked her up by her buttocks and kissed her. Before they knew it, husband and wife were ripping at the combat suits, trying to remove them as quickly as possible, lost in each other as they waited on the very precipice of Hell.

CHAPTER TWENTY

Eva rolled over, checking the clock on the bedside. It was eight-thirty. They had been alone for close to three hours. Replete and completely satisfied, Eva felt she should have been exhausted, but the opposite was true. She felt utter invigoration, as if making love to her husband had provided the spark she needed, the incentive to fortify her against what was to come. Or maybe she just needed to feel like a woman again and not a deer in the headlights of an oncoming car.

Madden stretched. "I've missed us being together. You had a lot bottled up in there."

"Never again." Eva climbed over the bed to her husband, making as much of a show of herself as she could and kissed him.

Madden reached to grab her and then paused. "We really should get those suits back on. If there is equipment to be carried, we should do our part."

Reluctantly, Eva agreed. Slipping back into the combat suit, she reveled in the silken feel of the material. This time, Madden zipped the suit tight, as she did for him and then patted his buttocks.

"Good boy."

"Let's do this."

As she entered the warehouse, all was calm and in order, for just a moment. A door crashed open farther down the structure, and Wolfgang Stufflebeam came streaking toward them.

"Do you see it? Can you see it from your room?"

Confused, Eva looked at Madden.

"No, sorry, what were we supposed to see?"

"Game time, people," Wolverton announced. "Load up."

Eva turned, ran back into their apartment, and threw open the curtains. "Oh dear God."

Across the bay, the evening sky had turned a strong shade of red as bolt after bolt of lightning rained down, hitting the ground and generating a fog where they struck the water of the bay. Only now did the constant cracks of thunder reach them.

"This is it," Eva gasped.

"Damned right it is," John Wolverton said from the entrance of their apartment as he surveyed the near-blinding pyrotechnics. "Hope you two lovebirds worked the kinks out of those costumes. They are about to get a damned sight heavier."

Eva followed Madden and Wolverton back into the main hangar, where the Shikari were bolting on armor to their combat suits. Not one of them looked the least bit self-conscious. Eva presumed they were used to wearing this gear.

Gila nodded at her from nearby as Matt Tanzer loaded her up with a backpack and combat belt, to which he attached all manner of gadgets. Gila appeared to sag under the weight.

"Your turn," Wolverton said and nudged Eva toward J.D. Shelton who stood next to a table, his face calm.

"Pay attention now, Director. Any one of these items could save your life. First, we have the belt. In pouches on both sides from front to back we have cord, lighter, flares, combat knife, skin glue and emergency first aid. You'll find sterilized gauze, pre-threaded needle, and pre-filled local anaesthetic. Anything else, call for the medic. The pack now."

Shelton placed a huge black backpack on the table.

"How am I supposed to carry such a large pack?" Eva looked the pack over with apprehension.

"The price you pay for a descent to Hell is more than just your soul," Shelton replied. "Here on the left you have a two-way radio, activated by depressing a button on the side like so." Shelton pressed the button and whispered something too quiet for Eva to make out through the thunderous barrage from outside. However, all of the Shikari who were ready paused and then laughed.

"You have a sidearm on the right strap, holstered, safety off. Inside you have rations; water, food and compressed air which should last you a week."

"Only a week?"

"A week is all you have," Swanson said from a nearby table where Madden was getting the same treatment. "If you don't complete this mission by then, all calculations point to earth being overrun, with or without the big sacrifice."

"Also, you have several c-four charges in case you need to blow yourself out of a hole or are... beyond redemption. Okay, try this on and I'll show you the best part."

Eva placed the belt around her waist. "There's no clip."

"Touch your right thumb to your pinkie."

Eva did as bidden and the belt snapped in place. "Wow, what just happened?"

"The suit isn't just protection. It's an exo-skeletal structure, magnetically charged and capable of bearing great loads." Shelton placed the backpack on her shoulders and while it was noticeable, the weight was in no way overbearing.

"Finally the headgear. Do you prefer a screen or three eyes?" Shelton held up two garish-looking helmets. One had a dark screen to cover the eyes and twin mounted cameras above each temple, while the other was a metallic monstrosity consisting of a facemask with three lenses.

Eva looked about the team. There were a mix of both in use and everybody was watching in expectation, as if the decision mattered more than she understood.

"I don't like having my face covered. I'll go for the screen."

Those bearing the twin cameras cheered, raising automatic weapons aloft.

"I'm definitely having the three eyes," Madden said, eliciting a similar response from the other half of the team.

"Power off!" Forrest Kyle yelled, cutting power to the warehouse. "Masks down, directors."

In the darkness, Eva fumbled with her headgear, finding it heavy and cumbersome until it became one with the combat suit. Once the helmet was in place, the screen faded up until Eva saw nearly as good as in daylight.

"Amazing," she said, holding her hands out in front.

Madden was doing the same. "It's all so clear. What is this? Night vision?"

"A modified form," said Swanson. It adapts to utilize background radiation, natural light, whatever it can find. Call it intelligent night-vision."

"And why the power down?"

"We have been tracking the movements of the enemy on each incursion," said a voice identified as Wolfgang Stufflebeam on the corner of her screen, which aside from the view in front, had information and statistics feeding streams to the periphery of her vision. "They are drawn to power sources. We suspect they are draining them."

"Time to load up, people," Wolverton ordered, throwing open the rear doors of two heavy transports.

The Shikari roared as one, jumping into the transports in their eagerness to face what was outside. In the commotion, Eva found herself separated from her husband, in the back of a transport next to an anonymous figure in armor.

"Don't worry, Director," Jenn Day said from behind a three-lensed mask. "I'll keep you safe until you find your daughter."

The diesel engines of the transports roared into life and the two vehicles pulled out in convoy, hurtling into the night. The lightning over the bay had intensified, the noise a pounding disharmony, threatening to deafen Eva.

"There are more portals coming on line," Scope said over the radio. "One has already opened, up in the residential area inland at Mount Salem."

"This might be a stronger push for dominance," Swanson added.

As they pulled out onto the main road leading across Montego Bay, Eva got a decent look at the open portal. The sky was a sooty-red from the fires raging up in the woodlands adjacent to the aperture. The white portals of the realm beyond winked into existence but closed just as quickly. People were running from the direction of the fires, but with the portal forming at what appeared to be the airport, once they reached the highway, they began to mill about.

The stench of the smoke was overpowering even from this distance. Eva tried not to think about what was going on up there. Where there were lights, darkness followed. As such, Eva was able to track the demon's progress toward the center of the town.

"This is going to be close," Luke Wolverton said. "They are coming down the hill at an incredible speed."

"They know we are down here," Madden answered. "They are coming for us. The Well of Souls has Eva's blood on it. They can track her anywhere on earth. They can feel we are on the move."

This was all very confusing for Eva. The headgear provided names and voices but with the masks down. She looked about as every new voice spoke; the Shikari remained completely still as they discussed tactics since they were used to the situation.

"How far to Rose Hall?" she asked when there was a pause.

"We are at the hip strip now, or what's left of it," answered Scope. "Maybe another six or seven miles."

"We aren't going to make it without a fight if this continues," John Wolverton indicated.

Outside, people were looting the shops, many with bodies lying prone on the floor where there had been a stampede. Several shops were on fire. Hell truly was coming to earth and it had nothing to do with demons.

"If they really knew what was coming, they wouldn't worry so much about clothes and watches," Jenn Day observed next to Eva.

"Roadblock!" called Swanson; Eva presumed he was in the lead transport. "What the hell are they doing?"

Gunshots fired. Behind the barricade, the lighting had coalesced into another circular aperture, sullen and red. In the distance, a body filled the opening.

"They have another giant moving through," Ellen Covlioni informed them. "Chatter is mostly screaming from the airport, but you can see for yourself."

"They are serious this time," Wolverton decided. "Elliot, Bishop, Kyle. Get out there and clear this road."

One of Eva's companions, presumably Kriss Elliot or Rachelle Bishop since they had no heavy ordnance, jumped from their transport. Eva watched helpless as her three companions lay down fire with their automatic weapons, mowing down the Jamaicans forming the block like grass.

"There," decided Kriss Elliot, his South African accent clear and crisp enough Eva no longer needed to glance at the screen in her helmet. "We can move..."

Feedback rang through everybody's earpieces. A red signal popped up on Eva's screen.

"What... what's a red screen mean?" Madden asked.

"Kriss, no!" shouted Forrest Kyle.

"Kyle! Get in here now!" Wolverton ordered. "You can't do anything."

"Oh dear God, look at them," Gila said. "They are getting back up. They are changing to demons here and now."

"The guilty no longer need Hell," Emdy Sengupta observed.

Eva craned her neck to try to get a decent view out of their transport, but the front vehicle blocked them. All she could see was a couple of bodies moving with slightly jerked motions.

"This is an ambush. Go! Go! Go!" Wolverton shouted and the front transport shot off ahead of them.

The door was wrenched open and what had once been a Jamaican man, tall and powerful, stuck its head in, trying to focus on Eva. Of course, they were all dressed the same and this must have confused it. Eva stared in dread at the face. A rictus grin, lips peeled back, eyes faded white; he had become a demon in an instant.

The creature focused in on her, the guttural noise emitting from its mouth some sort of triumphant roar. Outside, more of its kind shambled toward them from the side of the street. It reached for her leg, hands now clawed and scabrous.

As it did so, a single shot was fired. The demon launched backward out of the transport. In close quarters, the noise made Eva's ears ring. Bishop lifted her mask up and nodded. Eva smiled in thanks.

A moment later, their transport tore off after the first. Eva watched, mute with fear as they passed twenty or thirty bodies, each in various stages of standing, or growing abhorrent extensions as they began to transform into demonkind. Above, the sky turned a brighter crimson as the fires joined the glow of the portals. As they shot off into the night, the glow followed them. It was everywhere.

"This is it. This is the big play," were the first words Eva heard as the ringing in her ears eventually began to subside.

"What happened to Kriss Elliot?"

"One of the Jamaicans got in a lucky shot. Right up under the chin," J.D. Shelton informed her. "His head pretty much exploded in his helmet. He was gone in an instant.

"I hope this plan of yours works, Swanson," Madden said from the other transport. "Jamaica is being overrun."

"There are more roadblocks ahead judging by the satellite imagery," Ellen Covlioni apprised them. "If there's another way to Rose Hall not involving the one place all of demonkind is waiting for us to pass, I suggest you take it and take it damned soon."

"There are woods and a golf course on the right up here," Madden answered. "You should be able to just drive over them straight to Rose Hall. The only building in the way would be the Montego Bay convention center."

"Easy," Luke Wolverton replied from the lead transport. "These babies can handle a bit of cross-country. Follow my lead."

"Hold on, Eva," Jenn said from beside her. "This could get a little rough. These boys like to drive fast and hard. "

The transports shot off the road and onto the golf course, their headlights the only light aside from the red atmosphere. If anything, they gained speed across the grass. Eva maintained a tight grip on handles beside her seat as they thundered across the golf course, hitting bunkers with tooth-jarring regularity and slowing for nothing. There was another glow up ahead, but Eva could not see the source.

"We have a problem here," Luke Wolverton informed them. "We might have to find another way around. The entire woodland is on fire."

CHAPTER TWENTY-ONE

"Keep going," John Wolverton decided. "These rigs can take a lot of heat."

The front transport plunged into the boiling woods, flames rising a hundred feet into the sky where the tinder-dry woodland had succumbed to the fire. Eva's transport followed right on its tail. As they surged headlong into the furnace, Eva beheld rivers of flame pouring down between trees where ground level foliage had caught fire. Trunks smoldered, cracks in the black-charred bark revealing glowing wood underneath like a network of veins. Where there was no fire, the ground shined red.

"It could be worse," said Matt Tanzer in an out-of-place upbeat voice.

"How could this be worse?" Luke challenged.

"Well, we don't have him chasing us! Look left."

Above the burning skyline rose another of the Behemoths, all muscle and steel-tough hide, facing away from them as it smashed at the ground in the distance. The answer became clear as it raised one fist encased in ice, the wing of a passenger jet trapped within.

"More than one Hell seeks domination," concluded Eva.

"Trust me," added Madden. "You don't want one of those bad boys on your tail."

Only a few days ago, the tsunami was still all too real for Eva. This was a rollercoaster ride without end.

They passed through the flaming forest and across a wide-open space. To their left rose the enormous complex of the Montego Bay convention center, all-aglow in the fire on this strange red night. Bereft of material, the jokers in the squad remained silent as they plunged through the gloom, reliant entirely on the strange night vision afforded to them by their helmets.

"I'm sorry about Kriss," Eva said to the group, in part because nobody had mentioned the incident and because the silence was as oppressive as the red mist outside.

"He knew what he signed up for," Bishop said. "We all do. I can promise you if he had time for a last thought to go through his mind, it would be he regretted not being able to make it all the way to Hell."

There were general murmurs of agreement at this sentiment.

"If I know Kriss Elliot," said Porter Rockwell, "he will probably be waiting for us on the other side, all horns and forked tail, asking for his gun back."

This brought laughter all round. This close-knit group feared nothing and she took reassurance from the fact.

"Here we are. Rose Hall." Swanson's voice had an air of finality to it.

The transports stopped and the Shikari piled out into the darkness.

Eva lifted her visor, looking up at the imposing house just above them up the slope. It glowed pink in the ruddy darkness, a solemn reminder of the chaos inflicted on this once-beautiful island.

"Everybody inside," Swanson whispered over the radio link. "Let's not give whatever's out here any obvious sign of where we are."

Eva climbed the steps to the house, following close to one of the two with the mini-guns. There were no lights on inside and it loomed over them, arches full of darkness, windows full of gloom.

John Wolverton pushed the already-ajar front door open with the tip of his shotgun, masked face peering into the hallway beyond. By all accounts satisfied, he stepped in.

"Nobody's home but stay frosty. Full sweep of the building before we relocate at the portal."

The team scattered, each of them an army unto themselves.

"What is this place?" Eva asked Madden, standing in the hallway with Gila and Swanson, the latter of which looked like a skinny cousin in his suit and tie.

Madden flipped his mask up. "Rose Hall is currently a museum. It used to be a plantation mansion a couple hundred years back, with crops, slaves, and everything such abhorrent mastery of others entailed. It also plays host, so they say, to the ghost of Annie Palmer, who apparently murdered several husbands. Her tomb is on the grounds outside. Local legend believes she perished in a much more sinister place."

Despite the company, the darkness crowded in on Eva. As they spoke of the dark subject, the house became much more oppressive. Eva kept a close watch on anything moving through her visor, edging closer to her husband.

"Evidently whoever was here this evening left in a hurry," Scope said as he opened a door and waved them into the room. "This place is abandoned. Trashed here and there but this room should suit our purposes."

Eva followed her husband, sticking close. They entered the room to the aroma of Jamaican cooking. Eva realized it had been almost the entire day since she had actually eaten anything. Her mouth began to water.

The room was huge, chandeliers hanging down the center of the room, the only entrance the doors through which they had come and one small service door at the other end.

Down the far side lay an enormous buffet.

"Someone was feasting here this evening," Gila picked up a plate still piled high.

As the Shikari entered the room, many attacked the food with gusto, not standing on ceremony. Only once the entire squad was present did Porter Rockwell seal the doors with a foam spray.

"Keeps the light in," Swanson said.

"But you also said they were attracted to energy."

"Not this type," Rockwell answered and slammed a cylindrical object onto a table. An eerie yellow light erupted from the cylinder. Shortly after, two more were placed across the room.

"The glo-stick from Hell," Madden muttered.

Eva had already begun to head for the food, too hungry to reply. She pulled her visor up in anticipation.

On the table, there were platters of jerk-chicken, beef, patties, spiced buns, and a myriad of curries. Eva picked at random, soon filling her plate. Finding a place nearby to sit and eat, she waited. The mood in the room was expectant.

"Okay, so this is how it is, people," started John Wolverton. "You rabble are used to taking and obeying orders, so here's the chain of command. Doctor Gila Ciranoush is the mission specialist, and as such, de facto commander. After her you defer to Director Scott and then Madden Scott after her."

"Take orders from a demon?" Luke scoffed. "Not a chance."

Wolverton senior cuffed his son round the back of the head. "They both have mission-critical information and it's their daughter we are rescuing. You will defer to them as if you follow me. I am below the Directors in this chain of command, but I'm still above you miscreants."

"You need to understand what you are going up against here," Gila said, pulling her mask off. This is not just another mission, stepping into the wilds to kill a mark or rescue a hostage. This is the realm of the dead, the underworld. We have no idea what to expect there. Flames? Brimstone falling from whatever passes for the sky? Maybe. Fields of grain swaying in the wind and manicured rivers? Less likely, but why not? This is a place out of time, out of our reality. Hell is an alien world."

"They don't belong here," Madden took over the briefing. "I can tell you from brutal and bitter experience just what it does to them. I am a hellbounce. Part human, part demon. Moreover, I am the creature I became in Hell, born again in my human form. The demon suffers. Every waking moment is torture to it. All the demon wants is the human shell to lose the battle within so it can erupt. The problem is the demon in the hellbounce has a limited shelf life. Consider a fetus taken outside of the womb only halfway through a pregnancy. It's not long before nothing living remains. Well the longer a demon is in Hell, the more the atmosphere, the very air, tortures it. Hellbounces, whether intended or not are a failed experiment. The demons coming through now don't have the same frailty. They have a longer shelf-life and although the atmosphere is difficult for them, it's getting easier."

"How do you know this?" Bishop asked.

"The demon in me is weak. So weak I suspect I was only in Hell for an instant, but there's still a connection. I still sense what's happening. These repeated attacks are balancing the numbers, eroding the barrier between the realms. I have strength beyond mortal man. I can fight them hand to hand. I have done so and won."

"Your Johnson's all well and good," Bishop challenged. "So you are a demon-hybrid warrior. Tell us something of use."

"I can also read any language as if it is English. Let me prove it. Jawara, write something down in your native script."

J.D. Shelton took one of the menus from a nearby table, jotting down characters with a pen. He held the menu aloft. Eva couldn't read of whatever language it represented.

"Not all demons are evil..." Madden trailed off as he considered this.

Shelton nodded, confirming these were his words. The looks directed at Madden from the squad now contained at least a modicum of respect.

"I would amend my previous statement," Madden corrected himself. "'All demons are evil. It is just some are useful. You have to remember this struggle is biblical in every sense of the word. Demons can't abide the touch of anything holy, sanctified or not. I carried the Scroll of Judgment in Afghanistan and only the weakness of the demon inside kept it from killing me."

"What might be down there could be construed as biblical," Gila said, taking back the reins of the briefing.

"Clearly there is organization down below. The random occurrences of hellbounces bring chaos to the order they are attempting to achieve, but we might yet be ill-prepared."

Eva spoke up. "The last time I witnessed a portal there was something behind it, a structure of sorts. If anything, it looked like a tower, with lights. When I stood on Mount Gehenna, I perceived a similar view. There was too much organization. We have to gamble Hell is not just this mystical place of legendary creatures fighting and devouring each other as we always imagined it to be. What if Hell is in its purest and simplest form the various circles and pits but within, it is a place of massively developed technology? Our perception of all recent events has involved the demons fighting off something worse than what is invading their territory. They may perceive their antagonist the way we perceive them. There are entire scales of difference."

"You have seen this creature hunting the demons, have you not?" John Wolverton asked.

"I have. It was terrifying beyond words. Scales and eyes and enormous teeth. I don't think it really knows what this place is. It hunts demons, devouring them. Maybe its purpose is to feed. To balance the scales. It certainly doesn't like me; I stabbed one of its eyes out when it got too close. It knows fear now. It knows pain."

"You stabbed out its eye?" Bishop sounded impressed.

"I wasn't thinking straight at the time. I had just visited my father's tomb and found out everything I believed was good in my life, everything you have recorded in the files you have studied, was a set up. It was arranged for me to be in a place where they could guide me toward a single destiny: I would give birth to a child they could steal and use against humanity."

"I like to think some good came of it," Madden said, squeezing her hand.

Outside, the cracks of thunder resumed, quite close. No light made it past the seal around the twin doors; Porter Rockwell had done a very good job.

"We are only guessing, of course, at what we will find," Gila concluded. "We could pass through a portal right into the middle of an army, though we have made a calculated guess such a small portal as we expect to find will lead to somewhere more discreet. They want a massive incursion to knock the balance in their favor. Until the balance tips, we estimate the portals will keep closing, though it is likely the balance is found sooner rather than later. It won't remain the case for too much longer."

"I do know this," Eva said, placing her plate down on the table, the food barely touched. "There must be an atmosphere down there, however harsh. A woman I once trusted to keep me safe took my Nina across the threshold. They were alive when the portal collapsed. If they breathe, there is air. If there is air, what makes it? There has to be a geography of sorts. Cities? Rudimentary if we are wrong about their technology. Massive and complex if we are right."

"What such resource would also mean is if they are advanced, they might bring examples with them," Swanson said dreamily.

"Oh no," Eva countered. "We are not going this far into danger to go sightseeing and bring you back trinkets. There is one goal and one goal only."

"It's too late, Eva. The portal technology, the very science giving us insight enough to find the gateway below this mansion, came from Hell, though we did not know it at the time. By helping themselves, Rosier, Iuvart, and their masters have opened a can of worms nigh on impossible to close. And ARC has the lid on it."

"Not yet it doesn't," Madden argued. "This is not about power and prizes."

"All I'm saying is *if* you come across anything useful, hold onto it."

"The portals are on the increase again," said Scope as he focused on a small black plastic gadget.

"Where?" Swanson asked, concern overriding his lust for demon technology.

"Everywhere. The lists of places being overrun are moving too fast. This shows a clearer picture."

Scope flicked a switch and the gadget projected a picture on the wall of the room. A flickering image of the earth showed red dots concentrated in several areas of every major continent.

"They aren't large, but they are numerous and effective."

"I need to get out of here," Swanson said, the worry-lines creasing his face. "The response needs co-ordination. ARC is the only organization to have a truly global reach now. I will remain in constant contact as long as I can. You might learn something down there to help us. Once you are in, I expect all hell to quite literally break loose as they lose track of you."

"Chopper already en route, sir," came the reply from the sniper. "If it makes it past everything wandering about outside, it should be here in the next five minutes."

"You think they won't expect us to sneak through?" Eva was dubious as to Swanson's theory.

"That is our hope, yes. They will be so concentrated on you here they keep searching. Remember, they want you in Hell on their terms, not yours."

Eva gazed around the room. The black-suited team, fully armored and dripping with weaponry, was definitely not what she would call 'their terms'. How far she had come since the day she had left Brian, looking for an escape. How the experiences had changed her?

"And if they find us? If they take what they need and swarm the earth? If the entity beyond breaks its chains and overwhelms there... and here?"

"Then Heaven help us, Eva. Heaven help us."

CHAPTER TWENTY-TWO

"Time to move out," Wolverton decided. "Let's find the way down."

Eva rose, expectant. She looked at Madden and he smiled back, the smile not moving beyond his lips. It was grim. She knew this could be a one-way trip. Madden had accepted the truth long ago. What this would do to him she had no idea.

Eva crossed the room to Swanson. He considered her as she approached.

"If there is anything I can do from this side, I will make sure it happens."

The thud of helicopter blades began to sound amidst the thunder. "My ride's here. Stay safe, Director Scott. Don't do anything... unusually crazy."

Eva pulled him close, kissing his cheek. "You look after the earth. I expect it in good working order when I return."

"You find your daughter. I expect to meet her when you return." To the rest of them he said, "Good luck and God speed. Our fate rests with you now."

Porter Rockwell ripped the sealant from the door so Swanson could force it ajar. In an instant, he was through and gone.

"He'll be safe," Madden assured them, his cold arm now fully sealed and armored, placed around Eva's shoulder.

"They aren't after him," Eva agreed, trying not to sag under the weight of Madden's arm. "Just everybody else. Aren't we following him?"

"Not by that route," Emdy Sengupta answered. "Our path lies down a different route." He indicated the service door. "There's a charnel house once covered by part of the mansion during its construction. We need to find a cellar underneath the kitchens. The cellar should give us access with little difficulty."

"Director, I have to ask," Wolfgang Stufflebeam, one of the heavy ordnance experts spoke now.

"Ask away," she replied, turning to him.

"Well, lady, we are going to Hell for you, the enormity of which may or may not have escaped all these intelligent people." This brought hoots of derision from other members of the team. "What if we get there and we can't find your child?"

The noise stopped. This must have been playing on their minds, too.

"I have faith we will. I can track her. If we can find a way to rescue her, we will. But if we can't..."

"If we can't, Nina Scott, a baby only weeks old and our primary objective, is not the only target," Gila said, pressing buttons on a small device in her hand. Two objects popped into view, rotating on the visor just out of Eva's view above her head. She strained to look for a moment before pulling the visor down.

"These are the Well of Souls and the Scroll of Judgment." The dagger and scroll rotated independent of each other in her field of vision. "They are your secondary objectives. The scroll is the only item keeping the portals from opening permanently. If we can take it, we buy a little time. The dagger has a similar importance. But we are there for the child."

"Don't forget," Wolverton reminded them, "you will be in the fight of your lives when we get there, from the second we pass through until the last instant of your miserable lives. If the scroll is the only object keeping these portals from staying open, we find it and take it back. We will be writing a new 'Revelations' even while people up here are living the old. This will be YOUR Testament. The records of this journey will be YOUR Gospels. What happens now decides the fate of humanity."

Wolverton placed his meaty paw on Madden's shoulder. His bad shoulder. Eva gasped, but with the armor, the giant Shikari leader seemed unconcerned. His gesture was a show of faith in her husband.

"If we have to die so others may live, so be it. But we are gonna cause merry hell before we do!"

The Shikari cheered and yelled. Eva found herself doing the same. The enthusiasm was infectious and she began to understand why this unit was so tight, why they feared so little. Individually, they were each a force to be reckoned with. As a team, they felt unstoppable.

They moved into an ornate hallway, ancient polished tables bedecked with violet-colored flowers and roped off from the public. They stuck to the carpeted walkway, respectful of the building and its history. Lightning flickered in, sparking a million flashes of tiny light from chandeliers in the window, dazzling Eva. Pulling her visor down, she concentrated instead on the augmented vision the cameras on her helmet provided.

A small doorway led from the hallway into a room full of stainless steel counters covered with hastily abandoned dishes, preparation cutlery strewn everywhere.

"Something really spooked these people." Madden picked up a large wooden spoon from a nearby bowl and placed it on the counter.

A moment later, it began to move as a series of rapid vibrations made the room hum. A groaning came from somewhere deep beneath them, a low and moaning sound making Eva's skin itch.

"Scope?" Wolverton turned to the sniper.

"There are readings from below but no movement."

"Portal," Swanson said through Eva's headset.

"You certain?"

"Yes, John. I'm back at Freeport. The demons are most everywhere but not here. The only power we are using is to interface with the ARC global network, but it's more than enough for what we need. You lot had better get a move on. There are portals opening and closing all over the world now, along with reports of frozen responses: as many as the ice demons take, more swarm through. Worse, energy readings indicate the big one is powering up."

"The big one?" Eva asked. "The portal in the Gobi Desert?"

Gila nodded in silent response.

"How did you…? Never mind. Yes. The readings are off the charts and nothing has appeared except for a few flickers of lightning. Our only positive there is the fact it is in the middle of nowhere, which is not much of a positive given they merely need to set foot on our soil to have an effect."

One corner of Eva's visor became a screen panning across the Gobi Desert. It should have been empty but was instead packed with tents, temporary buildings, row after row of assault helicopters, and dozens of fighter jets.

"If they want to take our planet, they will find we do not go meekly. There are similar setups across the globe. Have you located the cavern yet?"

"We are on the way down."

"Good. It looks like the secret won't last long. They are starting to converge on Rose Hall."

Off to the far side of the kitchen, there was a cry of triumph as Matt Tanzer held what looked like a camera against a wall; it showed what was through the wall on the other side.

"It's behind here, and there's a locking mechanism. This was built with intent." Tanzer ran his hand over a section of paneling, and there was a click as he found the hidden door. A section of the white paneling made its way open, becoming stuck after a few moments.

"A narrow gap is not gonna let most of us through," was Tanzer's critical observation.

"I can get through," volunteered Eva, grabbing a nearby broom. "Maybe I can clear the blockage."

"By all means," Tanzer replied, the resignation on his face showing he didn't believe there was anything she could do help. She would show him.

Eva dropped her kit and squeezed through the gap, looking down the stairs beyond. In the augmented vision of her visor, walls and ceiling were covered in grime, refuse, and rubble on the steps indicating a long-term lack of use. Some of the smears on the wall caused Eva to turn away in disgust.

"Something bad happened down here," she said, turning to attack the rubble causing the problem. It was stubborn but with a little brute force it began to dislodge. A thought struck her: *If these suits are used as an exoskeleton for strength, can the same strength be directed externally?* Setting her feet, she pulled the door, the experiment working.

"Eva!" Madden shouted from in the kitchen. "Are you all right?"

"Sure, just housekeeping."

"Hurry, they are almost here."

She fought against the detritus, the muck proving resistant as she attempted to dislodge it from the floor. "Try now. Get J.D. to shove against the door."

"Ready," J.D. said, as one enormous meaty hand gripped the edge.

Eva set herself and pulled, as he pushed from the other side, and with reluctance, the door gave way, protesting with a loud metallic shriek as it did so.

"Noise won't help keep us hidden," Madden said as The Shikari passed through. "Let's hope the demons are as stupid as they are fierce."

J.D. Shelton came through last and together they pushed the door shut. In an instant, he had sealed the frame of the hidden door with a substance similar to the one Porter used at the kitchen door but with a much more acrid smell.

"The door will hold for now." Shelton looked dubious.

"How do we get back out?" Eva was worried now.

"Director, I don't think anybody in this squad has any doubt about your ability to find your daughter, but not a one of us expects to be coming back this particular way."

The man had all but admitted he knew this was a one-way ticket. "Then why are you going? Have you nothing more left to do in life?"

Shelton laughed. "It is for the thrill of it. When we complete this mission, there are no others who will ever be able to say the same."

Eva made her way down the steps with J.D., the staining on the walls growing more pronounced as they descended the stairs.

"Can we go through?" she heard Madden ask.

"No, not yet," advised Swanson. "The portal is not in full phase. It's flickering in and out of existence, and you could end up doing an Asmodeus if you enter at the wrong time."

Eva shuddered, remembering the gruesome scene when Gila unloaded an assault rifle at the Orpheus superstructure and they all believed Asmodeus was sliced clean in two as a result. Now she knew it to be the work of Belphegor, who had posed for generations as his partner. Nothing was as it seemed.

"It seems the energy used by the large portal at the airport is a primer for this. What you are seeing is a residual portal, an eddy in the current of energy, if you will. It's why they aren't using it. Remember, they want mass infiltration, overwhelming force. They no longer care for clandestine movements."

"Well, could we not inspire them to attack again? Give them an incentive?"

"What did you have in mind?" Swanson asked.

Eva came out into the cavern, meeting Madden's eyes as he said, "I could injure myself; such an act might draw some attention."

There was a crunch under her foot. Eva glanced down and caught her breath. The partial remains of a human skull with empty sockets glared up at her, loose teeth scattered nearby, bones gleaming white. She looked about. The entire floor was littered with bones, some human, and some animal. The room had a scent of death, cloying and musty. The charnel house rumors were true. It was about ten meters across, domed, and judging by the markings, carved out by human hands. The Shikari were scattered about the room, where rough brickwork contained many more bones and racks of skulls, the bones organized by size.

"Who were these people," she breathed.

"I think the mystery surrounding this house is justified," Gila observed.

A flicker drew Eva's attention. In the center of the room, a pale rose glow emanated, glowing and then disappearing entirely.

"The portal," Madden supplied.

Eva stepped around the bones as best she could, wincing where the snap underfoot indicated she hadn't been so careful.

"Watch your step; you do not want to slip and break bones. Injuring yourself would just draw the others down here, and now we are trapped in, I don't think being injured is an option."

"I'm not the issue. Madden, you need to let your guard down. You need to lose control. They sense you more clearly the more demonic you become. You are the weakest hellbounce, or at least you were. You can open the gate."

To the rest of the group, Eva added, "One thing you have to know about the denizens of hell is their perverse attraction for defeating those of lesser stature. From what we learned, Madden's demon is as weak as they come. He was like catnip for demons."

"So if he exposes his demon side, however briefly, it might drive them crazy and set off another chain of portals," Swanson concluded.

"It might also induce a full-scale invasion," Eva warned.

"Will this be enough to allow passage for fifteen people?" Madden looked doubtful. "CERN needed a phenomenal amount of energy to stay open and this doesn't even have a power source."

"It does as soon as you let loose," Bishop growled.

"Let's find out. Hit me."

"I can do it," John Wolverton volunteered.

Madden grimaced. "I don't want my head taken off, though I know you mean well. This has to be under my control."

"My turn." Eva slapped her husband hard in the face with her right hand. "Think of how weak and useless you have been the last year. Think of how you couldn't defeat Brian without the demon inside. Think of how different you feel with it now. Embrace the power, the rage." Eva threw a punch to his stomach, causing him to double over.

Madden grinned through the initial assault and then a strange look came over his face. Rage mixed with fear. He held his hands out, the rippling of his skin showing the slight emergence of the creature within.

The Shikari raised their weapons, all guns ready to obliterate him.

"Wait," Eva cautioned, her hands held aloft. "Madden, hold on to it. Concentrate. Look at me. You did it several times before, when you first bounced. When they tortured you at the airport. When you held the Scroll of Judgment. You could have let go, but you didn't. You are stronger than you were. Prove them all wrong."

Madden wrapped his arms about his middle, heaving deep breaths as sweat broke out on his forehead. He closed his eyes and swallowed.

"It's working," said Gila, her eyes on the instrument Scope held for her.

"What the hell is happening to your body?" Luke Wolverton asked, looking at Madden.

"It's... my true form. You don't... you don't want to meet it."

"You've done enough," Gila decided. "We have piqued their curiosity. You can let it go now."

"There's a portal opening in Kingston," Swanson advised. "The flow of energy is enormous. It should light this one up like a beacon."

Madden had his hands on his knees, bent over taking deep breaths. Eva dropped to one knee to check on him.

"I'm okay," he said. "I wouldn't want to go there on a regular basis. It's stronger than I remember."

Behind him, the dim glow of the portal increased from a faint rose, becoming bright pink, and then as it gained strength, turning white. It hung, shimmering in the air, putting the rest of the cavern in stark relief. The whole room had turned a nauseating shade of white, and from within the portal came a groaning noise. The source of the sound they had heard upstairs.

"It looks a lot like the wrong type of portal," Madden uttered, apprehension clear in his voice.

"The energy readings are fine," Gila affirmed. "We are good to go."

At the top of the stairs, a shriek of protesting metal betrayed the fact they were no longer alone.

"Get in there!" Swanson shouted through Eva's headset.

"You heard the man!" Wolverton echoed. "What are you waiting for? An invitation? Eternal damnation waits. Get on in there! Go! Go! Go!"

Porter Rockwell winked at Eva before lowering his visor and jumping through the portal, disappearing in a flash of light. Up above, screams of rage at a target lost followed them down. The Shikari then began to pour through the aperture until only Gila, Wolverton, and Madden were left standing with her.

Gila smiled, placing her hand over Eva's. "See you on the other side." She turned and entered.

"You in control?" John Wolverton asked, the huge man stooping to check on Madden.

"Yes," panted Madden. "I'm fine."

"Good. You're next."

With no words, Madden turned to the bright white light and stepped forward, becoming one with it.

"This is it then, Director. No way out now. I've got your six."

Eva nodded and turned to face the shimmering light, about to do the one thing she feared above all else. They were there, waiting for her on the other side. With no alternative, she would step into the lion's den.

"Abandon hope all ye entering here," she said and stepped into the gateway.

CHAPTER TWENTY-THREE

Is this what it feels like? Walking toward the light?

The blinding luminosity played tricks with her senses. Shapes, images came and went but nothing definite materialized. Eva had no idea if she was moving forward or backward. There was a chill in this place, yet at this instant, in this moment between worlds, she had the feeling she was being watched, and the watcher was not happy to see her.

With a jolt, the light ended, replaced by darkness. Eva experienced a moment of pure panic as she dropped in mid-air, and then her feet hit a surface. Hands grabbed at her; acting on pure instinct, Eva fought to get away.

"Steady," came Madden's voice. "I've got you."

Eva relaxed at the sound of her husband, reaching up to touch his face. "You're still you."

"Were you expecting anything else?"

"She feared you would resume your true form, demon," Rachelle Bishop said from nearby.

Eva's eyes began to adjust. They were in a narrow gap, an alleyway. The walls were high, reaching up beyond the limits of her vision. If there was a sky, she could not see it, but there was an angry red glow coming from somewhere. She sniffed the air. There was a metallic tang and the acrid stench of burning, but otherwise it was breathable. Cold but breathable.

"Well, that makes sense," Eva decided. She looked round to see the Shikari had their masks on and oxygen tubes in.

"Lucky for you," John Wolverton's critical voice observed from behind her. "The rest of you save it. You never know when you might actually need breathable air, but the Director here has proven luck overrides preparedness."

"Makes it easier to understand why earth isn't completely alien to them. Where are we? What is this place?"

Madden looked around him. "I'd be tempted to say this is home." He was about to elaborate when a massive roar came from overhead and an enormous and black object passed over the top of wherever they had emerged. The object crawled, as if oblivious to the small group of newcomers.

Eva reached out to touch the nearby wall, finding it smooth. "It feels like glass or very polished stone."

Jenn Day plucked a dagger from her belt and began to scratch the surface of the wall. After a few attempts, she gave up. "Nothing. Not a scratch. Not a damned mark. What sort of material is impervious to razor-sharp steel?"

"A material not of Earth," Emdy Sengupta remarked, making notes on a small screen with a stylus. "Let us suppose for a moment all of this were made of diamond..."

Luke Wolverton put his arm around the diminutive Bangladeshi. "Let us suppose you don't start thinking avaricious thoughts in Hell. You might not have to die here in order to become a demon."

"While you are using your brain," John Wolverton said to his son, "what do you make of the portal from this side?"

Eva turned, and for the first time, noticed from this side, there was nothing to indicate a portal. "Where has it gone?"

"It's still there," Luke said, his voice full of wonder. "If there are more like this, they could swarm earth in no time at all. There would be no need for enormous expenditure of energy."

Luke stuck his arm into the portal and then pulled it back, staring at it. He turned to the gathered Shikari. "Be right back."

Before anybody could stop him, Luke jumped into the portal.

"Idiot," John fumed.

Then just as soon as he was gone, Luke returned, thrown out of the portal with force, bowling into Ellen Covlioni and Wolfgang Stufflebeam, who grunted at the collision.

Luke stood with help from Covlioni, his face somewhat battered, cuts on both cheeks. He winced, bending down again to rub his shins. "There's a step up. Bashed my legs."

"What happened to your face?"

Luke reached up, his eyes betraying the pain he felt as he touched his jaw. "It's a message from the demons on earth. We are not welcome through this exit. The demons were waiting for me. They appeared afraid of getting too close, but the room was packed with them. As I came through, I was grabbed by a humanoid with dark grey skin. It didn't look like the other demons. A cowled figure told me if we attempted to use the gateway, we wouldn't make it out of the cavern alive. They then proceeded to do this."

"In a second?"

Luke appeared confused. "It was much longer. I might have only been there for a minute or so, but it wasn't a second."

John Wolverton clipped his son on the back of the head. "And that's from me for such a dumb move."

"There's a time differential," Gila concluded. "Let's say a second here is a minute there. More importantly, it appears they intended to drive us into the cavern and keep us there. They know we have crossed over, so they were expecting us."

A chill ran down Eva's spine. She closed her eyes and felt for the connection, the distant spark she'd had so briefly experienced with her daughter.

"Madden, I can feel her. She's still here."

"Good news," her husband said.

Gila took a couple of steps toward the exit of the alleyway, where Porter Rockwell and Forrest Kyle waited, guns in their hands. "Let us see what we can find. Time to move out."

Very well practiced, the Shikari eased around the end of the alleyway, guns first, not making a noise. Eva found it difficult not to hit something or someone with the enormous pack she carried; yet they avoided all contact, wraiths in a world of the dead.

She crept forward as the team dispersed to the right, hugging the wall on the right-hand side of what appeared to be a massive thoroughfare, ten meters wide. Her visor down, Eva followed Madden as he tried to replicate the stealthy movements of the team ahead. Once she got around the corner however, she stopped suddenly.

"My God it's enormous," Madden said, clearly in awe.

He wasn't wrong. The walkway stretched off into infinity, walls climbing higher than the tallest skyscraper. Sheer and black, the walls were punctuated by an occasional circular exhaust vent, spewing black vapor into the sooty darkness above. From time to time, there was a green glow from somewhere in the structure, but it was far too high up to make any difference to them on the ground.

"How are we ever going to find Nina in this?" Eva whispered. "Maybe we aren't going to. This could be Hell, or it could be a part of something much bigger. Maybe this is my own personal Hell; to be left wandering a labyrinth for eternity, my baby out of sight but not out of mind."

Madden clutched at her hand. "You didn't die. You don't belong here. Don't think like anything should change. I have the feeling it is easy to give into despair here."

They walked on, hugging the side of the street for what must have been hours. During this time, nobody said a word. The sentries moved with determined purpose, but Eva became distracted. There was a humming coming from deep within the ground, like the sound of an engine deep within a ship. The vibrations reached up to tingle Eva's feet through the soft soles of her combat suit, yet it was impossible to say where it came from. The only breaks in the endless walls were a series of small exits like the alleyway they had arrived in. Eva started counting them at one point but gave up after a couple of hundred.

"One thing is clear," Rachelle Bishop observed, her voice low. "You were spot-on about the technology, Director Scott. This all seems very automated. But where is everybody? How would all of this run with no maintenance at all?"

"We don't know enough about what's going on here to make any sort of a judgment call on this place," John Wolverton said from the back of the group. "We keep going until we find a different point of reference."

And so, it went. Eva walked, yet the end of the labyrinthine walkway never seemed any closer. Behind her it appeared exactly the same. She realized even if she wanted to go back to the portal, she now had no idea which of the alleys was correct. In fact, she couldn't be sure they weren't walking in circles.

"Light, up ahead." Porter Rockwell whispered over the headset.

Eva looked up in hope. The comment had stirred the Shikari into action, and they began to move with purpose. It was faint, but up ahead there was a red glow. Anything breaking up the monotony of this street was good.

The glow grew in intensity as they neared, Eva preferring to watch the feed from Rockwell's cameras, as he was just a little bit closer. And then they came upon it; Eva's heart dropped.

They stepped out onto a ledge, a shallow gradient tipping away from them, down toward the hub of the most enormous city Eva had ever seen. In the distance, every building seemed as big as a mountain. Above it, the sky was blood red, swirling despite the lack of wind. A blast of heat hit them from below. Circular vats of molten liquid opened and closed in rhythmic patterns, to what end Eva could not fathom. Lighting danced across the sky, static charges given no release in the swirling mass above them.

"Dear Lord above," Wolfgang Stufflebeam uttered. "Those buildings. They must be thousands of feet high. We've only been traversing one structure. Look."

There were other walkways down to what Eva presumed was ground level, every building a mountain. Metallic structures reached up hungrily from the ground. Filled with pipework and lighting, there was a massively industrial feeling about the superstructures, as if they were all interconnected. Above the buildings, winged machines moved at an imperial pace, clones of the ship recently passed by.

"It's as if a machine was trying to replicate the jungle in Mount Salem," Madden observed, unknowingly echoing her very thoughts. "I wonder if its creators ever realized what beautiful structures they were building?"

He wasn't wrong. Enormous spiral structures formed from what looked like crystal or glass topped many of the distant buildings, glowing red. In a macabre way, given the location, there was a dark beauty to it all.

"It's the peaks behind," said Scope, studying the distant horizon. "They are erupting, spewing objects out for what must be miles. If this city is this size, who knows how big those mountains are. As it stands, I think we are at some sort of viewing platform. Take a step off and it all misaligns."

"These buildings could all be made of volcanic material," Madden said.

Some of the Shikari turned to stare at their demonic guest, no doubt still considering where his loyalties lay.

"What?" he asked, reacting to their stares. He reached out and placed his hand on the stone. "This could be a form of basalt, granite, obsidian."

"Granite is metamorphic, not volcanic," Eva corrected him.

Madden turned to her, a comeback already hovering on his lips. He lifted his hand from the stone, and as he did so, the surface retracted, sliding with a faint hiss up into the surrounding structure. Revealed underneath was a flat screen with the rough outline of a hand.

"Did Iwake it up?" Madden asked.

"Tanzer," Wolverton said, "you're electronics. Look at this."

Matt Tanzer stepped forward, examining the plate. Eva watched through the screen in her visor. It took some getting used to; she felt detached from reality this way, as if she were not here.

"It looks like some kind of screen, a sensor perhaps. What is this even doing here? It seems very random."

Tanzer placed his hand on the screen. Nothing happened for a second and then a sullen red glow came from around his hand.

Tanzer appeared confused. "Nothing."

"Maybe it's not meant for mortal hands?" Madden's suggestion felt appropriate to Eva.

He stepped back up to the screen, placing his hand on the sensor. The glow this time was instant and strong. More of the stone paneling retreated, sliding back with a rippling effect until a control panel was revealed. A screen filled with strange glyphs blinked into life above, as did the panel surrounding it. All glowed a deep red.

"Those are the same characters we saw back in Worcester," Eva recalled, the memory chilling her. "They were in the hospital, in Gideon's hidden room."

Madden stared at it for a moment. "Amazing," he breathed.

"What? What do you see?"

Madden glanced at her for a moment and then back at the screen. "This appears to be a portal with access to a network. A massive network. Cities, zones, information, politics, history, economy, it's all here. It's like they have computerized Hell."

"But how...?" Eva asked.

"Can you access a map?" Gila suggested.

Madden concentrated for a moment and the screen flickered,

widening as a picture filled the void. It was covered with mountainous regions, several large bodies of what appeared to be water, and marked with borders and cities.

"Amazing," both Gila and Emdy offered.

"This map," Gila continued. "It is as if every map or description of Hell has some semblance of accuracy. It's like somebody who saw this drew the De Jorio map of Virgil's Hell. What's the light mass in the center?"

Madden zoomed in on a region surrounded with glyphs. "Ice."

"Does it say where we are?" Eva asked, in no doubt now her daughter would be right at the center.

Madden pressed a couple of buttons and the map zoomed out, shifting rapidly to the right, centering in on a peninsula at the end of a long and narrow stretch of land. Eva's heart sank when she realized the distance the map indicated.

"We are in the city of Cain, the citadel of Leviathan."

Madden was about to say more when Emdy Sengupta lurched backward. A mammoth creature of deepest shadow, fully twelve feet high, picked him up with ease. Eva only had a moment to study the demon, humanoid in shape with glowing coals for eyes, as it in turn examined Emdy. It pulled him close and sniffed. Its eyes widened.

"Mortal," it growled and threw Emdy as hard as it could off the balcony into mid-air where he sailed out before crashing down the side of the building.

"Fire!" Wolfgang roared, letting rip with his mini-gun. Forrest Kyle joined in, and the rest of the Shikari did soon thereafter. Despite its size, the demon disintegrated under such a ferocious assault, letting out a roar of pain before it collapsed to the ground. Black blood spilled out, running down the superstructure and gathering in pools. An alarm sounded, a foul shriek of a klaxon. From the path they had taken echoed howls of rage.

"We have to get out of here!" Eva urged. "Look at the blood."

The demon blood, fatally corrosive back on earth, had begun to flow back toward its owner. The demon twitched. "All those bullets. They did nothing," Eva said, terrified.

"They slowed it," Wolverton countered. "We have to get down there. Emdy has the key recording equipment."

"Which won't mean a hill of beans if we are all dead," Eva argued. "We have to get out of here."

"There are hundreds of them," Scope informed the team, only making the situation worse. "We must have walked right by them all. The only way is down."

"Go," Wolverton decided, clearly unhappy. "Protect the Directors at all costs.

CHAPTER TWENTY-FOUR

IF IT HAD EVER OCCURRED TO EVA THIS JOURNEY TO RESCUE HER daughter was a bad idea, it was rammed home now. The headlong flight down the ramp from one gigantic structure to another was as hopeless as it was crazy. There was nowhere to hide and now an angry mob of indestructible demons was baying for her blood.

The slope gave the Shikari the advantage of an initial burst of speed, but Eva was not fit and trained like they were. Soon, she began to falter, her knees jolting with every step, pain shooting up through her legs despite the support of the combat suit. The faltering way Gila moved betrayed evidence she was feeling it, too

"We have to get to Emdy," Wolverton said through the team's radio, which only functioned now due to a small generator Emdy Sengupta had been carrying in his kit. John Wolverton was right. Without power they were completely lost.

The air became oppressive, the stench of sulfur too much for Eva. She felt small, overburdened.

"I can't keep up," she gasped as the team peeled off from the ramp to scamper along the surface of the superstructure.

"You have to!" Rachelle Bishop shouted. "You are dead otherwise."

Above them, the demon was on its knees, recovering as the blood returned. In moments, it would be on its feet, a squadron of its kind ready to fall on the interlopers with fatal prejudice.

Eva stumbled on the surface they traversed, catching her tired feet on seemingly smooth stone. She threw her hands out to stop herself crashing and both Madden and J.D. Shelton caught her.

"We got you," J.D. said with a nod.

Behind her mask, Eva smiled. "Thank you."

In short order, they reached the crushed remains of their colleague.

"Quick, retrieve the pack," Wolverton ordered. "We don't know what being here means when we are dead."

He was right. Eva watched the crumpled corpse of the late Emdy for signs of movement. For the moment there was none, just the trickle of blood where the impact had ruptured his body. The suit kept the worst of the wounds hidden.

"Got it," Ellen Covlioni declared, holding a small black box aloft. "It's still in good order."

"Where do you think they got the idea for black box recorders from?" Wolverton replied. "Move out, those things will be on us in seconds. Head for that exhaust port. Let's see if our oxygen was worth bringing." Wolverton pointed to one of the mouth-like apertures emerging farther down the terrace, and the Shikari broke into a run. All except Eva and Gila, along with Madden, who remained with the two stragglers.

Eva tried her damnedest, but despite the combat-suits' assistance, her equipment weighed her down. She jogged for perhaps two hundred meters, watching her protectors disappear up ahead. Up above, an ear-splitting roar caused everybody to stop and turn.

Now remade, the demon stood at full height and pointed at them, snarling and hissing in some unintelligible language. Several more emerged from the walkway behind. The group proceeded at leisure down the walkway, seemingly not concerned in the least about their route of escape.

"It's a trap," Eva concluded. "Wolverton, it's a trap. Stay away from the exhaust vent."

"How can you be sure? It looks like a good escape."

"Remember who you are here to protect, Commander," Gila warned.

"You heard the Director," Wolverton shouted, plainly unimpressed about having his authority questioned. "Move away."

This caused an immediate reaction in their pursuers. Robbed of whatever fate they had intended for their victims, the demons began to lope down the ramp.

Eva watched, numb, feeling intense heat behind her as the exhaust erupted liquid flame, the viscous fluid pouring down the side of the stone building. And then a gap opened in the surface of the building.

"Quick! In here!" Madden yelled.

Eva glanced at him.

"I didn't say anything," he said in confusion, but it was too late. Following their re-direction, the remaining Shikari gathered around Madden and Eva. They entered the dark passage without a second's thought.

"Keep going," Madden appeared to call. "Eh? What?" he said a moment later.

The passageway was narrow and high, tall enough for the demons, but in no way wide enough to accommodate their bulk. Eva heard a heavy grating from behind as the stone door slid shut.

Eva kept her eyes trained on Madden's back, trying not to think about the roars of frustration and the scratching of talons at the now-closed entrance behind them. The air felt stolen from her lungs, as if there was not enough to breathe; the onset of a panic attack. She forced herself to keep moving. Despite their proximity to danger, it appeared they were safe. She did wonder how Madden had found it; was there knowledge returning from his previous visit?

In time, the corridor opened into a cube-shaped room, with a larger version of the data portal across one wall and several stools fixed to the floor and just too high to look comfortable. Everything was black, a red glow from a strip across the center of the ceiling the only illumination. A low-level hum sounded around them, making the walls vibrate.

The gloom didn't matter to Eva, wearing the mask as she was. The cameras enhanced everything, and she grabbed Madden in the surety for now at least, they were safe.

"What was your confused conversation all about? How did you know to find this refuge?"

"I didn't," Madden admitted. "That wasn't me."

"Damn well sounded like you," John Wolverton accused. "It even came from your direction."

Several of the Shikari nodded and made noises of agreement; Eva could see from their body language despite the training and equipment they wore, many were shaken by what they had seen outside; what had nearly happened to them was a new experience for most of the group.

"He didn't call you in here; it was my command," said a hooded figure in a black robe, stepping out from the narrow corridor behind them. The voice was eerily familiar to Eva, sounding just like Madden.

"I have been watching you since you appeared. You should not be here."

"Who are you?" Madden demanded, clearly shaken by the imitation of his voice. "Show yourself!"

The light strip across the middle of the room grew brighter and several bulbs began to glow around the room.

"Great," Eva moaned. "More red." It felt as though she was back at school, learning how to develop photographs in a lab.

"Such is the nature of Hell. Heaven is golden light; earth is green and blue. Here it is red and black. Welcome to Hell, Eva Ross."

This stunned her. "Ross... Who..."

The hooded figure pulled back the material shadowing his face, revealing a small man with little hair and a very familiar face.

"Janus?"

"Hello, Eva," he replied with a shy smile.

"Janus!" Eva threw her arms about him, hugging him tight and causing him to wince.

"Careful, careful…"

Eva stood back. "What is it? Are you hurt?"

"All in good time," he replied. "First off, you military types. You might as well unload for now; you aren't going anywhere. I'm sorry; I can't offer you any sustenance. There is no such thing in this domain. It doesn't mean anything here."

Madden extended his good hand, which Janus clasped. "It's good to see you, old friend. We have so much to thank you for."

"Stop," Rachelle Bishop said, a harsh tone to her voice. Eva turned to see her with her assault rifle levelled in Janus' direction.

"How is it we come to a place no rational person even believes exists, get chased by monsters out of nightmare, and just happen to be saved by an *old friend*?"

"Someone didn't do their homework," Madden said with a wink. "Janus Lohnes was the unsung hero of the mountain, not to mention responsible for saving my life several times."

"Both of our lives," Eva added. "He stabbed Iuvart with the Well of Souls, right through the heart, took the Scroll of Judgment and brought them both here, where they were meant to be in the first place." She turned to Janus. "You owe me an explanation. What were you doing on Mount Gehenna?"

"I go wherever I am needed," the small man answered.

The cryptic nature of his answer infuriated Eva. "Are you needed here?"

"Perhaps. My fate hasn't been determined yet, although it certainly helped you. When I fell through the portal on Gehenna, I landed far from here, much farther to the West if direction has any meaning."

Janus pressed a button on the control panel and a screen perhaps four by three meters emerged, the same map from earlier glowing in scarlet hues on the screen.

"There, to the South, in the middle of the map below the inland body of... whatever it is. If anywhere could be called the Gate of Hell then the location is there. It's not a city like this but an immense construction nonetheless. It powers the portals. I came through one of the secondary portals there; they are saving the primary aperture for the main push. Leviathan and his army were waiting for us. I believe you saw the endless hordes as the Scroll's seals were broken.

"When the portal failed, the blowback sucked everything in after me. There was an influx of demons, hellbounces, minions, beasts, and phantoms. More than you could imagine populated the earth. Behemoth tore a swath through the army, swelled as it was with all the returnees. I bore the corpse of Leviathan's underling, his avatar on the mortal plane in my arms.

"To say Leviathan was not pleased would probably be the biggest understatement in the history of existence. He had me imprisoned here in his great city of Cain, the city of Envy. That was not so long ago. His entire army is awaiting his order on the plains to the southwest, and is only one of several armies vying for supremacy. They would destroy each other in a heartbeat were it not for the ice."

"So what happened to you?" Eva persisted. "Why are you in this state?"

"When I was brought here, my jailors were not gentle." Janus shed his robe to reveal the tattered remains of the combat gear he had worn in Afghanistan. The clothes were shredded and under every tear there was a bruise or a gashed cut weeping pus.

Without hesitation, Jenn Day moved to treat Janus, a medpack in hand.

Janus raised his hands to ward her off. "No, don't bother. There is no healing in Hell for those not attuned to the source."

"The source?" Day looked confused.

"It's an energy field, the only nourishment in Hell. You saw an example of it when you gunned the demon down. Anything attuned to the source is essentially indestructible unless torn to pieces. If you are linked, you are immortal to some extent. Machines use the same energy. It comes from the souls of the awaiting– those who have died and whose fates have not yet been decided."

"How can you use souls?" Gila asked. "If you are good in life you go to Heaven. If you are bad you come here."

"Sorry, Ms. Ciranoush, but you are wrong. When you die, you go to Hell. Everybody goes to Hell."

"It goes against everything we believe in."

"He's not lying," Madden said, reading the screen. "It's well documented here. The Elysian Fields are basically a sorting pot for Heaven, with those worthy ascending, those who have sinned serving a form of personal penance. If they pass, they ascend. If not, they remain, either as a source or as a citizen of Hell. There is one exception only. An anomaly they have found it impossible to replicate."

Madden turned away from the screen. "The Hellbounce."

"The one way back to the mortal plane not involving massive quantities of energy, and the one process they haven't perfected," confirmed Janus. "These records corroborate the fact. The Hellbounce as you call them are an abomination to most. Then the others convinced Abaddon to take on and defeat Satan. When the ice began to coalesce around Tartarus, no one paid any heed. When the minions of Crustallos became visible, taking Hell's denizens almost at will, it became a viable option for all demonkind. My own personal Hell will be to bear these wounds with no hope for absolution. When the ice overtakes me, as it inevitably will, I will accept white eternity with good grace."

"If we can't heal you, we can make sure you are at least clothed," Jenn Day decided, pulling another of the skin-tight combat suits from her pack. "Put this on."

"We are here because someone we put our trust in repaid us by abducting my baby daughter," Eva said to Janus as he pulled on the armor. "I think we need your help."

Janus pressed another button and the screen zoomed in on an area close to the center of the map.

"It's real," Madden breathed. "Tartarus."

"It is indeed. Most of Earth's fables and legends have some basis in truth. Greek myths of the underworld appear to have been closest, but every religion, every society has their version of what happens to you when you die. In truth, you select few consist almost entirely of the population of mortals who have found their way into this domain before their time."

"We have heard the name Crustallos. Who is it?" Eva asked.

"Everybody here knows the name and all speak it in fear," Janus replied. "Crustallos is the primary reason for Tartarus. It is a prison built in what is considered the deepest pit in Hell, but the true pit lies under the city. Tartarus is a lock, a lock slowly being pried open from the other side. Tartarus was created to keep the entity of ice out of this reality and locked up in the limbo beyond."

"What is it?" Madden asked.

Janus placed one hand on Eva's right shoulder, his other on Madden's good arm. "Crustallos is evil, pure and simple. If it comes through, it will consume everything here with a hunger as unimaginable as it is insatiable. When it finishes here, it will bend its will in the mortal realm and from there to the upper realms. It seeks to consume everything. To destroy it all. You will have to steel yourself, Eva. Difficult decisions will need to be made and there is not a lot of time. It is my opinion somebody seeks to fully open the lock and they are going to use your daughter as a key. I think they are going to sacrifice Nina."

CHAPTER TWENTY-FIVE

Eva had suspected as much from the course of events and learning about her history on earth. But when Janus confirmed it, her stomach knotted, and her heart began to thud against her chest; the sound of blood rushing through her ears threatened to overwhelm her.

"It's different to hear it from somebody here, rather than guessing the facts in ignorance."

"How do you know all this?" Madden asked, his tone suspicious. "I can read these words due to my unique... shall we say heritage but what's your explanation?"

"There is so much for you all to understand," Janus told them. "Concepts beyond anything you will be prepared to accept. But consider this: Hell is an instant, yet it is also an eternity."

"You mean there is a time differential?" Luke Wolverton piped up from the far side of the room. "We sort of already guessed."

"Not quite. It's more like Hell is whatever you want it to be. An instant. Forever. Time is a mortal concept. Only in the mortal realm does it matter. Here, all denizens are immortal. In Hell as on earth, nothing changes without the use of will. There are some of the most brilliant minds on Earth who have less than pure souls and they embraced what they saw here. Engineers, scientists, artists, they created what you see around you, having had eternity to perfect their craft. Consider putting Attila the Hun and Genghis Khan, with Brunel, Edison, and Pasteur. Give them infinite resources and time. They could accomplish what on earth would be miracles. Your daughter is a baby for as long as she decides to be a baby. Demons take whatever form they choose for as long as they choose it, with few exceptions."

In a moment of insight, Eva said, "But once they are on Earth, they are subject to the ravages of time as are we all. They become stuck in the shape they choose in Hell."

"And hellbounces are the anomaly," Janus confirmed. "They are a reversion of the demon to the mortal form. The price one pays for returning to the life they lost."

"You haven't answered my question, Janus," said Madden.

"Not directly, no. It has been seven or eight months since you last saw me? It may have been millennia for me; there is no way of telling. As it is, when I was imprisoned here and Leviathan took his army to await the opening of the portal, I was afforded the chance to escape. I wandered the city, which must be thousands of miles across, avoiding the Guardians until I found this place by chance."

"The Guardians?" Eva asked.

"Yes, the strongest demons choose an unalterable form. They above all draw strongest from the Source and *it* refuses to release them from their form. You met the Guardians of Cain earlier. The Source is the only reason you were not ripped asunder. They can't get in here; this workshop was built for slender men, the engineers of Cain. We are near the surface of a power plant designed to generate energy in a workable form to help construct the buildings around us. It's all but redundant now, a neglected form overlooked by nearly everybody. It was perfect for me."

Janus tapped on the screen in front of him, looking far more like one of the Shikari now he wore his combat suit. "I learned the language."

The map zoomed out and Janus pointed to several glowing positions. "Asmodeus had Aquinas as his citadel. Nearest to us is great Forente-Lautus, the dwelling of Belphegor. Beyond her realm we have Narcis, the home of Lucifer, and Tervere where Mammon sits on his throne. Abaddon is master of Torpa and masterless Tartarus sits atop the growing ice. Once the ice reaches the heart of the city, it will be too late."

Eva's heart chilled at the mention of Belphegor. "Forente-Lautus, where they have Nina. I can feel her calling to me."

"I don't find it surprising if your daughter's there. Belphegor was always a master-manipulator. Word has it something befell Asmodeus. His acolytes have been going berserk, hampering the effort to permanently open the portal."

"You're right," Madden agreed. "We saw him cut in half as he stepped through the Orpheus portal under CERN. Belphegor passed through whole. We think a demon named Rosier may be involved."

"Rosier," Janus repeated, a flat look on his face. Belphegor has been gathering the remnants of Asmodeus' army, with Rosier controlling the leading force. He is pulling them away from the main army."

Janus attacked the interface with a flurry of touches, his hands too fast for Eva to follow. The map disappeared. A series of live feeds replaced them, each showing a milling mass of bodies beyond number.

"The denizens of this domain live at the absolute whim of their master. They go where they are commanded, do whatever they are ordered. There are no logistics. This is not an army requiring a supply train. When the floodgates open, they absolutely will not stop until Earth drowns under a sea of blood. However, there are divisions. Abaddon was encouraged to attack Satan and he jumped at the chance. But when he was victorious and took the throne of Tartarus for his own, the ice began to form; the seal began to weaken. Eventually, Abaddon fled back to Torpa with the belief he could defend his own citadel with greater success."

"The instant the sacrifice touches the seal, Hell will be saved."

Madden turned to Eva. "Be saved? They always said the breaking of the seals would be the point the mortal plane becomes overrun."

"What if it were down to the will of the individual?" Eva asked. "What if they choose a different path?"

Janus appeared to mull this over for a moment. "It's possible," he conceded.

Ellen Covlioni approached the terminal. "Is there any way to get some of this paneling off? I'd like to have a look and see if we can boost the signal on our gear. Maybe we can contact ARC."

"You can certainly try," Janus agreed, and pressed a button causing the entire interface to withdraw and open up a collection of wiring.The panel looked very alien to Eva.

"Madden, why don't you help them? You can read the language. Maybe you can find a solution?"

Madden crouched down by the interface with Ellen, Parker Rockwell and Matt Tanzer, leaving Eva free to talk.

"What I don't understand is why Satan, if he was the key to all of this, allowed himself to be toppled?"

"They have a saying in Hell: I'm only demon. The politics of the place are no different from earth. Especially since Hell is comprised of the fallen from the mortal realm."

"If what I read was correct," Madden said while shoulder-deep in the terminal. "Satan was Heaven's greatest servant. Those dwelling up there were actually responsible for opening the path to the nether realms. Tales were concocted, classic stories spiced with just the right elements of truth, and implanted in the minds of mortals. It's as Janus said. Hell is a stepping stone, a sorting stop for those in life who were worthy and those who were not. Purgatory is a test, a measurement of whether your mistakes were too much to prevent ascension."

"And those who remain are tied, bound if you will, to a master.

Madden, correct me if I am wrong, but don't you feel an overwhelming sense of belonging? Do you not feel drawn somewhere?"

"I do, a little," Madden agreed. "It's no worse than the feeling of discomfort when on earth. Maybe it's because I'm not entirely a demon."

"They have trackers on everyone, except me, as I am not demon. Your friends here do not have them either."

"What about me?" Eva asked, noticing Janus had not included her in the general sweeping motion he'd made.

"They know you, Eva. If they are paying attention to the Well of Souls, they will know you are here. However, on the off-chance they missed it..."

Janus touched a section of the wall behind them; it slid away, revealing storage. He reached in and withdrew what appeared to be some kind of black sleeveless jacket which shimmered as the material moved. He handed it to her.

"It's light as a feather," she said, astonished. "What is it?"

"A self-regenerating body-armor. You get hit and this repairs the damage. In addition, it draws on the source like a mobile hotspot. It masks your signature. Your daughter is out there, Eva. If we are going to find her, we don't want half of the population of Hell dogging our every step. This city is full of wonders man was not meant to see, technology which would wipe out human existence in moments. But this armor is unique. Demonkind has never seen its equal"

"If such terrors exist," Rachelle Bishop challenged, "why haven't they been used already?"

Janus smiled. "Cain is the city of envy, young miss. Do you think Leviathan would risk any of his treasures being lost to his rivals? They are guarded with jealous ferocity. Demon politics is the only factor keeping them from uniting in a common cause. Leviathan wants humanity for himself, to swell his numbers. The lock in Tartarus is crumbling and demonkind is terrified beyond reason. Despite this, those in power will play their games until the very end of time."

Eva turned the armor over in her hands. It felt alive, humming in response to her touch, the electric blue shimmer pulsing like the skin of a cuttlefish. "How do I put this on with all this gear?"

"Simple. Cast it all off. You don't need this gadgetry, none of you. Your weapons do no permanent damage; you are not going to fight your way to Nina Scott."

"And yet we will carry it all anyway," John Wolverton ordered.

"You might," Eva contradicted him and proceeded to remove the gear she had been given in Jamaica. Keeping the belt, Eva shrugged herself into the armor and a strange thing happened. The material began to adjust to her body size, fitting her contours.

"I'm not going to need any of this," she said to John Wolverton, who glared down at her. "You heard the man. Most of what we are carrying is redundant. We don't hunger; we don't heal. We can't destroy anything with bullets. We can't fight our way past a demon horde. We just exist in this eternal moment.

"I'll tell you..." Wolverton started to say, but at the same moment a single note sounded, so loud it made Eva's whole body shake. She threw her hands over her ears, squeezing her eyes shut. The clarion call was loud enough to reduce mortal man to whimpers, cowering on the floor. The note was pure but had an air of desperation about it.

The initial shock subsided, and while the noise was still deafening, Eva was able to look up. Several of the Shikari had thrown up, and Gila had a nosebleed. Only Janus was unaffected.

"You get used to it," he revealed when the note finally ended. "It means Hell is under attack again and is to muster the forces to defend their positions. The same call happens when a portal opens to Earth. The two often coincide. The troops rally, but when they aren't fighting a common enemy they are usually clashing themselves. Their actions serve only to strengthen their foe. It's an insane situation you have wandered into."

"Where is the enemy attacking them?"

"In the regions around Tartarus, mostly. But sometimes their foe goes hunting in the midst of the armies. As tenacious as demonkinds' defense of Hell is, this is a war on the back foot. We have to go right through the middle of the battle between demons and the realm beyond if we are to rescue your daughter."

"They are finding easy pickings on earth," Gila said, rubbing her forehead.

"If you want to get Nina, the time to do so is now. They will be distracted. From here we can do nothing. They know I am on the loose, but I am a distraction to be hunted down whenever they see fit. The Guardians, who are not much more than mindless automatons, encountered something. They won't know what."

"We aren't making any headway with the communications," Madden confessed.

Eva peered over his shoulder into the mess of technology. Free of the encumbrance of the extra gear, she found moving about much more pleasant. The new armor gave her a warm feeling.

"It's the Source," Janus said from behind. You are in a way tapped in to it while wearing the armor, but it was made to fit only one person. Nobody else in Hell can take it from you now. If they did, it would serve them no purpose."

Wolverton looked her over. He was clearly unimpressed she had chosen to discard her gear, but he appeared mollified somewhat at the fact she still wore her combat suit plus the new armor. "At least wear the helmet," he suggested. "We can communicate with the radio at least."

Eva smiled and fitted the helmet over the top. The visor was somehow enhanced by the armor, the picture clearer than before. Eva kept this fact to herself.

"How are we going to cross such a vast space?" Madden asked. "If this is all in proportion, it must be tens or hundreds of thousands of miles across."

"Patience, hellbounce," Janus replied, his voice a mystery. "Your questions will be answered, but for now, let us see if the coast is clear."

. . .

Janus led the Shikari back out of the refuge. Eva's visor now showed two definite red marks against the list of names. Members of the Shikari who were no more. They concerned her more than the possibility of the demon giants waiting for them outside.

"Nothing," he said, his voice amplified in Eva's helmet. "They have moved on. Their attention span doesn't last for long."

Eva gazed out over the immense vista, appreciating the alien beauty of the structures and distant volcanic peaks now they weren't being chased. In the sky, the smoke gave way and finally allowed her to see beyond. In the distance, vapor trails swirled blue in an infinity-shaped sign around a celestial body.

"What's that?" she asked, pointing skyward.

"I don't see anything," Bishop said, squinting. Eva realized the armor had given her much more than just protection.

"You're seeing the mortal plane as observed from Hell. The one immutable fact about existing here is you never forget where you came from. Until all of this started, there was never any chance you were going to get back. There is no way to contact those you hold dear."

A yellow signal faded into view on Eva's screen. There was a crackling noise for a moment, and a voice faded in, faintly, as if a million miles away.

"Hello? Eva? Wolverton? Madden? Can any of you hear me?"

CHAPTER TWENTY-SIX

"Director?" Wolverton responded, years of what must have been Special Forces training betrayed in a second by his response to authority.

"Swanson?" Eva said. "Can you hear us?"

"Like you were next to me, Eva. John is a bit fainter. Can you boost the signal?"

Eva glanced at the leader of the Shikari and shook her head.

"No, Director Guyomard. I'm afraid it's impossible. Eva is on a somewhat different frequency."

"Well, isn't this a first?" Swanson's voice dripped self-congratulation. "A communication between the earth and the afterlife. Recorded for posterity."

A blue flashing light appeared on Eva's screen, becoming a bar filling from left to right. 'Upload complete' flashed a couple of times and then disappeared.

"Good, the transmission works," said Swanson. "Eva, where in the name of all right and good have you been? It's been three weeks since you entered Rose Hall."

"It's only been a matter of hours here. Suffice it to say we noticed a difference in the rate time passes from this side."

"How? Have you all grown old?"

"Time doesn't mean anything here, Director," Janus added, standing close to Eva's microphone. "Your boy Luke decided to test it out and nearly got his head lopped off for his troubles. He told me what happened."

There was a pause. "Whose speaking now?" Swanson asked, his voice cautious.

"Janus Lohnes, Director."

"Janus...What are you...? Well I never. I regret not having had the chance to thank you for all you did. You are as much a hero as anybody who stood on Mount Gehenna. More so, even. I'm not even going to begin to consider how it is you are there with Eva and the rest, but you can be assured it gives me confidence to know you are with them."

"You recover quickly from surprises, Swanson," Eva watched Janus as she said this. He gave away nothing.

"Eva, if I have learned one immutable fact during my ARC career, it is there is always something else out there to surprise you. This is just another example. How safe are you to talk?"

"We have a signal blocker, so the transmission can't be traced. It is second nature in Cain. Everybody is suspicious."

"I'm just watching the footage. My God that is stunning. Cain? The name of the place in which you are standing?"

This frustrated Eva. "Swanson, this is Hell. This is not a science trip. We are here to rescue my daughter, not build a common bond and hunt for souvenirs. None of this can get out of ARC. It would be best if nobody but the Council ever saw these pictures. Better still if you deleted them all."

"Your footage goes no further than the Council," Swanson confirmed. "Do you know how long the connection is likely to remain open?"

"It is all tied in, Director." Janus turned to look off into the distance. "The portal you have no doubt just recorded has been opened with the Well of Souls, the dagger with which I slew Iuvart, the same blade you discovered in Qina. While those portals are open, I suspect we can speak. The more you converse with us, the more worried you should be. It means demons are on earth and neither you, nor the enemy has stopped them."

"We are monitoring all locations, Janus. There is nothing open at this time. The containment policy we have developed is in force and working. Forces are marshaled at every major incident point and where we don't stop them, the ice portals normally clean up. Our ally is most efficient."

"Then let me be the first to tell you our information is no longer accurate. Your *ally* is anything but. The enemy of your enemy is not your friend. And portals are currently open. Otherwise, we would not be having this conversation. Have you checked all locations? All? Antarctica, for example, and underground locations? Earth is Earth, Director, and a demon population in the remotest of regions will have the same effect as an army sacking a city. I suggest you look again, for they are filling your world with demonkind and you are missing it."

"And to make matters worse," Gila supplemented, "Ivor Sarch is here in Hell."

"Rosier is..." The line began to crackle.

"Find those portals, Swanson," Eva shouted. "Stop the demons!"

"The clarion call has ended," Janus said, his voice regretful. "The portal is closed. We need to get out of here if we are going to find your daughter. Now is the time they start paying attention to the smaller details while they regroup."

Janus led them down from the terrace, the shallow gradient of the massive stone building easy enough for Eva to traverse with the unburdened combat suit. Nobody else had shed a thing and Eva suspected some had even incorporated her load into their own.

"Where are we headed?" she asked Janus, who kept alert, his eyes forever on the move.

"Into the city, the distance of a couple of these buildings, although it will feel like a trek to you. These buildings are like mountains."

The Shikari fell into formation about Eva, Porter Rockwell at the front, rifle in hand. John Wolverton was at the back, his sawn-off shotgun resting on his right shoulder. All masks were down. Between them, they could have passed for demons. They trailed up the side of the building, a few feet apart. There was no sign of the terrace they had emerged from; the pyramid-shaped enormity had too many. They were perhaps a third of the way up from the base by now.

"There's movement back behind us," Scope said across the headset network.

"Don't worry," Janus replied, now wearing Emdy Sengupta's triple-lensed helmet. "The Guardians of Cain are ferocious, but they aren't intelligent and can't see so far. We are well out of range. They also tend to stick to the borders of the city, which is what this building is. You will find the rest of the city completely uninhabited, unless Leviathan decides he would rather run from battle and await his destruction alone."

"What are the chances of Leviathan returning?"

Janus appeared to consider this. "More than average; he doesn't tend to play well with others. It depends how his personal plans progress. After the setback, he would have lost a lot of standing. Those who are perceived as weak don't last long. Look at his predecessor, for example. Beelzebub championed the last major incursion; the information is recorded in the Book of Revelations. With the failure of Beelzebub's attempt, Leviathan, then one of Beelzebub's lieutenants, was able to supplant his master. He knows more than anyone what is at risk. The only thing keeping him in power is the fact the Tartarus lock is now at a breaking point."

"You seem very at ease with all this," Madden observed from

behind him. His voice served to ease Eva's building panic at the prospect of this deserted city filling with indestructible demons.

"What is there to do but wait and hope? The portal you used is now guarded from both sides. They wanted you here and they may not realize it yet, but they have you."

"How long until the next portal?" Gila asked. "Maybe if there was some kind of discernible pattern..."

"It's becoming more and more erratic. Often, the portals are engaged in response to the enemy assaults. They take of Hell; Hell takes of Earth. From what you say, they have been trying to entice you or capture you, but it all takes energy which is drawn..."

"From the Source," Eva completed.

"Right. It is not inexhaustible, and it is being depleted. It takes many demons to open each portal, every one severing their own link to the Source and transferring it to the gates. It is this transference drawing the enemy on. The hellbounce is a mistake they never wanted to expose to Crustallos. It's like blood to a shark. An easy source. It's a creature leaking energy, completely in flux. Crustallos smells them across space and time. Yet the demon captains need them to maintain a presence on Earth. You saw what happened in the barn the first time you met me. The loss of control of any form, be it injury or personal choice, acts like a beacon. The more the lock in Tartarus crumbles, the easier it is for those beyond to reach past Hell. Thus, the portals appear on earth with greater frequency Crustallos and its minions are taking demons and converting their life force for its own use. Worse, I believe somebody here is aiding them."

Eva shared a glance with Madden. They had reached the base of the pyramid now and walked a path between two of the buildings, rising like black, stony titans into the sky above them. What passed for sky now seemed an impossible distance away. Lightning danced above them, from time to time touching down on one of the buildings, causing the entire structure to glimmer white atop the red.

"Belphegor," Madden said at length. "It has to be her."

Janus stopped, backing under the shadow of the building they passed. He motioned the Shikari to do the same. Porter Rockwell remained at the border between light and shadow.

"How can you be so sure?"

"She returned to Hell shortly before us, right?"

"So the records say."

"And her return heralded upheaval, yes?"

"As unprecedented as it was, it was not unexpected. What are you getting at?"

Madden removed his pack and headgear. Unzipping his combat suit, he pulled it down, exposing the extent of the crystalline disease.

Eva gasped. It had reached his neck and was beginning to creep across his chest. "You never said it had gotten bad. It's only been hours since we..."

Madden looked himself over. "I hadn't noticed. I don't feel any different."

"What is this?" Janus asked. "You are something other than human it seems. Something other than demon, too."

"When we were at a facility on Lake Bodom in Finland, there was a woman there. She claimed to be an employee, but she touched my hand, chilling it instantly. We saw her later on, from the earth side of the Orpheus portal as she crossed through. It was Belphegor. She was almost entirely crystalline by then, and from the way she moved, very weak. Unless it was just a deception."

"And you suspect you are undergoing the same transformation. She became infected and somehow you did as well."

"It's not unreasonable to believe." Madden shrugged.

Janus turned to Eva. "What about you?"

"It never affected me, but I was pregnant with Nina when we she touched me. The cold never touched me."

"Nina saved you then," Janus said. "She is a very special being."

"How do you know?"

"Let me take a look at your arm." Before anybody could stop him, Janus took Madden's arm in both hands, turning it over and back again. It did not escape Eva's notice he had adroitly deflected the question about her daughter.

"You shouldn't have grabbed me," Madden said. "You aren't protected. It will infect you as it did me. We think Nina is the only reason Eva was safe."

Janus let Madden's arm go and Madden pulled back, out of harm's way. While he reclothed, Janus held his hands up, contemplating the crystalline tinge on the tips.

"It will spread now, as it is in me, as it did in Belphegor. I don't know what I am becoming."

Janus held his hands out, palms up. "You are what you choose to be, Madden. This cannot take it from you."

Before Eva's eyes, the crystalline tips of Janus' fingers began to shine, at first a pale yellow, fighting with the ice for supremacy of the flesh. In moments, his hands were awash with white light. Pure and full of vitality, Eva felt herself drawn to the glow, as if it could heal all of her woes. A moment later, the light faded, leaving Janus' hands normal, no crystalline coating.

"What did you do?" Eva asked, full of wonder.

"That was the soul, asked for purpose and given form. In Hell, the soul is born. It is at its purest state, even in those awash with sin. One can work wonders should we just look inward. Even you, Madden Scott. You may have been reborn part demon, but your legacy cannot prevent you taking control of your destiny, even in the deepest pit of Hell."

Madden looked at his arm, disbelief written plainly on his face. "How?"

"You have to look within, my friend. Your soul is the only power capable of overcoming the darkness; the place where the battle for your body is being fought lies inside of you. When you find the location deep within your core, where fire meets ice, you can take a side."

Eva thought she had seen it all. "What are you?"

"Me?" Janus winked. "I'm just an ARC agent. I found my core and my purpose here in this city. To help you."

"With a rather special assignment it appears," Gila said, her voice wavering between surprise and acceptance. Eva was not sure which feeling was stronger in her friend at this point.

"Madden, keep looking inward. The rest of you move out."

Eva turned back to Janus. "I want my daughter back, Janus. We came here to undertake one task. How do we get from here to wherever we need to go?"

"Can you still feel her?"

Eva closed her eyes and reached out. A tiny spark responded, and for a second Eva was full of rapture.

"She's over there," she pointed right at the wall of the overhang sheltering them.

"Forente-Lautus," Janus replied. "It is unlikely Belphegor or whatever she is becoming will lead you to Tartarus without first trying to take you at her own stronghold. We must be cautious. There have been strange readings coming from the region, though there has been no obvious activity."

"So what do we do?" Madden asked. "Just walk in there? Ask her to please give our daughter back?"

"More or less. Up there is a docking port. Have you noticed the transports passing over? They are used when times are less desperate. They draw on far less of the Source than portals."

"You want us on one of those moving cities?" Eva was nonplussed.

"Not one of those. I was thinking something a bit more discreet. You will see. Whatever you need, the chances are you will find it in Hell. We need to get up to the apex of the tower. If we can make the ascent without being detected, we stand a chance of hitching a lift."

In the distance behind them, from maybe a third of the way up the building, there was a howl. Several others answered the initial caller both from behind and ahead of them. The net was closing.

"They let us go," Eva said, fear threatening to overwhelm what passed for reason in this insane place. "They set a trap for us."

With this realization, the Shikari came alert, guns raised and pointing in all directions.

"You won't be able to stop them," Janus warned. "You want your daughter and I will take you to her. But first, we have to outrun the guardians."

"Great. How do we run faster than a gang of giant demons?"

CHAPTER TWENTY-SEVEN

It was conceivable the Guardians could move far faster than any of their party on foot. Eva had never felt so small in the face of such immense odds, not to mention the scenery dwarfing them; ants never felt this size, she was sure of it.

The party hurried along a yellow-lit black path between the bases of two of the buildings, the stink of industry hanging in the air like a fog. Eva wanted to retch.

"Movement, in the distance behind us," Scope announced, walking sideways. Eva followed his cameras on her visor. There was definitely motion back there, something big. It was closing in on them.

"We have no choice," Janus decided. "Run for it. Follow me and stay close."

Janus broke into a sprint, Eva close behind him. The Shikari kept easy pace with them.

"How far?" Wolverton shouted above the noise of running. "We have no cover out here. If they catch us, it's gonna mean our slaughter."

It was hard for Eva to concentrate on the path in front. The cameras of those looking back cycled through on her screen, each one showing the large form gaining definition as it hurtled toward them. Panic began to rise, her legs aching as she grew tired. But then the armor glowed a faint blue, and somehow she was given a second wind as if infused with energy. Confidence replaced panic; the armor had replenished her spirit as much as her body.

"There," Janus called, pointing to a small doorway ahead of him to their right. "Hold them off while I get this open."

The Shikari deployed into two teams of five on the walkway. Clearly practiced, the teams formed around Forrest and Wolfgang, each wielding a mini-gun. Bishop, Day, and the Wolvertons were across the road by Wolfgang, the rest closer around Forrest. Only J.D. Shelton remained with Eva, Madden and Gila, the hulking mass of the man made all the more fearsome by his alien-appearing mask.

"If they get past the best of us, somebody needs to keep you safe," he said and reached around to his back. He slid out an impressive-looking curved sword from a sheath concealed there, the edge glittering and curved like a wakizashi, the shorter of two swords once worn by Samurai. "If they get past this, I always have my hands."

Janus worked at a furious pace on the small control panel of the door while in the distance the Guardian closest to them increased its pace.

Scope began to fire the sniper rifle he had constructed from his kit, barking as he squeezed off rounds. More than once, the demon tumbled to the ground as its legs were taken out. But always, it was straight back up, as if it operated on more than four limbs.

Eva was afraid to look, but other than removing her helmet, she had no choice but to watch, so she shut her eyes.

A hungry roar reverberated around them and Eva felt Madden put his arm around her. The gesture was appreciated and she leaned into him.

"Almost got it," Janus said, his voice stressed. "Take the limbs out if it gets too close.

"Now!" John Wolverton ordered and Scope ceased firing. The

two mini-guns erupted into action, the whirring scythe of bullets cutting down the Guardian, its legs severed. Eva felt the thump as the body hit the floor. The creature growled at them, not the least bit put off, while it reached for its legs.

The rest of the team opened fire, decimating the severed limbs.

"It's no good," Luke Wolverton called, "Its growing new legs."

"Worse," his father added, "it's not alone."

At this, Eva's instinct was to open her eyes. As soon as she had, she wished she had remained oblivious. Three more Guardians bounded toward them in the distance, eyes glowing, teeth bared.

"We can't take down all three of them," Ellen Covlioni warned, her voice barely audible above the hum of machinery and the frenzied attempts of Janus to get the door open."

"Let's give them a little something to think about," Forrest Kyle said with a grin, picking up the RPG he had placed at his feet. Taking only a moment to aim, the rocket seared off down the walkway, exploding at the feet of the three demons. Two did not stop, leaping to each side of the third, which took the brunt of the damage, its torso ripped apart. Eva turned away.

"We need more!" Wolfgang shouted, raising his mini-gun.

"No!" Janus replied, "I've got it!"

The door slid open, and before Eva could think, Shelton ushered her inside, his sword still in one hand. Madden followed and then Janus, the rest of the Shikari piling in behind. John Wolverton was last in. As he began to issue orders, a great grey paw grabbed his shoulder, talons digging into his armor, causing him to drop his shotgun. Behind him, in the narrowing gap of the open door, a face leered, wolf-like muzzle trying to force the door back open. John was stuck.

"Get out of here!" he shouted, "That's an order!"

Without thinking, Eva grabbed the shotgun, jamming it into the mouth of the Guardian. She squeezed the trigger, blowing a hole through the back of the Guardian's head. John nodded thanks at Eva as J.D. pulled him free. Just for a moment, she could see a gore-splattered second Guardian through the gap she had made. It pulled its fellow aside, lips peeled back, ready for the kill.

Eva felt herself pulled back by more than one hand, and the door slid shut.

A roar of frustration sounded from the other side and the door was quickly dented as the demon sought access by force.

Eva turned, finding everybody watching her, looks of approval on their faces.

"Told you," Rachelle Bishop said, the tone of her voice all warmth, "she's a badass."

"What now?" Eva asked. "These doors aren't going to keep them out forever." As if to emphasize the point, another dent appeared in the door, the demon gaining fury and a second voice as the less injured of the Guardians healed and joined the assault.

"Into the next room. I'll bar the door. By the time they beat down both we will be long gone."

Madden crossed the room to the next door, holding his hand over the sensor as he had done with the terminal outside.

The door slid open in response, revealing a much larger room beyond, filled with more of the gloomy red lighting and a strange series of railings in the middle.

"Go on through, Janus instructed them. "I'll be but a moment."

Eva hesitated, curious as to what Janus was up to but he stared at her until she moved. Once she was inside, the door slid shut

"This is for your own protection," Janus said over the radio and the communication from his helmet went dead.

"Hey, how did he cut the signal?" Matt Tanzer's comment echoed the general feeling as the team grumbled.

Eva kept silent. She alone could see a fuzzy image coming from his camera. It was indistinct, a hazy blue. But there was a definite glow. A door opened and the glow shot forward, as if directed in a beam. The Guardians moved beyond for a moment and then were still. Or no longer there, Eva could not be sure. How had this happened? Did Janus know she had seen him? Eva touched the armor. Had it sought to repair even the lost connection?

The door slid open once more and Janus stepped through, regarding her as he did so. His face was unreadable. Eva had never seen someone play their cards so close to the vest. She caught a glimpse of the first doorway. It was wide open and nothing lay beyond it but a few smouldering piles.

"Please, if you will, stand between the rails." Janus pointed to the center of the room.

"What about the Guardians?" Asked Gila. "Are we safe?"

"For now," Eva answered, preventing Janus from having to say anything. "Hurry."

The team gathered in the center of the room, Eva holding to both the rail and her husband. He gripped her hand, squeezing it tight.

"Hold on," Janus warned and the whole room appeared to lurch, sending the Shikari stumbling.

Eva's arm was nearly torn from its socket, only the combat suit and the close proximity of similarly unbalanced bodies keeping her upright. In between the railings there really wasn't anywhere to fall.

After a moment, she regained her balance, finding they were moving up the inside of the pyramidal wall, the near-silent whir of a motor propelling them.

"This speed is impossible," she said, watching the wall blurring past. "We should be flat on the floor with the g-force."

"Is it impossible or just unlikely?" Janus asked, echoing her thoughts. "The subtlety of the Source makes anything possible."

"How does it work, this Source?"

"The soul gives off power. Free will, the ability to choose, makes mortals powerful. On this plane, you can see souls as energy which is tapped. It flows like a river, and as long as it does so, everything works. The problem is the more portals opened without success, the more power is depleted. The soul retreats to its host, the ultimate refuge. At heart, every mortal is capable of great compassion. It's experiences shaping man and ultimately sealing mans' fate once they reach here. The soul in its purest form is a beautiful entity.

"As they flow about Hell providing energy, imagine if you will, each soul suffers its own purgatory. It is the quality of the soul determining if they go onward, but it is the same quality tapped into for power while the soul lives. It is ultimately the same quality keeping your body from collapsing into a sticky mess beneath you."

"If I could only get a look at the technology," Eva heard Ellen Covlioni whisper to Scope, who was kneeling, examining the floor.

"Don't," Gila intervened before Eva could say anything. "I don't care what Director Guyomard has promised you in return for his trinkets. If you start lifting panels and this thing goes wrong, we could all end up permanent residents. Once we have Nina safe, you are free to collect. By then, it might be too late."

The team remained in silence for the rest of the journey, Eva marveling at the sight of the city as crystal windows began to reveal the height they were gaining. Walkways crisscrossed the buildings; there was no need to ever descend to ground level. Where they had entered the portal was indeed the edge of the city; beyond lay a black wasteland, lit only by the scarlet glow of the sky. Beyond the limits of land, enormous waterspouts stretched up from the ocean, a haze around them causing them to glow red.

Above all, in the middle of the city, rose a tower not unlike the legendary tower of Babel. It was impossibly large and formed from concentric circles. When the lift began to slow and opened out onto a terrace just below the rooftop, Eva went straight to the edge to stare at it.

"Leviathan's citadel," Janus said from beside her. "Naturally, it had to be bigger and better than any of the other demon lords' towers. Leviathan was perfectly suited to master Envy."

"So what now?" Eva looked around. The small but wonderful

feeling her daughter was somewhere here made Eva impatient. "You said this was a docking port."

"And a docking port it is. This is all automated. Transports carry the populace from city to city and port to port on an enormous loop. It taxes the Source less. When one shows up, we board it."

"And what if there are already passengers?" Madden asked, a wry look on his face. "We didn't get all this way to be stopped on a bus."

"The port before this is Tartarus, Madden. I can promise you there will be nobody to greet us. At least, none from this realm. The transports are very frequent as they are on a loop. There is one now."

A rectangular box-shaped vehicle with small protrusions for wings and the overall look of a very basic shuttle landed with a gentle bump on the large platform, about thirty meters from Eva. In an instant, the Shikari had weapons out, all pointing at the door now opening. Nothing came hurtling out at them.

Porter Rockwell approached the doorway and peered in, the light on the end of his rifle moving back and forth in quick succession.

"It's clear," he whispered. "Boarding."

"I suggest we get a move on," said Janus, moving forward. "They don't stay down for long."

Eva took his lead and climbed aboard the shuttle, moving to the front. Inside, there was little in the way of seating other than a pilot's chair beside a small set of manual controls. Eva stood and watched. Behind her, the rest of the team unloaded their kit and began to check it over.

"What now?" She asked.

Before Janus had a chance to reply, the transport lifted into the sky above Cain, circling the city before moving in the same direction where Eva knew Nina was being held.

"You just can't appreciate the enormity unless you're airborne," Luke Wolverton said, awe written all over his face. "There must be hundreds of buildings like the one we ascended."

"And Cain's by no means the largest city in Hell," Janus

provided. "Cain is positively a backwater compared to Aquinas and it pales into insignificance compared to the Gates of Hell. It is part of the reason Leviathan is in the vanguard of the army. He wants to increase his numbers and is prepared to gamble his armies, even in the face of possible destruction by Crustallos."

"It doesn't appear any of this area is affected by the ice," John Wolverton observed.

"You are correct. But it's a very similar story to Earth. If the wrong place falls, all falls. There is no denying this fact and all of Hell knows it. If they open a big enough portal to earth for long enough, Hell will empty out and this entire domain will be at the mercy of those beyond. From there it is only a matter of time. Crustallos will assume control and feed on whoever is left here. When he has gathered strength, the mortal realm is next. The only place the assault can be bottled is here. It was always here. Satan knew this and he risked his future to maintain the equilibrium. His followers never understood what he sacrificed to keep those beyond in check."

"You talk of him as if he was some sort of hero," Gila observed. "Is he not *the* Devil?"

"No, Director. Satan came down here knowing he could never leave. He was a willing sacrifice. The Devil was one of Heaven's greatest champions."

CHAPTER TWENTY-EIGHT

It felt somewhat surreal to Eva, as the alien vista below roared past. The tiny transport in this strange world of enormity felt so fragile, so exposed. The land beneath them was colossal; they had been moving at what must have been several times the speed of sound for hours by her reckoning. At the very least, Eva felt a primal sense of terror.

This ship, traversing a place most feared and some dismissed as story, used power taken from the souls of dead people, some of which were destined for Heaven, and all of which could be snuffed out at a moments' notice by either overuse or an attack from the ice domain beyond. Around them the red sky swirled; Earth or a representation of it was occasionally visible in the sky. They were joined to Hell by a near-constant river of souls moving from one realm to the next. Where the cloud was thickest, it glowed, assaulted at all times by a barrage of lightning, too bright to look at but too frequent to avoid.

And to top everything off, Satan, the being whose destruction had created this whole mess, turned out to have been some kind of hero?

Eva watched Gila and Janus in fierce discussion. This apparent revelation had caused a stir amongst the Shikari, but Gila, with her years of historical research, had taken point.

"You know the truth already, Director," Janus said, keeping a remarkable lid on his temper. He pointed out the window at the front of the transport. "You read the Nag Hamaddi scrolls, the missing passages. All of it is true. For those caring to see the truth and read the history, it was written as a warning. One they chose not to heed."

"But you are trying to make out Hell is not a place of evil!" Gila's retort was borne out of a desperate need to cling to faith and doctrine many on earth believed, not the least of which were the Coptics to which she and Swanson Guyomard both belonged.

"My statement is not an assertion. This is the truth. All souls come here to be judged and it was necessary for the realm to have a leader, a guardian if you will. Satan guarded the entire realm, not only the lock at Tartarus. Those flocking to his side saw their own truths. Dissatisfaction with their lot in Heaven, this provided a way out involving a choice other than serene obedience. They could have fallen to Earth but they fell much, much farther."

"Better to be a prince in Hell than a slave in Heaven," came Madden's sardonic quip.

"There are no slaves in Heaven," Janus shot back. "Those coming down here twisted their own perceptions. It is not the evil of the place but the actions of those dwelling here. Nobody was meant to fail the trial to pass the gates of Saint Peter, some just take longer to do so."

"So you are saying even someone like Hitler would be capable of reaching Heaven?"

"After a long enough period of purgatory, yes. Satan's only fault was he was too busy managing the souls waiting ascension. He never saw the exceptions, those who were so close to being damned they could be extracted from the Elysian Fields. The subversion of this process was in part responsible for creating the hellbounce. Consider it as a natural restoration of the order, whatever those down here might believe the real reason to be."

"Except now the key once hidden by the process, the Well of Souls has been returned, and it is getting out of hand," Eva deduced.

Janus sighed. "That is very close to the truth, Director," he agreed. "It was never meant to be returned. Nor was the Scroll of Judgment. They are the keys to the process by which souls enter Hell and then ascend. If someone with any less than pure intent unlocks Tartarus, not only is Crustallos released, but all souls here are instantly exposed. An almost-infinite source of reluctant demons are borne, to be grabbed by whatever demon prince finds them first, or to feed Crustallos as it journeys onward."

Janus stood, moving forward to the front of the ship. He turned. "We are past belief now. Faith is trusting in an ideal, beyond all logical conclusions. Consider this, all of you. What is faith when all the facts are in hand and you can make a logical decision? Organized chaos."

Eva followed Janus to the front, leaving those behind to continue the debate.

"You almost gave yourself up there, you know."

Janus turned to her. "What do you mean?"

"Whatever you really are. Your knowledge speaks volumes, but I still saw what happened in the entrance back in Cain."

Janus watched her, possibly gauging if she was a threat and then smiled. "Always the psychiatrist. Always watching. Why have you said nothing?"

"Because you are helping us."

"Is that all I am to you, Eva? A useful tool."

"That's beneath you to even think so, Janus. You are dear to me, whatever you are. I could not have gotten this far without you. But they are going to believe what they believe, without something bigger to convince them otherwise."

Janus leaned against the window, the combat suit not even creasing as he pushed his arms up above on the glass. He bumped his head against the screen. "I can't. The ramifications... they could be colossal."

"Just keep doing what you are doing, my friend. Get me to Nina and let's worry about what comes after if and when it happens."

"Are you not afraid?"

Eva laughed. "Yeah... beyond all reasonable doubt. Out there ahead of us is a little girl you helped protect and she has nobody. I am more afraid for her than I am myself."

Lightning flickered around them, springing up from nowhere. In moments, the entire sky was full of it.

"What now?" John Wolverton called from the back of the transport.

"The frontier," Janus replied. "It's nothing to worry about. Each of the domains has a nominal amount of protection, which is lightning in many cases. The only way to get through it is on a transport. The Source is not affected by the lighting; in fact, it is augmented. You might want to hide your eyes though. You will still go blind if you stare at it."

"Masks on, people," Wolverton ordered.

Eva did as bidden, the cameras on either side of her headgear adjusting until the increasing light outside was barely an irritation.

"You can't fly above it?"

"No, we're at the limit, the definitive boundary. Only souls pass further on their journey toward judgment. Some white flashes you will see aren't lightning, they are the enemy seeking to circumvent the seal, reaching through to earth to grab at the demons already there. Easy meat. Until it is released from its prison, the boundary is the only path for the enemy."

"That's why it could only watch me," Eva said in response.

Janus blinked in confusion.

"I visited my father's grave before I came here. Crustallos, or at least I now presume that's what it was, watched me from a portal, its eye right up against the aperture. It was immense."

"What did you do?"

"I threw a dagger and burst the eye," Eva replied and Janus burst out laughing.

"Only Eva Scott would look the ultimate horror in the face and throw a knife." He turned to Madden. "Your wife is magnificent example to us all."

"She's worth saving," Madden agreed, watching her.

Eva could see the love in his eyes, love barely concealing the pain behind it. He didn't think there was a positive end to this journey for anybody, especially himself.

The lightning began to fade, electricity fizzing around the surface of the transport until they had passed completely through.

When Eva lifted her visor, she glanced back. The lightning formed a wall as far as the eye could see. Beneath them lay a large body of water, flat and dark, reflecting the swirls of red as the sky continuously stirred.

In the distance, there was a glow. Steady and yellow. It rose on the horizon, a thin band of light coming from what must have been land beyond the water's edge.

"Look" Eva said, Gila coming to stand beside her. "That's so beautiful."

"The Elysian Fields," Janus answered. "The birthplace of the soul. It is the home of the Source; the engine of Hell."

Many of the Shikari moved forward to watch as the light grew. Eva lost track of what she perceived as time. Everybody watched in silence as they came closer to a place every one of the men and women on board the transport anticipated and feared. The field of souls. Eva felt the trepidation around her. The chances were somewhere beneath them loved ones waited, enduring the purgatory that would grant or forever deny them their place in Heaven. Eva wondered if she would see her father; was there anything she could do to help him? This realm had technology. Could any of it send him on his way?

"Don't even consider it," Janus warned. "If you mess with the natural order of events, what happens? Unforeseen consequences, rarely ever good for them or for you."

Eva flushed, guilt in her mind. Janus was watching her. She glanced at those around her. Judging by their faces, her thoughts were not unique.

The steady glow filled the horizon now, stretching off into the distance to their right and ending abruptly at the base of a titanic mountain range to their left. Its peaks scraped the bottom of the swirling cloud, the contact causing a near-constant barrage of lightning as land battled sky.

In time, the transport reached land. Beneath them, the entire surface glowed yellow. Unlike the sickly light of icy apertures, this glow was healthy, emitting warmth, even comfort.

"What are the mountains called?" Gila asked.

"I don't know," Janus replied. "All I can tell you is the left range leads to Forente Lautus and the right to Tartarus. Between them, all is as below, though I have never seen it until now."

"Can we go down?" Eva asked, not put off by Janus' warning.

"There is no way."

"Oh, I don't consider no to be an answer. We are still headed in the right direction. What's the matter if we fly a little lower?"

Madden sat at the controls. "This should work. It's designed to come off automatic." He pressed a button and the transport veered off course, sinking until Madden grabbed the control stick and gave the transport guidance.

The vehicle dropped from the sky at a rate making Eva's stomach rise in her throat. The yellow glow gained definition, a sea of light becoming an infinite number of small points on the ground.

"There's nowhere to set down," Madden warned.

"Head back to the water," John Wolverton advised. "There was open space on the shore."

Madden did as told, and a short while later, they reached the end of the light, though at reduced speed it seemed to take a lot longer.

Landing the transport on the ground with a bump, Madden let go of the controls. "What now?"

"Let's go take a look," Eva decided.

The door slid open, and Porter Rockwell took point, stepping out with caution onto the alien landscape. Eva followed, visor raised. Curiosity overcame any sense of trepidation. The terrain was unyielding, volcanic rock smoothed to a shine over an indefinite amount of time and the glow reached with defiance into the sky just beyond a small rise.

Eva followed Rockwell, aware everybody else was close behind.

Rockwell stopped. "Oh my God," he breathed, his voice full of awe.

Eva moved past him, taking a couple more steps. For as far as the eye could see, crucifixes pierced the ground. Arranged in perfect lines, the crosses appeared to be of similar material to the buildings in Cain. Tethered to each cross, stood a nebulous, glowing yellow humanoid form, arms crossed, hands secure in fists up by the shoulders, eyes closed. The faces of all Eva could see were perfectly calm, serene even.

"You should not be seeing this," Janus warned. "That said- you should not be here in the first place."

"Are... are those souls?" Eva could not quite grasp what she was seeing.

"They are. Each in what they perceive to be their own personal hell. You can observe what they are going through by touching the posts to which they are tethered. I would rather you did not do this of course but when has anybody ever been able to stop the great Eva Scott?"

Eva smirked. "Funny. You try and guilt-trip me into standing fast. An interesting psychology."

"Believe me, there are things I would rather you not do. But stop you I will not. If you feel you must experience somebody else's Hell, please go right ahead."

There was plenty of distance between each cross. Several of the Shikari followed Eva into the field of souls. Eva picked one at random and placed her hand on the top of the post.

She was transported into desolation, watching a scene from above. A man walked through a ruined city, cars rusted to the ground when a cataclysm occurred. The foundations of fallen buildings thrust up toward a sky formed more of flame than cloud. It was Earth gone to Hell, she realized. Eva felt a profound sense of nakedness and loss at the ruin of her planet. The man walked on, black-suited, unseeing, suffering his own personal purgatory.

Eva blinked. Nobody had moved an inch. She must have only touched the post for an instant yet it felt like a lifetime. She took a few steps past the first post and touched another.

A pit, a huge fiery pit. At the center stood a colossus of a demon, all fangs, horns and muscles. It pulled people on chains down toward it. The soul felt a pull and the demon grinned. It was Satan, or the soul's perception of Satan in this horrible scene of torment. As the soul moved ever closer to obliteration, it began to heat up, pain lancing through its very core. Yet, because it was no longer mortal, there was no release. Eva screamed in silence along with the soul; this one had been bad in life. Very bad. As it reached the demon, the soul reappeared at the edge of the pit, for the torment to begin again. Eva let go.

And jumped. Again, how little time had passed. The Shikari were all still close and Madden watched on, as if he had not seen her suffer. Eva walked further into the field and touched a third post.

She found herself watching, helpless, as a massive wave began to form in the distance, the water retreating as it drained from around her feet.

"Get out of here!" A voice yelled. She could see it was the hollow nimbus of a man, not quite there, but real enough to experience the fear of a potential drowning.

"It's going to hit us. Run! Run!"

Eva turned and watched in terror as the wave built in the distance. It must have been a hundred feet high, frothing at the top as it crested. Eva tried to leave but found herself bound, her feet glued to the ground.

"Get out of here!" The voice yelled at her, unable to change the words. "It's going to hit us. Run! Run!"

"I... I can't!" Eva replied.

The man just stared at her, then looked at the wave. It surged over them...

Eva screamed. Blinking, she saw Janus had one of her hands.

"I couldn't leave," she said, starting to sob.

"I know, Eva. I kept you in there. I need to prove this point to you. This helps nobody and risks you."

"You bastard, Janus." Eva drew great racking breaths between sobs as she tried to control herself. "I couldn't leave."

"Look how far in we have come," he said, his voice calm.

Eva looked about her. She swore she had only come two or three deep into the field but now there were maybe twenty souls between her and the rest of the Shikari. The team watched her, helpless. J.D. and Porter Rockwell attempted to restrain Madden with little success. Eva let go of Janus' hand. "What happened to me?"

CHAPTER TWENTY-NINE

"You were getting drawn in. Giving too much of yourself to their suffering." Janus waved his hand about them, indicating the sea of souls. Eva slowly mastered the fear inside her, the feeling of panic subsiding as she gained control.

"Hell, and purgatory in particular, is a very personal experience. When souls are judged, our greatest fears are laid bare for all to see. The rest of your team learned after one touch of a cross. What is it you hoped to accomplish?"

"I... I don't know. I want what everybody wants, I guess. A happy ending."

"I am taking you back out now. Do not touch anybody. The reason you are so far in is because you were allowing yourself to feel their pain. Any longer and we might have lost you entirely. Any demon may come and feed directly from the Source should they so wish, but they know it can be an addiction. I read accounts of those who became lost in here forever. There is no record of what happens to them."

"Do the souls give up? I saw some pretty nasty experiences."

"Some do. The lost souls stay here forever. It was the farming of such souls that gave rise to the hellbounce. Never affect the natural order. You can watch the experiences but most here are steeled against the pain, having already failed their purgatory. You are a soul in a mortal body, Eva. You don't belong here and the consequences are unforeseen. In addition, you care too much."

They were about half way back to the transport when a shaft of pure white light surged around a nearby soul. Warmth exuded from the light, as if the glow of the soul in purgatory was healthy; pure joy radiated from the beam of light. Eva found herself crying and laughing at the same time. Everything felt right. No, she corrected herself. Better than right, everything felt perfect.

The light faded and the soul once occupying the cross was nowhere to be seen.

"What did I just see?"

Janus smiled. "The rapture. A soul ending purgatory and has being embraced by Heaven. It's a wonderful sight. Better at the other end. Imagine a demon but with none of the inner chaos. Wrapped in serenity, completely at peace."

"Angels..." Eva breathed.

"Indeed. The white glow moves the soul onward. A red glow is what the demon clans watch for and there are more than enough of those."

"What about the hellbounces?" Eva looked at her still-struggling husband as they neared the Shikari.

"A different matter entirely. There is a special place reserved in hell for the hellbounce."

Back on the transport, the Shikari compared horror stories. Eva was content to sit and listen in silence. She held Madden's hand, protective of him now she had seen just what he could have gone through. The words *endless steps* and *falling* made her shudder.

"Makes you want to go back and atone for every little thing, doesn't it?" Madden observed as Luke Wolverton finished a particularly gruesome telling of his experience. Eva doubted it was without embellishment; as in every tightly knit group, there was an element of one-upmanship going on and by the sounds of it, those who had partaken had all met the worst mass-murderers in history.

"If I get out of this, I can promise you that is exactly what I will be doing. If you want to make the world a better place, don't tell them how. Show them." She turned to her husband. "Did you want to see your kind?"

"Don't you want to rescue our daughter?"

Eva closed her eyes and reached out. Nina responded, surrounded by a feeling of calm. Since the connection had been restored, Eva's confidence had grown. She was confused as to why Nina radiated such contentment, while Eva had such nagging feelings.

"Nina is fine. I get the impression she doesn't much like who she is with, but they are treating her fairly. She says we have to do what we need to do before we come for her. We still have time. It is as if she knows us better than we know ourselves."

"Janus, we need to find the hellbounces," Madden called ahead. "There's something I have to do."

"It's on the way to our destination," Janus replied. "I don't know what you expect to find there, but I expected you to ask."

The transport skirted the edge of the mountain range previously on the left of their route. Eva watched, fascinated, and in no small way mesmerised, by the Elysian Fields, which stretched to the horizon on their right. To their left, the once-volcanic range rose steep and imposing, jagged ledges jutting out at them, forcing Janus to fly the transport quite a distance out.

"There must be millions down there," she said, leaning on Madden as she watched. Her eyelids grew heavy from the hypnotic effect of the carpet of lights. She was exhausted and this was the first time she had felt any measure of safety. Wherever this so-called population of demons was, they were not here.

"Win or lose, there will only be more." Madden gazed past her out the window. "There is no real win."

"He's not wrong," Rachelle Bishop said from Madden's other side. "We saw a Jamaican turn into a demon right then and there. If instantaneous change becomes the rule rather than the exception, if demonkind takes a secure foothold on earth, there will be no need for Hell. We need to find your daughter and get out of here, fast."

"And this entity coming through from beyond?" Eva looked around the Shikari. "If we rescue my daughter and leave stones unturned? If Crustallos reaches Hell? Who is there to stop it if we turn tail and run?"

"Leave them," J.D. Shelton, huge but so unassuming, finally spoke up from across the other side of the transport. "Be damned with them. Crustallos may never come through. We rescue your daughter, we find the keys if we can. Then we get out." Others made noises showing they were in agreement. John Wolverton sat silent, watching the proceedings.

"Finding Nina won't be the end," Eva warned them. "Crustallos was after me. Do you think it will stop if it reaches here? It was after me for a reason."

"You..." Shelton began to argue and John Wolverton stood up.

"We go with the Director, to the bitter end if need be. That is what we signed on for. We stay until victory or death. Just because you have seen things here frightening you, proving you're the mere mortals you think you have ascended beyond, does not take away the fact you have a job to do. Now you carry out your assignments, or you answer to me."

Shelton glared at Wolverton for a moment and then grunted. He nodded in Eva's direction and stared forward.

"I feel the same way," Eva said, trying to explain. "I do. I just want there to be a home to return to, and have it remain a home."

"We are there," Janus said from the pilot's seat and immediately

Eva leapt forward, eager to be out of the uncomfortable situation. She was sure the Shikari, as trained and dedicated as they were, just felt like baby-sitters on a rather dangerous vacation.

As Eva stared below, a marked difference hit her. "They aren't yellow."

"True but they aren't red either. Hellbounces are something in between. Be very careful out here."

The transport touched down and Porter was first off, followed by J.D., Eva, Madden and Gila. Janus and the Shikari trickled out, coming to a halt in a group behind them.

The valley ahead was a steep-sided affair, black rock from two spurs of the mountain above reaching round to form a bowl. Inside were figures similar in form to the souls they had seen before, but these had more definition. Eyes closed, the faces were visible, as were clothes. They all glowed orange, the energy from them undulating a few meters above their heads as it rose from their bodies. The major difference here was they were untethered, hanging a few feet above the ground. The figures moved as dandelion seeds floated on a breeze, an unseen force sending them in random directions. They were spread out across the valley. The bowl must have been miles in diameter. Sometimes, the bodies hung in groups. It appeared they had just been randomly left. In the middle of the valley, the energy coiled, rope-like and twisted up into the sky where it passed through a small aperture and disappeared. The sky was especially red above this valley.

"They... they look like people," she said. "I can see their faces."

"This is what happens to untethered souls," Janus explained. "Not good enough for Heaven, but not bad enough for Hell. The Source must be pure, or nothing works. When impurities are found are moved here to the Valley of the Damned."

"A nice affectation," approved Madden.

Janus turned to him. "I am sorry, my friend, it is not an honorific. What you term *hellbounce* has no name in this realm other than lost. They have no chance at redemption. There are those who consider these exceptions to be an abomination. *These* are what have caused Crustallos to move so rapidly against this realm. The hellbounce emit energy like any soul, but it holds some of the essence back, leaving it in a volatile state. This orange glow is what attracts the ice on earth. It is ambrosia to them. The minions of this other realm, Crustallos foremost among them, sense it and can track it across space and time. Even across reality. It is also an indication the soul is, in part, back on the mortal plane."

A few meters away, one of the floating bodies winked and disappeared.

"You see? It is an example of the emergence. Back on earth, the body has claimed the hell-based part of the soul. The demon is loose, and will deteriorate."

"Like Brian," Madden agreed, awakening feelings of suppressed dread in Eva.

"Hellbounces create a lot of energy. Their souls are intense, as we know in Madden here. But they are also disruptive. They can explode. These souls are impure; they influence the souls around them and can cause ripples in the Source. As soon as it is identified, a soul deemed impure is moved here. Away from the Source. The energy is left to dissipate. Hell's minions have tried everything to repeat this, since part of them on Earth is better than all of them in Hell, awaiting destruction. They are not meant to go to heaven. They will never ascend in the white light of rapture. I'm sorry, Madden; but these are the damned.

Madden's face was pale, drained of blood. His arms had begun an involuntary twitch, swelling in places. "No, what you say can't be true. I can't have fought this hard for redemption and still be damned. I'm worth more than a bitter end."

He shook his head and then took off into the valley, stopping some fifty meters in down the slope.

"Madden," Janus called, "don't let your actions precipitate something unforgivable. There is danger in this for all of us."

Eva took one look as Janus and ran after Madden. When she

reached him, she found him staring up at a version of himself, eyes closed, a strong orange glow contributing to the light above them.

"Those are the clothes I was wearing when I died in the crash," he said, staring up at his nebulous twin.

"I keep expecting you to open your eyes and stare down at me," Eva said after a while.

"Let's see if I can," Madden answered and reached up to touch the glowing ethereal version of his mortal body.

"No! Stop!" Janus had come closer, standing a few paces behind them. The floating hellbounces had closed ranks, preventing him from reaching them. "You would end it all if you did make contact; you would lay the boundaries bare for anybody to cross. Heaven, Hell, Earth might all merge with the explosion. Past, present and future would become one and the same. There will be complete obliteration."

"You don't know what happened," Madden accused their guide, "but I was restored. I was human."

"No, part of your soul was always here. Your body may have walked the earth but it was incomplete, just a moral compass off by a few degrees. You must have felt it."

Madden put his hands on Eva's arms, gripping her tightly as the realization hit him.

She nodded. "Maybe the reason why you felt so empty is here. I trust you, love."

"Madden, you are something else," Janus continued from beyond the barricade, his voice rising as he began to panic. "Why do you think they are all after you? The text, you read it. You draw them like a magnet on Earth. Here, who knows?"

Madden dropped his hands. "Janus, I must know. This is the reason I am the way I am. This population, this entire valley, they are related, but I am something different. My demon is the only one of its kind to have breached the barrier multiple times. Is this my Hell? Is this my own personal purgatory, to wander across the barriers for eternity every time there is an event? Is the hellbounce a blessing or a special kind of punishment? Are we doomed to lose control? Are we a weapon? Heaven's joke on the damned? Don't ask me why, but I have to do this."

Janus paced about outside the wall of souls, impotent inability to do anything his only companion.

"You should probably step back, or crouch down or something," Madden said, now looking up at his shadow-self. He discarded the gloves of his combat suit, dropping them next to his already discarded helmet. He reached out, his outspread hand of ice making contact with the chest of his doppelganger.

The two met, a red spark jumping from chest to hand. Madden gasped, his eyes widening.

"Madden?" Eva tried to get his attention but his gaze was locked on the face hanging before him.

The red spark grew, swelling into a light that encompassed first the floating soul and gradually traveled up his arm and directly into his chest.

"Madden!"

Her husband turned his head. His eyes glowed red, blazing with the same energy flowing in and around him. "Eva, it's wonderful. I understand now."

The red glow spread from his eyes, running across his face like veins, surrounding his entire body in a matter of moments. The glow began to swell, larger than Madden, threatening to touch her. Madden paid her no attention, looking back at his other self and the glow increased. One hellbounce floated a little too close and became tangled in the red light, trapped as if it were glue.

The eyes of Madden's ethereal twin opened and looked down at her. Seeing her so close, the eyes widened in fright. Madden's human face had the same look on it, eyes wide, tinged with panic.

"I can see you, Eva," the apparition mouthed, though the voice came from the being on the ground. "I can see... everything. Go, Eva. Go! Go! Go!"

Unsure which of them to look at, Eva backed away. There was a gap in the hellbounces swirling toward Madden and Eva dove through. On the other side, Janus grabbed her, and helped her up. "Out of the valley! He's gone too far!"

Eva glanced back. The red glow had begun to swirl above him as a tornado of energy formed a vortex, the base of which touched the apparition's head. Hellbounces swirled toward him as the energy whipped about. Madden began to rise in the air, lifted aloft by the red glow linking his body and soul. His arms rose to each side and the glow intensified.

"Evaaaaaaaaaa..." wailed a desperate voice from within the vortex. Madden's body arched back, his head screaming to the sky as scarlet energy erupted from his mouth. Body and soul merged and exploded. A concussive shock threw Eva to the ground, Janus shielding her with his body but not before Eva saw the souls in the Valley of the Hellbounce explode and wink out of existence.

Eva's head dropped to the ground as consciousness gave way to oblivion. Madden was lost.

CHAPTER THIRTY

"Eva?"

The voice was familiar, coming from above. Gentle hands rocked her, encouraging her to move. The armor hummed about Eva's chest, repairing both it and her; the blast must have done more damage than she had imagined. It was easy to believe she was safe, those concerned with her well-being close by, until the unspoken query from Nina jolted her awake. It seemed concern was not a one-way street.

Eva groaned, trying to move about and receiving a shooting pain in her neck for her troubles.

"Hang on, wait. Let the armor work out the kinks." It was Janus speaking. The memories began to flood her mind.

"Madden!"

She opened her eyes, looking about. The angry red scars etched in the cloud above her, staring down, causing her to squint, reminded her all too well of where she was. There was a distinct concentric pattern in them where the force of the explosion had traveled up, pushing at the cloud and sending it streaking in all directions. Such a pattern must have been like a beacon to any choosing to see it.

To her left, Janus pressed down on her with firm hands. "Wait. It looks like you have some broken bones."

Eva drew a panicked breath, causing a coughing fit. Her neck felt better already.

"I can see why you gave me this armor rather than anybody else. Because I might get caught in the crossfire."

"I thought of it because you don't listen to anybody and put yourself in harms' way rather than take a cautious approach to anything you do."

Eva stretched. The pain was subsiding. She sent a mental jolt to Nina, reassuring her. "Where is he?"

Janus glanced back in the direction of the bowl-shaped valley. They had been blown out by the explosion and lay just beyond the rim. "I haven't looked. Eva, I won't kid you. I don't know what happened back there. I have no idea if he is even with us."

"Why haven't you looked?"

"I daren't. Whatever he did was unprecedented in all I have studied. All of our... all of *my* history has never seen such a reaction."

Eva pushed herself up, Janus resisting for only a moment. "Whatever it is you are not telling me Janus, now is not the time to shrink away from bearing witness to the truth. He's my husband and Nina's father. I'll not let her grow up not knowing what has happened here."

Eva climbed to her feet, aching all over, though the pain of healing bones was becoming bearable. She stumbled to the edge of the valley and stood there, her mind numb. A red mist filled what had once been a valley of souls. There was no sign of her husband, or anything else, just a stygian glow, an after-print of what had happened.

"Eva!"

She turned at the sound of a man's voice, imagining for a second it might be Madden.

John Wolverton approached, rifle at the ready; Porter Rockwell, J.D.Shelton, and Rachelle Bishop were close behind.

"What did he do?" He looked past her down the valley. "We

were at the rim. When the bodies closed in, we couldn't see a thing. It looked like someone set off a bomb."

"Madden reached out for his soul," she responded, her body going numb with the onset of shock. "He set off some sort of chain reaction. The hellbounces were all destroyed. There's nothing left but a memory."

"Then who is walking towards us?" Bishop asked, pointing past her.

Eva turned. The red mist was clearing and from within strode Madden, smiling. Forgetting everybody around her and ignoring her own pain, Eva threw every fiber of her being into running toward him. She hurtled down the uneven ground, nothing else in her vision but him. As she reached Madden, she jumped at him, throwing her arms about him and smothering his face with kisses.

"Eva love, we have company."

"I don't care. I thought I'd lost you," she said in between kisses and then locked her arms about him and kissed him.

Eventually, she allowed him to catch his breath and led him out of the valley holding his waist tight.

Back at the entrance to the valley, Janus and the others greeted Madden with surprise, a little fear, and an overall abundance of awe. Janus in particular seemed dumbstruck to see her husband still standing.

"I don't suppose you would care to tell us what went on in there?"

Madden stared at her for a moment. He looked about, brows furrowed as if unsure himself.

"I don't know," he admitted. "But look at this."

Madden held out both hands. The skin on them was identical.

"You're healed! Madden, but how?"

"Janus was right. It took something special for me to be able to take control of my own body. Stand back. There's more."

Madden turned his hands over, so his palms faced up. Without warning, a claw-like appendage shifted from underneath the skin on his left hand, stretching it to impossible dimensions. Madden just watched.

"You aren't stressed," Eva said in amazement. "How are you doing this?"

"I have complete control of the demon inside of me." Madden glanced at the emerging claw and it settled. He wiggled his fingers. "I can no longer lose control. Whatever happened to me down there… Well, let's just say I see everything through new eyes. I willed the ice away from my arm."

Eva stood amazed. He was whole again. She looked about. Janus had fallen to his knees, looking at Madden with something close to adoration.

As for her husband, Madden watched them, at peace with himself for the first time since Eva had known him.

"I understand the hellbounce now and in the instant I touched my counterpart, I ended them. There is no recourse; demons will no longer haunt the earth as an abomination."

"Miraculous," Janus declared. "What else do you see? What else can you tell us?"

Madden opened his mouth to continue, but the clarion call once again sounded, deafening everybody. There was a strange double-tone to the sound.

Janus motioned to them all to put their headgear on.

"Hell is attacking and under attack at the same time."

"What just happened," Swanson's voice crackled into life. "Gila, Eva, can you hear me?"

"Swanson, something miraculous has happened. Madden has cured himself. He's no longer a threat."

"Explain."

Eva grabbed hold of her husband, hugging him tightly again.

"He found a way to destroy all the hellbounces. He has control of his body."

There was a pause. "Eva, I'm sorry to break it to you like this, but whatever he's done there, it has sent twenty thousand hellbounces crazy here. They've shifted into demon form all over the world, and they are tearing several cities apart!"

Eva frowned at Madden. He stared back, mute, for a moment, then as one they turned and ran for the transport.

"Come on, Janus, John, everyone!"

The Shikari began to jog after them.

"Do you care to tell us what is going on, Director?"

"This was a set up. They wanted Madden here. How do you think it was so easy for us to just set down and go exploring. This isn't a stroll in the Alps. We are in Hell, for crying out loud. This place is teeming with evil and they probably will be here any moment."

"Twenty thousand demons loose on Earth," Madden said, shaking his head. "How could I be so naïve?"

"We have to get airborne," Eva said, jumping aboard the transport and hurrying to the front. "We have to rescue Nina. I think this was a set up on a grand scale."

"Director Guyomard," Janus asked, "what is the status of the main portal? Is there any sign?"

"Janus, the Gobi Desert is lit up like the fourth of bloody July at the moment and it's not stopping."

"The hellbounces... Eva, you are right. I think this is the beginning."

"Of what?"

"The end."

Janus sat down at the controls and within moments, they were airborne. Not a moment too soon.

Eva watched in mute horror as wave upon wave of horrific demon form came surging to the very spot they had just vacated, roaring up at them, climbing atop each other as if they could form a column and rise into the air after the transport. The noise of their rage was audible even above the clarion call, which was unending.

"Keep your headgear on," Ellen Covlioni suggested. "I'll work on filtering out the goddamned foghorn."

"Nina is troubled," Eva decided. "We need to get to Forente-Lautus now."

"They know we are here," Janus flicked a few buttons on the control panel, causing the transport to shudder. "I would say the normal transport paths are being watched. Time for a little improvisation."

"What do you mean?" Gila asked. "Isn't everything controlled here? Surely any deviation out of the normal would attract their attention."

"We approach the city from the seaward side. It's atop this mountain chain and all observation faces inward, since there is nothing but endless abyss to defend from on the rear of the city. You couldn't sneak up on Belphegor's domain with one of those giant transports if you intended to launch an assault."

"But you could if you had a small team aboard one of these tiny ships," Gila concluded. "Janus, you're brilliant."

"We have to move with haste. They can tell where we are and they will attempt to follow us now they know we are in transit."

Eva watched the ground, already so very distant. It was impossible to tell whether there were demons moving beneath them. "Can they sense our auras?"

"In a way, but nothing so profound." Janus held up a small device, another mystery black box. "It's used for tracking unusual energy readings. Hold it up where you feel Nina strongest."

Eva took the box and reached out to her daughter. When they had communicated, she held up the device. The box hummed in her hand and projected a screen, highlighting two glowing yellow nebulous forms. They were small, as if a great distance away, to the right of their flight path.

"Forente-Lautus," Janus confirmed.

Eva turned, pointing the device at the Shikari behind her. The projected screen nearly blinded her, the mortals it sensed being brighter and larger due to their proximity.

"This looks like similar technology to ARC's demon aura sensors."

"It is in fact the same device, just attuned to a different wavelength."

"Impossible," Swanson said over the headset. "We developed demon aura tech ourselves. Ivor Sarch..."

"Ivor Sarch," Eva repeated. "Swanson, was anything developed for ARC he was not involved in?"

"He made many of the key breakthroughs," Swanson's reluctant voice admitted.

"Again, Rosier. If we can track them, will they be tracking us?"

"I'm uncertain," Janus admitted. "This technology is not widely used given the appearance of mortals in Hell is an extreme rarity. They use it for tracking rival clans. If they could work out how to track different signals then maybe. It comes down to how important Rosier ranks our being here."

"If he doesn't know about you, I expect he assumes we are floundering about, directionless."

Janus grinned. "Director Guyomard, can you pipe through some of the footage of the invasion?"

The small screen on Eva's visor faded into life as real-time footage was piped through the tenuous link. Several instances of demons pouring through portals akin to the one back in Afghanistan and being met by very heavy resistance cycled across her field of vision.

"It's carnage. They are being slaughtered, but they are not stopping."

"What about the main portal?"

"The portal has formed, but is not yet open."

The screen faded to a picture of an impossibly huge aperture, hundreds of feet in diameter with a shimmering silver surface. About a half-mile back, row upon row of armed forces awaited the call to arms; tanks, missile batteries, helicopters, and endless battalions had formed up.

"Swanson, where are those other portals forming?" Madden asked, his voice cautious.

"The three most vicious battles are in Tokyo, Haiphong in Vietnam and Kyzyl in southern Russia."

"Which is going worst for us?"

"Easy. Kyzyl. We have nearly been overrun twice. If it continues, we are going to have to reallocate forces from the Gobi desert to compensate."

Madden frowned at her. "Swanson, the clarion is sounding here, but from what you say there is no major movement. They are waiting for something. Whatever you decide, don't pull the troops from the Gobi Desert."

"And lose the containment at these other portals? Madden what you suggest borders on lunacy."

"It is not as mad as allowing the army on this side of the portal to cross over. If they're successful, it's game over for humanity. Swanson, I'm so sorry. It seems in finding myself, I have provided them with the key to bypassing the locks on their own prison. The Scroll and the Well might be the only thing to stop them coming through now."

"Is there anything you can do from your side to slow things down?"

"The Well and the Scroll were going to be used to force open the portals," Janus mused. "Maybe we can use them to shut it all down."

He glanced at Madden, but if a thought was shared between the two, Eva did not see it.

"Yes," Madden agreed. "We have to at least try. Permanent stability of an open portal could mean permanent closure is also a possibility. Of Hell and of the realm beyond. It is the choice we have to make. Join Hell and Earth and protect it from the ice, or seal the breach."

"Would you be able to get out in time?" Swanson's voice sounded genuinely concerned, a stark contrast to the violence still cycling across Eva's screen.

"No idea," Janus admitted.

"It doesn't matter," Eva added. "A dozen or so of us for the entire human race." She took Madden's hand. "Besides, at least we will be here together. A family."

"Yes," Madden agreed. His face was unreadable, but she was certain there was something he wasn't telling her. Mastery of the demon had changed him. There was no going back.

They had rounded the end of the mountain chain. To their left was the infinite abyss of the dark water and on their right the forbidding precipices of the peaks at the edge of Hell.

"It's funny to think beauty exists in such a place," John Wolverton said from behind her. "At least there's no pretense. Everybody is evil. Everybody seeks domination over every other being down here. It's the purest truth there is."

Madden leaned against the window, perilously close to the cliffs. "There is nobody down here to make the sacrifice needed. Everybody is hell-bent on the annihilation of the human race."

"It's not annihilation," Gila said, "but self-annihilation. Somebody down here realizes the value they bring. When there are no mortals left, if the fight continues, there will be no demons. In a way, it provides the victory. Someone has to change the order of events."

"Before we figure out our grand plan, first we must travel into the stronghold of one of Hell's deadliest foes. Nina is there and if it takes every one of us, we shall snatch her from the clutches of those holding her. It's time to show Hell you don't have to be a demon to make a difference."

CHAPTER THIRTY-ONE

The ominous nature of the task facing her was not lost on Eva. As they crept along the edge of the mountains, she realized they were not approaching an empty city, guarded by near-mindless automatons. There was no guarantee Forente-Lautus was empty at all; with Belphegor back in Hell, the city could be teeming with demons.

Everybody else was quiet after the discussion with Swanson. In the background, Eva heard a conversation between Swanson and Gila. The channel had remained open since the so-called destruction of the hellbounces. Their communication with Swanson, if nothing else, was evidence enough the game had nearly played itself out.

Madden was discussing protection detail for her with Wolverton should the worst happen to him. The Shikari, as usual, remained very quiet but alert. They were used to being in hostile situations, living off their wits. She smiled as she remembered the calm acceptance of the fact they were more than unprepared for this. She honored their choice to accept the death of comrades quickly, not dwelling on the incident, and moving on.

Once more, Madden's arms encircled her, and Eva leaned back, taking brief comfort from the warmth of his body, somewhat excessive now the demon was truly part of him and not an alien being trying to escape.

"So am I safe?"

Madden snorted, shooting a short blast of air down her neck.

"Those guys are so professional, it makes me sick. It's like talking to a brick wall. I honestly think they take all of my ideas on board and dismiss them without a second's thought."

"They do know what they are doing, love. It's what they have been trained for."

He turned her toward him. His eyes were so dark now, so solemn. "If I had my way, you would remain here, safe, while we rescued Nina."

"Out of the question. My daughter's up there. I can guide us right to her."

Madden nodded at the Shikari. "They made the same comment; we go as a unit."

Eva smiled, the small victory assured. "They can protect us better if we are together rather than assigning babysitters."

"They can protect you," Madden contradicted. "They don't consider me part of the detail any more. I can look after myself. Just stay close to J.D. He is your shadow."

The transport moved away from the sea as they followed the peaks of the mountain chain. The first Eva saw of Forente-Lautus was a series of sparkles in the distance as lightning flashes glinted off crystalline surfaces. The city grew in size, and Eva was gradually able to discern the geography of Belphegor's citadel.

"It sits atop four of the highest peaks in Hell," Janus provided.

"It's beautiful," Eva breathed, not looking away.

While not in any way as large as Cain, Forente-Lautus expressed a delicacy in the structures emerging from the peaks. Small domes everywhere, towers only a few stories in height were joined by walkways impossibly wrought from crystal, far too delicate for the brutal nature of the domain. All the stone was black, back-lit by an eerie yellow glow emanating from the entire structure.

"If this were anywhere else, it would be a fairy-castle," Janus said, clearly as in awe of the city as Eva herself was.

"Instead, the beauty hides a mystery and evil," replied Eva.

The Shikari moved up to have a look. None appeared unmoved by the sight.

Janus stepped up from the console. "We are now on a standard flight path, bringing the transport to the base of the citadel. Be ready to run. This is likely to be a very different experience from what we saw in Cain."

"Where are we going?" Eva asked as the transport lost height, the mountainous city looming over them.

"Did you see the domed tower at the top?"

Eva nodded.

"Belphegor's Citadel. She resides there whenever she's in the city. I'll bet that direction is where you feel Nina strongest."

Eva reached out. Nina was content for the moment, high above her. This left Eva uneasy. Why was her daughter so at home here? "Yes," she said, the disappointment not hidden in her voice.

"You didn't think this was land at the gates, pop in and grab the babe, and home for supper? The citadel is comprised of nine concentric circles, the seventh of which we land on. Belphegor is at the top. So we need a lot of luck."

"Do you know how to reach the top level? I mean you haven't been here, have you?"

His smile was grim. "I studied the layouts during my incarceration. No more do you need to know."

As predicted, there was movement in the distance as the transport began to dock, but when the time they landed, the dock was clear.

Porter Rockwell took the lead, assault rifle at the ready despite

Janus' warnings. Forrest Kyle and Rachelle Bishop came next, and then Eva was ushered out. The dark stone structures around her caught her attention immediately. "It's normal-sized," she observed. The glow lighting the citadel came from thousands of tiny eerie yellow lights. It didn't look as majestic to Eva eye-level with it.

"Not everything is out of proportion like Cain," Janus whispered across the comm. "Belphegor has always had quite refined taste."

Eva recalled the blonde woman who threw the little girl to the howling mob; the noises as she was ripped apart would forever haunt her. Belphegor was evil incarnate. "I would have called her twisted myself."

The team hurried across the transport bay, heading toward an arched exit. Inside, there was a pile of material up against one wall.

Rockwell poked at the pile with his rifle and it fell apart, a body rolling to the ground, several others exposed underneath.

Eva suppressed the urge to scream.

"Demons," Madden hissed.

John Wolverton knelt down, examining one and pulling the robe it wore back with the end of his shotgun. The face was frozen in a mask of rage, lips peeled back, nose wrinkled in a crystalline snarl.

"Dead demons. Something has destroyed this one. The head has been turned to crystal."

Madden reversed his shotgun, hitting the head with the butt and shattering it into tiny pieces. Beneath, black ichor began to seep around the edges of the crystal as the wound opened.

Wolverton stood, about to say something, but Scope raised his arm, fist closed. A sign indicating they weren't alone, as Eva had learned.

As one, the Shikari backed into the shadow of the archway. Moments later, a trio of robe-wearing demons passed by, sparing furtive glances for the dock and the transport awaiting take off.

As the trio moved on, Eva whispered, "They were terrified. Could you feel it?"

"I have an idea," said Janus. "Grab those robes. Rockwell, Kyle, Bishop. Throw them on."

Kyle and Bishop looked dubious but Porter Rockwell, wrapped himself without delay. "Good plan," he said, his mask sticking out from under the hood. "We look like them, maybe they will leave us alone."

"Maybe they will lead us right to the top," Eva added.

"Something is wrong here. Things are not as they should be. We need to hurry before we lose them."

Janus was right. By the time the three in front had donned their robes and rearranged their weaponry to the satisfaction of all, the demons were out of sight.

Eva thought she would never get used to the prospect of such creatures in close proximity. Despite Madden, in the face of all she had gone through, there was just something inherently wrong about them.

The team moved briskly, a pace threatening to leave Eva breathless had it not been for the body armor. The health flowed into her, replenishing energy as she lost it. She spared a moment to thank the souls whose essence she was tapping, whether they heard her or not.

After a short while, they came upon another trio of dead demons, the humanoid bodies so similar to their own, yet disfigured by a crystalline attack.

"We aren't alone in wanting to find answers it seems," John Wolverton noted as they stripped the robes from the cadavers. In the distance, the group they had trailed were stooping over another set of bodies, heads together as they discussed their findings.

"This one's colder," Jenn Day noted as she pulled the robe on.

"This was more recent. It's not been long since this happened."

Eva peeked out at Janus from beneath the heavy robe she now wore. It felt like velvet but she shuddered to consider the robes actual point of origin, or body. At least there was no demon stench, for which she was thankful. Unlike those she had met on earth, this group had been spared the proclivity to emit a dirty aroma.

"Keep following them," Janus directed. "They are heading in the right direction.

Eva felt uneasy about this. "Is this wise? Don't you feel this is a little too simple?"

"What choice do we have, love?" Madden said. "Nina is up there, yes?"

Eva nodded, the feeling still tugging at her.

"And they're leading us up."

"But we are going in the front door. Uninvited. Following a trail of devastation caused by what one can only presume is something from the next realm. Frozen heads? Doesn't anything about this weird you out?"

Madden grinned "This is Hell, love. Like I said before, what choice do we have?"

The path stretched into the distance, following the concentric circles of each tier. The demons had long since left them behind, the obsidian walls of Forente-Lautus guiding the Shikari toward the peak of the mountain and uncertain doom. On occasion, Eva caught a glimpse of the land outside. They really were isolated here, thousands of feet above the foothills. Belphegor had chosen her citadel well.

Swanson's continual chatter provided her with updates. The demons were threatening to overrun Kyzyl and were becoming more resistant to the weapons of earth as their numbers swelled and the balance of lifeforce shifted.

More disturbing was the increasing number of demon corpses littering the path they followed. All had been dispatched in the same way, heads frozen, looks of rage on their faces as if they had been tricked out of life and only realized this at the end. Eva had an uncomfortable feeling. Something bad waited for them.

"This is wrong," Janus said quietly as they reached the seventh of nine tiers. "Forente-Lautus shouldn't be deserted like this. Belphegor hasn't yet sent her army to the Gates of Hell. There would have been a record of it."

"You don't say." Madden nudged one of the demon corpses with his foot. The demons were ice-cold now. This was recent. "Whatever is responsible lies in wait ahead of us, can't you feel it? We are walking into a trap with no means of escape."

Madden's fear worried Eva and began to make her desperate. "But Nina is up there."

"And Nina's the only reason I don't lead you back out right now, love. There is a game at play here we are destined to lose. The only option we have is to not play *their* game and make our own rules."

"What did you have in mind?" Gila asked.

"Well, for starters we ditch these robes. They weigh us down, restricting our movement and hiding us from nobody. What good are we if we get there and are exhausted?"

Taking his cue, Eva dumped the robe she had worn in a heap on the floor. With the lack of contact, she felt better.

"Quick, take them off," she said, tugging at the robes the nearest Shikari wore. "There's something wrong with them."

Used to commands, the team removed the robes, casting them aside.

"The Director wasn't kidding," Ellen Covlioni said, awe mixed with fear in her voice. The view from her cameras popped onto Eva's visor, changing color as Covlioni cycled through the different lenses. When the screen showed what Eva presumed to be infrared, a pulsing light appeared around the hood of the cloak.

",". "This robe is sucking energy out of me," she deduced." Must be why I was starting to feel bad."

"Perhaps the demons were affected in the same way," Madden proposed. "Perhaps their very life force, their connection to the Source was being drawn out of them."

"But who would have the power to make them wear these robes against their will?" Eva asked.

"Anybody given the power of Command," said a cold voice from above her. "Take them."

Eva had no chance to look for the source of the voice; as she turned her head, robed demons sprang out of doorways opening out of seemingly solid walls. To a man, the Shikari were disarmed with barely a shot being fired.

Eva closed her eyes as rough hands grabbed her. Sharp talons threatened to pierce through her combat suit and the demon pulled her arms back so she had to bend forward. Her shoulders screamed in pain as she was bound.

"Remove their helmets," the voice said. "Without them they are all but useless."

A series of guttural laughs came from around her as the masks were ripped from the armor, wiring hanging out as they were tossed aside. Eva closed her eyes and braced her neck as she was shelled like a nut, her helmet hanging off before it dropped to the floor. The cameras hit the stone and sparks flew as at least one of them smashed. Similar noises surrounded her. Eva looked up to see the unmasked faces of the Shikari; familiar but strangely distant; it had been a while since she had seen anybody's face.

John Wolverton had a face like stone, his beard sticking out and his eyes wide with rage. He watched Eva without comment and nodded. He had a plan already.

She shook her head, the movement imperceptible. This was not the time. Nina felt so close, almost in the next room. She began to come even closer, pleading for her mother. The anticipation grew.

"You think technology is the answer," said the voice. "Always the answer. In this domain there is a technology developed beyond anything you can comprehend. Hold them up!"

Eva felt something sharp poke her in the small of her back and she moved forward, causing the pain in her shoulders to become red-hot agony. The vest, deigned to heal gradually, was of no use against such sudden violence.

The doors to the next circle opened and more demons came through. No more than a few dozen, those stepping down all wore the robe, all had the snarling faces of rage worn by the dead demons. These were close to death themselves, yet still they did the bidding of...

"Elaine?" Eva gasped, astonished at the diminutive figure following the demons down the steps. "What have you done with my daughter?"

CHAPTER THIRTY-TWO

Elaine Millet smirked at Eva. Throwing her hood back, she cast her eyes over the assembled group. Small in stature, her red hair flowed unbound down her back, decorated with small bones like the headdress of a tribal queen.

Disbelief vied with rage for mastery within Eva, the battle completely even and ultimately impotent since she could do nothing. The memory of the woman in front of her standing on the other side of the Orpheus portal, Nina in her arms, surfaced. But this time there was no baby.

"What have you done with my..."

Elaine pointed, and the demon holding her shifted its grip so both of her hands were now bound by one clawed paw, two fingers of the other pressed across her lower jaw inside her mouth.

"If she speaks again without permission, you can snap her jaw off. She does not need to be able to speak to bleed well."

Elaine stepped close. The wide eyes on her face did nothing to hide the insanity lurking behind them. But where was Nina?

Eva began to panic. From her connection, her daughter should be right there in front of her. She struggled against the demon gag, silently trying to shift out of her binding.

Elaine leaned forward, until their noses were almost touching.

"She's not here," Elaine whispered, studying her for any sign of reaction. "She's alone, in a great deal of danger, probably hungry, no doubt cold. But she's not here."

Elaine cackled, dancing a few steps away and removed a small metal device from the back of her head. Instantly, the connection Eva assumed had been with her daughter was lost, and a new, yet mysteriously familiar connection, this one a lot further away, replaced it. Pain, fear, discomfort. Nina was in trouble. The real Nina.

Eva tried to thrash her way out of the demons' grip, but it was hopeless. Tears leaked from her eyes, but she could not move.

"There. Your anguish is all I needed to see. Now you know how futile it was to come after your daughter."

Elaine spun away from her, the look of avarice, of pure unadulterated desire on her face evident as she had spotted Madden.

"Futile but ultimately necessary."

The demon turned Eva so she had no choice but to watch. Elaine stepped close to Madden, his head held back. He watched her without interest, as if she were just not there.

"You can try to hide it all you like, lover. You know how you feel about me, how I felt about you on our glorious trip across the Baltic Sea. She will never be able to feel what passed between us, you know. Her fate is not yours, my King."

"You are insane," Madden growled.

Elaine patted him on the cheek and turned away, idly walking around the rest of the captives, stroking Luke Wolverton, who glared at her, nostrils flared.

"My, this one looks like he has some stamina," Elaine said of J.D. Shelton. "I may keep him after Belphegor is done."

She turned back to Eva. "Just for use of the body, of course. I don't need the mind. *Mens sana in corpore sano.* A healthy mind in a healthy body. You tell me Eva. Which of us is the more insane? You feel your daughter? Is your mind not delusional?"

"Not as much as yours. You never had my husband."

"But I do now. I have all of you. Belphegor will do with you what she will, but after she's done, you are all mine. Take them."

Eva felt another sharp shove, her captor removing its hand. The taste of demon flesh in her mouth made her want to retch. It was carrion and cinders and a foul wrongness all wrapped into one. Behind her, Elaine fell into step alongside Madden.

"I still want you. I am in need of a champion, a partner, a King. Belphegor gave me orders, but my mistress gave me the command over her armies. She has gone to the place where the lock will be rent asunder and there she shall rise above all. She shall have no need for this mountain when she ascends and I will take it as my home. Our home."

Eva remained calm. Elaine was trying to goad her, much as she had on the journey through Scandinavia. Her insanity had only gotten worse.

They climbed the steps to the ninth and final circle. At the top, two enormous stone doors rested open on hinges well hidden in the wall. The inside of each was covered in similar glyphs to those shown to them by Janus in Cain, carved into the black stone and given life by a network of tiny red lights.

"Wait here," Elaine instructed the guard. "If any cross this threshold, do with them what you will."

Eva felt herself released, blood flowing back into her arms with agony.

"They won't be any trouble, will they my King?"

"No trouble at all," Madden answered, voice neutral. He had plans; Eva could feel it. He turned to the Shikari, his face away from Elaine. "Meek as kittens, this lot."

Sure of victory, Elaine led them into the enormous antechamber, the doors closing behind them. The moment the doors were closed, Elaine reached for Eva, murder in her eyes.

Madden was quicker, moving like lightning, intercepting Elaine's hand even as it reached out to grasp at the back of Eva's head.

Surprise was written all over Elaine's face. Shock and evident betrayal; she had had a genuine belief Madden had been falling for her.

"Why?" she gasped as his grip tightened, the knife she had intended to use dropping from her free hand. To Eva's amazement, it was the very same knife Iuvart had carved her arm open with on Mount Gehenna. The Well of Souls.

"You would never understand," he said, his voice gentle and full of compassion. I may have been reborn a hellbounce twice now, but you are more lost than I ever have been. You have been damned to believe your own version of reality in the twisted paths of your mind. You're truly in Hell."

Elaine's face registered wide-eyed betrayal, and then hardened to rage and vengeance. Eva stepped back, out of harm's way. She could sense J.D.'s proximity, just waiting to step in.

With the change in emotion, the last flicker of sanity disappeared from Elaine's face. "If I can't have you, nobody can. I'm stronger than you and I..."

Madden must have recognized the imminent violence, for he shifted his stance, using the newfound demon strength to throw Elaine clear across the antechamber where she crashed into the inner doors, landing senseless in a heap.

"No," Madden said with a release of pent-up satisfaction in his voice, "you aren't."

Eva bent to retrieve the knife. The blade still glinted with conchoidal perfection as she turned it in her hand. She felt more complete with this weapon; her blood and therefore an element of her soul resided within it. There were many victims, past and present, who would feel the same. In a moment of vengeance, with Elaine lying prone on the floor, blood tricking from her nose, Eva took the first step toward ending the woman who had stolen her child.

"Don't," Madden warned her.

"She deserves it."

"Perhaps, but not from you. Don't become part of this domain. Don't become a citizen of Hell."

Eva turned to her husband, helpless to deny him. Behind them the Shikari watched, Wolverton at the front, as Eva struggled to make the right decision.

"It's not something you can walk away from, Director," John said, his voice calm but deadly serious. "We all know we are damned in the long run. Every one of my team has killed. Don't become one of us."

Eva's resolve began to waiver, she opened her mouth to apologize, but a grating noise from behind forestalled her. A chill up her back made her turn. The doors had cracked open, frigid air seeping through and a mist billowing across the floor. A bright white light shone through the crack and Eva closed her eyes. She had been here before, in this situation.

When she opened them again, the doors were opening inward, away from them. The ice portal shone like a deathly moon from the center of Belphegor's throne room, the white glow impure, nauseous. Beyond the aperture, Eva could see nothing. This time there was no enormous eye beholding her.

The doors ceased moving, banging on the inside of the chamber with a boom sounding awfully final to Eva, and she realized there was no escape.

Silence descended and a figure no taller than Eva walked into view, coming right through the portal. The white light glittered off its skin and radiated right through the crystalline body. The noise of the steps was like glass tapping on stone, and Eva now understood what had happened to the population of Forente-Lautus.

"The demons aren't here. Those are the Guardians of Forente-Lautus. The demon army has been ordered to Tartarus. The lock to the next realm is being tested."

"Where it will be broken," said the figure in front of them, the voice like gravel dropping on glass, a horrible, raspy noise. Eva wanted to cover her ears.

The figure paused, turning its head and cocking it to one side to stare at her. Its lips peeled back, revealing crystalline teeth glittering like diamonds.

Eva recognized in the shape of the face, the stance of the creature, the woman she had met twice before. It was the same woman who had fed the girl to the mob, the same woman who had touched and nearly frozen Madden. Is this what he would have turned into?

"Belphegor," Eva said.

"Exerrocks," the creature grinned. "Belphegor is no more." The crystalline entity turned its attention to Elaine, who had begun to stir.

"M... mistress," Elaine mumbled, groggy from the impact with the door. "I brought them to you, as you asked."

"You tried to kill one and take the others, which I did not command," Exerrocks grated in response.

Elaine's face paled and she began to cry.

Eva wanted to feel sympathy for the woman, but from a great distance a cry pierced her soul. Nina was now fully aware of her mother and was terrified for her.

"We need to get back to the transport," she whispered to Madden. "I know where Nina is."

"Patience, mortal," Exerrocks replied, holding Elaine's head by her chin, as if examining a trophy. "You will all be going there. As for you," the crystalline form regarded Elaine once more. "You have served your purpose and shall reap your reward."

"Mistress?" Elaine's eyes brightened with hope. "You would grant me... eternal life?"

"So that was her plan," Gila muttered from behind Eva.

"You will be one, forever, in the realm of my master. In the realm of Crustallos."

Elaine opened her mouth to answer but as she drew breath to speak, Exerrocks stood, taking a step back. Crystalline tentacles unfurled from her back, where angels would have had wings, snaked in the air for a moment, and then plunged into Elaine's middle.

Elaine tried to scream as she was lifted aloft, blood fountaining from her mouth and pouring down the crystal lances impaling her.

Exerrocks opened her mouth in a silent outburst of joy, flexed her shoulders and ripped Elaine in two. Gore splattered everywhere as the two halves of the body were waved for a second, before being thrown into the portal. The white aperture glowed pink for a second before resuming its sickly hue. Exerrocks turned to Eva.

"Now!" shouted John Wolverton. As one, the Shikari pulled out handguns and opened fire at the murderous creature in front of them. The bullets struck true, shattering the tentacles still covered in blood. But as fast as they were falling, new tentacles erupted from her back, surging forward. The tentacles whipped low and swept the floor, causing everybody to lose their footing and fall to the ground.

"Do you know where you are?" Exerrocks asked. "Do you truly comprehend? Nothing comes out of nothing. You all arrive here in time. You are just flesh sacks full of energy for my master to devour. Your rightful place is grovelling on your bellies at his feet. You have the right blood in you, Eva Scott, of the line of David. Yours is a mongrel line of unfit descendants, impure and inbred. Your blood is needed. It does not have to be inside you."

A tentacle lanced out, reaching for the fallen Well of Souls which was now just out of Eva's reach. As it began to curl around the handle, a foot smashed down on the tentacle, shattering it.

"You dare?" Exerrocks hissed the words and the sound pained Eva's ears.

She looked up. "Janus? What are you doing?"

Janus stepped in front of Eva. "You will not have her, sub-creature." He kicked the obsidian blade to Eva, who picked it up once more.

Exerrocks laughed, what once might have been a pleasant noise, now sounded like shattered glass. "There is nobody in this realm to stop me. Crustallos is coming."

"That has not yet been decided."

Arms spread wide, Exerrocks launched a tentacle at Janus, who sidestepped it with ease. How had he moved with such speed?

Confusion clouded the crystalline face of their enemy. Several tentacles sprang from behind her, all thrusting at Janus. Some he smashed, others he simply dodged. One tentacle lashed for Eva, the blow knocking the Well of Souls from her hand again. It span end over end, slicing Eva's outstretched leg. The blade bit into her calf muscle, straight through the combat suit.

As blood seeped onto the blade, Exerrocks eyes lit up, glowing white. In the chamber beyond, the portal began to swirl.

"Blood on the blade!" a guttural voice, one Eva recognized from beyond the breach, roared. "Take her now."

Exerrocks moved toward Eva, straining against the tentacles now constraining it. This was what Janus had been waiting for. Instead of smashing the crystal tentacles, he wrapped them around his left arm and pulled the creature off balance. In an instant, he had jumped past her, pulling her with him into the main chamber.

"Go! Find Nina! I'll try to catch up if I can."

"Janus, no! Not again. There must be another way?"

"Only you can find her Eva!" Janus pulled at the tentacles, keeping their crystalline foe unsettled and focused on him. "Save your daughter! Save her and save your world!"

A tentacle detached itself from Janus, snaking through the doorway toward Eva. Janus grabbed it, throwing his enemy before him. Spreading his arms wide, he motioned with his hands, bringing them together. The doors began to slide shut. Just before they did, Janus shimmered. Two wings made of white feathers so pure they glowed began to unfurl from his back. Janus uttered a word. Eva had no idea what the word was but the impact of it was instant. Exerrocks screamed in pain, as did Eva, but it was the sweetest pain she had ever experienced. She felt rapture threaten to overwhelm her. The doors sealed, one word lingering in the air. "Go..."

CHAPTER THIRTY-THREE

The thick stone doors had sealed, but still the noises filtered through. Whatever was going on inside was nothing less than cataclysmic; Eva winced at every blow, every cry of pain.

"What the hell is he?" Madden whispered from behind her.

"I don't know," was Eva's honest answer. "A Guardian Angel maybe? But you heard him. We shouldn't wait around to find out."

"We aren't waiting anywhere," John Wolverton said, moving to shield Eva with his enormous frame. The rest of the Shikari crowded close, backs turned away from the outer doors. "Clear!"

Matt Tanzer depressed a switch on a small silver remote, and behind Wolverton the door exploded, fragments scattering everywhere, the chamber filling with dust.

"They might have taken guns, but we have many weapons," Wolverton added as the dust settled, and the ringing in Eva's ears faded.

Eva climbed to her feet, eyeing past her protector as she stretched and checked her extremities. The cut on her leg had already healed thanks to the armor yet the Well of Souls still glowed where her blood had touched it. She picked it up, holding the knife by the hilt with care.

"Some weapon you've got there," Wolverton said, admiring the blade. He was interrupted from any further comment by a body collapsing to the ground beside them.

"Matt, no!" Jenn Day's cry of anguish was plain and undoubtedly personal.

Eva tried to peer around the crowded bodies of the Shikari, but there was no way through. Only when blood began to trickle across the stones beneath their feet did Eva realize what was wrong. "What happened?"

Madden took her by the shoulders, turning her away. "He was caught by shards from the door. You don't want to see it, love. It's not worth the anguish. Come on, we need to get out of here."

Madden led Eva with firm but gentle force in the direction of the doors, his strength not giving her a chance to even turn.

Eva ducked into the gap created by the bomb, peering beyond. Several of the demons waited, hunched over. One collapsed, its violent thrashing on the ground a hazard in itself.

"Wait!"

Jenn Day came up to them, her face glistening from tears still flowing. An instant was an eternity in this domain.

"You don't go first, Director. But you don't look back."

Day stepped through the gap, Shelton and Porter Rockwell following her. Madden then indicated Eva should move.

Outside, the Shikari had small arms at the ready, but the demons were almost still.

As short as she was, Day seemed six feet tall when she walked up to one of the demons, measured it, and threw a punch knocking it flat. She waved her fist around, cursing and then punched the floor. Ice shattered from her knuckles.

"Damn thing's head froze as I punched it."

"The Guardians," Eva surmised. "That's what these are. That's why they aren't with the army. They protect only the city.

Belphegor can command them, but I think she is sucking their energy, feeding on the life force much like Crustallos has been doing."

"Maybe she is channeling the energy through the portal," suggested Gila.

Eva watched her dear friend. She was holding up well, but she had no business being here; she had nothing to prove.

"We have to get back to the transport," Wolverton advised, pushing his son ahead of him. "The job is not finished yet, not while any of us has breath left in our bodies."

"First the gear," Eva countered. "Then the transport. We aren't much use to Swanson if we can't contact him."

The Shikari accompanied Eva, Gila and Madden back through Belphegor's citadel, doubly alert now since all they had were a few handguns and makeshift cudgels. As before, their only company was the series of demon corpses, life-forces long since desecrated by Belphegor.

It was not long until they made it to their cache of weapons, everything untouched from where it had been strewn when they had been caught. Stufflebeam and Kyle picked up their mini-guns, caressing the instruments of death as if they were lost pets. Even John Wolverton reclaimed his shotgun with a degree of reverence.

Eva retrieved her helmet, one camera smashed, the other hanging loose.

"Wasted. The recording equipment is gone," Ellen Covlioni muttered. "They destroyed almost everything ripping the armor off."

"Not all," Gila countered. "Mine still works."

Eva placed her own helmet on, feeling more secure for having it there. The visor flickered for a moment and then became a clear view of a desert full of lightning.

"Swanson?" She said more out of hope and the need to hear the security of her own voice than of any expectation of an answer.

"Eva? What happened? There was a blip and then you all went silent. Are you all right?"

"Matt Tanzer is dead. Elaine was here but she is dead, too. She captured us and took us to Belphegor. Except *she* is dead too and an entity calling itself Exerrocks has her body. Oh and Janus is fighting her. He's probably dead as well."

"Nina? Tell me you have your daughter."

"She's... she's not here. They have her in Tartarus. We were misled. They wanted us here the entire time."

"I only lost you for a second," Swanson said, confused. "All this happened in one instant?"

"Maybe the time differential isn't constant," Gila suggested. "This is a very strange place after all. We have no comparative measurements."

"Time to move," Wolverton said. "Let's go, Directors."

A roar behind them betrayed the presence of several Guardians, those not yet sucked cold. They rushed in the direction of the escapees, their smoldering eyes glowing beneath the cowls hiding the details of their faces.

"What was that?" Swanson asked.

"You don't want to know." Eva replied, already moving.

Jenn Day remained where she was standing.

"Move it, soldier." Wolverton ordered.

The small blonde turned to them. "Matt isn't leaving. Neither am I. I'll buy you some time, sir. Get out of here." The acceptance of her fate was written as plain as day on her face. She would die here.

"Jenn!"

But Day had turned away, her own rifle slung across her back, Matt Tanzer's machine gun in her hands.

"Go!" she shouted, echoing Janus' last words. Not turning to check if they were leaving, Day let rip with the machine gun, walking with steady purpose toward the Guardians.

Madden pulled at Eva, encouraging her to leave. "We can't save them all, Eva. She's made her decision."

Eva ripped free of her husband's embrace, hurrying past him to where John Wolverton was striding down the arched hallway.

"You aren't going to stop her?"

"As your husband said, she made her decision," Wolverton growled, not turning his head.

"Well, what sort of stupid comment is that?" Eva asked, outraged.

Wolverton set his jaw, snarling without answer and strode on at a pace Eva would have had to run at to keep up.

"What the commander means," Forrest Kyle said from just behind her, "is Jenn ignored an order, thus defying the chain of command. Everybody follows the Mir-Shikar without question. It's his one absolute rule. The only time his rule is broken is when somebody wishes to leave the Shikari."

"And how many times has *his* rule been broken?"

"Never."

Eva swallowed, fearing the next question. "Are there any other circumstances in which one would leave?"

"When you knew you were about to die," Madden said, his voice somber.

Forrest had a grim smile on his face as he swept his mini-gun in an arc, covering the angles Wolverton left open. "Tanzer and Jenn were lovers second, Shikari first. You didn't see but he was torn near in half by shards from the doors. Protecting her. She's sacrificing herself for us, so let's get out of here, Director. Let's not waste our second chance, use the radar you have in your head, and let's get your daughter back. For her. For Matt. For any more of us yet to perish."

"Aren't you scared?"

Forrest grinned. "Crapping myself. Wolfgang over there used to be a close friend with a former Shikari, name of Magnus von Black. Crazy guy. Insane, I think. He was killed in Cambodia before all this got bad. He used to say, 'At least I will die in the proper place, doing what I love'."

Eva's heart pounded as she watched the hallway through the armor-enhanced vision of her remaining camera. There was an organic quality about the construction, as if Forente-Lautus had been grown, not fashioned. There was a brooding menace about the place. It wanted nothing more than to swallow her up.

They reached the level of the transport. Something had changed.

"This is not where we climbed up before," Porter Rockwell said, frowning. He went to one of the great gabled windows. "No water. We aren't on the same side."

Eva looked about them, the threat of menace felt as real to her as the panic coming from her baby daughter. "It's the city, the very building. It feels us within and doesn't want us to leave."

"Double-time it," Wolverton ordered. "I want us out of this labyrinth. Two-by-two cover formation, our guests in the middle, Wolf and Forrest at either end."

Eva found herself shuffled next to Gila in the middle of the Shikari, jogging while her remaining escorts arranged themselves in pairs. This was as close to blind panic as the Shikari got. The walls pressed in.

It all happened so suddenly. A wall to Eva's left just dropped away, a knot of Guardians spilling out into the middle of the group and laying into them with savage ferocity. John and J.D. got involved immediately, the latter finally having cause to unsheathe the sword he carried on his back. Wielding the wakizashi with brutal efficiency, Shelton cut the Guardians down as if he were felling trees.

Another wall popped open.

"It's a distraction!" Wolfgang roared, opening fire with the minigun, but it was too late. Ellen Covlioni had become separated from the main group and the Guardians grabbed her, stepping back from the fight as a wall began to rise from the floor, closing the hallway behind them.

"Do it!" Covlioni yelled.

Eva turned to see several of the Shikari with grenades in hand. Without hesitation, they threw them over the closing wall.

"Run!" Wolverton roared.

Eva flew headlong down the hallway. She was indistinctly aware of the explosion behind, the life-signs of Ellen Covlioni flat-lining and turning red on her screen. All she could think was they were picking them off, one at a time.

Around her the sounds of footfalls indicated she was not alone, but she kept her eyes forward.

"There! Turn right!" John Wolverton's command caused Eva to turn for the passage without thinking, her feet sliding out from under her. She collapsed on her side but as soon as she was down, strong hands were picking her up and shoving her through a contracting entrance, a door being lowered.

The Shikari piled through the entrance, the door grinding into the pathway behind them. This was not happenstance.

"Madden? Where's Madden?" Eva yelled in a moment of panic, searching the survivors for a familiar face.

A hand took her shoulder from behind. "Here, love." He turned her, removed her helmet, and gazed into her eyes before a rumble caused them to look skyward.

All of Forente-Lautus shook as an explosion rocked the citadel above, white light bursting out in several different directions. The top circle crumbled in on itself.

"Get in the transport," Wolverton's voice was not to be ignored, Shikari or not.

"Wait," Gila cried, "something's happening."

Amidst the beams of light shooting into the sooty sky, a single speck shot alone, arching down toward them. Eva stood mute, uncomprehending, as the speck grew and became a figure. A body glowing white, tinged with blue, two enormous wings supporting its descent.

"It's no demon," Madden said aloud.

The glowing figure hurtled out of control toward them, wings collapsing as the speed of descent increased. It was as if Eva was watching a peregrine falcon stooping for the kill.

"Get inside!" Wolverton shoved Eva.

She climbed into the transport but only far enough for the structure of the machine to protect her. Above, the citadel exploded outward, sending lumps of polished volcanic stone in every direction. Madden watched from over her shoulder as several crashed onto the landing bay, leaving impact craters several feet wide.

"We have to get airborne," Gila shouted. "Madden, you are the only one who can fly this thing. Get us out of here."

"No!" Eva shouted. "We can't leave yet!"

The glowing being had become a streak of pure light as it plummeted, a bar of brightness doubtless never before seen in Hell. The force as it hit the landing bay was nothing less than cataclysmic, the impact rocking the transport, tipping it over on one wing, sending Eva falling out and rolling down the side of the impact crater which was now all remaining of the once-level surface.

"Eva, are you all right?" Madden called from the safety of the transport.

"I'm fine," she shouted back. The light was fading. She scrambled down to the middle of the crater, fully twelve feet lower than the rim. What was left of the nebulous being was a broken man, wings torn and mangled, a face covered in cold burns, missing skin and one ear. The body was well muscled yet spent.

"What are you," she wondered.

Against all odds the head moved, one good eye opening and focusing on her.

"Eva, help me," croaked the voice.

CHAPTER THIRTY-FOUR

"Madden, get down here! Bring J.D. with you!"

Eva examined the ruined body. It was seeping the same black ichor the demons had done.

The eye of the creature watched her, calm, trusting. "Don't leave me here," croaked the voice of what had once been her friend.

Eva smiled, smoothing back the curled white hair that had replaced the balding countenance of her friend and protector. "You never need worry. I would abandon you about as much as I would my own daughter."

Janus tried to smile, but the pain was too great. He arched back, coughing, more of the black blood erupting from his mouth.

"What's all this then?" Madden asked as he scrambled to the bottom of the crater. He caught sight of the body lying beneath Eva. "What IS all this?"

"It's Janus. We have to get him out of here, fast. We aren't safe. You two need to carry him up to the transport; be as quick and as gentle as possible."

"Janus... This is Janus? Are you sure?"

"Madden, I'm not going to sit here and try to prove it. Have a little faith. You two are the strongest. Just be careful. We need to get out of here. Now."

Madden and J.D. shared a shrug, and between them, picked up the ailing body. Eva held on tight to the Well of Souls, leading the way. Behind her, the two men struggled up the slope.

"Eva, he weighs a ton. Are you sure this is necessary?"

"I am. I made a promise."

On the transport, the reaction was nothing less than awe as the ruined body of what was Janus was brought aboard. The word *angel* was whispered around the gathered Shikari, who made room for them to lay the body down. There was no comfort to be had on the floor of the transport so Eva knelt, resting Janus' head on her knees.

"Where to?" Madden called from the pilot's seat.

"They think we are going to head straight for Tartarus. As much as I want Nina back now, we need to detour. Head straight for the Gates of Hell."

"Are you insane?"

"Without a shadow of a doubt. We have a score to settle first."

Janus coughed, the black blood thick and oily, seeping onto Eva's combat suit.

"Careful," a very subdued Rachelle Bishop warned, her dark hair hanging loose about her head, unkempt and ignored. "He's bleeding acid. It will burn you."

"No..." gurgled Janus. "Not... demon blood. Divine... blood. Demons are... tainted... corrupt."

Janus fell into an extensive bout of coughing, each spasm forcing more of the fluid out of his wounds. It had gone everywhere. Eva was soaked with it, but she did not care. She smoothed his hair, comforting him as much as she was able. How did one heal an angel?

The coughing subsided, and Janus rested for a while, his chest barely moving.

Behind them, the sky lit up brightest white until it was so bright it threatened to blind, causing everybody to shield their eyes. A moment later, the transport shook as a shockwave slammed into them. The transport tilted but quickly righted itself.

A croaking noise sounded from Janus. Eva realized he was attempting to laugh.

"Don't. Save your energy."

Janus opened his one good eye. It was clear, lucid with the clarity of one not left long on this earth. No, in this Hell, she corrected herself.

"My life-force is almost spent, Eva. The explosion. I set off a chain reaction in the portal. I hope...I pray it was enough to end Belphegor. Thought I had enough left to land but Crustallos tried to suck me dry."

"But what... Who are you?"

Janus continued to speak. "I wrote the Scrolls. The...Nag Hamaddi. You were meant to know sooner, but the demons...Iuvart stole them. All is back on course. Madden..." Janus closed his eye, squeezing it tight as the pain threatened to overwhelm him. He reached up and grabbed Madden by the back of the head, drawing him near. "Madden... Heroes don't always walk in the light. Do what must be done. See... See it through. Make the right choice. Protect them."

Janus let go of Madden then. He looked up at Eva, a tear leaking from his eye. It mingled with her own as she found herself unable to hold her own tears back.

"Eva, are angels just ascended demons? Or are demons fallen angels? Look after your girls, Eva. They matter. Listen... Listen to me. Find the gate. Tell them... Tell of my sacrifice. They won't understand otherwise."

Janus slumped, his face becoming drawn. He began to take short, shallow breaths, whispering a phrase every few seconds. Eva leaned down, her ear near his mouth.

"The creator named me Metatron. I am Janus. Your friend."

Janus took one shuddering breath and ceased to be. In moments, his body desiccated, crumbling to dust in front of her until all left remaining of Janus was a single feather, purest white at the end, stained black with blood everywhere else.

For a while, there was silence, the hum of the transport's mechanics the only noise. Eva stared at the feather, eventually tucking it between the armor Janus had given her and her combat suit. She began to gather the dust. In silence, Rachelle Bishop and J.D. Shelton both helped her, creating a small pile. Without comment, Porter Rockwell produced a pouch and they scooped the remains in, sealing it. Eva looped the pouch around her belt, patting it with reverence. In the distance, somewhere to the North, Nina approved, though she was still scared.

Eva looked up. Gila was watching her from beside Madden, who was back to piloting the transport. The visor on her helmet was raised, her black hair protruding at random angles from the sides of her face. She was talking in low tones, presumably to Swanson.

"He was a brave soul," John Wolverton said, kneeling beside her.

"You all are," she replied, still staring at the floor where Janus had perished. "Ellen, Jenn, Matt, Emdy, Kris. How many of you is it going to take? I had to come here. You had a choice and we have lost nearly half your squad for what?"

"We are closer to your daughter. We have your dagger."

A plan began to hatch in Eva's mind. "The dagger... Gila, tell Swanson I think I have a way to forestall the enemy."

"He can hear you." Gila flicked a switch on the side of her helmet. "You are on, Director Guyomard."

"Eva? I'm sorry about Janus. He was a worthy man."

"He wasn't a man. He was an angel. With his last breath, he insisted he was Janus but said he had another name: Metatron."

A stunned silence followed her comment. Eva looked up from her contemplation of Janus' remains to see most of them staring at her.

Gila's mouth hung open.

"Metatron. Are you sure?" Swanson's tone had changed, becoming grave in tone.

"I heard him as clear as I hear you now: 'The creator named me Metatron' were his exact words. Why?"

"Metatron is the mouth of God. The one responsible for communicating His will since to hear the voice of God directly is beyond the capability of all but the most high."

Eva placed her helmet on her head. "The name doesn't mean anything to me. Show me what's happening on Earth."

"It's very strange. See for yourself."

Eva watched the screen as the fighting was replaced with pictures of the sky. It was growing dark everywhere, a strange red mist beginning to coalesce.

"What are we seeing?"

"We don't know. The atmospheric center on Utö has reported marked increases in the level of atmospheric sulfur. Not enough yet to do any harm, but pretty soon we won't need to worry about demons for hiding from acid rain."

Eva pulled her visor up and glanced outside. The Earth she saw had red gas swirling about it in much the same way they had seen the souls moving onward.

"The fighting. It's a distraction," she realized aloud. "They are terraforming Earth, making it habitable for demonkind."

"Eva, what you say is madness."

"No, it makes sense. The air, it's breathable here, but it's not particularly pleasant. They don't need to do a lot to make the environment perfectly habitable. The longer we focus on the demons, the less we concentrate on the ice. What else is going on?"

"The Gobi Desert is full of the weirdest energy readings. Off the scale from anything we have seen before. It's not just the portal out there."

"It's their hidden city, where the Convocation of the Sacred Fire intended take me. You may well be right; we are not alone."

More pictures flashed up. Saddening but not surprising. Riots, mass praying, placards reading *God Has Abandoned Us* and *The End is Coming* were popular. One in particular caught Eva's attention: *Your God is dead.*

"People are degenerating into their animal state, doing what they feel necessary to survive. Riots, looting. It's all going on. Any religious focus is overwhelmed. Order is disintegrating completely. It's gotten real *Old Testament* here. Even in Geneva, the city center looks like the scene of debauchery before Moses returned from Mount Sinai."

"We are doing the demons' work for them," Eva agreed, feeling distraught mankind was so easily swayed to madness. "Hells' army will just walk in and assume control. Swanson, you are going to have to make an effort to counter this."

"What would you have us do, Eva? We can't. We don't have the manpower, stretched thin as we are. I'm taking an incredible risk, sacrificing many men without telling them why because you want us to hold the main portal. You are going to have to take action from your side. Is there anything you can do to help?"

"I have an idea. Just stand ready and mobile. I'd hate to cause another Sangster because we were on the ground, unarmed, and too large to have an effect."

Eva watched the distant ground as they edged nearer the Gates of Hell. She had pondered Swanson's understanding of her cryptic comment. Surely, he understood? The Jamaican airport was too recent, too crucial.

A city came into view, black, domed like the shell of a beetle, with one large tower piercing the sky from the center. Yellow ribbons cut across the surface, undulating in a strange manner, yet never intertwining. It was a very alien structure. The transport lowered without request so she could have a look.

"It's Aquinas," Madden said, slipping his arms around her. The comfort was welcome, though Eva missed Janus' insight.

"The city of Asmodeus?"

"The very same. It looks ruined, too. Abandoned. If I am right, the surface is shattered and covered with the lava pouring down from the tower. It appears Asmodeus didn't want anybody assuming control of his city or his armies if he was destroyed."

"And we destroyed him. Maybe we should command his minions to withdraw. At least we are rid of one more of their kind."

Eva turned within the circle of his arms. "Madden, what did Janus mean when he said, *do what must be done*? What have you read you have not shared with anybody else?"

"The truth?"

Eva nodded, not trusting herself to make a sensible comment.

"I don't know. He said I would know when it was time for me to rid myself of Belphegor's infection. I have a feeling this is another of those riddles. I think the time will come soon."

Eva leaned her head back on his shoulder, taking comfort in the security she felt with him around. "Nina is tired, but she can't sleep. The noise, I think, is disturbing her."

"Noise?"

"She can't elaborate; she can't see it."

"Madden, Eva, get up here," Gila called.

Grabbing her helmet, Eva followed Madden to the front of the transport.

"Look," Gila said as they reached her, pointing in front of them.

A portal swirled lazily in the distance; the sky around it was shades of pink and red. As they approached ever closer, a structure in the region of the portal became defined, unlike anything Eva had ever seen before.

"This is new" Eva couldn't quite make out the shape of the structure, even with her enhanced camera vision.

Madden tapped a few of the demon-glyphs and text began to read across the screen in front of him.

"The Gates of Hell. It's a city. THE city, from which all attempts are made to break through the veil and colonize the mortal plane. It's the sole purpose of this construction."

"But it has to be thousands of miles across."

"Maybe more," Madden agreed. "All the power of the Source is focused here, concentrated on one portal. It has been the one factor combining the purpose of the demon clans and giving them direction. They know their time is at an end unless they can withdraw to a safe harbor."

"Are you getting this, Swanson?"

"I am. The council is here, such as it is. There aren't a lot of words able to do this justice."

"Look below," Madden advised.

Eva's heart caught in her throat as she watched the ground come into view, every square meter covered with a writhing mass of demon spawn.

"There must be millions of them down there," Swanson said. "How can we defeat so many?"

"We don't engage them," Madden answered. "There is another way. Technology is the key. The timing is critical. Swanson, what you see is only two, maybe three of the seven armies of Hell. These below are subject to Lucifer and Leviathan, plus whatever remains of Asmodeus. This doesn't account for Abaddon, Mammon, Belphegor and the remnants of Satan's army."

"It sounds like we don't have a chance."

"You don't. If this portal opens and the army makes it through, Earth is gone. I get what Eva meant now and I sincerely hope you do, too. We had to come here. Eva has a task to undertake. Technology can be undone. Knock out a keystone and the bridge falls. This is just a massive bridge. As Eva said, be ready."

Madden rose from the controls, removing Eva's helmet. He looked at Gila. "You too."

"We need the guidance," Gila protested.

"Not here, you don't. If we are right, this is the focus of everything technological in Hell. If there is a signal coming from your equipment, do you think it is wise to alert several million demons? Or indeed those ships?"

Madden pointed behind him, out the front of the transport. Several larger transports, looking like enormous weaponized bugs, had risen from the city to block their path.

Everybody in the transport ducked out of view.

"Great," Eva hissed at Madden. "What do we do now?"

Madden grinned. "Something really stupid."

CHAPTER THIRTY-FIVE

Eva examined her options, high and dry as the ships moved forward to inspect the transport.

"Hide!" Madden hissed. "Up against the bulkheads, where the walls are thickest."

Eva ducked down, finding herself sharing a space with Rachelle Bishop. Across from them, J.D. Shelton tried to cram himself into a gap Eva would have had a hard time squeezing into alone.

"What about you?" Gila said to Madden in muted tones.

"I'm half demon. Maybe I can use it to my advantage for once. Stay quiet. I'm going to attempt interference with their systems.

The transport moved forward at a casual pace, not slowing, as if it were going exactly where it was meant to go. One of the enormous ships pulled close, Madden piloting the transport close to the port side of the titanic fuselage.

A series of glyphs appeared on the screen at Madden's terminal. He squinted as he read, pressing a series of buttons in quick succession. A moment later, the ship left their side, moving off to undertake other tasks. Curiosity had been satisfied.

"It's all right. You can get up now."

Eva scrambled from her space, pausing to pull Rachelle to her feet. Unlike before, when the Shikari were content to wait, to a man they now watched the scene unfold in front of them.

"What did you do?"

"Inverted their scans and sent them back. What they saw was in fact the make-up of their own crew."

"You can fake readings?" Eva was impressed.

"It just came to me. This little ship has all manner of tricks if you care to... read the instructions."

Madden sat back on the pilot's seat. He must have realized his words were self-defeating since he was the only one left on board able to read the alien language. Eva watched his face fall, kissed him on the cheek, and settled back to regard the scene below.

The city spread out as far as the horizon, metallic towers sparkling with lights, chimneys belching smoke into the sky, and lightning jumping from the surface to a floating level of the city, supported entirely by a series of vertical jets. It spread above them into infinity, a technological marvel the likes of which Eva knew they would never see on Earth. Between the two levels hovered the portal, shining like an unholy beacon, Earth's sun visible through the hazy portal.

And in front of the portal, an immense plaza as wide as it was long, with every meter packed with demons of various sizes.

"There he is." Eva pointed at the vanguard, where a series of giant demons similar to their pursuer in Lake Geneva stood, restless.

"That's Behemoth?" Wolverton asked.

The giant creature stood on two legs, flexing claws and gnashing fangs, staring down the portal, which dwarfed even its hulking size. It had taken the defeat badly. From their great height, Eva shuddered, pressing closer to Madden. The memories of the same monster facing her down in Afghanistan were not those she cared to revisit.

"I thought you were brave, but you looked Behemoth in the eye? You are more worthy of a place in the Shikari than anybody I have ever met."

There was a tone of newfound respect in John's voice, and the rest of the team nodded in agreement.

"I wasn't the only one there," she admitted, the memory of facing down the armies of Hell now a waking nightmare. Everything she had seen through the portal was laid out beneath her, the horror of it all magnified. "The demons I saw. The boundless hordes; they were only a fraction of this. The portal showed an army. This is the entire population."

"So this is Leviathan and Lucifer's army?" Wolverton asked in a dour tone.

"You sound disappointed," Madden noted, turning the transport directly toward the aperture.

"I just expected them to be here, waiting on thrones or some such grandiose gesture."

Madden watched him for a moment and then chuckled. "Oh, I get it. You wanted to challenge one of them directly. John Wolverton, who took on a Prince of Hell for the fate of all mankind. The war isn't going to be won through the use of force."

"Was a fight not your crazy plan?"

"Trust me; they are nearby. But the great captains aren't going to reveal themselves with the threat of the ice realm so close. Don't forget there is a bigger picture, as little as we have seen of it. No, facing down Hell's champions is not the plan. What happened last time Eva shed blood?"

"The portal opened," Eva answered quickly.

"And they were using the Well of Souls to recreate their undertaking because it contains your blood. At least they were until Belphegor retrieved it. Your blood can open portals, Eva."

"You crazy son of a bitch," Luke Wolverton accused Madden. "You would sacrifice your own wife?"

"It is not nearly as bad," Madden replied. "We just have to get close enough to the portal."

"But my blood wasn't right. The portal collapsed..." Eva smiled with the comprehension of Madden's motive. "The portal collapsed.

It's what has been happening every time they open one. Do I need to stick my arm in the portal?"

"I doubt it. We just need you to cover something in fresh blood and toss it in. Your blood is right enough for what we need, love."

Madden had moved the transport to within a few miles of the portal when the vibrations began to appear. At first, a subtle hum, shuddering as they continued to fly right at the portal. By the time they were within half a mile of the aperture, the turbulence was knocking the team off their feet; violent shakes hitting them out of nowhere. Eva held tight to Madden's shoulder, her legs loose as she attempted to ride the strange bucking affecting their craft.

"I guess this is why nobody else is coming so close," Madden shouted above the noise. "We aren't going to be able to throw anything in from in front."

"What about from the side?"

"The angle is too narrow. We might miss, and then it's all over."

In the midst of her desperation, Eva saw the solution. Attached to his back, Wolfgang still had his RPG. He saw Eva eyeing his weapon and grinned, evidently comprehending her thought.

"If we can't get close enough, we have to use something smaller, more mobile," he shouted above the whine of the engines and unpacked the launcher.

Eva took out the Well of Souls. "You know, we aren't going to have a lot of time once I cut myself with this. It will be like a beacon to the millions below. Nina is worried for us. She is not alone and she is no fan of whoever is holding her. After I do this, whatever happens, we go straight for my daughter. Promise me."

"I promise," Madden replied, his voice sincere. The time had finally come.

Eva winced as the obsidian blade cut open the all too recently healed scar on her arm. The six-pointed star now had a new line across it, blood beading along the incision. Wolfgang handed her the rocket and she smeared blood across the warhead, streaking the grey weapon red.

Below them, ships began to rise, converging on them. A massed roar from the millions below chilled Eva to the bone.

"We aren't inconspicuous anymore," she concluded.

"Open the door," Wolfgang instructed as they moved out of the turbulent path of the aperture. "Forrest, grab my belt."

Forrest Kyle stood to one side of Wolfgang, leaning away from the weapon on his friend's shoulder.

"As close as I can get us," Madden shouted above the howl of the vortex outside. "It's now or never. Do it!"

Wolfgang fired, filling the transport with smoke.

It felt like slow motion to Eva as she watched the rocket sear across the gap between them and the portal, hitting the energy of the aperture and exploding. The effect was instantaneous. The portal stabilized, becoming clear. The other side was filled with desert framed by mountains, the sunshine bright and the sky a red-tinged blue. The demons on the ground began to surge forward, roaring with the mindless lust of conquest. Some of the ships converging on them began to change course, heading for demonkinds' salvation. Some, not all.

Eva rammed her helmet on. "Swanson, are you getting this?"

"Eva, you had better damned well know what you are doing," came back the disbelieving voice of the ARC Director. "You have just started the Apocalypse."

"Keep them occupied," Madden shouted above the din. "You need the portal open but you need to bottle them up from your side. I'll give them something to think about. Send jets, missiles, whatever you have with the ability to fly and destroy a standing structure. Send a goddamned hot air balloon with grenades if you can! I have no idea if this is going to work, but if this structure is disabled, they have no way of sending through a force sufficient to hold ground on Earth. Send them now!"

Beneath them, the surging demons were met with a withering

display of force as they were fired upon from earth. The second the demons crossed the threshold they were cut down by everything the mortal plane could muster and the bodies were already piling up. Some got through, drawing fire away from the portal, and as fire was drawn from the entry point, more made it across.

Then the ice portals appeared, Crustallos taking easy pickings from the dead and dying. So concentrated was the attack from beyond the aperture itself began to freeze, much as the sky had once done over Gehenna. The magnitude of power expended was incredible. Still, demons made it through.

One of their pursuers, a city-sized transport itself, began to head in the direction of the portal, closing on it rapidly.

"Swanson," Eva warned.

"We see it. Whatever you are going to do, do it now. We have a little surprise for them but it will take all of us."

"There are structures over the portal on this side," Eva advised. "If you knock them out, they should collapse on top of it."

"Move out of the way," Swanson replied. "We are ready."

Madden pulled the transport up above the portal. "Guys, hang on. I'm not exactly sure what the consequences of this will be but..."

Madden pressed a button on the console, and instantly, a blinding white light radiated from their ship.

Eva threw her hands over her eyes and even her own body failed to block the light. There was a yell from nearby, but from whom she could not tell. In time, the light faded. When Eva removed her hands from her eyes, she could see everybody else was similarly dazed.

"Madden, what did you just do?"

"They call it a soultap. It's a mass-release of energy from the Source, Hell's electromagnetic pulse. I basically drained the soul-energy from everything around us and released it all in one concentrated burst. The portal won't close but anything big and floating should no longer have the power to move. For a while."

"It's worked," Gila shouted, her head stuck out of the still-open door.

Below them, the larger ships were falling out of the sky, the transport within touching distance of the portal dropped like a stone on top of innumerable demons. The front of the transport lit up as a missile from the other side exploded on its surface and several silver blurs streaked past it, entering Hell from the Earth side.

The Shikari began to cheer. A squadron of three F-22 raptors skimmed the surface of the fallen transport.

"Orpheus Leader, take point. Orpheus two and three, good hunting," Swanson said over the airwaves.

"Roger, base."

Eva watched, fascinated, as the planes shot off over the sprawling metropolis below, fading into the distance. Dependent on the energy from souls, Hell had nothing as agile with which to respond, despite the superior speed. A few of the smaller transports blinked out of existence as they completed their sluggish turns, but by the time they were lined up to follow, the raptors were already on their way back.

"Targets identified, missiles locked. Directors Scott and Ciranoush, good luck and God's speed."

As the planes came back, still in formation, six missiles roared ahead of them, heading up to what Eva presumed was the framework of the portal. Much like Orpheus, this would be the demons' downfall.

"Get out of there, Shikari," Swanson warned. "Those warheads are nuclear."

Several events occurred at once. Madden threw the transport into a turn, building up speed. The missiles passed the portal and one of the demon transports collided with them, knocking their small ship sideways.

"Hold on!" Madden shouted.

"The missiles missed!" Eva yelled, distraught.

The three fighter jets passed through the portal, gone in the blink of an eye. A second later, the missiles detonated and impacted the superstructure. A series of blinding flashes accompanied severe buffeting from the shockwaves; the damaged ship beside began to drift downward, spiralling out of control.

"The bump saved us," Madden said, the relief clear in his voice.

Eva watched the demon transport crash into the superstructure below, then looked above. Where the missiles had exploded, only twisted metal and a small mushroom cloud remained. Many of the engines maintaining the height above ground were gone and the raised superstructure began to buckle. Even from miles away, the massive structure still appeared too close. Yet from as far away as Eva was, the portal appeared to settle to the ground. The city below disintegrated, many parts of falling around and even through the portal.

"There," Gila's voice was heightened in its excitement. "Watch the portal."

The sheer weight of the collapsing upper level caused the portal to tilt. There was a scramble to escape as the army began to comprehend their doom. They scattered in every direction including through the collapsing aperture. Having seen Asmodeus do the same, Eva knew the army beneath were in for a painful end.

The portal winked out, the framework shattering under the monumental stress of unsupported metal and everybody on board cheered. Eva hugged Madden, kissing him in the heat of the moment.

When the commotion died down, Eva turned to see John Wolverton standing by the still-open door.

"We are not without loss ourselves."

His voice was somber. Eva searched about, seeing everybody. No, not everybody.

"Porter,"

"He fell out during the soultap," Madden presumed.

"He must have done. We have lost another of our family, but we continue, steadfast until the end."

"Until the end," the remaining Shikari intoned.

Eva found herself saying the words also, not knowing why.

"I didn't see him anywhere near the door," Madden said, somewhat confused.

"Who knows what happened," Wolverton replied. "Yet fell he did. Fall we all will if our fate it is to die in service."

"Swanson? Director?" Gila was tapping the side of her helmet. "Maybe the blasts knocked out the communication."

Eva retrieved her own from the floor where it had fallen, placing it on her head. "Cameras still recording; they are fine."

"Directors Scott and Ciranoush, good luck and God's speed," quoted Madden. "The pilot knew this might happen. The way back is shut. The only way to open a portal now is..."

Eva held up the Well of Souls. She swallowed. "We aren't going to be alone for long, are we? All of Hell knows I have this. I just cut my arm open for crying out loud."

Bishop took one look and reached for a kit. "You are starting to look like a self-harm victim."

"Rachelle, don't worry." Eva examined her forearm. "As you can see, I have clearly had worse. The knife is so sharp the cut has already dried. Now it's not just the handiwork of Iuvart scarring my arm."

"Madden," Scope called from the rear of the craft. "Put your foot on it. We have company."

Eva turned with the rest of them to look aft. In the distance, the Gate of Hell was in flames, transformed from order into chaos. In front of the ruined portal, the entire sky was filled with ships, every one of them gaining on the tiny transport.

"Only one place left to go," Madden decided. "It's time to ask the Devil for a door."

CHAPTER THIRTY-SIX

The fleet behind was gaining on them. There was no denying it. Every time Eva looked forward to see where they might lose their pursuers, there was nothing. Every time she glanced back, the vanguard of the fleet was closer.

"Where are we?" she asked Madden, leaning over her husband.

Madden examined a map on the screen labeled with demon glyphs. "There's a long and complicated name but let's just say we are crossing over the sea surrounding Narcis, Lucifer's citadel. No, we are not taking a detour."

"How far to Tartarus?"

"We are here," Madden pointed to a small island in the middle of the inland sea. He moved his hand North to a mountain ridge crossing the center of the map. "Tartarus is there."

"What's that the blacked-out portion of the map?" John Wolverton waved his hand over the northernmost portion of the screen.

"That's ice. Crustallos has one foot in this realm. The entire northern ocean is frozen."

In the distance, columns of smoke billowed from the shore. Not smoke, Eva corrected herself, ash. Lightning sparkled up around the columns, jumping out to fork mid-air. They were headed straight for it.

"Is there any way around?" Eva looked back once more. It felt like the lead ship of Lucifer's army was within touching distance.

"None. We just have to speed up as much we can and hope it's enough."

"Does this ship have anything left to give?"

Madden pored over the control panel once more, his face frustrated. "We've ridden her pretty hard. With the soultap, the circuits were fried. If we could do it once more we could drop them all in Lucifer's pond but there's no hope of escape in the ship's condition."

"There's always hope." Eva felt the call of her daughter growing closer. They were on the right path, whatever stood between them.

"Fly into the ash cloud." Madden speculated.

"Are you nuts?" Everybody else on board echoed Bishop's exclamation.

"Think about it. This transport has no turbines to get clogged. It doesn't rely on electricity. It is driven entirely by the energy of souls, of which there are millions. We might pass right through with no damage. They are huge. They have a much greater chance of being slowed than we do."

"Do it," Eva agreed. "It's about time we took some risks, don't you think?"

Given what they had already been through, the comment made the Shikari chuckle.

Eva turned to them. "If anybody has a better idea, I'm open to suggestions. It seems to me we are out of options."

A rumble from beneath caused them to halt the discussion and crowd the window. A colossal ship was emerging from the cloud above the lake on all sides. Glowing red along the top and sides, it was oval in shape with stunted wings that dragged the cloud up as it rose. The vehicle was so vast it looked about to engulf them from below.

"Lucifer," Madden whispered.

"He was never at the Gate," concluded Gila.

"It makes perfect sense," Madden agreed. "What general with brains ever led from the front?"

The ovoid ship continued to rise, angling after them as they sped past its outer reaches and dwarfing every pursuing ship nearby.

"The size is ridiculous," Eva observed, fascination overcoming her fear for just a moment.

"I would suggest it's the upper half of Narcis itself," Madden explained. "Lucifer takes his vanity very seriously; he remains apart from most others, hence the great lake."

"Not now, though. I have what he wants. What they all want."

"We go through the ash cloud. At least we will lose them for a moment."

Eva waited motionless as they approached, the twin columns of lighting-pierced ash rising far above them, flattening out where the limits of the prison prevented any escape. She could feel the hairs on her head start to rise every time a bolt of lightning jumped out from the nearest ash column. Beyond the columns lay white mist and a cloud bank.

"Whatever is beyond is hidden," Madden observed, echoing her thoughts.

"Did you need the sensors to gain understanding?" Luke Wolverton asked, "or did you like, use the force?"

Luke was just dismantling the stress of their plight. Madden guffawed at the comment. "Okay. I want you all to hold on," Madden cautioned them. "Make sure the door is sealed. We don't want any more accidents."

Eva found her place next to Rachelle once more, the familiarity of the space and company a comfort. This time, J.D. remained standing.

"I want to see what's coming," he said by way of explanation. Given the fate of so many of his squad, Eva could well understand why he might take such an approach.

. . .

They waited in silence for the unescapable. While the sky was dark because of where they were, the edges of the ash cloud wiped out any remaining light. In the darkness of the transport's interior, the only light was the red glow of the pilot's console.

"We have lost all signals now," Madden advised quietly. The transport wobbled in the cloud as they rode the thermals from the volcanic source beneath.

Eva shut her eyes and squeezed back into the bulkhead.

"What's it like, having a little voice in the corner of your mind?" Rachelle asked her, more Eva suspected to take her own mind off their peril than to actually understand.

"It's a comfort, for the most part. Knowing there is always somebody there, sharing your experiences, your feelings. There's a very special quality to Nina. She is an old soul in a young body. She looked out for me before I even knew I was pregnant. Now to have her nearby, well I would rather be stuck in Hell with my daughter than be kept apart from her. She's worried right now and eager to be back with me."

"Doesn't it just weird you out, though? Knowing your thoughts will never be your own?"

Eva shrugged. "What's really so unusual now? Maybe it won't continue once we get out. I just don't know."

"True. Things are never gonna be the same again if we get back from this."

"So you would think, Rachelle. But as far as humanity is concerned, the threat is neutralised. As long as we do something with this knife, they can never reach Earth. They don't need to know any more than they already do. If we get back, we should take the secret of true Hell to our graves..."

"I'm getting readings," Madden announced and everybody jumped up, the worry about the ash cloud forgotten.

"Where?"

"In front, behind, everywhere."

A burst of lightning revealed shapes quite close to them. Metallic, reflective objects looming within a stones' throw.

"Pull up!" Eva urged her husband.

His eyes wide as if he had had an epiphany, Madden glanced at her and did the precise opposite. "No. Dive down. They will be expecting to trap us up the top, so we fall down in the middle of their floating city. Hold on!"

Madden plunged the transport into a near-vertical swan dive, the ash thinning as they exited the column.

"Dear God," exclaimed Scope, who was the first to spot what was in front of them. Beyond his comment, there was stunned silence.

As far as the eye could see, armies of demons swarmed across the ground, moving in two directions. Below them, one army moved forward in the same direction as the little transport, their advanced elements already clashing with a different army moving from their right. Above, fleets of transports jockeyed for position; they had entered the middle of a colossal battle, but one clear fact overrode all else.

"They aren't waiting for us," Eva said, confused. "They are moving against each other!"

This other army drew everybody's attention. As they fought, huge ice bombs began to rain down from the transports on the right, freezing the first army, decimating their ranks.

"Well, we know where Belphegor's demons went," Gila said. "Whose are these?"

"Could be Abaddon," Madden mused. "The honest truth is it doesn't matter. They are already engaged and if Belphegor's army is moving this way then they intend to take Tartarus. They don't know about the Gate of Hell."

Madden piloted their transport beneath the underbelly of a massive freighter, staying as close to the larger ship as possible. As they emerged on the far side, the tide of battle suddenly changed, the ice-bearing ships making a beeline directly for her, Eva felt.

"They know about us, now! Madden, do something."

Madden turned, helpless to react. They were about to be crushed between the two fleets, neither apparently caring for the welfare of their passengers as long as in the destruction, the Well of Souls was captured.

Then from behind them, Lucifer's floating fortress appeared, alongside the rest of the pursuing craft, plunging into the melee. Madden threw the ship into a downward spiral in an effort to avoid the crash. Everybody inside was thrown to the right as the transport lost its balance. Madden remained the only person upright, hanging on with grim tenacity, fighting to regain control of the transport.

The transport continued to plummet, but gradually Madden managed to steady the ship. Leveling out just above the fighting demons, Eva watched, fascinated and horrified at the same time, as one set of demons— with tentacles and glassy blue visages, fought the breed of demon she was more familiar with— all claws and teeth. However, when the combatants saw the transport flying so low, they forgot their quarrels and jumped after them.

Above, the Leviathans in the sky began to crumble as they collided, debris falling much as the Gates of Hell had. Those avoiding the crash took aim and resumed the hunt.

"Those demons," Gila said, her voice quiet and clearly shocked. "They were like Exerrocks. Completely turned."

"Now we know what she was doing and why there were no demons other than the Guardians in Forente-Lautus," Eva responded."

"We also know why the ice is still in abundance," Madden added, inspecting the monitor. "It's growing. The ice is within touching distance of Tartarus. Closing the portal to Earth hasn't prevented anything. If Tartarus is unlocked, chances are they can just force their way through. They still mean to bring the three domains into line. We have to get to Nina now. We have to put an end to this."

There was an edge to her husband's tone. He didn't mean *rescue* but *get to*. It was too much to hope they would all get through this and somehow live.

The race was on. The map on the screen moved perilously slow no matter how fast they went. At this low level, the demons jumping for them were no more than a blur, a mere impression of movement, and their reactions far too slow and basic.

As the mountain ridge supporting Tartarus came into view, a shockwave knocked Eva off her feet.

"It's the ships behind us," Gila shrieked. "They are firing on us."

"They don't want us reaching Tartarus intact," Madden called back. "Dammit, I'd hoped they would all get caught up in the fight."

"They are, Madden. They are bringing the fight with them."

Eva looked back. The ships were all there, assaulting each other as much as they were firing on the small transport. Occasionally, one would drop out of the race, the damage sustained too great. All the while, beneath them, the masses fought or tried to pursue them.

"Why are we so low?" Eva asked. "We risk one of those demons getting lucky and hitting us."

An ice bomb exploded off the starboard wing, coating it in a frozen sheen. The transport began to veer off course. With the weight, they began to sink toward the enemy below.

"What do we do?" Eva appealed.

"Nothing. They got in a lucky shot, but we're nearly there. Look below."

Eva peered down; the fighting had ended. The ground was clear.

"No demons."

"Right. They were firing on us out of desperation. There's a good reason for them wanting us down now. Look ahead."

The ground rose toward them, their peril increasing. Ahead of them, the mountain range divided, a cut appearing in the middle. In the center of the cut, there was a building. Not a complex city full of technology or spectacular beauty, but a simple temple structure. Four enormous pillars rose around the temple, the top of each emitting a glow drawn into a dazzling beacon of light directly above a central convergence. Above, ice arched down from behind the building, an enormous wave of it, ending in a point just above the light.

"We've seen something like the ice before. On Gehenna."

Eva recalled the nightmarish visions. The sheet of ice had appeared from nowhere, reaching toward the portal.

"If only we had those horsemen to drive it off as they did before."

"What do you think the demons are so afraid of down here? Those horsemen were the Guardians of Tartarus, forced into a different shape by Leviathan. Once the portal failed, they were released to their true form. Only a madman would try flying in here now."

"Then why are we..." Eva stopped, staring, with a slight whimper.

Around Tartarus, three forms arose. Snakelike, impossibly thick with muscle, they dwarfed the temple. A ridge of spines rose along the back of each and writhing about each other, the sightless demons turned to face the approaching fleet. Gargantuan mouths opened, revealing glowing depths, as if the creatures were themselves made from the volcanic pits of agony for which Tartarus itself had become legend.

"The blind Guardians of Tartarus," Madden provided. "You don't need sight to see."

The three Guardians plunged into the rock of the mountainside with ease, sending showers of stone up into the sky. Moments later, one of the Guardians appeared behind them, erupting from the ground and striking the largest of the ships.

"They won't suffer any assault on Tartarus. They repel it with vigor."

"Let's hope we are small enough to fall off their radar," Eva responded. "Does this say how Satan was defeated if he had these to protect him?"

"Subterfuge. Abaddon did not meet with him with the intention of a fight. Yet he came out as ruler of Tartarus. The problem was..."

"Look out!" John Wolverton shouted.

Madden twisted away from her and Eva followed his glance. In front of them rose the immense trunk of one of the Guardians, reaching over them to snap at a pursuing ship. They had not been seen, but they were not the target. The Guardian bit the leading ship in two, causing it to explode.

Madden tried to veer their transport out of the way, but with the ice on the wing, his efforts were useless. The transport clipped the wormlike body of the Guardian, sending them spinning out of control into the mountainside. Eva slammed into Madden as the transport crashed upside down. The windows shattered as a shard of black volcanic rock penetrated the transport, impaling it. They were almost within touching distance of Nina. Eva protected her head with her arms. This couldn't end now. Not when they were so close.

CHAPTER THIRTY-SEVEN

Eva stirred. She had landed on something soft, and was thankful for the cushioning. The cabin of the transport stank of fear-induced sweat. She wasn't able to see anything in the near darkness.

The soft surface underneath her began to wriggle, and a strangled moan came from her right. Climbing off was an effort, her senses thrown off by the sudden change in angle. The ship must have been upside down; Eva didn't remember so many slopes inside.

"Next time we crash, you can be underneath," Madden groaned.

"Are you all right?"

"Nothing a good shot of tequila wouldn't fix. What about you?"

"Fine. We need to get out of here; they are coming. If any demons make it past the Guardians and we aren't out of this wreck, we are done for."

A light shone from the rear of the transport, nearly blinding her. She raised her hand to cover her eyes, squinting. "You want to point your torch someplace else?"

"Good," John Wolverton said, satisfied. "All accounted for. How you ended up in the front and the rest of us back here is a mystery."

Eva climbed through to the back, the light revealing they were indeed upside down. "Is everybody all right?"

"A bit cut up, but we will live."

"Take what you can. We won't be coming back here."

Eva retrieved her helmet, which was definitely the worse for wear, and out of sheer defiance more than any real hope, jammed it on her head.

"Still with us then?" Swanson's voice came through the communicator.

Eva stopped in her tracks. "We closed the portal, Swanson. You shouldn't be here."

"You neutralized the biggest threat, Eva, and the whole world will never know it. They would thank you if they did. But the other portals are open and demons are pouring through. We focused on the Gobi Desert to our detriment. They are killing indiscriminately, and their victims are becoming demons as soon as the light fades from their eyes. There is no going to Hell. It is coming to us."

There were no words to describe the guilt Eva felt at choosing the wrong course of action. The horror unleashed on Earth had not been prevented.

"There was no way we could have known," Gila said sympathetically.

"The balance is too far shifted in their favor to matter now," Eva replied. "We saw evidence of it in Montego Bay and now we have proof here. We must get up there and find Nina."

"And do what?" Swanson asked. "Eva, if there is any action left, great. However, from our side, we are beaten. You should just hide and await the inevitable."

"No!" Eva screamed. "We haven't come all this way for nothing. Keep fighting, Swanson. One way or another, everything ends."

The smashed side-window proved a useful point of exit and within a few moments, the remaining ten stood outside of the ruined transport. The mountainside was stark and treacherous, black shale threatening to fall away with every step. They had landed on a steep slope, the rock ledge keeping the transport from sliding down to oblivion.

"Up there," Scope pointed. "The slope flattens out. We should be able to make it along the ridge to the city."

"And then what?" Rachelle asked as they began to stumble up the slope.

"We find Nina and the Scroll of Judgment," said Madden, "and we destroy them."

Eva stopped. "We destroy it. Not them."

Madden said nothing, climbing the slope.

Eva climbed after him, confused and hurt by his lack of answer.

When they reached the plateau, Eva stopped Madden. "We destroy it?"

Madden took her by the shoulders, but Eva shrugged free and stepped back. "What do you think you are going to do here? What do you see happening?"

"Do you understand what not seeing this through to the bitter end could mean? Do you understand what it could do? To them? To us?"

Madden tried to take her by the shoulders once more, but Eva slapped his hands away and stomped off ahead of him.

From behind her, he said, "Would you really want to live in a world where you are a slave? One way or another, someone is conquering right now. I would rather kill us all than have you exist in a world where you aren't free."

His words were fatalistic. He must have come to some inner decision about this long ago.

"You are changed, Madden. Do you remember what it is to be human?"

"I lost the luxury of knowing long ago, love."

Her eyes brimming with tears of betrayal, Eva turned and resumed the march ahead. Madden was prepared to kill their daughter to end this. Humanity lost.

. . .

The sky above was black. It suited Eva's mood. Nina tried to console her from afar, and Eva tried her best not to let her daughter share her feelings. Through the ash and sky-borne volcanic debris, a white globe began to shine. Ahead of them, the ice above Tartarus seemed thicker, more robust

"It's nearly over," Gila observed.

"You figure?" Madden's every work broke Eva's heart. Just having him nearby was too much pain.

"This is Tartarus. Everything else has been true about what we have seen. Is this not the prison of the Titans? Under here should be Cronos, the one-eyed Cyclopes and the hundred-armed Hecatonchires, Typhon the hundred-headed father of Cerberus, the Sphinx and whatever others there are.

"It's a prison for gods. The two hundred fallen watchers. The nine circles of Hell. They are all metaphors for the protection around Tartarus and the protection is failing. Up there is the focal point of this entire realm. In every picture, in every depiction of the devil and the frozen core in Hell, it was always this. It's not the deepest point of Hell; it's the most central. Everything else has been put here to protect this, and Crustallos is driving them away from within its prison. How much power must you have when the prisoner behind bars drives the guards away and opens the doors?"

Eva climbed over the brow of the ridge, accepting J.D. Shelton's help. Around them, flames licked the sky, turning the underside of the ash cloud threatening to choke them a sooty red. Down below them a series of narrow stone bridges appeared to be the only way up to the temple. Around her, the air had grown hot, making it difficult to breathe. Eva put her hand out, resting on some rock only to pull her hand back with a curse.

"What is it?" Madden asked.

"Hot," Eva said, not prepared to waste more words than necessary on her murderous husband.

"Such devastation," he said in response. "We are at the seat of Hell, and it's a ruin."

"This must also have been part of the city," Gila answered.

Eva could not help herself; Nina pulled at her consciousness, now so close. Was everybody out to torture her? Yet, she looked.

Ruined walls and broken columns sprawled off into the distance, as if the entire city had been shaken at its foundations.

"What sort of being has the power to do this?" Forrest Kyle wondered aloud.

"One with no other need than an unending hunger and desire for release," Madden answered. Eva knew every traitorous word was meant for her.

"What do you think is coming through? Why do you think Crustallos is choosing this place for its attack? Crustallos is a titan. THE titan. The others imprisoned here? They are part of the lock. The energy from all of them is what keeps it shut. Why else have the most powerful entities trapped in this place?

"The power of human souls is part of the same lock. The price all men must pay is preserving the realms. Hell is a place of evil because of the impurities in the human race; man's nature is to sin. But there is more to hell than demons, the focus of which is Satan."

"What are you saying, Madden?" Gila asked, her voice worried.

"I think without Satan, this all fails. Satan was the key. Something has to restore the chains. Someone has to bind the ice."

Eva climbed down what was left of the destroyed path to the bridges below her, paying scant attention to the surroundings. She felt truly in Hell now. Not just in the physical sense, as insane a concept as it was, but in her mind too. There was little she could do to stop Madden if his honest intent was to end them all. Her feet skidded on loose stone underfoot, and she fell back, Madden catching her.

Not acknowledging him, she shrugged out of his arms and continued.

Above them, the sky brightened as ice expanded, threatening to dome over the entire range.

"Not long now," said Gila. "The domains are preparing to align. This is all coming to a head."

They rounded an outcrop, and Eva stopped. There was nothing between her and Nina but two slim stone bridges. The three Guardians writhed above the temple, veering away by reflex as they encountered the ice.

"I thought there were four Horsemen," Eva wondered aloud. "There are only three Guardians."

"In the ice," John Wolverton answered her. "Past the temple."

It was true. There was a fourth Guardian. It had become trapped in the growing sheet of ice and had perished.

"Crustallos has a mighty plaything," Gila observed. "The Guardians are reputed to be the offspring of Typhon himself."

"There's no time to stop and stare then," Madden decided. "We have to cross these bridges while they still stand and get into the temple." He took the lead and Eva followed close behind him. The pathways of Tartarus were wide enough only for two people to walk abreast, the bridges supported by chains on both sides. Eva felt extremely lightheaded as she crossed the first span. Far beneath them, the entire chasm was filled with fire. The lava in the pit beneath was making the very air burn. She tried to concentrate on staying in the middle of the bridge with the regrettable result of having to look at Madden's back.

Just for a moment, Eva considered pushing him. He had betrayed her with his intent and surely deserved such an end. Eva's hand actually began to rise in the initial stages of the act, when a feeling settled over her.

"Nina," Eva gasped.

Madden stopped and turned. "What is it?"

They were only midway across the first span of rock and dreadfully exposed.

Eva looked her husband in the eyes, terrified to admit what she knew to be true. "She... she agrees with you. God help me, Madden, you should burn for your intent, but our daughter is more of a hero than I could ever hope to be. She says, *One must perish, or all perish.* She says it is your decision alone. Whatever you choose will decide the fate of us all."

Madden's face hardened and above them, the three Guardians became aware of the intruders on the stone bridge. There was a calm feeling of acceptance from Nina.

"The choice has been made," Eva said, closing her eyes, knowing in her heart nothing would sway Madden from his dreadful choice to kill their daughter. "We have to..."

"No!" Madden shouted and turned, running for the other side. "Come on! Before they get here!"

Up above, the Guardians had been spurred into action and began to twist around each other as they navigated their way around the city and toward the bridges.

"Run!" John Wolverton shouted, his powerful voice causing Eva to comply without thinking.

As best as she could, Eva sprinted across the first span, the heat from below and the stink of sulfur making her lungs burn as she gasped for breath. She stopped on the rock pillar joining the two bridges. There was no sign of the Guardians, but from the vibrations underfoot, they were not far off. The pillar started to shake. Cracks began to appear.

"Run, Eva!" Madden shouted from midway down the next bridge.

"I can't," she gasped. "The vest is weakening. It's too much."

"No! Nina needs you! One last time you get to see her before the end! One last time we will be are a family!"

Please, came Nina's single word from the temple above, and without thinking, Eva staggered onto the second bridge.

Her pace held up those behind her, John and J.D. compensating by each taking an arm and dragging her along the remaining bridge.

They were two thirds of the way across when a rock-splitting roar blasted them from beneath.

Eva had the misfortune to stare down and catch a glimpse of the open mouth of the nearest Guardian as it twisted up to consume them. She willed it to take her, accepting the inevitable. The feeling lasted only a moment before the Shikari picked her and dragged the rest of the way.

The Guardian continued on its deadly assault, surging up to the bridge while another erupted from the rock face they had just started crossing. The two monsters slid past each other, scaled bodies destroying the walkway, dragging the chains with them.

Eva found herself thrown ahead by the two man-mountains supporting her, landing in the arms of her husband. Stunned, Eva remained there for a moment.

"Keep going," Madden urged, pushing her up and into the arms of Wolfgang and Forrest who continued this unusual relay. "Get away from the edge before they hit it again."

It was too late. Most had crossed, but Scope was still on the bridge. Eva watched events unfold, helpless as her failing body couldn't even match the healing properties of the armor she bore. Scope ran toward them, J.D. reaching out from the edge of safety, urging his fellow Shikari onward. She found herself dragged into a narrow corridor between high stonewalls. The bridge erupted upward as the third Guardian consumed it from beneath. In an instant, Scope was gone, but the Guardian was not done. Even while Eva was dragged away, every man and woman in the dwindling team trying to save themselves, J.D. remained where he was. The chains on the bridge had become entangled in the teeth of the enormous monster in front of them and had wrapped around the arm of her protector.

The Guardian turned its head, gazing down on him with sightless eyes, and then whipped the chain up in the air, blasting hellfire from its mouth and roasting the mortal body in the blink of an eye. The chains flailed as the Guardian arched its body, coming loose, and depositing the corpse of the fallen Shikari on the ground where he had so recently been standing. Its work done, the intruders on the bridge dealt with, the Guardian disappeared into the abyss.

Smoke curled up from the corpse into the sulfurous air. Nobody moved. When the vibrations had subsided, Rachelle Bishop crept from the security of their hiding place to examine the body. Kneeling down, she tried to turn the huge body of their fallen ally over. With a bit of brute force, she managed it and the body rolled, settling onto its back. J.D. was burned to a crisp, half of his face charred black. Eva bit back a sob, knowing it was not the Shikari way. The head turned and Eva's heart froze.

"Rachelle get back. Get back now."

J.D's eyes had opened and one was milky white. He watched her.

CHAPTER THIRTY-EIGHT

"Demon!" Wolfgang yelled, but it was too late. In the second it had taken his cry to be uttered, Shelton's remains thrust a hand up, puncturing Rachelle's torso with a fist. Bits of rib stuck out her back where her kit had been punched off by the force of the blow.

The demon peered round the body, wiggling its charred and bloody fingers as if examining its new found powers for the first time. Watching Eva, it cast the body aside, the lifeless body of her once-reluctant friend sliding across the rock plateau to fall into the abyss beyond. All remaining of her was a bloody smear on the ground.

"No!" Wolfgang bellowed, bringing his mini-gun to bear. The weapon spat a stream of bullets with such fury the demon should have been cut down in moments. However, this was a demon based on the dimensions of the immense J.D. Shelton, and as such, was nigh on impossible to floor. As the bullets tore into its torso, the wounds healed almost immediately. The demon looked down at its body, not even attempting to shield it from the bullets, smirking with contempt at the efforts to maim.

"It's Tartarus," Madden shouted when Wolfgang ceased firing.

"It draws the Source here. For all intents and purposes, it IS the Source. You are gonna have to tear Shelton to pieces."

The demon began to close on them.

Luke Wolverton pulled out a long metal weapon not unlike an extended crowbar, spinning it in one hand like a marching band spun batons. "Let's see what we can do with this." He nodded at his father and stepped forward into the circle of battle, ducking the demons' first effort to grab him. The demon Shelton was large, but had yet to comprehend and master the skills the body it now possessed was capable of.

Wolfgang elected to drop the mini-gun and circle the demon instead, a large curved knife in one hand. The demon was still focused on Luke and was easy meat for a few moments. Wolfgang jumped and hacked at the demon's thick neck.

The white-eyed monstrosity turned at the impact, grabbing the blade as it bit deep, pulling the dagger from its neck, a gush of black blood catching Wolfgang on the left arm, hissing as it corroded through the combat suit.

Wolfgang howled in pain as the fluid found his skin, but like the true Shikari he was, he clamped his mouth shut, and switched the blade to his other hand. Luke joined him and together they began to stalk their quarry.

The demon moved toward Luke and as it did so, Wolfgang lashed out with his knife, carving close to the bone as he aimed for the joint of the demon's left arm.

The demon howled in frustration and turned to face Wolfgang, at which point Luke danced in, swinging the bar. He had more success, connecting to the demon's right knee and shattering the bone.

The demon shrieked in pain, going down on one knee and rolling onto its back when the joint gave way with a crunch.

There was a splintering and bone stuck out below the knee joint of the demon. The resulting scream had ghostly echoes of a voice Eva remembered well: the voice of J.D. Shelton.

"It's him," she gasped. "He's still in there." Eva moved to approach the fallen demon.

Madden grabbed her as she took her first and very-nearly fatal step. "Eva, no!"

"But you heard him. He's caught. Trying to get out!"

"Eva it's not a hellbounce. You can't talk it down and get it under control. It's a fully formed demon. You go down there and it will kill you; you will probably end up exactly the same way and I don't want to lose you. You will not lose control. You will lose yourself, and then we will lose this fight."

The demon seemingly recognized the struggle on the periphery of its fight and began to croon to Eva, the voice of a whimpering Shelton. Eva felt the lure of his call and stepped back, understanding the danger.

"Now!" John yelled and his subordinates rushed the felled demon.

Injured, but not incapacitated, the demon reached out with both arms as its two assailants attempted to cripple it more, catching both of them by their weapon arms and bringing them around to collide. The force of the collision made Eva wince. Bones shattered as Luke and Wolfgang caused each other's instant death. The force was such Luke's face had caved in when the bodies were pried apart. The demon grinned at Eva, and she saw her own fate. Nina cried out in her mind.

Turning away, the demon Shelton threw the bodies off the side of the abyss, watching them fall.

A force rushed past Eva with such intensity she was sent sprawling. When she looked up, John Wolverton had the creature in a full Nelson, hands locked behind its head, the demon's arms flailing in the air. Such strength Eva had never seen in a mortal before. The demon thrashed with wild desperation, but John planted his feet, swinging from the waist. The demon screamed and John heaved his arms, fracturing bones. With an almighty roar, he threw the demon from the very spot his son had disappeared mere moments before.

Eva crept from their hiding place among the ruins. John stood on the edge, staring into the abyss.

"I'm sorry," she said.

"They knew the risks," he rumbled. "Luke being my son made no difference to his being in the Shikari, nor to the risks he took. He was a hell of a soldier. They all were."

John turned away from the cliff edge. Looking up at the path they had to climb, he moved past her. "I'll build a wall to them if we get out of here." He clapped Forrest Kyle on the shoulder, causing the heavy ordnance specialist to drop his teammates' mini-gun. "Whatever's up there, Forrest, I've got the feeling we aren't going to need all this weight. We certainly aren't going to take it with us when we go."

"Go where, sir? We are already in Hell. There's nowhere left to run."

Wolverton looked proud. "That's the spirit, lad."

"It's time to end this, however we can," Madden decided. "The ice is closing and if you haven't noticed, all this heat isn't leading to a drop of water. There's nobody left here to destroy it seems. Good thing too, we are running out of Shikari."

Madden's crude attempt at humor made Eva groan inside; the last thing a man who had just lost his son would want to hear would be morbid one-liners. Yet both John and Forrest broke out in grins.

"Remind me to have you inducted into the team when we find our way home. Your knack for not staying dead might be an asset."

Eva took a deep breath. The armor had done its work and her lungs were fine. "Let's finish this." *Nina, I'm coming to get you.*

The trek to the temple was steep, the carved rock path switching back on itself as they climbed.

The anticipation had been building for Eva since they finally turned in the direction of Tartarus, and now the tension was threatening to make her sick. Eva took deep breaths to steady her heart.

Nina was close, though a force was messing with the connection between them. It faded in and out, remaining full of love and trust.

At the top of the switchbacks, the core of Tartarus leveled out, the four massive stone pillars reaching hundreds of feet above them. The light curling through the air was weaker than when they had first seen the city from across the abyss. The ice-dagger reaching down from the sky was now piercing the light.

"This is almost over," said Gila. "If the light from Tartarus is the lock, then the ice is a crowbar with infinite possibility but only one goal. Crustallos is ready to ascend. We need to get to the structure directly underneath the light."

"I'll bet that's exactly where we find Nina," Madden replied, his tone neutral. He still had plans. In the back of her mind, so did Eva, and she bore the Well of Souls close to her heart. She prayed he wouldn't make such a choice she would have to use it on him.

Ahead of them, a wall prevented access to the core of the temple. It was about twenty feet in height, seemingly impenetrable, made of a dark grey, red striped rock.

"That's different to everything else we have seen," Eva noted.

"This is probably the oldest place in Hell, given the nature of the city," Gila responded. "We should go around until we find a way in."

"I don't know if we have time," Eva replied. "Something is happening in the middle of the temple, and Nina is involved. I don't think we can afford to go exploring."

"You got any explosives left in your kit?" Madden asked Forrest.

"I have one more rocket left," the Shikari offered.

"Lovely,"

This panicked Eva. "No. Wait. What if we hit an object and hurt Nina?"

"We don't have time to waste, love," Madden replied. He pointed aloft. "We need to snatch our baby girl away from eternal damnation, and we need to do it now."

Eva leaned back on a nearby wall. As she did so, the wall started to crumble away from her. She turned, alarmed, and examined the rock. Poking at it with one finger, the mortar disintegrated, even the very bricks turning to dust.

"This place," she murmured. "It's ready to fall apart. John!"

Wolverton turned from his contemplation of the barrier in front of them to look at her. Eva poked at the wall, watching it crumble. He came over, prodding at the damage she had done with the butt of his shotgun. The side of the building gave way, and Eva jumped back.

"This lock isn't just ready to crumble," he said. "The very fabric of Hell is crumbling and we are at the weakest point."

"A rocket is going to incinerate everything here," warned Eva. "We might never find my daughter."

Wolverton considered this for a second. "Forrest, give me your pack."

"Anything in particular?"

"No, the entire pack. You have your rifle. You need nothing more."

A quizzical expression on his face, Forrest detached his backpack and handed it to his commander.

Wolverton balanced it in both hands, measuring the weight. The grabbing the pack by the straps he spun a few times as if throwing a hammer, letting go of and sending it sailing toward the wall.

The pack hit the wall about ten feet up, disappearing right through the middle. The resulting hole quickly filled with crumbling rock, the damage causing a domino-like effect on the side of the wall nearest them.

Watching it was mesmerizing. As the wall crumbled, a cloud of dust built up and Madden had to pull Eva out of its path.

"Will the hole be enough?"

Madden looked determined. "We will have to hope it is. The ice is accelerating. We don't have long.

The dust cloud rolled past, disappearing off the edge of the cliff, and settling on the switchbacks they had previously climbed. Madden didn't wait for everything to calm; as soon as they could make out the greater structures around them, he was off.

Eva stuck close to her husband, ready to ward against him as much as she was to aid him. They reached the wall, finding it now a pile of rubble about four or five feet high. Madden began to stumble over the ruined brickwork. Eva followed his steps.

He reached the middle of the wall, the structure still standing thirty feet away on either side. Behind her, Eva heard Gila and the Shikari follow. She corrected herself. John and Forrest. There was no need for such formalities any more.

"There's something in there," Madden said. "A building of some sort."

"Go," Eva urged them. The sensation of her daughter was stronger than it ever had been. "She's in there."

Madden climbed down the rubble, Eva sliding after him. When finally she was free of underfoot encumbrance, she hurried to catch her husband.

"Well, blow me," he said, and Eva smiled at seeing what faced them.

"A church?" John climbed down the rubble and came to stand beside them. "Who would have thought it?"

The church stood right in the center of Tartarus, directly under the nexus of light and ice above, now shaped like a wasp's sting and seemingly lowering toward them as Eva watched on. There was a pressure being exerted from above. She felt the weight of the ice above her. More profoundly, she felt the weight of humanity, of what had been and what could possibly be if she failed here.

The church itself was a fairly simple affair. Eva took the time to enjoy the simplicity of the gothic structure as they neared the building. The roof was gabled, three pointed arches moving from end to end where a tower rose with four points at its tip.

"What's it doing here?" Forrest asked, staring up at one of the stained-glass windows.

"Maybe it's always been here," Gila answered him. "Maybe it was constructed entirely so we would have a place to stand or so Nina had a roof over her head."

In the distance, the three Guardians waited, immobile, expectant, gazing sightless at the center of Tartarus.

"They know something, too," Madden observed.

"Or they just wait for destiny," retorted Eva, her excitement reaching fever pitch.

John turned to her. "It's your daughter in there, Director. How do you want to play this?"

"No weapons," she cautioned.

Wolverton opened his mouth to protest, but Eva forestalled him. "If the walls of this building are crumbling like the rest of Tartarus, I want my daughter safe before you start fighting. Swanson, can you hear me?"

There was a crackling noise on the other end of the comm-link, perhaps a little more than static, perhaps not.

Gila shrugged at her. "Looks like we really are on our own."

"Then it's been my pleasure," Eva said, fixing her gaze on each of them. "You have done more than anybody should be prepared to ask of you, and the world will probably never know of the sacrifice made. Yet, should we make it back, Earth will be a different place. Larger for what they have seen and the knowledge there is an existence after death. Smaller for the immediacy of Hell and proof something worse lingers beyond. If any of you make it back, remember what we have seen. Strive to make it better. Make an effort to encourage them to remember what it is to be human."

Eva turned to face the wooden door of the church, so out of place in these dark caverns of stone.

"There's only one thing left for me to do."

She reached out and gripped the cool iron handle.

CHAPTER THIRTY-NINE

Eva stepped through the archway into the Church of Hell, as she had dubbed it and stopped, stunned. There was nothing out of place. The walls were grey, made of limestone and carved with exquisite detail, frescos and bas-reliefs of angels and pious worshippers from end to end. Arches guided the way to the nave, the pillars nothing less than stunning. The inside of the vaulted gabled roof was darkest oak, the patterns mesmerising. The aisles held heavy wooden pews of the same material and where those ran out, wooden seats. Church candles were placed about the altar, fresh-cut flowers twined about the columns supporting them. Red carpet became blue as the aisles changed. Even the smell was musty and old, as if this church had been transported directly from some small village.

"Wow," Madden said in admiration. "They spared no expense here. Even the stained-glass windows look real."

The windows were multi-colored and filled with pictures. Only when Eva got close to one, she found the content was not of angels and prophets but of dark creatures, sacrifices, and blood. Rivers of blood. To her right, on a raised dais, a scroll waited. Six seals had been opened, leaving only one intact. This was a place of worship but not aimed toward Heaven.

"The Scroll of Judgment," she said. Her grip on the Well of Souls tightened. "We are in the right place."

Mother, a voice called in her head and Eva looked about, seeing nothing.

"Nina, where are you?"

Eva turned to cross the aisles toward a sealed-off area containing an organ when Forrest stopped, pointing toward the rear of the church.

"There. I saw something move in the shadows. Careful. It could be a trap."

Eva ignored the warning, running down the central aisle and dodging around a thick granite column. Behind, there was a smaller archway leading into the tower. Thick red cords hung down where one would presumably ring bells but they were of no interest to Eva. On the cold stone floor, at the bottom of the tower, in near-darkness a form lay, naked and wriggling.

"Nina!" Eva threw herself forward, skidding to a stop on her knees and picking her baby daughter up in arms hungry for the feel of her child for far too long. Madden was close behind her and they both wept for joy at the sight of their little girl, safe again for the moment with her parents.

I knew you would come, the tiny voice spoke inside her mind as the knowing eyes Eva had missed beyond the point of heartbreak gazed upon her.

Madden gasped. "Did you hear her?"

Eva smiled, stroking the tiny face and cooing at her. "It is how she communicates. Madden, your daughter is as much a gift as she is gifted." To Nina, she said, "I'll never let you go again."

Gila passed a blanket forward, tears glistening on her cheeks, and Eva quickly wrapped her daughter. John and Forrest came forward to check on the target of their mission.

"She looks a strong one," John complimented Eva. "She must get her strength from her mother."

Eva smiled, radiant once more and winked at Madden who responded with a mock-scowl.

Nina exuded a feeling of comfort and satisfaction as she rested in the crook of her mother's arm and Eva reveled in it. The feeling was short-lived however, as Nina's eyes widened, and she whimpered.

Beware!

"We aren't alone in here," Eva relayed her daughter's warning.

John and Forrest brought their weapons to bear, turning to face the doorway of the main church. Outside, white and red lights gave the stained glass a grisly glow. As Eva watched, the pictures came to life, the scenes full of beheadings and blood stained altars. Blood ran from the scenes down the walls and out onto the floor of the church. The demons in the glass danced with glee, laughing at them, mocking them. Above, the roof began to turn white with frost and a spike of solid ice sundered the central gable, fracturing the vaulting, and sending a waterfall of oak splinters to the floor of the church.

"Enjoy your reunion while you can," croaked a crystalline voice, "for it shall be brief enough."

From behind the organ on the left of the church, limped the mangled form of Exerrocks, the crystalline form of Belphegor. Undefeated, the body was nonetheless heavily damaged. Her torso was rent nearly in two, a huge gash right through her stomach and more across her shoulders. One leg was twisted and an arm hung useless, but her eyes terrified Eva most. They burned with a hatred for Eva beyond description.

With one hand, Exerrocks dragged the lifeless body of Porter Rockwell, blood welling from dozens of lacerations. She waved her hand about, spraying more blood through the air. "Do you like what I did with the place? I took the memories from this mortal's brain, as I ripped it from his head."

Eva couldn't help but look down. It was true. Exerrocks wasn't just dragging Porter by his head. She was using the hole in his skull to drag the body with her.

"Your tame angel was not good enough." The acid tone with which Exerrocks spoke threatened to render Eva senseless. Until Nina sent a thought to her. *Listen to my voice. She is still being manipulated. Mother. There is always a choice, even here.*

"He never ended me, not with all his Holy might, all his devout righteousness. Still, I am here. My God is stronger than yours is. The time is upon us. In this anointed place, at this appointed time, finally the true God will arise."

"Believe what you will?" Eva shifted the weight of her daughter to her other arm. She'd missed Nina but had never had the chance to get used to the continual weight of a small and constant weight. "Did you learn nothing during your exile on Earth?"

An ice smile formed on the damaged face of the crystalline-demon. "Mankind feeds demonkind and in turn the demons nourish me, His herald. When Crustallos has His victory, all will be His."

"I guess just because you are supernatural, it doesn't make you any smarter. It is self-annihilation bred by attempts at survival."

"No, it is more. We are beings from a higher plane. Banished to an eternity of darkness by those you pretend to worship in your pitiful ignorance. By creating this domain, your God was always doomed to destruction. It is in your nature to destroy, mortal or otherwise." Exerrocks dropped the body of Porter Rockwell like a dirty rag and held his ruined arms aloft. "Even those you place above all others are not without the urge. You are equally culpable. There will be no willing sacrifice to ensure your existence this time. We are chaos. We are beyond Hell."

Eva suspected Belphegor, in her state, would not be alone, and then a shadowed figure moved to her side.

Right then however, Madden distracted Eva. He turned to her, keeping his back between Eva and their opponent.

"That's it!"

"That's what?"

Madden took her hand, rolling back the combat suit until the twin scars on her arm were revealed. He squeezed it tight.

"When I ask you to do something, no matter how insane, will you do it? Will you do it for me, Eva Scott, my wife?"

His face was as serious as she had ever seen it. This was not a request he was making lightly. He squeezed her arm again, right over Iuvart's scar.

"Ow! Yes Madden, anything."

"Do you love me?" he whispered.

"Yes, you know I do."

"Say it. Eva, this is important. Never forget how important it is for you to tell someone you love them without prompting."

Eva smiled; what had gotten in to him? "Madden, I love you. We are in the deepest pit of Hell, in a place crazier than any we have ever been, and I love you."

Madden took her head in his hands, his big strong hands, pulled her to him, and kissed her. The feeling was electric but why did it feel like there was regret coming from his side of the kiss?

"Remember. Whatever you see, it's me. I'm a hellbounce. The only hellbounce left and I am completely in control."

Madden kissed Nina gently on the brow. "I do, daughter. I understand. I love you, too."

He winked at her and stepped forward.

Belphegor, distracted from her companion, hissed at him as he moved directly under the slowly descending ice. "You are an interference, demon. Nothing more. It is time you met my Master."

"What's he doing? John growled, hulking his shoulders and preparing to join Madden.

"No. Stop. He asked us to trust him."

Madden shed the top half of his combat suit, flinging it to one side where it hung on one of the candles. Clad only in his black combat boots and trousers, he flexed his muscles, his already-massive shoulders growing larger. His hair hung down his back, caught in the sweat glistening on his skin. "We shall see, herald. I am the interference who will end what Metatron started."

"I think not," contradicted Exerrocks. "I have someone who would like to test your statement. Come forth..."

The shadowed figure pushed past Exerrocks, throwing back its cloak. Eyes burning with a luminous fire glared out from under the heavy brow of a skull with no humanity in it whatsoever. The mouth split open and the same light shone out. The top of its head ended in two thick horns swept back behind. It shed the cloak entirely.

"He doesn't stand a chance," Forrest said, his voice betraying his fear.

Eva found it hard to disagree. The demon appeared to end in spikes wherever there was a surface. It had a narrow waist and massive shoulders, legs ending in cloven hoofs. The demon oozed malevolence. A tail swished behind, covered in more spikes. All told, it stood a good two feet above Madden. The demon let out a roar causing the windows to shatter, glass spraying all over them. Eva covered Nina with her own body.

"I should have ended you at Nag Hamaddi," the demon rumbled. It reached behind Exerrocks, pulling a shining trident from the shadows. "No matter."

"Sarch," Madden said, his voice neutral. Eva could detect no fear in his voice.

"Rosier! King of Hell! Overlord of the demon hordes and the TRUE heir to Tartarus!"

Rosier bellowed once more and came charging toward Madden, crushing the heavy wooden pews as if they were kindling. Gripping the trident mid-way down its shaft, Rosier threw a punch with the weapon.

"Madden!" Eva screamed, but her husband stood his ground, bringing his own arm up to meet his opponent. Rosier's giant fist should have crushed him, instead the two fists met as equals. Madden's arm had changed, the skin becoming blood red, morphing from the man she had married to the monster that had always remained hidden. The skin changed all over his body, rippling as though a million dominos had been set off at once. In moments, his skin gained spikes of its own, the hair turning black, and ears pointed. Madden glanced back at her as he fended off the assault of his larger opponent. His eyes were black-rimmed yellow and his teeth were now fangs, black as ancient ebony.

"Get back," he said in a deep voice no longer his own and grabbed his opponent's arm, bringing Rosier around and sending him colliding into Exerrocks. The pair of them crashed through the wall of the church, rock flying everywhere. Cracks ran from the hole in the roof where the ice had pierced through.

"This whole building is destabilizing," John warned her. "We have to get out of here. You are no use to him dead!"

Unable to speak for the fear consuming her, Eva merely nodded, allowing them to escort her back through the arched entrance. When they got outside, Eva paused. The temple of Tartarus had disappeared. They were on a plateau, beyond them infinite space in which floated rocks resembled a belt of meteors. Giant planets converged on them, one icy and white. From it, a column of incandescence twisted through space, linking it to the ground where they stood, like an umbilical cord. The universe unfolded about them. Infinite and hungry but not from this universe. This was the realm beyond, waiting to become one with Hell.

"Where are we?"

Gila looked about them. "This could be the true lock. What if the church, in fact the whole of Tartarus, was just a metaphor? The portals are aligning. If this is the prison containing Crustallos, and he is close to breaking free, it stands to reason we might see this."

Ahead of them, the church, its roof impaled by the ice, began to break apart. Parts of the wall rose above, sucked into a glowing maw consuming every object it touched. Behind, a dark planet blocked out further light in an eclipse, throwing shadows over them.

The ice spike proved to be the tip of the connection from the other planet and it began to lower toward the church floor as the building dismantled. Soon, the only structure left was the altar on which rested the Scroll of Judgment.

Madden continued his fight with Rosier, and despite being much smaller, it seemed to Eva they were evenly matched. Exerrocks watched from near the ice and Eva looked around them. There was a pattern on the rock.

"This is the lock," she said, realizing what she was seeing. "The same pattern from the wall in Iuvart's crypt. I saw this when I was in there." She looked up. The tip of the ice couldn't have been more than ten feet from the pattern.

"We need to stop it," she decided.

Mother. Cut your arm with the blade, and then cut mine.

"Cut my arm?" Eva said aloud, confusing those around her.

Nina gazed at her, calm, unafraid. *He needs our blood. Yours, mine...his on the blade. Cut our arms with the blade and throw it at him.*

"He was right. That does sound crazy. Gila, would you hold my daughter please? Don't panic at anything I might do."

Her three remaining companions stared at her as if she was a madwoman, but Gila took Nina without comment.

Across the empty stone plateau, Madden wrested the trident from Rosier, throwing it into the air where it was sucked into the maw. Beyond, in the darkness, Eva sensed an eye watching her, expectant, malevolent. Crustallos saw her. Tendrils began to writhe up from the dark planet beyond. Crustallos was at the breach.

Madden grabbed Rosier by an oversized arm and turned, throwing him over his shoulder where he skidded to the very edge of the rock. Almost.

Regaining his footing, Rosier roared in anger at the smaller opponent and began to swell in size. Five, ten, twenty times the size of Madden; Rosier very quickly dwarfed him.

"Now to end you all."

Madden held out his hand in appeal. "Eva, now!"

Eva stared in utter helplessness at Madden's demon form for a moment before holding her arm up and slashing it with the Well of Souls. Right across Iuvart's six-pointed star. She screamed at the pain.

Of her own accord, Nina held her tiny arm aloft, reaching out of the bundled blanket. With care, Eva ran the blade along her forearm. The blood mingled and the blade began to glow.

Exerrocks had been watching them, but only now perceived a threat.

"No," she hissed. "You cannot."

"Eva, throw it!" Madden pleaded, while above the giant Rosier raised a gargantuan fist, ready to crush him out of existence.

Eva reached back and hurled the blade end over end at her husband, her lover, her soul mate. Exerrocks launched her one remaining tentacle at the blade, but as they made contact, the Well of Souls sheared right through it and into Madden's open palm.

Madden's hand pressed shut, his own demonic blood mingling with the essence of his wife and daughter.

"No!" Exerrocks screamed in crystalline panic.

Madden held his hand out at arms' length, watching the blood well in the cut, glowing red and deepest black. Looking right at her, he mouthed the words *I love you* and blood dripped from the open wound onto the Scroll of Judgment.

The seventh seal popped open.

CHAPTER FORTY

There was calm. Complete and utter silence descended about them. One by one, all of the lights from the alien universe winked out, leaving them in darkness on the plateau.

Eva reached for her daughter, gripping her tiny hand in her own. If this was the end, at least the people she cared for most were nearby. If only she could hold Madden, the end would be worth it. But there was no way of seeing him. Darkness had never been so complete.

After quite some time, the light returned. They were no longer facing infinity but were back on the ground in the middle of Tartarus. As if controlled by a greater being, the sound returned, a wail growing louder and louder. It was Exerrocks, except it was no longer the broken monster. The crystal being had disappeared, replaced by a blonde woman whose face was a mask of utter anguish.

Madden remained on the altar, one knee on the ground, the Scroll of Judgment unrolled and trailing from his right hand. Rosier still towered above him, and released from whatever mystical force had held them all in place, bellowed, and launched his fist down at the tiny being below him. The force of the blow was full of menace, full of fury, and guaranteed to crush him to a pulp. Yet as Rosier's fist struck home, Madden raised his left hand above his head to ward off the blow. The fist struck a golden shield of pure energy, lightning crackling from the force of the deflection.

A golden sphere of light about him, Madden stood. His eyes glowed the same bright color as the shield, and he wore his human form once again. The same golden glow came from his wounded hand, as it did from several other cuts on his body. His skin seemed scarcely enough to contain him. He was a being of pure light. He was stunning. Absolutely beautiful.

Rosier moved to strike again.

"Stop." The word was simple, spoken in a quiet tone of authority, yet his one word stunned Rosier to motionless silence. Eva was sure the word had been heard throughout all of Hell and probably all across Earth. Maybe it even made it to Heaven.

"I am the lamb; I have broken the seventh seal. I am the sacrifice you hoped for, the being you feared."

He walked over to Belphegor, regarding her with caring, regretful eyes. "Belphegor, my sister. For the kinship we once bore, the same kinship you ripped asunder when you misled your brother into rending my former body, I regret what I must now do. This was never the master plan. It cannot be allowed. I willingly place myself between you and this domain. Crustallos will not pass to this realm much as our kind will no longer walk amongst the mortals. You made the wrong choice and will spend eternity explaining why. I am Satan, Guardian of Tartarus. I am Madden Scott, resurrected angel, demon knight. This is my domain, and thou art banished."

Belphegor dropped to her knees; tears streaming down her face. "Master," she pleaded. "Have mercy, I beg of thee."

Madden stepped back. Belphegor attempted to stand but the same golden glow shielding him now kept her clamped to the ground. A crack opened up, full of blackness. It rent the rock apart until Belphegor hung suspended over the infinite nothingness.

Eva peered in. It seemed to go on forever, but at the bottom, a great eye stared unblinking at them. A malevolent eye, hungering for what it could not touch.

"Go to him, my sister. May you find him more benevolent in nature than the children of man found you."

As if the floor had become quicksand, Belphegor began to drift lower, her face a mask of terror. Madden waved a dismissive hand at the ice and the point halted its advance. In chunks, it broke apart. Deafening cracks rent the spike into several long masses, all of which fell past the slowly descending Belphegor. Everything hit the eye in time. A roar of pain echoed up the crack in the ground.

Madden approached Eva then, the majesty of his bearing threatening to overwhelm her. Standing in front of her, he radiated power. He was the demon. He was the Lord of this domain, a being without equal.

He tilted her chin up, pleading with her to behold him.

Eva was frightened but allowed herself a glance. He was the same. Her husband once more. His eyes were golden now instead of brown, but there was no more demon about Madden Scott. He took their daughter and stroked her face, passing Nina to Gila. Madden turned back to his wife. He kissed her gently and the force of the touch made Eva's legs give way. He clamped his arm about her waist; Eva never wanted to let him go again.

"I think we can close the lock off now," he said, his voice richer than before. Madden waved one hand at the crack, which began to repair itself.

As the rock healed, Eva looked sidelong at the being her husband had become. She realized he had let his guard slip when all she saw was a being of energy, white and pure. Around them, Tartarus was a similar mix of energies. This platform upon which they now stood was just for their benefit.

"How long will she fall?" Eva asked.

"An eternity. Long enough to be very, very certain she is the only meal the dark one will taste for the foreseeable future. Just before the end, as Crustallos reaches out to claim her, I will summon her back here.

Eva opened her mouth to voice outrage, but Madden held up a finger. "She is a leader, and I need her."

"You know," Gila said in as neutral a tone as she could manage, "you are in fact the dark one now, especially with your latest decision."

Madden laughed. "My choice is a matter of perspective. Please bear with me. My immediate tasks are not yet finished."

Madden waved his hand, a vision of unending demons milling around on earth appearing before them.

"Come home," he said, gentle but commanding. "You aren't meant to be there. Our time on Earth ended long ago."

About a third turned back, hearkening to his call, but it appeared the majority of Lucifer and Leviathan's army pressed on. They clearly didn't believe the voice they were hearing.

"So be it," Madden decided. "Lucifer, Leviathan. My brothers, remember my sin."

Madden raised his hand, a golden glow enveloping it. One by one, the demons began to incinerate, lighting up the darkness in their incandescence.

Madden turned his gaze upon Rosier next. The giant demon stood above them, head hung low. Madden nodded and the demon began to shrink, becoming more human as it did so. By the time he was normal once more, he had regained the face of Ivor Sarch, the traitorous administrator.

"If justice were equal, you would have gone through the breach with your mistress," Madden warned, his voice stern but gentle.

Rosier dropped to his knees. "Master," he begged," show mercy. I sought to increase my station. I was not duped. There was no... you were gone. We were dying."

"That you would take responsibility for your actions is the one reason you remain, Rosier. I would make use of you. Aquinas needs a new Prince. Lust needs a new Lord."

Disbelief mingled with excitement on Rosier's face. "You would grant me clemency? Advance me"

Madden placed his hand on Rosier's shoulder. "You have seen the consequences of your actions. There is no end beyond this realm, just a hunger we must prevent escaping ever again. Do you understand? We are servants, not masters."

Rosier stood and glanced at Eva and her companions. "What about them? They do not belong here."

"They will soon depart. Return to your great city of Aquinas." Madden spoke aloud to his realm. "All of you return to your cities. We have a purpose. I would see it fulfilled."

Rosier shimmered and disappeared, leaving Eva, Gila and the two Shikari with Madden.

Next, the King of Hell turned to Gila, still holding Nina.

"May I hold my daughter?"

Gila passed the bundle containing the daughter of the new Satan to him without comment.

He took Nina and folded back the edge of the blanket so he could see her face. "Thank you, my child. Such a noble act for one so young."

"You are welcome, Father," a voice said aloud, though Nina's mouth did not move.

This spurred Gila to clear her throat. "Madden... Satan...My Lord? I have questions. So many questions."

"You may have them, but the answers are mysteries for a reason and should remain unanswered. Already, you have seen what no mortal is prepared to behold. Our true nature and purpose. Yes, Director, even Hell has purpose. It is your decision to reveal what you will. I will answer your earlier question: the world knows Satan, the Devil, and the Prince of Darkness. They shall continue to do so. Madden Scott will fade with time.

"As for the rest of what you have seen, there will be those worshipping you and those deriding you. Should you reveal the truth, they will not be prepared to hear it. Tell Swanson he has my thanks.

Do not disband Anges de la Résurrection des Chevaliers. They will be needed more than ever now. Belief has a funny way of warping the mortal mind."

Madden raised his hand to send her back to Earth and paused. "One more thing: marry your boyfriend. Ran Byron has waited long enough. Be well, Gila Ciranoush."

Madden's hand glowed again and Gila became transparent. In a moment, she was gone. Madden turned to the Shikari.

"I have a task for you, if you will undertake it?"

Wolverton appeared dubious. "I'm not sure where we stand on taking requests from the Devil, but go ahead."

Madden grinned. Whatever else he might be, he had retained his sense of humour. "Look after Eva. Watch over my girls. They are vital. More important than you could ever know."

Wolverton nodded. "I will make the task my life's work. Is there anything you can do for Luke, or the rest of my team? They died so you might become what you now are."

Madden smiled, genuine sympathy in his eyes. "I am sorry John. There are some laws even I cannot break. But suffice yourself with this. They won't be long in my realm. That much I can guarantee."

John nodded. "It was worth a try." He extended his hand. "It's been an honor to stand at your side."

Madden took the proffered hand with his free hand and gave it a firm shake. "Some heroes do walk in the light, though they seem shrouded in darkness. Forrest Kyle, John Wolverton, be well."

Though he still held the hand of the Shikari, Madden glowed once more, and the two warriors faded.

Madden now turned to his family, Nina in one hand and Eva in front of him. He passed their daughter to her.

Eva stroked the face of her baby, her clear eyes taking everything in.

Madden bowed forward and kissed her once more, leaning down to kiss his daughter's tiny cheek once they were finished. But for the momentous shift in the universe, they could have been a family.

"Imagine this," Eva said, lost in thought.

"What?"

"How am I going to explain to my mother I'm married to Satan?"

"You don't. You married Madden Scott, and he died saving you and Nina. It's true enough. Each event did happen."

Eva reached up to touch his face. The ever-present stubble was there and she stroked it, holding onto his chin. He looked no different from the day she had first met him, not a year ago in the bar in Worcester.

"I don't want to leave you again, Madden. Life be damned. I want to remain here with you."

Madden reached around her, squeezing tight, leaving just enough room for Nina.

"You will have your time, love. This is not the end of us, but you have to go back. You have to protect Nina and raise her. She is special in ways you do not yet understand. She is my only current link to the living world, the only child, despite popular belief, sired by a demon. In a manner of speaking, at least, she needs you. ARC needs you. The world needs you."

"You told John 'girls'."

Madden winked. "You picked up on that, eh?"

Eva put her hand down to her middle. A pulse, similar to Nina, but at the same time, markedly different warmed her mind. She looked at Madden quizzically. He just smiled.

"What about my needs?"

Madden cupped her chin. "You are stronger than any woman I've ever met, Eva. I knew it the night we met. Everything we've been through has prepared you for this moment. I'm always with you, Eva. I shall always be watching, forever rejoicing in every happiness you find."

Madden stroked Nina's head, his hand glowing gold once more, as he placed a benediction on his daughter. "I love you too, my little Nina," he said in response to the unspoken words flowing from their child.

He leaned forward, kissing her brow. "I love you, wife."

The air about her began to mist, Madden and everything around him fading.

"Madden, I love you... Madden, Madden!"

The mist cleared and Eva found herself standing on a beach, beautiful coral sand underfoot. Waves lapped with gentle rhythm at the edge of the sand, the sea farther out as calm as ever Eva had seen it. Behind her, the majesty of Rose Hall sat above the treeline. A few cars crept along the nearby highway, and off to the West, the sun hung sullen and red just above the horizon. It was warm, a beautiful evening. Eva sat on the sand, holding Nina in front of her, the two of them watching each other in silent communion.

After a while, Eva noticed she wasn't alone. Off to her right, a couple walked along the beach, headed straight for her at a leisurely pace. Eva waited for them to reach her.

"I checked under the museum," Gila said, as she reached Eva and her daughter. "The portal is gone. They are all gone."

A flash of regret, only momentary, saddened Eva. "Well, that's it then. How long since you got back?"

"A couple of weeks." Gila took Nina from her, desperate, by the look, on her face for a cuddle.

"Long enough for me to fly to Geneva and set a few things right," Swanson Guyomard continued for their colleague. "And then get back here to find you. We weren't leaving until you showed."

"How did you know where I was?"

"You bear a unique signature," Swanson advised her. "Since you entered Rose Hall on the night of lightning, three months have passed. We waited for the readings the Shikari instruments recorded to reappear. Since there is no demonic activity, no portals at all, it was just a matter of time."

Eva touched her chest. The regenerating armor was still there, though it had fallen silent, no longer attached to the Source.

"You won't be able to do anything with it," she warned.

"You let me be the judge. I hope you are considering Geneva as a place to live. You still have your position on the Council and we need to rebuild."

Eva looked out at the setting sun, the red ball on the horizon surrounded by a golden glow, a light shining from two eyes, with her forever. The bond of love was strong with her daughters, and because of them, her husband.

"One day, Swanson. I already have a job for the next twenty years. Then, I'll think about it."

EPILOGUE

"Mommy, look!"

The precocious and very excitable Nina Scott jumped up and down, pointing west along Ninety-Sixth Street, her brown curls flying in all directions. The Manhattan skyline was enormous. Eva couldn't get used to the sight, even though Worcester was not without its own set of tall buildings.

It was early July, around eight in the evening. Eva had promised her six-year-old daughter a trip to the Big Apple. Nina had been fascinated by the heavens from the moment she had first seen a book on the subject. So, when an article appeared on ABC news about the impending 'Manhattan-henge' it became the little girl's mission in life to bug her until she said yes.

As it was, the sun was setting, a huge ball of fire hanging midway down the Western end of the immense road. Nina stopped bouncing, mesmerized by the spectacle. Around them, onlookers were annoying the traffic and risking a ticket by stepping out in the road to take selfies with the sun behind them. Eva was content to watch.

A fussing came from her right hand; the small hand gripped securely in it belonged to a little girl with a riot of curly blonde hair.

"I'm bored," Samantha Scott said, a frown dominating her face.

The sun continued its journey down, gradually misaligning with the buildings. Streetlights began to glow. The red sky was a painful memory but a good one.

"We've seen enough," Eva decided. "Nina, come on, love."

A pout replaced the awe on Nina's face but she assented to her mother's wishes. Taking her other hand, Nina dragged at first, to catch the last flickers of the Henge.

They began to walk back to their hotel not two blocks away when Nina stopped suddenly. She turned to look at a huge mural on the side of a brickwork building.

Nina pointed and the silent words echoed in Eva's head. *Did they draw him?*

The mural read 'Satan Rules' with an enormous face spray-painted in great detail behind the words. The face was a depiction of a man. No horns, no wings and certainly no forked tail. The man had brown hair tied back in a ponytail, a bit of stubble on his chin and a wise, knowing look. It appeared as though he was watching them. The murals had been popping up everywhere in street art lately.

They did, Eva confirmed. *The pictures used to look like a horned monster, but I think he showed the artists the real truth.*

"Are you responsible for this mess?" asked a voice from behind them.

Eva turned to face their accuser. It was a little old lady with a furious face and an abashed-looking husband standing a few steps back.

"Really, influencing the young in such a way? Disgusting."

Eva glanced at Nina, who beamed back. So like her father. "It's hard to think you were ever this age, lady. In the end, we will all be one. You will meet him soon enough."

The old lady stared at their t-shirts and her eyes widened. "Disgusting," she said once more for good measure. "Come along, Christopher!"

The elderly couple tottered off, leaving the three of them alone with the mural.

"Mommy, why was the lady mad?"

Eva looked down to the mural on her own t-shirt. It also read 'Satan Rules'.

"She was mad because she didn't understand."

"Would Daddy understand?"

Eva knelt, looking at her two girls. Both wore t-shirts in a similar style to her own, bearing the words 'Daddy Rules'.

Eva gathered her two daughters close, hugging them tightly. "I think Daddy would understand just fine."

The End.

Dear reader,

We hope you enjoyed reading *Hellbeast*. Please take a moment to leave a review in Amazon, even if it's a short one. Your opinion is important to us.

https://www.nextchapter.pub/authors/matthew-harrill-horror-author-bristol-uk

Want to know when one of our books is free or discounted for Kindle? Join the newsletter at

http://eepurl.com/bqqB3H

Best regards,
Matthew W. Harrill and the Next Chapter Team

ABOUT THE AUTHOR

Matthew W. Harrill lives in the idyllic South-West of England, nestled snugly in a village in the foothills of the Cotswolds. Born in 1976, he attended school in Bristol and received a degree in Geology from Southampton University. By day he plies his trade implementing share plans for Xerox. By night he spends his time with his wife and four children.

http://www.matthewharrill.com/

BOOKS BY THE AUTHOR

The Arc Chronicles

Hellbounce, Book 1

Hellborne, Book 2

Hellbeast, Book 3

The Eyes Have No Soul

COMING SOON...

His hands balled in fists, Zophiel dropped to his knees, his robes spreading about him. Tears of purest light streamed down his face, glistening like the first rays of dawn on the morning of the first day. His head hung low.

"Metatron, my brother, is dead..." The whisper came from clenched teeth. The lips peeled back as his shoulders trembled, the feathers on his enormous wings starting to shake as grief very evidently became rage. Those nearby took a step back.

"They did this." His eyes opened, and the crystal blue had been replaced with irises of darkest night. "Release Nibiru," he growled. "Unleash the host."

"Zophiel, no," Ioviel gasped. "The world will end."

"The world has ended."

The ARC Legacy

CPSIA information can be obtained
at www.ICGtesting.com
Printed in the USA
LVHW031140080221
678694LV00001B/9